Raves for *The Godstone by* Violette Malan

"Malan doles out the details of this fascinating world sparingly, keeping the reader engaged in the many mysteries, including why and how the level of technology seems to change as the travelers move through different Modes along the Road. Well-drawn characters and a quest that's eventually revealed to be as epic as they come add depth to the story, but the standout here is this strange, highly original world. . . . An original, enigmatic fantasy about reluctant heroes drawn into a quest to save the world."
—*Kirkus*

"Malan transports readers to an exciting world of high-stakes magic in this epic fantasy series launch. . . . Malan's elaborate worldbuilding and nuanced characters help keep the pages turning on the way to the slow-building climax. The unexpected plot twists and a subtle hint of romance will leave readers eagerly awaiting the next installment."   —*Publishers Weekly*

"I like to think I have my own preferences nailed down, and then a totally original book like Violette Malan's *The Godstone* comes along and thoroughly delights and surprises me. . . . There's a confident briskness to Malan's pacing; nothing seems to drag over *The Godstone*'s 300 or so pages. The momentum is only aided by the superb dialogue throughout. Fenra and Arlyn's banter is so pleasant, so assured, that it at times reads like classic English literature. Readers would be wise to pick up this exciting start to a new fantasy series."   —BookPage

"Come for the characters and themes, stay for the plotting and worldbuilding, or the reverse. I loved it."   —Nerds of a Feather

"I couldn't put it down! . . . *The Godstone* was a satisfying, self contained fantasy with just enough weird to pull you in and keep things fresh."
—Powder & Page

"*The Godstone* is an adventure story. And a quest. And a story about being forced to dismantle a comfortable persona in order to do what desperately needs to be done. Which just so happens to turn out to be saving the world."
—Reading Reality

THE
COURT WAR

A NOVEL

VIOLETTE MALAN

DAW BOOKS
New York

Cover design by Faceout Studio, Jeff Miller

Edited by Sheila E. Gilbert

DAW Book Collectors No. 1943

DAW Books
An imprint of Astra Publishing House
dawbooks.com
DAW Books and its logo are registered trademarks of Astra Publishing House

Printed in Canada

Library of Congress Cataloging-in-Publication Data

Names: Malan, Violette, author.
Title: The court war : a novel / Violette Malan.
Description: First edition. | New York, NY : DAW Books, Inc., 2023. |
Series: The Godstone ; book 2
Identifiers: LCCN 2023008302 (print) | LCCN 2023008303 (ebook) |
ISBN 9780756417895 (hardcover) | ISBN 9780756417918 (ebook)
Subjects: LCGFT: Fantasy fiction. | Epic fiction. | Novels.
Classification: LCC PR9199.4.M3278 C68 2023 (print) |
LCC PR9199.4.M3278 (ebook) | DDC 813/.6--dc23/eng/20230303
LC record available at https://lccn.loc.gov/2023008302
LC ebook record available at https://lccn.loc.gov/2023008303

ISBN 9780756418946 (PB)

First paperback edition: March 2024
10 9 8 7 6 5 4 3 2 1

For Paul

Acknowledgments

Of course the first people to be thanked are, as always, my wonderful editor Sheila Gilbert and my incredible agent Joshua Bilmes, without whom there would be no book in your hands. I would also like to thank my regular weekly video correspondents, who gave me encouragement, gossip and company during a very strange and unusual Covid-afflicted time period. Here they are, in the order of their calls: Barb Wilson, Tanya Huff, Shari Cohen, Patti Groome and David Ingham. My thanks also go to my irregular video correspondents: Jenn Shannon, Steven Price and Mary Jo Henry, Kerri Elizabeth Gerow and Marie Bilodeau. You know who your friends are when they sit down and talk to you even though you're not feeding them.

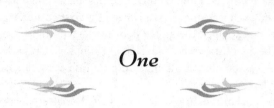

One

FENRA

I NOT-QUITE SLAMMED THE door of the clerk's office behind me. No, I could not meet with the council, third-class practitioners no longer had that right. No, I could not present a petition myself, I had to get a first-class practitioner to do that for me. Except all the first-class practitioners I knew were on the council and I could not meet—I wished I *had* slammed the door.

I got down the stairs and out of the building without noticing any of the people I must have passed. Once outside I slowed down. The sun shone, as it always did in the White Court, and the orange trees were in bloom. Their scent remained remarkable, regardless of whether I saw the council or not. The question was, how long would any of this last?

When Elva and I had gone to bed the night before, our room at the Hotel Ginglen had an oil lamp, but this morning the light was a candle with a copper reflector, and the hotel had become an inn. Most of the secondary streets weren't paved anymore, and I would prefer not to describe what had happened to the sewer system. The Mode had changed overnight, and not for the better. I knew how to stop it, but I couldn't do it myself, I needed to meet with the council.

I rounded the Phoenix building and had the East Bridge in sight when I heard my name called from an upper window. The voice had meant nothing, but the face was familiar.

Predax. Predax Ap Gervin. So, he had made it back alive. I was suddenly ashamed that I had never thought to check. "What is your room number?" I called up.

"Seventy-two, but it's complicated. I'll come down."

"Wait," I said before his head could disappear. "I know the way." Meeting a friendly face encouraged me, though as an apprentice Predax could do even less than I. As I turned the first corner, went up half a staircase, and stepped through a door in the landing, I had a sudden image of the apprentice who had lived in room seventy-two in my day. Her name was on the tip of my tongue. Tall, very fair, she always smelled of lemons.

I ran up another twisting staircase, opened a battered wooden door and strode down the narrow corridor, took three turns to the right and two to the left, and there was Predax standing in an open doorway. To my surprise, he threw his arms around me, hugging me tightly enough to shut off my breath. "Predax."

"Oh, sorry. It's just—somehow I thought I'd never see you again."

I smiled, shaking my head, as he gestured me into his room. Inside was the same tiny sitting room I remembered, with two easy chairs, a desk, and a miniature woodstove right in the center of the room for cold nights. Through an open arch, the bedroom, almost exactly the size of the sitting room, held a bed, a wardrobe, a washbasin, and the window where I had seen Predax. He had put a small, padded bench under it, along with a hexagonal table more commonly used for wine glasses, which held the remains of his lunch.

"Is Elva all right? Did you, uh, take care of everything?" He waved his hands in the air as if to show me what he meant by "everything."

I caught hold of his practitioner's wrist with my right hand and brought it back to his side. *Forrans* had been loosed on the world that way. I was careful to smile. "He is, we did, and," I waggled my right hand, "we did not."

"Tell me, no, wait." Predax shifted some practical artifacts off the padded chair in the sitting room and offered it to me. He found me a clean glass and poured me some orange squash from the pitcher that sat next to his half-eaten meat pie. I did not know how thirsty and dry I was until I took my first swallow. All the while Predax rattled away.

"So, I got home safely," he was saying. "I took your horse, like you told me. He seemed to know where he was going, so I let him have his head, and he took me to Ginglen's Hotel."

"It's an inn this morning," I said. I did not remember suggesting Predax take Terith, but he had been in Ginglen's stable when Elva and I arrived in the City three days ago. "I need to see the council." Abrupt, but I had no one else to help me, and Predax seemed glad enough to see me. "Have you a first-class friend?"

He impressed me by not asking any questions, just nodding slowly, and narrowing his eyes. "Maybe I can do better than that. Are you staying here in the Court?"

"No, since Elva is with me, we preferred to stay at Ginglen's."

The boy's face brightened when I mentioned Elva. I had forgotten they were friends. "And Arlyn Albainil?" I moved my head to the right, and then to the left. Predax blew out a sigh. "I'm sorry. I never really knew him, and I never got a chance to apologize for . . . well, you know."

Holding him down while Metenari cut his wrists and siphoned off his blood? I managed not to say this out loud.

Predax stopped chewing on his lower lip. "Is this about the God-stone?"

"Predax, I will tell you everything—" *probably*, "but can you help me?"

He studied my face with concerned eyes before answering. "Do you have some time right now?"

I stood up. "Absolutely."

I was not quite so eager a few minutes later, however, and I slowed as we approached another familiar building. "My mentor, Senior Lorist Medlyn Tierell, had his offices here."

"And my new mentor, Lorist Tamari Otwyn, has hers here now."

Wonderful. Tamari Otwyn. The name sounded familiar, but . . . surely it wouldn't be.

Though the door stood open, Predax tapped three times and waited until a voice called to us to enter. I had had a glimpse of the Lorist once before, when she had found Elva, Arlyn, and me in her office. She looked exactly the same, middle height, short fair hair standing up in spikes, an oval face with a nose like a knife blade. With luck, she would not recognize me.

Altogether, this was not turning out to be my lucky day. Judging by the sudden stiffness of her face, she remembered me very well. For a moment I thought she would just order me out, but after a glance at Predax she gave me a short nod.

Predax ushered me in and closed the door. "Practitioner Tamari Otwyn," he said formally. "This is Practitioner Fenra Lowens." He went to a side table covered with the complicated paraphernalia used by coffee fanatics, raising his eyebrow to me. I shook my head and wasted one of my best looks on his back as he turned away.

Tamari Otwyn stood and offered me her right hand. "Fenra Lowens, as I live and breathe. Call me Tamari," she said, still stiff, but with a small smile, and indicated the armchair in front of the desk. She had changed the furniture, so at least the office didn't feel like Medlyn's anymore. "Predax has told me so much about you, I feel I know you already." Her tone gave nothing away.

"Fenra needs a favor," Predax put in before I could respond. I should have realized that any mentor worth having would have questioned him carefully before taking him on. Especially in this case. It's a rare thing for an apprentice to lose his mentor, it's usually the other way around.

Her smile fading, Tamari sat down. "Let's hear it."

"I need to see the council," I said.

Tamari glanced again at Predax before she spoke. "Why?"

I took a deep breath in through my nose and set my hands down on my knees. "How much did Predax tell you about the Godstone?"

She nodded slowly, pursed her lips, and leaned forward over her clasped hands. "I've had access to all of Practitioner Metenari's research, in case there was any way of finding him. From what I read, it's pretty clear the Godstone is a dangerous artifact made, or perhaps found, by Xandra Albainil so long ago that the documents concerning it read more like myth than lore. According to the official record, he disappeared while still looking for it. According to Predax, Metenari found it, and the thing possessed and ultimately killed him."

I raised my eyebrows. So Predax had told her what really happened, and she had not only believed him, but she had also kept it to herself.

"What Predax could not tell you is that after the loss of Metenari, we . . . I returned the Godstone to where it came from." I waited, and when she did not respond beyond lifting one almost colorless eyebrow, I continued. "The Godstone is a part of a much greater sentient being. A being that was injured by its loss, and which now can begin to heal, with our help."

"And you need help from the council? To heal this being?"

I leaned back, closing my hands around the arms of the chair. "Unfortunately, it's more complicated than that."

"Naturally. Why should it be simple?" She signaled to me to continue, but suddenly every word of the summary I had prepared for the council vanished from my brain. I was more exhausted than I had realized. I wished Elva was with me. Predax could vouch for part of the story, but Elva had been a witness to all of it. I took a deep breath and reminded myself that Tamari Otwyn was a lorist, just like my mentor, and not liable to dismiss any story before giving it consideration.

"Have you ever wondered why the world is as it is? The changes from Mode to Mode? The Modes themselves, for that matter?"

This was not what she'd expected. Tamari leaned back as Predax set a glass of iced coffee in front of her. "Current philosophy supports the idea that the world was created this way for practitioners. The Modes and the changes fuel the practice."

I liked the way she said "current philosophy." She was not wedded to one pattern of thought. "Think of the World as a human body," I said. Now came the tricky part. "Systems, organs, patterns made by veins, muscles, arteries. Each individual piece of the body has its own function; each part is necessary for the whole to be healthy. If one of the parts is missing, or ceases to function as it should, the body as a whole is damaged. Like the human body, the World can take a lot of punishment, a lot of abuse, before it begins to fail. It can even lose parts of itself, and still live." I waited until Tamari took a sip of her coffee before continuing. "The sentient being I speak of is the world around us." I paused, but, again, she had no reaction beyond raised eyebrows. "The world around us and everything in it, the Modes, practitioners, mundanes, rivers, mountains, animals, *everything* is a piece of one organism. The World had already begun to fail, and when Xandra Albainil tore the Godstone from it, it lost the ability to act in its own defense, and it lost the ability to heal. The injury was too great to overcome."

Tamari set her sweating glass down on a thin slice of cork clearly intended to protect the walnut desktop. "'Think of the world as a body.' You're saying that the world we live in is a living, sentient being and we're just parts of it, which is nothing more or less than the Dadian philosophy."

Did I detect of a note of skepticism? "I've met it," I said. "I've spoken with the World directly. It needs our help."

I watched her carefully, but I did not expect her face to relax.

"Why us? Why practitioners?"

"We are the only ones who can see it. The only ones who can see the differences in the Modes." I leaned forward. She *had* to listen to me—she might be my only chance. "It's our job to travel through the body of the World, checking that the Modes are working well, growing and evolving, increasing in number. Through traveling we keep the World healthy and disease free—and long ago, before even the Godstone incident, we stopped doing it."

"And the Red Court?"

I could not tell whether she just humored me. I spread my hands. "I have to admit I do not know their purpose exactly, but you notice that there are far more mundanes than practitioners. They must be a vital part of the whole, even if I cannot say at the moment what that is. We use our patterns to power *forrans*," I continued. "We study existing *forrans*, or we create new ones to accomplish specific tasks, but it is our own patterns that power them. Practitioners are the World's pattern. Our movement through the organism strengthens that pattern and keeps the World healthy. When we stopped traveling, the World's illness began. When Xandra Albainil tore the Godstone free, the World began to die."

I waited. She remained silent, staring into the distance, a faint smile on her face. Was she laughing at me? I had once found all this almost impossible to believe, and the proof had been right in front of me.

"That theory would certainly explain some of the differences in the records."

I nodded. "The older records mention as many as seventeen Modes. Now we have only, what? Seven? Nine?"

"Something like that. We don't go out to check the Modes with any kind of regularity—oh, that's what you're saying is wrong . . . you're saying that the Dadian philosophy is the accurate view of the world, of life in general, and that we should all be living according to its tenets."

"Yes."

"And you want me to convince the council of this?"

"Get me in to see them. Get me a chance to explain. It's vital."

"You don't ask much, do you? Unless—is there some way for the rest of us to meet and speak to this being? Can you summon it?"

I looked from his mentor to Predax and back again. "I would not know how to begin. It always summoned me."

Tamari leaned back in her chair, arms crossed over her chest, whistling without sound. "I'm probably the only person currently at the Court who has even *heard* of this philosophy—who even knows that our lives used to be different. Most people believe we've always lived the way we live now."

"Less work this way, that's for sure," Predax said.

I liked that he felt comfortable enough with his mentor to speak up freely. With Metenari he had always been timid.

"A philosophy that let people stay in the City if they wanted to instead of all that traveling around with their apprentices in tow? Of course it's popular. But if you haven't any proof . . ." She slowly shook her head.

Something suddenly struck me. I searched their faces. "You are not arguing with me, either of you. I claim to have met and spoken with the World. How do you know I am not insane?" *Or lying?*

This time Tamari's smile reached all the way to her eyes. "As a practitioner who specializes in healing, do you know when someone is ill? Even if they don't know it themselves?"

"Yes, of course."

"Well, I can't *always* tell if someone's lying to me, but I can tell whether you—your pattern, if you will—I can tell if it's bent or twisted. You're clearly not crazy, so what you're telling me could very well be true." Her lips pressed into a thin line. "No matter what, you should have your chance to present your case to the council."

I opened my mouth and shut it again. All practitioners have areas of special strength, and some have additional quirks. Tamari was evidently one of these.

"Now, how much of your part in this can I tell them?"

I spread my hands. "Whatever you find necessary."

ELVANYN KARAMISK

"All right. Oleander, you're up. Tell me what you're going to do."

The boy stepped up to the line chalked on the cobbles. Oleander had done them a couple of favors in the past, and Elvanyn Karamisk would have been happy to teach him marksmanship for free, but the kid insisted on paying his way. Oleander worked as a lampee by night, lighting the way for people who were out late, and a runner by day, delivering messages and packages, so this was an attitude Elva respected.

"Plant my feet, but keep myself relaxed." The boy wriggled his shoulders to loosen the muscles. "Point the pistol up, toward the sky, *then* bring it down to bear on the target. Inhale, exhale, pull the trigger. Oh, good morning, Practitioner."

From the look on Fenra's face, there wasn't much good about her morning. Elva smiled at her anyway. He always smiled at her, ever since he'd met her in the New Zone and followed her back here, to the world where he'd been born. Even though that world no longer existed.

"Good morning, Oleander, Doms." She nodded at the men behind him. They'd only been back in the City three days, but Elva didn't like to be idle. Itzen, co-owner of the inn with his partner Ginglen, *was* getting his lessons for free. The others, a City guard hoping to improve his marksmanship and therefore his chances for promotion, and two merchants who frequently took their dinners at the inn, were being charged twice what Oleander paid. "I am sorry to interrupt your lessons. Please continue."

The long mews behind the inn made a perfect practice range. The narrow yard let Elva place targets at different distances, with the farthest set at fifty yards. At that distance there was no chance of penetrating the far wall with a pistol shot, so the only things in danger were the inn's chickens.

Elva knew he and Fenra would be welcome to stay at Ginglen's Inn as long as they liked—with or without paying. He couldn't find anyone willing to tell him what favor it was Fenra had done for them, which probably meant it was illegal. There were very clear laws limiting what practitioners could and couldn't do in the City. Rules and restrictions from both Courts. As usual, all this political maneuvering did nothing good for the people.

"Oleander, take your shot. Everyone else, return to your own places. Itzen, turn the glass when everybody's in their spot. I want you all to be loaded and your shots taken before the sand runs out."

Keeping only half an eye on his students—they were past the stage where they would hurt themselves through carelessness, or so he hoped—he joined Fenra at the opening of Terith's stall. The horse poked his head out and snuffled at his ear.

Elva might have kissed her if they'd been alone, but he and Fenra behaved formally in public; anything else would have made them too noticeable, too memorable. Practitioners and commoners—what they called "mundanes"—didn't fraternize, except in the professional sense. They hadn't been away from the City very long, but even so, relations between the two Courts had deteriorated.

He looked her over carefully, assessing her mood. She had left that morning with her black hair severely braided, the whole of it powdered with white, in the current fashion. Her dark skin glowed, though he could see lines of fatigue around her eyes. She hadn't been sleeping well. Her braided hair, naturally darker and curlier than his, started to come loose as she took off her hat. He tucked a strand behind her ear. She was dressed in practitioner's colors: black shoes and white stockings, topped by yellow knee breeches, a crimson waistcoat, a white shirt and cravat, and a black long-skirted coat with embroidered crimson reverses.

"Tell me," he said.

"I could not get an 'audience' with the council," she said. She quirked an eyebrow at him to make sure he hadn't missed the emphasis. "But we now have a friend who can."

"Who would that be?"

"You'll never guess." She glanced upward to the windows of their rooms. The owners might be their friends, but the inn was still a public house, and the other guests were strangers. After what they had already been through, they knew it paid to be cautious. Whatever Fenra had to tell him, it could wait until they were in private.

Shooting had stopped and Elva looked around to find his students checking their scores on the targets. Politely not watching them, Oleander grinned wider than ever.

"That's all for today, Doms. Same time tomorrow for any who can make it."

Itzen took charge of seeing that all the pistols were returned, and put them, along with all the shot and the powder horns, into one of the inn's lockboxes. Fenra had put a locking *forran* on the box that only she and Elva could open. He took charge of the box and followed Fenra inside. The hallway smelled fantastic. *Just about dinner time*, he thought.

Ginglen had given them a suite with two rooms, the same one Fenra and Arlyn had used when they had first reached the City a little more than two months ago. Elva usually slept in the same bed as Fenra, but they had separate bedrooms for the look of it. Just like the guests, not all the inn servants were in the full confidence of the owners and their friends.

Elva came out from their bedroom carrying his own revolvers and found Fenra sitting on the common room's dining table swinging her feet. "Admiring your shoes?" he asked her.

"I believe I prefer boots." She looked critically at her left ankle. "All the hose and garters and things we have to wear with the breeches—it takes so long to dress."

"Were they boots before?" Fenra nodded.

As a mundane, all the Modes looked the same to him; only practitioners saw the changes. That's what made them practitioners. "Are you going to tell me?"

"You remember Predax Ap Gervin."

"You saw him? How's he doing?" The kid was once Santaron Metenari's junior apprentice, before the practitioner had been possessed by the Godstone.

"He has a new mentor, the newest member of the White Court council."

Elva whistled softly. "A space opened up when Metenari disappeared?"

"Something like that. Predax tells me Ronan Sedges now has Metenari's place as Headmaster, and that move opened up a slot for Tamari Otwyn." She grinned. "Metenari would be rolling in his grave, if he had one."

Elva unfolded the thick cloth he used to protect the table. He laid out his cleaning rods, the bottle of oil, and some fresh pads of cotton waste. "Otwyn's the one who took over your old mentor's offices and workroom, isn't she? Did she recognize you?"

"She did. But she did not seem to hold it against me."

Elva could tell from the shadow on her face and the way she touched the locket resting under her cravat that she was thinking of her mentor. Fenra slipped down from the table and sat in the upholstered armchair near the cold fireplace.

"I could practice those clean for you. In fact, I am fairly sure I could create a *forran* to keep them permanently clean."

Elva looked up, cotton waste in one hand, oil bottle in the other. "I suppose you could, but then what would I do to relax?" Fenra shut her eyes, the corners of her mouth twitching. "So Practitioner Otwyn is going to take your message to the Council, is she? You were able to persuade her, so that's a good sign." He set down the clean revolver and picked up the other.

"I am not so sure how persuaded she is. She may simply believe in my right to present my case." She rubbed her temples.

"You should have your day in court, no pun intended." He set the piece down. "Are you absolutely sure you can't contact the World again?"

He had barely finished speaking when the floor suddenly jolted sideways and Elva was thrown from his chair. He immediately rolled on his shoulder toward Fenra, but she had jumped to her feet, legs spread and knees braced as though she stood on the deck of a ship. The floor continued to shake, the table walked over to the window, and his revolvers danced off the top of the table, followed by glasses, a pitcher of water, and two plates. Another abrupt heave and Fenra fell to her knees, cutting her right hand on a piece of broken glass. Elva was able to get to his feet only after the third attempt, and his footing still felt untrustworthy.

"What was that?" He wasn't surprised to hear a tremor in his voice.

"I think the World has just contacted me." Fenra headed for the door. Elva grabbed up jacket and guns to follow her.

WITTENSLADE CAMDIN VOLDEN

Witt turned one way and then the other, trying to see every angle of himself in the three-part mirror in his dressing room. His tailor had been right after all, the peacock *wasn't* too bright a color, not once the coat was combined with a dark blue waistcoat and a fuchsia cravat. He smoothed back his hair automatically, though it was too short to matter.

"The wig."

The wigmaker's assistant set a stool down behind him and the wig-maker herself stood on it to place his new periwig gently down on his cropped head. An expert, she didn't even have to adjust it. She'd done it right the first time.

He drew his brows together, tilting his head to one side. "That's a new shade, isn't it?"

"We put a little bluing into the powder, Dom." Witt could tell from her tone how pleased she was he'd noticed. Most people wouldn't, he knew. "It makes the white brighter."

"I like it. Yes. That'll open a few eyes."

"We expect other people to be asking for it once they see you, Dom . . ."

Witt knew exactly what she was getting at. "And of course you may sell it to them, but wait a week. I insist on being seen to lead the fashion." The wigmaker then fastened a miniature tri-cornered hat to the wig. Witt tilted his head to one side and then the other before nodding and turning his back on the mirror. "Now, if you will all excuse me."

He waited until the tailor, the wigmaker, the cobbler, and all their assistants had bowed their way out of his dressing room before turning to his valet. "Well, Arriz? What do you think?"

"I think your father is spinning in his grave."

"Why? I've dressed like this for years."

"But you're attending the chamber today. Dressed like that," he added when Witt did not respond immediately. "Not even your shoes are black."

"Yes, well, that's the point, isn't it? Begin as I mean to go on. Isn't that what he was always advising me?"

"I didn't know you were listening." Arriz handed him his ebony stick and his fan with the fuchsia cords, and straightened his cravat.

Witt hadn't been in the Chamber of the Red Court since the ceremony when his father became First Courtier. The old man had still had hopes and expectations of him. Even at the age of seven, Witt had known better.

From what he could see now, the room hadn't changed much. His seven-year-old self had been much impressed; he'd never seen an oval room before. He was a little embarrassed to admit that he still found it impressive. Though the color scheme needed help. Fine, it was called the Red Court, but other colors existed, for the Maker's sake. He grinned. It was now the fashion to use county people's superstition-based way of swearing. He looked forward to introducing it to the chamber.

Centered in the room was an oval table made from some dark wood, stained oak perhaps. From the look of it, the top was polished often, but the wear of years was difficult to hide by polishing alone. There were eleven high-backed wooden chairs around the table, each of them upholstered, seats, backs, and arms, in dark red velvet. Though Witt couldn't tell if the darkness was due to color choice or dirt. They were comfortable enough, he found when he took his father's chair—his now.

Witt's grandmother had told him that the Red Court once had twelve courtiers. "Fools never thought they'd disagree," she'd said, laughing. "Soon learned they had to have a tie-breaking vote. Idiots."

Witt's father hadn't liked that he spent so much time with his grandmother. "Fool" was the nicest thing Witt had ever heard the old lady say about his father.

As he looked around the table, Valter Fenger Denson caught his eye, lifted a brow. Witt smiled and gave the new First Courtier a shallow bow. The older man sat back in his chair, satisfied. Unlike Witt's father, Denson had never cared what clothes or colors he wore. Witt still called the old man "uncle."

An important vote had been postponed when his father had suffered a stroke on his way home from the last session of the chamber he would ever attend. They'd decided to postpone the vote until he recovered. A mistake, as it turned out, since he hadn't. Much as he disliked the man, Witt had tried to send for a doctor from the White Court, but the family advocates had overruled him, showing him his father's stated wishes. The stubborn old fart would rather die than be helped by scientific medicine. Maybe the old man thought he'd pull through without. Well, as Arriz said at the time, he'd thought wrong.

After the old man's funeral, the Court sent Witt his summons to attend, along with a thick file of papers outlining the current issues. Witt skimmed through all of them, but paid particular attention to the "Matter of the White Court," his late father's particular project. "Matters" between the two Courts had finally reached a point where diplomatic relations had been all but suspended. They had even put a halt to proposed implementation of new technology, though Witt had heard rumors of a new type of lighting.

There were a few raised eyebrows as the other courtiers came in and saw him sitting, in all his colored finery, in his father's seat, though Witt thought that was more because he wasn't wearing mourning than because he hadn't dressed in the chamber's red and black. Denson smiled at him again, and that was enough for the rest of them to find his clothing acceptable. *Sheep.*

"First, I would like to formally welcome Wittenslade Camdin Volden to the Chamber of the Red Court. We all had great admiration and respect for your father, young man, and we know that you will represent him well." Denson looked around at the rest of the courtiers, nodding as if he saw agreement on their faces.

All Witt saw was a boredom that matched his own. Except maybe for Riva Anden Deneyra. She looked at him with appraisal and speculation in her bright brown eyes. *Not quite old enough to be my mother,* he thought, giving her a shallow bow. Her expression did not change, but somehow he was sure she had smiled at him, which surprised him more than a little. The widow didn't have a reputation as a flirt. On the contrary, gossip said.

"The motion before us is the one we postponed due to the late Courtier Volden's illness. Now that he is ably represented by his heir, we can conclude that business. Courtier Deneyra, will you state the motion?"

Riva Deneyra cleared her throat and, if it was possible, sat straighter. "The motion was made by Courtier Ebanol," she said in a low, rough voice, "and seconded by the late Courtier Volden, that the City take aggressive action against the White Court, subduing them into an obedient submission."

I wonder who worded that, Witt thought, stifling a smile. He suspected he saw a twinkle in the widow's eye as well.

"Discussion has already taken place, and I now call for a vote. Those in favor?"

"If I may?" Witt tried to sound diffident and bored at the same time. "I wasn't a party to the original discussion," he added after the chief courtier gestured his permission to proceed. "I saw in the material sent to me that this was considered a good time to move against the White Court, but the Maker knows it isn't clear to me. Why now, in particular?"

Several of the courtiers pressed their lips together—in exasperation, Witt hoped.

"Because the White Court is experiencing a period of instability," Courtier Ebanol said. "It's come to our attention that in the last year or so there's been serious dissension among the members of their council. The infighting that resulted with the appointment of Santaron Metenari to the position of Headmaster—a compromise, may I point out—was exacerbated when the practitioner disappeared two months ago, just after taking office. His rival, Ronan Sedges, is now promoted into Metenari's place, but even his position is not secure. Now, while this state of instability exists, is the time for us to make our move."

"Thank you." Witt stifled a yawn behind his fan. "That's very clear."

Witt already had a pretty good idea how the vote would go. It was all his father had talked about before the stroke permanently stopped him from talking. *Speaking of infighting*, Witt thought, stifling another smile. In the meantime, courtiers who had started out on one side of the debate had switched over, and back again, undoubtedly because of persuasion of one kind or another—which probably included blackmail, in some cases, Witt thought.

Five ayes, five nays, with his father casting the deciding vote. Witt knew his father had held his vote in reserve, quiet, until there was a tie to be broken. Everyone knew which way his father, and subsequently Witt, was expected to vote. The vote went around, ayes and nays accumulating. He noted Riva Deneyra voting nay. Finally, the vote came to him. He knew he was expected to vote "aye," like his father, but now that he had to speak, he hesitated, languidly moving his fan. Since when did he do the expected?

"Nay," he said.

A deadly silence met his words, but before anyone could speak the whole room shook. Glass cracked in the windows, chairs tipped over spilling courtiers onto the floor, along with papers, pens, and inkpots. The shaking continued, sharp and unnerving for what seemed an endless time, until it died away with a rumble.

Well, well, Witt said to himself, *looks like my dear father really* is *spinning in his grave.*

FENRA

"This way," I called over my shoulder. Even if I had not felt the rift in the World's skin as if it were a cut in my own, I would have known from the chaos in the streets where to find it. Elva was close on my heels. People made way for us as we ran, some of them calling out to ask me what had happened. As we got closer to the rift, we found people on the ground, some of them holding broken limbs, others crying in the arms of friends or loved ones. I ran by without speaking, but Elva called out as we ran that we would come back and help when I had dealt with the danger. *Optimist*, I thought. It must have been hard for him to leave these people without stopping. Elva had spent the last few decades in the New Zone as the High Sheriff of the Dundalk Territories, someone who protected and looked after the people where he lived. However, the greater emergency at that moment was the damage to the World.

The space around the great crack in the pavement was clear of people, though not of debris. I could see where a building had fallen into the opening, broken in half like a stick of candy, rooms, furniture, chairs, rugs, wardrobes, and fireplaces all mixed together as if in a child's toy box. People close to the edge had formed a human chain to help others crawl out of the building, lifting them as carefully as they could until they reached what had once again become solid ground.

"Is everyone out of there?" I called to those closest to the edge.

"This is the last." A young woman in a City guard's uniform called to me over her shoulder from where she was coordinating the rescue.

I began to rub my palms together. "Can you get everyone further back from the edge?" I heard Elva calling out to people to back away.

I pulled my hands slowly apart, bright green lines of light reaching from fingertip to fingertip. As I clapped my hands softly, over and over, the strands of light multiplied until they were beyond counting. I tossed them into the air, chanting a *forran* aloud as the net formed by the light settled like a lace tablecloth over the ruined building. Almost immediately, the entire structure began to crumble, bricks and mortar returning to sand and mud, wooden furniture to branches and leaves, and so on. Finally, the whole thing disintegrated, dissolving into its original state of being, and slid into the fissure.

I jumped in after it.

A layer of my mind heard Elva calling my name, and wanted to answer, to tell him I was safe, but I could not break my concentration, not even to reassure him. The net of my own light caught me before I had fallen very far. I spread it thinner, until I could feel every inch of the fissure, rocks, soil, bodies of insects, and bones older than the City itself. I thought about how I healed a broken bone, how I could see, feel, the sharp edges, the places where the bone had chipped and pieces floated loose in the body. This break in the earth was just like that. *Bigger*, I told myself, *but the same.*

I twitched at the net of light, pulling it in toward me, tweaking it until it matched my own pattern, the structure of my own body, the thing that made me a practitioner. I flung it out again like a fisherman throws out his nets. Everywhere it touched it began to contract, pulling the broken parts together, shifting little pieces back to where they belonged. Gradually the sides began to draw closer to each other. I had to move as slowly and as gently as possible so as not to cause another quake. "Just like closing a wound," I said aloud. "Gently. Do not pull anything else out of place."

Fenra. Fenra, come.

My whole body shivered, but before I could respond, I heard Elva call me again, and I started up the nearest slope toward the edge, drawing the fissure closed behind me as I moved. I could feel the sweat sticking my shirt to my back, loose strands of hair tickling my face. My arms felt like lead, but I could not drop them yet. Not yet. The part of my mind that listened to Elva thought of how sore and tired I would be when this was over.

The next thing I knew, I felt Elva's arm supporting my back. He held a mug of something that could have been ale to my lips and told me to drink. When I opened my eyes I saw several worried faces hanging over us.

"She's all right," someone called out. "She's waking up." I winced as people around us began to clap and cheer.

"You're a hero," Elva said, setting down the mug and smoothing my hair from my face.

I caught his hand in mine. "We must get away from here before anyone else finds out."

⬦

TAMARI OTWYN

"Excuse me, Chief Councilor." This time I stood up. "I believe I'm first on the agenda."

Ronan Sedges looked up from his papers in surprise. "Practitioner

Otwyn, I know you're new, but surely you realize that yesterday's earth seizure takes precedence over any other matter?"

"But I may have an explanation—"

"You're acquainted with Fenra Lowens, then? Do you know where she is?" Sedges still had his eyebrows raised as far as they could go. He thought it made him look sarcastic. I thought it made him look like a fish.

I pressed my lips together. That was the third time he'd interrupted me. I shut my eyes in frustration and slumped into my seat. I should just gather up my notes and leave.

"Third-Class Practitioner Lowens was seen at the site of the fissure that opened in the Ottway area of the City's west end." Sedges went on just as if I wasn't there at all. "It's unclear at the moment what her connection is, but I would like to ask the council for a warrant requiring her presence."

Nubin Sonsera spoke up from the other side of the table. "I heard that according to witnesses she repaired the fissure." If he started using the nail file he fidgeted with, I planned to stab him with it.

"Did she?" Omasi Dekadent had her hands folded in front of her like a schoolgirl. "Really? A third-class practitioner manages to repair a fissure so deep the bottom couldn't be seen? I don't think so."

"I heard she barely passed her exams, at that." Zavala Rankin, the last new councilor until I came along, sat to my left. I knew her better than I knew anyone else, but we weren't friends. Too gossipy. "Who knows, she may have been clumsy enough to cause the earth seizure herself."

"Councilor Otwyn, you have something to add?"

Sure, *now* they wanted to hear from me. My gut told me this wasn't the time to bring up Fenra's request—if they knew she had an explanation for all of this, they would blame her even more. I gestured at the books and papers on the table in front of me. I didn't like Fenra much, but I wanted to be fair. "I wondered whether the recent changes that have been experienced here in the City might have anything to do with the Dadian philosophy, whether there might not be something in there that might help us."

"Excuse me." Zavala liked to draw attention to herself. "But someone told me they saw Fenra Lowens being escorted by your apprentice— what's his name again?—sometime yesterday."

"I was about to add," I used my crispest tone, "if I had been given a chance, that I did see her yesterday morning."

"So you *do* know her."

I made a face and shrugged. "Not really. Turns out we had the same mentor and she wanted to visit his old office, like a farewell, you know? We had some coffee, we reminisced about Medlyn Tierell, and she left."

Was it my imagination, or did Ronan Sedges study me a little too closely? I responded by first putting on my best perplexed expression. "You're new on the council, Tamari, but you must learn to keep yourself more at a distance from the second- and third-class practitioners, otherwise you'll never have a minute to yourself. Did Practitioner Lowens say where she was staying?"

I shrugged again, but this time I barely managed not to make a face. Somehow they all managed to forget we were all second and third class once. "I never asked. I assumed somewhere in the guest halls, where else would she stay?" I recognized the looks on their faces, the same looks adults give children when they think the kids are too innocent to know what's really going on. And maybe they weren't so far off, at that. I'd thought they would want to fix things. I had expected someone to be sent out to view the scene of the damage. I hadn't realized that all they were interested in was finding someone to blame. "She shouldn't be difficult to find, though, should she?" I asked as innocently as I could. I touched the pearl studs in my right ear. "I mean, we'll know if she leaves the City, won't we?" But they only ignored me again.

"Very well. Do I have the agreement of the council for the warrant?"

I added my "aye" to the rest. As I expected, there were no nays, and I'd do no one any good by being the only one who didn't go along. Better to stay under the line of sight, if I meant to do what I'd decided to do.

The meeting adjourned shortly after, with no other business discussed. I gathered my papers and returned to my office, where I found Predax at his study desk. Though I might not like it, as far as I was concerned, the tremor, or seizure or whatever we'd decided to call it, supported Fenra Lowens' theories, and what the council wanted to do was worse than useless.

"Predax, do you know where Fenra Lowens is? No, don't tell me, just get a message to her. Tell her the council is about to issue a warrant for her appearance, to defend herself against charges for what she did yesterday. Tell her I have a very bad feeling about this." I sank into my chair a little more heavily than I'd meant to.

Predax nodded without speaking, the color fading from his face. No wonder—a warrant once presented would force Fenra to attend, and prevent her from leaving until the council was satisfied. I couldn't see how they could be.

"Don't be followed," I said to his back.

Fenra was no particular friend of mine, even if we did share a mentor, and until this morning I was just going to do her a favor for Medlyn's sake. But after my experience with the council, I had a horrible feeling she was right.

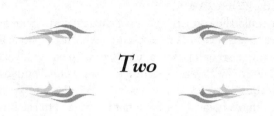

Two

W E WERE FINISHING lunch when Predax appeared in our open doorway, glancing anxiously between us and the servant who had come for the dishes. Predax held the door for the woman and shut it behind her. His breath came short, his face blotched red and white. Elva immediately refilled his glass of wine and handed it to him.

"Good god, man, sit down before you fall down."

I took Predax's wrist and found his pulse pounding. "What is it?" I said, tracing a small calming pattern onto his skin.

"You need to get out of the City, quick as you can."

"You explain, we'll pack." Elva went into our bedroom and left the door open as he stripped off his vest and shirt, pulling his New Zone clothing out of the closet. Like the revolvers—or anything else from the New Zone—this clothing didn't change no matter what Mode he was in. He tossed me a pack through the open doorway and I checked its pockets for any money we might have left. Not much.

"The council's been given a warrant for your appearance. You'll be asked to explain what you were doing that resulted in yesterday's earth seizure."

Elva paused halfway into his shoulder holsters. "'Resulted'? She didn't cause it, she fixed it!"

I met Predax's eye. I had a feeling my face matched his for pallor. "Can you prove I did not cause the seizure?" I asked Elva.

"There are lots of witnesses—" Elva stopped short when both Predax and I shook our heads.

"However many mundanes saw me fix it, they are not allowed to testify in the White Court."

"What could the council do?" Elva shrugged his shoulder holsters into place, fastened them, and tucked a revolver under each arm. He tossed me my shoes and jacket, and gathered up our saddlebags, handing them to Predax. "Get us some food, can you? And have you any money on you?"

Predax fumbled one of the bags, but I managed to catch both shoes and jacket. "You don't want to know," he said, answering Elva's first question. "At the very least she could be confined, and you'd never see her again. You'd die before she was released."

If anything could make me feel worse, that was it. One thing to know I would likely outlive Elva—unless we could return to the New Zone, where he apparently aged as slowly as a practitioner—but to rot away confined while he aged and died without me? Not likely.

"We cannot get far enough on the Road before they would be after us." I took one of the saddlebags from Predax before he dropped it again. You would think the boy had never saddled a horse in his life. Elva stopped with a shirt halfway into his pack and looked at me.

"The locket?" he said. "Can we take Terith that way?"

My hand went to the blue-enameled lump of gold resting against my skin just under my cravat. "Perhaps, if he were just a horse, but as it is, I cannot chance that he can survive in the vault."

Predax came downstairs with us but peeled off to the kitchens as we continued to the stables. Though I could not take him, I needed to tell Terith where we were going, and why. Minutes later, Predax was back with a much heavier saddlebag, judging from the way he was carrying it, with Ginglen Locast and Itzen right behind.

"I've brought what money I can spare," Ginglen said, handing Elva a package wrapped in heavy parchment. "Including the rent you gave me yesterday. Don't worry," he added when Elva started to protest. Lowering his voice, he said, "I'm charging the others extra. Good luck," he added, still whispering. "I'll go so I can honestly say I didn't see you leave."

His thin shadow followed him back into his inn.

"You had better do the same," I said to Predax. "Thank you, and thank Tamari for us."

"I don't understand. What are you going to do?" Predax reached a hand toward Terith but did not touch him. He had ridden my horse from the third Mode to the City, but still seemed nervous of him.

"No time to explain." I gave Terith a last embrace and slipped my right arm around Elva's waist. "If you will not go, will you at least stand further back?" I waited until I thought he was far enough away before opening the locket. I heard him draw in his breath when fog began to spill out of it, but I kept my focus on the connection between Elva and myself. Finally the fog cleared and we were standing in the vault. My legs trembled and I was happy to let Elva steady me.

"Sit down," he said, pulling out the nearest chair.

I sat a little more heavily than I had planned. "That was more difficult than I expected. Can you still see everything?"

We were in my old mentor's vault, a space many practitioners created to hold personal and private things. Living in the outer Modes, I had never needed a vault of my own, but Medlyn Tierell had given me the key to his just before his death. Medlyn had also left a *forran* running that would prevent mundanes like Elva from seeing the contents of the room. One of the last things I had done before we confronted the Godstone was overlay that *forran* with one of my own that allowed Elva to see and use everything in the vault.

So he was able to fetch me a steaming jug out of a walnut cupboard standing against the wall across from where I sat and pour me a cup.

"Apparently I need coffee," I said. I took a deep swallow before continuing. I could hear bitterness in my voice. "If the council thinks I caused the earth seizure, they are even less likely to listen to me than they were before."

Elva handed me a piece of travel bread full of nuts and dried fruits. "What about taking people to the beach where we saw the World? Wouldn't that help convince them?"

I pressed my lips together. "That place doesn't exist, unless the World wants it to, and I suppose it thinks it does not need to meet with me again."

As soon as the words left my mouth, the vault vanished, and I stood on a familiar pebbled beach, strewn with driftwood, seaweed, shells, and the bleached bones of fish. In previous visits I had been able to see far into the distance, but this time fog lay just offshore, and edged the rocks behind me. The wind picked up, tossing sand, bits of driftwood, and fragments of dried seaweed into the air, though it did not blow the fog away. I started walking, but the fog moved with me, so my area of visibility stayed the same. Eventually I saw a rock, just at the edge of the sea, with a figure sitting on it. The last thing I expected to see.

I slowed down, not sure whether I wanted to meet the thing on the rock. I knew it couldn't be Arlyn, the person I used to meet on a similar beach, when he was low and he needed me. Arlyn was dead.

"Arlyn?" I felt like a fool. I knew it wasn't him.

"I thought this form might be easier for you." The voice was similar, but the tone was wrong. Arlyn never spoke to me like that, not even when he was low.

It tilted its head. Arlyn used to do that too, when he was thinking something out, but never to the right, always to the left. Of course, it was not Arlyn. It looked as if someone had taken a drawing of him and animated it. When you got close, you saw that his clothes weren't separate from his skin, but were all of a piece, shirt, jacket, and trousers, and didn't hang properly. I could not see where the cuff ended and the wrist began. What was supposed to be his hair didn't move in the breeze the way mine did.

A better job had been done on his face, except for the eyes. Like mine, Arlyn's had been gray, but these had no whites, no pupils, just a chaos of movement.

I shivered. *No, not at all easier for me.*

It shrugged, the movement lopsided and uncoordinated. "Isn't this better? Don't you like it?"

"I do not know." It was the truth. Was this doll-like version of the man I knew better than the avatar I was familiar with, the giant figure made up of constantly moving pebbles and sand and seaweed and shells and rocks? I lifted my voice over the sound of the waves. "What happened? Why did the earth open like that?"

It looked away and then back at me, the way a person will when she tries to hide indecision. Or the way a person will when she tries to hide a smile. My stomach suddenly felt cold.

"Our pattern needs to be strengthened sooner, faster."

I opened my mouth and shut it again without speaking. The World evolved so slowly, I had thought I had plenty of time. "What has changed?"

"Not enough has changed. The deterioration that had already

begun before the Godstone left us has continued, and more rapidly. It must stop. See to it."

The next thing I knew, Elva had my face in his hands. "For a minute there, you weren't here."

I took in a deep breath and released it slowly. "The World would like me to work faster."

"Did it have any suggestions as to how?"

I shook my head. "When I asked it about the earth seizure, it did not answer me."

Elva poured another cup of coffee and handed it to me. "All right, getting the White Court to listen to you didn't work. We need another plan, and a safe place to think of it. I'd rather not stay here," he added after a moment's thought.

"I know of a place where it will take some time for anyone to come looking."

I planned to go directly to my cottage when we reached the well, but we were spotted by a threesome of eight-year-olds. One ran ahead while the other two stopped us and insisted on taking the extra saddlebag and "helping" us, as if I did not know the way to my own home. They chattered without stopping to hear the answers to the questions they were asking. Just as well, since I had no answers to give them. I looked around at the houses as we passed through the village and saw more or less what I expected, wattle and daub where there had been timber and dressed stone.

No, I was wrong, the mill building was still mostly stone, and I could hear the hard oaken mechanism creaking from here. From the sounds, they were closing the sluices, getting ready to hold back the stream until there was enough water to work the wheel. Ione Miller came out of the building, wiping her face and hands with an old linen rag that from the look of it had once been a tunic. She frowned at the children and they peeled away. Probably supposed to be at their lessons. Despite the chill, Ione wore only a short-sleeved, knee-length tunic belted with a leather thong, baggy trousers, and wooden clogs.

"You're back then, Practitioner. And Arlyn Albainil?" Ione looked past us down the track, frowning slightly.

"I am afraid he will not return from the business that took him to the City," I said, not sure how she would react.

Ione looked away before asking me, "Dead?"

"Dead, but successful."

Ione nodded, already planning what she would tell the villagers. "Good for him," she said finally. "Though unwelcome news for us." Arlyn's furniture had meant a great deal to the village. He always made his customers come to him, and that brought trade of other kinds.

"This is his good friend and mine, Elvanyn Karamisk."

"Not a furniture builder, by the look of him."

"Not at all," Elva said. "I'm a soldier by profession, though I've helped build a few houses."

"Good hunter?"

"It's been a while, but I'm sure it'll come back to me." Elva touched his revolvers and his sword in turn.

Ione turned back to me. "You're very welcome back yourself, Fenra Lowens, of course, it's just . . ." She shrugged. "It's been strange here without him these last couple of months, and now, knowing that he's not coming back . . ." She looked away again.

"Strange" understated it, I thought. Arlyn Albainil had lived in the village longer than anyone could remember. He had always been there, and now he was gone. They were even used to his not aging. In fact, they thought of it as a curse. They were more leery of me, even though I was the only healer in the entire Mode.

"I don't expect I'll need to tell people that you're back, the kids will do that for me. You'd better be ready for patients. There's been illness and injury since you left."

Another reason to come back. The village could not afford to be without both its carpenter and its practitioner. The mill alone would not bring enough business to keep the place alive. Arlyn had altered their lives all those years ago when he picked this place to stop his wandering.

"Then I had better be where they expect to find me," I said. She nodded and turned back to her work.

"This way," I said to Elva. I led him past the mill and up the path to the branching that led to my home. I had been right about the mud.

We wouldn't have known, before we became whole again, that the small facial movements have meaning. Even now we aren't always certain we understand them. We've always looked at the big picture.

This time, however, we are certain she believes us. Confused, yes, her face tells us that clearly. The strategy of looking like Arlyn Albainil works beautifully, distracting her. We know how to solve the problem. We're convinced we can't wait, we shouldn't have to wait, we don't want to wait.

Using Fenra's schedule, it could take generations before practitioners start doing what they should. Why? None of this is our fault. Just because things were done slowly before doesn't mean we need to go slowly now. We see it clearly now. We believe she listens. We believe she understands.

⌐

ELVANYN

Fenra's house sat a fair piece out from the center of the village—if you counted the mill as the center—and was definitely larger than he expected, considering that she lived here alone. Like the mill, both wood and stone had been used in the construction, and the walls were higher than most of the other buildings he could see. Perhaps the same people who had built the mill had built Fenra's house.

The inside of the house, on the other hand, was exactly what he expected. The wall farthest from the door held an open hearth. An iron ring to hold pots above the flames sat on four sturdy legs, a spit crossed where the fire would be hottest, and several cooking utensils, including what Elva recognized as a frying pan, hung on hooks around the fireplace as though they were ornaments. Everything else, from the bed in the corner on the fireplace side, to the smaller cots stacked along the side wall, to the worktable, and even the chairs and the floor, were covered over with books, scrolls, boxes, jars, and what must be practical artifacts since he didn't recognize any of them. Even though the door had been standing open, nothing was dusty.

Again, as he would expect, nothing had been touched. In the outer Modes, people believed in the practice, and knew what practitioners were. In the City, they called it science and were less respectful.

"I'm not sleeping on one of those cots," he said. Fenra took off her red-lined black cloak and tossed it onto an already overburdened bench before crouching down in front of the fire. It had been left laid, and she only needed to shift a few bits of kindling before lighting it.

"Of course not." Her voice had a smile in it. "Those are for patients."

"People won't talk about us sleeping together?" In the City mundanes didn't socialize with practitioners, let alone sleep with them.

"I am a practitioner," she said, holding a chunk of wood in her hand while the flames caught. "People do nothing except talk about me."

"Ooh, look who's so important."

She turned and threw the chunk of wood at him. He caught it in his practitioner's hand. "You know what I mean," she said, laughing. "I am not full of myself, it's just that no one expects practitioners to act like ordinary people, so they will talk if we are sleeping together, and they will talk if we are not. They used to lay bets on whether Arlyn and I were sleeping together."

"Which of course you weren't."

"Would it bother you?"

Elva gave it the consideration it deserved before answering. "Nope. It should have been obvious to anyone who saw you together that you weren't."

"Yes, well, not everyone is as perceptive as you." She moved around the room tidying things as they spoke, and Elva realized that the disorder wasn't, in fact, very disorderly. Crowded, definitely, but not a mess. There were two clean plates and some spoons in a bucket, and he sorted them out and returned them to their places in the kitchen. When Fenra didn't comment, he picked up four bound books and stacked them neatly on a shelf. He stopped halfway through folding a clean tunic, frowning at the cloth in his hands.

"Everything knows where it's supposed to go."

He spun around. "What?"

"You were wondering why you were not making mistakes helping me put things away." She waved around the room. "The written things are all parchment, and the rest is wood or some other natural thing."

"Sure." Fenra had a particularly strong bond with natural objects—which meant everything, in a way. That's why the World had spoken to her in the first place.

Elva frowned. He'd often seen Fenra tired, but the droop in both her shoulders and the corners of her mouth was new. She'd been discouraged since her abrupt meeting with the World. Abstracted.

"Listen," he said, sitting down at one of the two seats at the work-table and motioning her to what he could see was her regular seat across from him. The table was narrow enough that he could reach across and take her hands. "The White Court council is not going to do anything, is it?"

Her grip tightened and then relaxed. "Not now, no. Not if they are trying to blame me for the earth seizure." She looked through the door she had left open. "I need to think of some other solution. At least here I can be doing something useful meanwhile. The village is so much smaller now that the Modes have changed, it won't survive without help."

"I've thought of something that might help the village and the World at the same time." He smiled when she lifted her left eyebrow. "Back in the New Zone, when a new philosophy comes along, something that changes how people see the world and themselves, the people who believe in it open a school to teach it."

"Different philosophies have different schools?"

"Not necessarily schools with buildings and such, sometimes the followers just meet in the marketplace."

"And mine is a different philosophy, although not a new one. So, you are suggesting . . ." Fenra's chin went up, and the spark was back in her gray eyes.

"That you start a new court. That you start it here."

WITTENSLADE

The last person Witt expected to be shown into his sitting room was Riva Deneyra. She had changed out of her chamber clothing and wore a simple City suit of dove gray, with a dark green waistcoat, pale yellow shirt, and a white cravat with green polka dots. The footman had no doubt taken her hat, gloves, and walking stick at the door. Witt couldn't help noticing that the black ribbon braided into her hair as a nod to her widowed status somehow enhanced the single streak of gray.

She looked around, a faint smile on her lips as she took in the rose-papered walls covered by family portraits, and the tall narrow windows with their lemon swag drapery. "I like this room," she said, accepting the high-backed chair he offered her. "But then, I expected to. You're known for your exquisite taste."

Said the spider to the fly, Witt thought. *I wonder what she wants.* "Tea and chocolate," he said, nodding to the servant still hovering at the door. He'd kept his father's household intact, though it meant having more servants than one person needed. People thought it was extravagance, but Witt saw the practical side. Every single one of them gave better service since they knew they weren't really necessary and he could turn them out into the streets whenever he liked.

Riva Deneyra crossed her legs and seemed completely relaxed and ready to wait for the refreshments to arrive before beginning any conversation. Witt relaxed his face into his pleased-idiot smile. They didn't move in the same circles, even though both their families were courtiers. She was older, for one thing, and her marriage removed her from the unmarried or never-married set who had fewer responsibilities and were more likely to carouse. He couldn't remember whether she had children, and he certainly couldn't tell by looking at her.

"Yes, I have children," she said, her mouth twisted into a smile. "And no, I didn't read your mind, I guessed from the way you were looking at me. The reason I look so slim and trim is that I had a practitioner assist at their births."

A servant came in with a tray carrying a blue porcelain pot of tea and a green porcelain pot of chocolate, along with four cups, two blue and two green. Behind her came a second servant carrying plates of tiny, iced pastries, fruit tarts, and the twists of fried and sugared dough that were the rage at the moment.

"That was bold of you," he said, as if they hadn't been interrupted and she had just spoken.

She waved this away. "More women do it than talk about it, let me assure you. Many of us prefer not to risk dying for the sake of having heirs."

It made sense to him. He imagined being left with a living child after the death of a wife in childbirth, and it didn't strike him well. It would be even worse if you loved her, of course, as some men apparently did. And what if the child died as well? A hideous waste. "That would be why you support diplomatic relations with the White Court." He made it a statement, but Riva gave him a short nod anyway.

She took up the pair of silver tongs and added a slice of lemon to her tea. "Yes. Whereas you voted the way you did just to annoy your dead father."

"And the rest of his old cronies—did you see their faces?—let's not forget them."

"Oh, believe me, I'd like to. It can't be done, and I've *really* tried." She stopped to accept a small cake from the plate he offered her. "Which brings me to why I'm here," she said. He put on his most interested face. "You probably realize that those who supported my proposal of a trade agreement between the two Courts voted with me because of favors owed or given—and, frankly, because many of them expected your father, and then you, to vote against me."

"I take it no one is now falling over themselves to demonstrate their support?"

"Not enthusiastically." She set the cake down on the edge of her saucer. "A great hole almost splits the City in half, and a single practitioner reseals the chasm, saving dozens if not hundreds of lives and businesses. You would expect everyone to be falling over themselves to create stronger ties with the White Court. And yet . . ."

Witt drew himself up, his hands frozen in the act of dipping his fried pastry into his chocolate. He shifted immediately to get his trousers out from under possible drips. "So where do I come in? Why come to me?"

"I'm here to find out whether you are going to help me to move talks along, or sit back and relax, now that you've achieved your purpose in upsetting everyone." She leaned forward, fixing him with her glittering green eyes. "I need action, and I need it now, before the Red Court has time to gather its wits. If the two Courts were a little less like armed camps and a little more like counties bound by treaties and trade agreements, we'd have more than just easier access to medicines and medical care. As it is right now, only the rich can afford the permits and the fees required to have a practitioner attend a childbirth, for example. But we'd also have faster access to their technology as they develop it. I've heard that the White Court has something they call gaslights, not just oil lamps and candles. Who knows what else they might have of benefit to us?"

"I see." *And who did you hear this from, I wonder?* Still, he liked the sound of benefits. "And the people who initiated diplomatic contact, those people might benefit a little more than others?" He pushed the last bit of pastry into his mouth.

She blinked. "Why, yes, I expect that would be true."

He was careful to react as though her smile made him a little uncomfortable. He almost expected her to show teeth. He took a sip from his cup of chocolate, covering the lower half of his face. "So again, why me?"

"I see you as someone who makes up his mind, then *acts*. I need your youthful energy. This earth seizure has thrown the whole Red Court into the air. These fools will flounder about, meeting again and again, and finally, once their panic subsides, convince themselves to do nothing. Whereupon they'll have another vote, and like that!" She snapped her fingers. "Our chance of diplomacy disappears. I want to act now, while they're still dithering, open talks before anyone can stop us. I've made an appointment with the Council of the White Court for tomorrow at midmorning. Will you go with me?"

Witt sat back in his chair and furrowed his brow. She clearly expected him to swallow this flattery. He supposed he couldn't be annoyed with her for thinking him this big a fool when he'd spent the last five years trying to convince everyone of exactly that. He picked up another piece of pastry. On the other hand, he could see ways agreeing with her would work out well for him. If nothing else, he could satisfy his curiosity. He'd never been in the White Court, not even that one time his father had refused permission for him to go on a school-sponsored visit. Agreeing with Riva would give him a chance to see the place for himself. Non-practitioners weren't exactly forbidden to go there, but it was frowned on. And then there were the benefits. He wiped his mouth on a linen napkin. "I'll make an opening in my schedule." He gave a pompous and self-important nod.

Riva set down her own cup, folded her napkin, and stood. "I'll have my carriage outside at ten."

Witt got to his feet.

When she was at the door with the servant waiting, she paused and turned back. "Did you tell him? Your father. How were you going to vote? At the end, when it was too late for him to do anything?"

Witt didn't answer her, exactly, but he smiled, and she smiled back.

RIVA ANDEN DENEYRA

Riva Anden Deneyra settled back into the soft blue velvet cushions of her carriage, tilted her hat to one side, and straightened the fingers of her gloves. On the whole, that visit had gone better than she had expected, better, in fact, than she had hoped for.

"You look pleased." The young woman who had waited in the carriage re-crossed her legs to give Riva more room.

"He's a vain, arrogant little toad whose main concern is whether his manicure matches his vest buttons—followed closely by how many pastries he can stuff into his face," Riva told her friend. "I'm not sure he knows which purse his money is in."

"Won't that cause problems?"

"On the contrary, I can count on him screwing up." Riva patted her friend's knee. "He'll be perfect for taking the blame." He might be shrewd about money—many who were fools every other way were—but she could work with that too.

It wouldn't bring back her dead child, nor her dead child's dead child, but something was better than nothing.

She tried not to have favorites, but her daughter Stell was the child most like Riva's dead husband. Everyone thought it a political marriage, and so it had been, but that hadn't stopped them from becoming the best of friends and confidants. When Stell had wanted to marry the Crisspet boy, Riva had made no opposition, even though it meant her daughter would live over a day's ride from the City. If it did nothing else, money made things like distance less important.

But when it came time for Stell to give birth to her first child, Riva had wanted to send to her the practitioner who had helped Riva herself with all her pregnancies. The White Court said no. Told her she'd have to use the practitioner who lived in that county, which would have been fine had there been one. Nothing Riva could do changed anything, not bribery, not political pressure, nothing. They shouldn't be allowed to have so much power, the White Court practitioners. No one should, she supposed, but if someone had to, Riva wanted it to be the only person she could trust—herself.

Riva couldn't bring the White Court to heel alone, but with Witt to help her create the right distraction—and to fumble things at the right moment—and Fendall Dorst Vanaldren to bring her his troops, she thought she could succeed.

"When we get home, I must write a letter for the courier."

Fenra

"Let me just finish this, and I'll be right with you."

I always liked watching Ione Miller, and her father before her, working in the mill, checking the gears, choosing and setting the stone for grinding depending on the grain being ground, checking that the chutes were clear, and that the sacks were well placed to catch the milled grain—I found it relaxing to watch others work. Satisfied that everything progressed as it should, Ione left her assistants to watch while she came out with me to the sturdy wooden table set up in the shadow of the mill building. Here we would not have to yell at each other over the noise of the machinery.

Ione waved me to a seat, removing and slapping dust out of the cloth she wore tied over mouth and nose. It had taken a lot of persuasion to get her great-grandmother to wear protective masks, but every mill worker had worn them since. Ione slapped more dust out of her clothes before sitting across from me. She picked up the pitcher on the table between us and held it up in question.

"Settled in all right, now that you're back?" she asked me while she poured out two cups of the watered wine.

"I had a few visitors yesterday evening, as you warned me, but luckily only one urgency. The journey tired me more than I expected."

"They're saying the Road's more dangerous now, animals and ghosts and such." Ione spoke in the tone of someone who had never traveled on the Road in her life and saw no reason to start. "Seems to me the White Court should be doing something about it."

"Right on both counts," I said. "Anyone thinking of traveling should use the Wayfarers' Rests, and not camp off the Road. And as for the White Court, that's partly what I want to talk to you about. First, though, I would like to thank whoever kept my home clean while I was away."

"You're looking at her." Ione grinned. "No one else wanted to. They were afraid to touch anything. Now that you've thanked me, what is it we need to talk about? And 'as for the White Court,' what does it want now?" From her tone, Ione thought just as little of the Court as she did of the Road.

I might be able to use that. "How much will the village suffer with Arlyn's loss?" I asked finally.

A line appeared between her brows. "We've got a few of his pieces left in his shop we could sell—unless you're going to claim them?" I shook my head. "But once they're gone, they're gone. It's a pity he never took an apprentice."

And he never had. Neither in his life as the practitioner Xandra Albainil, nor in his life as Arlyn the cabinetmaker.

"The mill brings in a living for my family and my workers, since there's no river large enough for another one anywhere near." She turned her cup of wine around in her fingers, focusing on it as if she thought she would find different answers there. "In a good year we make enough to do maintenance on the mechanicals. But if I lose a gear, or we have a couple of bad harvests, all of that can change."

"I can help with the harvest," I told her. "I picked up a few things while I was in the City." How to help things grow, to be precise, though not exactly in the City.

"Did you, now? Well I won't deny that will help." Ione refilled her cup. "I know practitioners live a long time—you'll outlive me, and probably my children, not that I'll care by then. But what if you go away again? Will the harvests still be good?"

The responsibility I felt toward the village was purely subjective; our agreement covered healing and nothing more. But if the Godstone had taught me anything, it was that every part had its place, and its importance. I opened my mouth and shut it again.

"Exactly," she said.

"There's another idea that may help the village that doesn't rely on my presence alone," I said. "It should improve conditions on the Road as well. I would like to start a new court for practitioners, and I propose to do it here."

Someone shouted inside the mill and Ione tilted her head up, listening. When the shout wasn't repeated, she looked back at me. "Here. What would be involved?" She did not sound as enthusiastic as I expected.

"It would be small at first. I have no idea how many practitioners, if any, might join me right away, and how many others might come later, as we gain some reputation. We could house a few people in Arlyn's buildings, and if anyone else in the village has spare room." I leaned forward, my elbows on the table. "Then there's the old, abandoned fort." It had been a courthouse before the Godstone had damaged the Modes, but it was only a shell now, little more than foundations and one solid wall. "We can take that over, fix it for our classrooms."

Ione leaned away from me, frowning. "Small *might* be possible. We wouldn't want to be outnumbered by strangers in our own home." Her eyes narrowed. "And still less by practitioners. How much do you think we can ask for in fees?"

"Fees?" I could feel my face stiffen.

"Fees. You know, rents, meals." Ione twisted up her lips and slewed her eyes to one side. "Hadn't thought of that, had you?"

I felt like three kinds of fool. I did not look forward to telling Elva about this. In fact, I could see now that I should have brought him with me. He would never have let me make this kind of mistake. Knowing this didn't change how annoyed it made me.

"No, Ione, I had not thought of it." In the City the Court didn't pay fees, it collected them, and supported itself through that. Communities and inns along the Road paid a tax that financed the couriers, apprentices who carried the mail and other items from the City to the Outer Modes and back again. "I pay no fees." Even I could tell how lame that sounded.

"Sure you do, but it's all barter. In exchange for your service, the village supports you, gives you food, mends the things you can't mend yourself, even fixes your roof when it's needed, or cleans your house. *The village*, meaning us and the people in the other places you visit. But there's only one of you, and there's only enough extra for you."

"If everyone's harvest is improved, there would be more work for the mill—"

"Can you make the river deeper? Have more fish in it? Milling's one thing, but it's not everything."

I could, in fact, do all those things, but that by itself was not the solution, and I knew it. "Practitioners are more than healers," I said. "There are other things we can do, things that will bring people to the village the way Arlyn's shop did. Those people bring money and provide other business."

Ione stood up, brushing herself off again. "That's more the kind of thing I'm talking about," she said. "People to bring in money, to bring in trade. That's how your new court can pay its way. You think about this some more and come back to me. We'll see if you can come up with something the whole village can agree to."

I sat staring at the tabletop after she left, clenching and unclenching my right fist. I had been taking things for granted. Turned out the White Court was not the only place with a council who had to be convinced.

ELVANYN

Elva was checking the swing of Fenra's door when he heard her footsteps behind him.

"Is there a metal worker in the village?" he asked without turning.

"What is it you need?"

"It's more or less a yes-or-no question." He straightened to his feet and turned toward her, smiling and holding out a hand to her. "These hinges need to be fixed—or replaced entirely. I know how to do it, but I'm no expert." He'd picked up a lot of different skills during his long exile in the New Zone, but he considered himself, as the saying there went, "a jack of all trades and master of none."

"Arlyn used hinges in his furniture, but they weren't made in the village. The smith here did not do work fine enough for him."

"But there's a smith? Door hinges would be well within his grasp, I should think." Elva followed her into the house and went to the kitchen area, where he poured himself a cup of water from the glazed ceramic dispenser. "I can make them myself, if the smith lets me use his forge," he added.

He held up his cup toward her, raising his eyebrows.

"No, thank you." She seemed distracted, not meeting his eyes.

"The idea didn't go over well, I take it?" He took her gently by the elbow and led her to a seat, handing her his cup of water. He pulled up a stool to face her, looked at her face and took the cup away again, shaking his head. Once he'd put it down, he took her hands again. The calluses always surprised him, considering she didn't work with her hands. At least not in the usual sense. "You'd better tell me."

He listened carefully to everything she said, and everything she didn't say. He had seen Fenra angry, and frightened. He had even seen her cry. But discouraged? It worried him more than he wanted to admit.

"Ione asked me if I could hunt. That would bring in some money, or at least something to barter." He paused. "Maybe we are thinking too small? The mill runs only when there's grain to grind. Not a lot to do after harvest. What if we could make it more profitable? Set it up to do other things, in the off times?"

"We can help make the village more prosperous," Fenra said. "But would that be enough? Would the villagers want to use their new money on providing room and board for practitioners? And not many practitioners, really, mostly students and apprentices? Will they be willing to subsidize that kind of education?"

Before Elva could answer, Tally, one of the mill boys, ran into the house, stopping short just inside the door when he saw Fenra had company. Elva smiled at him and waved him in. Soon enough everyone would get used to seeing him in Fenra's house. He wasn't planning on going anywhere. The boy looked from one to the other, excitement bringing him up on his toes.

"Fenra!" he finally burst out. "The courier's here and she's asking for you."

Fenra glanced at him, one eyebrow raised. "She has a message for *me*?"

"No, she just asked if you were here, and when we said yes, she said she wants to talk to you in person."

Fenra got to her feet and picked up her walking stick, more out of habit than of need. She had not expected anyone to come looking, not really, or she would have told the villagers not to say anything.

"Wait. Don't move." Elva ran into their bed space, pushing the curtain aside. Fenra had set a personal locking *forran* on the chest at the foot of the bed. His hand hesitated over his revolvers, but he picked up his sword instead, fastening it to the loop in his belt. Fenra tilted her head in question when he joined her at the door.

"Precisely because you don't think it's necessary," he said, grinning in answer to her unspoken question. "You wait here, and I'll see what this is all about."

FENRA

"Practitioner Lowens." The courier followed Elva up from the road and took off her black cap, nodded to me, and replaced it on her cropped black hair. Because of the caps they had to wear, many apprentices kept their hair short. It was almost a sign of passing the third-class exam that they began to grow their hair out. Like all apprentices she wore gray, black, and white. In this particular Mode, leggings, shirt, and tunic under her cloak. "I'm Teke Urgal. Predax Ap Gervin's going to be really pleased I found you," the girl said, leaning on her horse.

I was not pleased at all. Who else was Predax talking to about me? Elva appeared relaxed, however, and I trusted his instincts when it came to judging people's motives.

"Come and sit down," I said, leading her toward the bench outside my door. "Will Carith be fine for now, or would you like to unsaddle her? I could give you some feed out of my store." Just yesterday I would not have added the last four words, but talking to Ione had made me much more aware of where the supplies to support the couriers came from.

"How do you know my horse's name?" the girl said, taking a seat at the other end of the small bench.

"She knows every horse's name, and most other animals' too, if they have names at all." Elva stood only a pace away, leaning his shoulders against the wall where he had the best vantage point, and his sword arm was free.

The courier looked from me to Elva and back again. Obviously, she had been told who he was, and I could see a thousand questions in her eyes, but she had something she needed to tell me.

"Predax says stay away for now, give Practitioner Otwyn a chance to get the council to at least listen to what you have to say," the girl began. "Lots of us know about what you did, when you fixed the damage in the City. We're not supposed to know, but . . ." She shrugged. "A lot of us are real excited about that."

I smiled and nodded, remembering how quickly gossip had spread through the whole Court when I had been an apprentice.

"Predax also told us what you spoke to Practitioner Otwyn about. We were talking, you know? And I mentioned that the courier circuit isn't as long as it was when some of us first started. A friend of mine—she's waiting to take her third-class exams—says there used to be another two Modes after this one, and now this is the outermost Mode."

"Nothing beyond us?" This fit with what I had thought myself, but it still came as a shock.

"No practitioner. And Predax said he wished he knew where you were, so that he could tell you this, and he says, now that he's had time to think, there's lots more that's happened within the last few months that maybe you should know. We've had reports of fetches and ghosts along the Road, and there are wolves in the Fourth Mode."

Which meant the earth seizure was just the latest phenomenon. I glanced at Elva and found him watching me. The Godstone, mistaken about the nature of the World, and the importance of the Modes, had tried to make changes, with near disastrous results. This dropping off of Modes was only part of it. But the World had told me restoring the Godstone would begin to restore its health and balance. Why wasn't that working? Was the World wrong? Was that even possible?

"Thank you, Teke."

The girl shifted in her seat. "I wanted to tell you that the . . . the topic you discussed with Practitioner Otwyn makes sense to a lot of us. I mean, it's an explanation, isn't it? At least more of one than we're getting from anyone else." A note of bitterness changed her voice. "Some of the council don't even believe me about the Modes. They think I'm just trying to cut short this phase of my training."

Riding the circuits was the last thing apprentices did before starting on their class exams. Afterward, the ones who had a calling for it, and couldn't pass the first-class examinations, used to became Wayfarers. Or removed themselves entirely from the White Court, as I had done.

"Any message for Practitioner Otwyn?"

"Nothing other than my thanks for Predax's warning and advice." I did have a message, I thought, but better I should give it in person.

"I'd better be starting back." Teke swung herself up on her horse.

"This is my route for the month," she added, "so I'll be seeing you again."

I sat watching the courier ride away. Elva joined me on the bench.

"Looks like you're getting converts already. We'd better put more thought into what we're going to do with them."

Three

TAMARI

"YOU MUSTN'T BE nervous," Practitioner Sedges said, reaching to pick up the folio that slid out of my hands onto the top of his desk. "We just want to ask you to think back. Are you sure Lowens didn't say anything about where she was staying, or if she had plans to leave the City?"

I hadn't been nervous when the summons from Sedges' office came, but maybe I should have been.

"We would just like to speak to her about the earth seizure," he continued. "I'm sure she has an explanation."

"That's not how it sounded in council," I began. His head jerked back, like a surprised turtle, and his eyebrows rose. He obviously hadn't expected an argument. Maybe it wasn't the smartest thing to do, politically, to talk back to the head of the council, but if I started letting him push me around now, I'd be doing it for the rest of my life. "I don't know what motive she could have for causing that kind of damage," I added, "if all she was going to do was fix it."

"I'm not saying she caused it on purpose, not at all. But don't overlook that she's only third class. The likelihood of accidents increases in the lesser classes, and she *was* involved with the disappearance of Practitioner Metenari—innocently, I'm sure, since she wouldn't have been able to hurt him in any way. Still, I'm sure the experience must have been very traumatic for her."

I didn't think his saying "lesser classes" rather than "lower classes" made him any less bigoted—but this wasn't the time. Everything Sedges said could be true, but it was only "could be." Predax hadn't been so traumatized by Metenari's disappearance, and he was the man's own apprentice. Predax was a good kid, smarter than he looked, and except for the occasional passing shadow, his spirit was intact. And furthermore, the same could be said for Fenra Lowens. She irritated me—she wasn't as calm and in control as she'd like people to believe—but she was one of the more stable practitioners I had ever met. She believed what she said, and I almost believed her myself. At least, I had no reason to *dis*believe her.

"We had the same mentor, you know?" I said finally. "That's more or less what we talked about."

"Nothing else? Nothing about where she is staying?"

This was getting annoying. "Nothing like that at all." Lucky thing I hadn't let Predax tell me anything. I could honestly say I didn't know.

"Well then, Tamari, I won't keep you."

"Sure, Ronan." *Begin as you mean to go on.*

"Here, let me take those." Predax stood waiting for me outside Ronan's office and relieved me of more than half of the scrolls, folios, and books—with pages carefully marked—I carried in my arms. I'd brought all my research with me, but I should have known Ronan wouldn't listen to me.

"I needed a cart, really," I said. "But I didn't want to look like a maid going to market."

"My friend Yunien tells me they're working on a floating *forran*—not a *forran* that floats, I mean one that—"

"I knew what you meant, Predax. I'll ask if I don't." I smiled and his shoulders lowered as he smiled back. *Metenari has a lot to answer for,* I thought. His two more junior apprentices, Jordy and Konne, were still without mentors and would be for some time until the gaps in their education were better filled—at least that was the excuse other practitioners gave. Even Predax had had much of his natural intelligence sapped out of him and replaced with nerves. I'd wanted to help the other two, but I'd only been a first-class practitioner for a little over a year, and what with my sudden promotion to the council, I'd thought I'd better stick to one apprentice for now.

Predax opened the door to my office and stood aside to let me go in first. I put the documents I was carrying down on a side table and left them for Predax to sort back into order.

"Why don't you get yourself something to eat," I said, with my eye on the clock. "I won't need you until mid-afternoon."

"What can I bring you?"

"Nothing, thanks. If I eat anything right now it will only make me sleepy."

I sat down behind my desk and wriggled. Nothing like your own chairs for comfort. "I'm giving odds Ronan Sedges practiced the chair in his office. It couldn't be so uncomfortable by accident."

Predax paused in the doorway. "Maybe he wants his meetings as short as possible."

"And I thank him for that." I could hear Predax chuckling all the way down the hall.

I sighed and rubbed my temples. I had that itchy feeling you get when you leave a job unfinished, but I'd done everything I could for Fenra Lowens. At least for now. I wondered if I'd ever hear from her again.

I pulled over the book sitting to my left and opened it to the marked page. I had plenty to do without worrying about Fenra. When I'd agreed to take Predax as an apprentice, I'd pulled my own work journals out of my personal library. I had a wonderful experience working with Medlyn Tierell and I thought I couldn't do better than to use my own records of that time as guides. Testing showed that Predax had a good grasp of the basic concepts—he knew what a pattern was, though his still wasn't very strong—and he'd mastered the basic *forrans* that didn't need patterns. I began to read my notes.

"Tamari?"

I tore the page I'd been about to turn. Fenra Lowens stood in front of the desk.

"You have *got* to stop doing that." I tossed down my pen. This was maybe the third time she'd just popped into my office out of nowhere. I hadn't liked it before, and I still didn't. "Or at least tell me *how* you do it."

Fenra smiled and pulled a gold locket out from under her shirt by its chain. I recognized it, though I'd only seen it once before. "That's Medlyn's locket." I kept my voice matter of fact.

"He gave it to me," Fenra said, closing her hand on it. "I also still think of it as his," she added.

Did she? Nice of her. It took me a minute to control my voice. "I know he was slowing down before the end," I said, waving her to a seat. "But I didn't know he'd made an artifact to get to his office." *What else does she know that I don't?*

"He did not. At least, not exactly." Fenra stood up again and held out her right hand. I stared at it for a moment before standing up and taking the offered hand in mine.

Fenra held the locket up in her practitioner's hand, fingernail ready to flick it open. "Ready?"

For what? "Sure."

Fenra opened the locket and fog began to spill slowly out. I found that I'd moved closer to her without being aware of it. An almost familiar pattern formed around us, soft, natural colors. The pattern moved, expanded, and settled. The fog disappeared, and I looked around at an oval room paneled in a dark streaky wood. Shelf after shelf held books and artifacts; cupboards and chests lined the walls where there weren't any shelves. A familiar shape drew my eye, and I let go of Fenra's hand to examine it.

"I know this model." My smile felt shaky. "It's one of Medlyn's. This is his vault, isn't it? He gave you the key to his vault." I looked away so she wouldn't see my face. *I was his last apprentice,* I thought, *but he gave this to her.*

"He did," Fenra said. "He knew me for so long, you see," she added, as if she'd guessed how I felt.

"Sure." I took a deep breath and let it out slowly, trying to push all my jealousy away with it. I like to think I managed. "Thanks for bringing me here." I hoped my voice didn't sound as flat to her as it did to me. "So, how does the locket work?"

"If I am anywhere other than the vault, the locket brings me here. If I am already here, opening the locket face up takes me to your office, face down to Medlyn's old rooms, which no one seems to be using at the moment. I assume there are other places, but I have not had time to experiment."

"I didn't know anything about this." And the little spark of jealousy was back.

"But you noticed his interest in transportation?"

"Of course, but I thought it was a . . . well, a hobby. He was such a fine lorist, I couldn't really imagine him as serious about something else."

"He was. I remember him working on unusual *forrans* even when I was his apprentice. And you know he gave the class in movement."

I clenched my jaw. Fenra led me to a round table just large enough for two people to eat at, or for four people to play cards. There were only two chairs, however. Probably Medlyn hadn't ever brought more than one person at a time. *He never brought* me *here.*

"I didn't know," I said after I'd taken one of the chairs. "That class hasn't been offered since before my time."

"Well, there never were many who could profit by it," Fenra said. "When it comes to movement, I can use someone else's *forran*, but I cannot write one myself. And even so, I have never seen one that works like this locket. I wonder why Medlyn never got around to sharing more of his work."

"I wish *I'd* seen more of it," I said, looking around. I think I was able to keep the bitterness out of my tone. It was stupid to feel the way I felt. Every mentor/apprentice relationship is different, and intimate in its own way. *Just keep telling yourself that.*

"Here, I can show you something right now." Fenra crossed the room to a cupboard made of some dark wood so smooth and shiny I'd give odds the surface would feel like satin. Fenra opened the right-hand door and took out a pitcher.

"There are glasses over behind you," she said. "If you wouldn't mind."

Looking around, I saw four glasses standing next to a model of a bridge. I took two back to the table and set them down next to the pitcher. Fenra had opened the left-hand side of the cupboard and taken out a covered dish of green-glazed ceramic, not unlike one my mother had used for years, and set it down on the table between the two chairs.

"Just a minute, I forgot plates." She crossed over to the end of the room and came back carrying two wide, shallow bowls and a handful of cutlery. "I do not know why these aren't kept with the glasses," she said after distributing them and sitting down across from me.

"People who live alone often do things like that," I offered, as I poured the wine. "When you live with someone else, the organization has to make sense to both of you." I felt I was regaining my equilibrium, and my stomach suddenly told me I was hungry after all. "So, what are you going to show me?"

"This." Fenra lifted the lid and the sudden aroma of chicken braised with sherry and saffron made my mouth water. "This is my favorite dish," I said as Fenra served me. "How did you know?"

"I did not know." Fenra smiled what I thought was the first genuinely gleeful smile I'd ever seen on her face. "Medlyn did."

"Well, of course he knew, but . . ."

Fenra raised a finger, still smiling. "There is a *forran* on this dish, and on this jug, and on a number of baskets, bowls, and other containers—even some of the chests. You are familiar with the standard *forran*, if I can put it that way, that makes a container constantly refillable, but only with the same thing each time?"

"And?" This was nothing new. The White Court had quite a little business placing *forrans* on water carriers and wine barrels—to say nothing of renewing them.

"Well, with these, each time you open, or pour, or uncover, you will find something different."

"So there won't be chicken and saffron next time?"

"There might be," Fenra said, frowning slightly. "If that is what you need. But it might be a dish of dressed greens, or soup, or something else totally different. I have eaten lamb stew out of this dish, and one time it held half a dozen warm meat pasties. This jug," she tapped the handle with her fork, "has wine in it now, but it's also had vegetable juice, and water, and coffee. Sometimes it depends on who is pouring."

"And Medlyn did all this?"

"Yes. Each item not only remembers what it once held, it remembers *everything* it once held. Medlyn created a *forran*—or a series of them, I am not sure—that touches different places and different times, and if that wasn't enough, it seems to know what you need before you open it."

"And I needed my favorite dish?"

"Evidently. You must be tired, or under stress."

"That's an understatement." I took another bite of chicken and chewed slowly, savoring the sherry, the garlic, the saffron and the almonds. "You're trusting me with rather a lot, aren't you?" I waved my fork around in a gesture that took in the whole room.

"I think it's you who are trusting me." Fenra put down her own fork and took a sip of her wine. I noticed she always kept her practitioner's hand free. "After all, without me you cannot leave here." She set her glass down and smiled. "But Elva likes you, and that counts for a great deal."

I chewed and swallowed. I told myself I wasn't nervous. "How do all the *forrans* keep powered, now that Medlyn is faded? Or is keeping them active what faded him?"

"Another item he shared with no one," she said. "Perhaps when we have time we can find out."

FENRA

I watched Tamari take everything in. A great deal of information in a small space of time. "I hear the council is still trying to blame me for the earth seizure."

Tamari picked up her glass and leaned back in her chair, frowning. "The way I see it," she said finally, "they're not even going to think about the Dadian philosophy. Not in the current atmosphere and not if they know the idea comes from you. They'll just think you're trying to cover up some monumental incompetence. No offense."

"None taken. Being associated with me won't make things easier for you."

She looked down, and back up, and waited without responding.

"Just as well, perhaps." It had all seemed so obvious when the World told me what was needed. "They would prefer things to continue as they have been, and so they would not see the seizure as evidence of the World's needs." I drummed my fingers on the side of my glass. "I have wasted time, and meanwhile the World continues to fail— perhaps faster than expected." I took a gulp of wine and put the glass down carefully. This was just what the World had been trying to tell me.

Tamari was nodding. "So, what will you do now?"

"I will start a new court in the Outer Modes. In my village, in fact." I would find some way to finance it, I thought. "I hope there are practitioners who will join me, but if not, I will take apprentices, students, and any others I find."

"You can't do that!" Her dropped fork rattled as it hit her plate.

"Really?" I said, stung by her tone. "Is there some *forran* that prevents it? Some ancient prohibition? You are the lorist, you tell me."

Tamari watched me for a moment. "Specifically against setting up a practitioners' court? Nothing that I've ever read. But there is something, and the council will be happy to use it against you." Tamari picked up her fork and pointed it at me. "Only first-class practitioners are allowed to teach."

I was taking a chance, but I decided to tell her. "I did not take the second- or first-class exams, true, but that does not mean I am not a first-class practitioner."

She sat back in her chair and studied me with narrowed eyes. Finally, her mouth twisted into a smile and she nodded. "I see it, now that I'm looking for it. Medlyn spoke to me about not taking the exam," she added, sounding as if something had just fallen into place for her. "The possibility of it, I mean. Did he want me to reject the Court and the City like you?"

"If you had felt as I did, he would have supported your decision, as he did mine. But I know he respected the decision you *did* make. Did you ever feel otherwise?"

"No, never." She looked comforted. I realized that her relationship with Medlyn—despite how uncomfortable it seemed to be making her at the moment—was at least part of the reason I trusted her. Though Elva did like her, I had told the truth about that.

"Well, then. It may be that the White Court doesn't want me to teach, but who is going to stop me?"

Tamari stayed serious for a few minutes, thinking over what I had said. Finally, she nodded, a small smile on her lips. "Especially if they don't find you. I'll do what I can to muddy that trail, but you should know that most of couriers know where you are. They're not talking yet, but they will. It's just too exciting to keep to themselves. I'll see what I can do to help. I'm not completely convinced by what you say, but there *are* old documents that support the Dadian philosophy—and at the very least, it explains some of the recent changes, which is more than anyone else in the Court can manage." She shrugged. "But they'll find you eventually. Just because there's no rule against it doesn't mean the White Court will stand back while you open a court that competes with them."

"When you have fought against the Godstone, and spoken with the World, it's difficult to be afraid of lesser things." *Remember that,* I told myself.

"Do you think—if the World would only manifest itself, that would be proof enough for anybody."

"If I could summon the World, I would, even though there will always be people who for reasons of their own will reject the proof of their own experience. But I am not the one who summons the World. It summons me."

ELVANYN

"That's not a bad shot."

Elva wasn't startled by the voice behind him; he'd heard the footsteps approaching. He put the arrow in his hand back into its quiver and turned around. "I haven't used one of these in a long time," he said. The tone hadn't sounded sarcastic, but you never knew.

"I was serious," the man said, coming closer now it was safe. "It's all the more impressive if you're unfamiliar with the weapon. You've got a good eye for a City man." The speaker was burly, at least half a head shorter than Elva, and looking shorter still because of the thickness of his torso and arms. He wore his graying hair cropped short and Elva thought he could see the faded remains of a very old burn scar on the man's left cheek.

"Good eyes are needed everywhere," Elva said.

The man held out his hand. "I'm Betrex Smith, and when it's needed, I'm the hunt master. I hear you're interested."

Elva took the offered hand. "Elvanyn Karamisk," he said. "What's the pay?"

"Two-thirds goes to the village," Betrex said, taking a seat on the bench outside Fenra's cottage. "The remainder we divide among us. Keep it to eat, sell it to someone else, whatever you'd like."

"Two-thirds seems a lot for the village to get."

Betrex shrugged. "They supply us. Most of us are unmarried, so we're given room and sometimes board in one of the hostels, or a private home. Things we can't grow or make ourselves. Then there's weapons repair—"

"Wait a minute, don't you do most of that? Aren't you paying yourself, then?"

"As smith, I get a stipend from the village." The man grinned, opening and closing his hands. "And let's not forget, I also keep all you rowdies in line. We're short a hunter just now, if you're looking for work."

"Won't that make your share smaller?"

"Think about it. The right person means we can hunt more in a shorter time, bring more back. That increases everyone's share."

It made sense. Elva nodded. "Sounds good. Count me in."

"You're living with the practitioner, are you?"

Elva wondered where this was going. "That's right."

"She saved one of my hunters last year, took a boar tusk to the leg. I'm not sure I'd want to live with her, but we're all glad she's back. Do you think she would ever come with you? It would guarantee a good hunt."

"What I can guarantee is she'll say no. She has a good relationship with the natural world, and she'd like to keep it that way." Elva gestured into the cottage. "Are you busy right now? I've got a couple of questions."

FENRA

"Come," I said to her. "I will take you back." I pulled the locket out from under my shirt.

"How are you getting back to your village?" She got to her feet, wiping her hands with her linen napkin. "Even if you managed to get out of the Court without anyone seeing you, I'm afraid I can't lend you a horse, and the public coach only goes as far as the Third Mode now."

"Not to worry," I told her as we grasped hands. "Our old mentor had a few other tricks up his sleeve."

"I suppose you'll let me know what they are, one day?" The hard note was back in Tamari's voice.

"I sincerely hope so." I opened the locket.

Once Tamari was safely back in her office, I returned to the vault. Of the twenty-three models on the shelves, most of bridges and fountains, the one I knew best was a fountain—more a walled spring, really—up on the hillside west of the village, dedicated to an old god no one remembered, though the spring itself still worked. Nowadays those people who did not have their own cisterns tended to use the newer fountain, on the other side of the main square from the mill. Medlyn had not made a model of that one.

I pulled Medlyn's book of *forrans*—I still thought of it that way, though it now had my name on it—from the shelf and reviewed the *forran* I needed. Even though I had used the *forran*/model combination several times, I did not feel confident enough to try it without first consulting the book. I fixed it once more in my mind, spinning my pattern around and through it. I set the book down on the tabletop and touched the model of the fountain. The nice thing about using this fountain, I thought, shaking my tunic straight as I stepped off the stone coping, was that the model deposited you well out of the path of the water. That wasn't true for some of the others.

I walked down the path leading to the village, dodging overhanging branches and telling myself to come back with something to cut them with. I had told myself to trim the path before, I realized. This time I would try to remember.

I found Elva replacing the hinges on my door.

"Did you find those in Arlyn's workshop?"

"No, ma'am, Smith gave them to me."

"*Gave* them?"

"An advance on my pay." He stepped back from his work and smiled at me. "I got a job."

My knees felt rubbery and I sat down on the nearest stool. "Sheriff?"

"No, ma'am. Hunter."

I listened as he told me. "Are you certain of being able to manage the weapon?"

He shrugged. "It's been a while, but I've used a bow in the New Zone. Besides, it turns out I have a good eye." He grinned like a small boy who was trying to get away with something. "I've had a lot of practice shooting. Turns out to be a transferable skill."

We went inside and I found everything tidier than I usually kept it. There were two wine cups drying, but other than that the table was cleared, and the dishes shelved. Elva brushed past me to the water barrel and ladled himself a cup.

I told him about my talk with Tamari. "She agrees," I concluded, "the council will not listen to me." I accepted a cup of water. "Oh, and can you remind me to take a tool and cut the branches that grow over the path to the old fountain? I almost put my eye out today."

Elva drained his own cup and set it down. "Why didn't you just ask the trees and bushes to pull them back?" I looked at him, my mouth fallen open. "You know, like you did the grasses and bushes in the New Zone?"

I closed my mouth. "Because I did not think of it."

"Using your magic this way is still pretty new to you," Elva said. "Don't let it skew your focus."

There was something important in what he said, but it took me a moment to track it down. Something that would solve our money problems.

In what was beginning to seem like another life, I had persuaded grasses and other growth to clear a small area of ground for Arlyn Albainil to draw a pattern. I had asked the rocks to move, and they had sunk out of sight. If they would sink for me, they might also rise. The problem was that I knew nothing about this subject.

"Elva, do you know anything about gold mining?"

WITTENSLADE

"What does one wear to the White Court?"

"Anything but practitioner's colors, I would say."

Riva's carriage was due to pick him up in half an hour, but Witt had already been dressing for three times longer than that. He had changed his shirt four times, his breeches and stocking once each—he could change neither cravat nor fan without also changing his manicure—and his wig twice. Finally, it seemed that both he and his valet were satisfied.

"I should come with you," Arriz said, and not for the first time.

"If we were taking my coach, certainly, but I can't expect Riva Deneyra to accommodate you. Guaranteed to make her wonder if I was up to something. You know all these people are paranoid."

"And you're not?"

"That's different. I *know* there's something to be afraid of. Everyone talks about the practitioners as though they were some kind of servant who'd gotten above himself." Witt looked Arriz in the eye. "What if everyone is wrong?"

The widow rolled up in front of his townhouse in an open carriage, painted green and gold, with stylized eyes on the sides making it look like a huge frog. Both her coachman and her footman wore livery in the same colors as the coach. Witt cast a glance over the pair of grays harnessed to the front of the carriage. They were well matched, but seemed sturdier, less light-footed and sleek, than was the current fashion. As he was very quickly learning, Riva Deneyra wasn't much influenced by the current fashion. He fluttered his fan at her as he descended his front steps and watched her nostrils flare before she managed to smile at him.

He saluted her as he reached the carriage, tapping the brim of his hat with his walking stick. Her footman opened the carriage door, jumping on the running board once Witt was safely inside and seated next to the widow. From this angle Witt could see that both her coachman and her footman were women. *I suppose that cuts down on the gossip*, he thought. *Or starts up an entirely different kind.*

"What are you smiling about?" she said, once they were under way. The day's overcast sky darkened her suit to a sea blue and dulled the gold of her buttons and earrings.

"I was just thinking that we'll have to come up with better terms for our servants if many more people start using women in the traditional place of men." *I wonder if I could wear earrings.* "Footmen, coachmen."

"Why not call them all servants?" she said. "Foot servants, coach servants, and the like?"

"You know, I think valets were once called body servants. In fact, they still are in some places."

"Wherever did the word 'valet' come from, then?"

"I've no idea," he said. "Though I suppose some dusty old scholar would be able to tell us, if we really wanted to know."

"If the rumors about practitioners are true, perhaps one of them can tell us."

"Which particular rumor do you mean?" Witt asked her with a smile.

"The same practitioner assisted at the births of my children. The youngest came along twelve years after the oldest, and as far as I could see the practitioner hadn't changed a bit. Same hair, same skin, same teeth. Not so much as a frown line."

"My mother looked the same at sixty as she had at forty."

"That's not uncommon," Riva agreed. "But my aunt claimed to have used the same practitioner, and that would mean this woman who looked perhaps twenty-eight had to be over sixty."

Witt turned in his seat and tapped Riva lightly on the arm with his fan. "Don't tell me you're worried about looking your age."

Her smile was unexpectedly genuine, reaching her eyes. "I'm more interested in finding out how long they live."

Their carriage was stopped at the East Bridge, where they were asked to step out. Witt opened his mouth to object, but Riva Deneyra stood without hesitation and took her footman—her foot *servant*'s hand to step down out of the vehicle. Clearly, she expected this. She stood until she saw the carriage safely parked in the waiting area and her servants comfortable before turning toward the bridge. Apparently, they couldn't take attendants into the Court with them. Witt reminded himself to tell Arriz he'd been saved a boring wait.

"If you would come this way, please." Dressed in gray trousers, short black jacket, a white shirt, and a small black cap, the person speaking was obviously an apprentice. Witt had seen several around town, though not lately. There was something different about this one, however, and it took Witt a moment to realize that the young man—at least five years younger than Witt himself—wasn't nervous like every other apprentice he'd seen. This boy was almost bouncing on his toes.

"Have you been here before?" Witt asked Riva, seeing that she didn't look around her as much as he did.

"I contracted my birthing aide myself." She stopped and turned completely around, taking in the whole of the gardens they walked through. "It was sunny then too." She turned to the apprentice. "Is it always sunny?"

The boy grinned again. "This way, please."

He led them past a long pool dotted with pink water lilies and surrounded by orange trees bearing fruit, across a narrow patio, and up a wide, shallow set of steps. They crossed the courtyard at the top of the steps and passed through an archway into a cool, tiled hallway. Witt trailed his fingers along the blue and green tiles on the walls. *I like this,* he thought. *I could do this at home.* It would be nice and cool in the summer, and for the winter he could always hang tapestries.

The apprentice opened a raised-panel door on the left and motioned them to enter.

"Please have a seat," he said. "The practitioner will be with you shortly."

They had barely made themselves comfortable on the other side of the table when a woman only slightly older than the apprentice and dressed in practitioner's colors entered, taking a seat across from them. Though if what the widow had said was true, Witt thought, there was no way to know for sure how old either of them was. The apprentice who had been their guide came in behind her, carrying a large folio. He sat down to one side, opened the folio, took out a pen, and waited.

"I asked to meet with the council." Riva's voice was cool, but edged.

The practitioner looked the widow right in the eye and raised her brows. "I am the practitioner Tamari Otwyn, member of the council and here as their representative. I understood this was a . . ." The woman stopped to clear her throat. "A routine petition." Just as Witt was thinking that she didn't seem very sure of herself, the practitioner turned her head slightly and looked him in the eyes. In the instant that their eyes met and held, Witt saw that she knew him, the real him, not what he made very sure other people saw, and while the thought made a little sweat form on his upper lip, it didn't scare him as much as he would have expected. In fact, what he felt was offended. He was sure of it.

TAMARI

"Find out what they're whining about now and get rid of them," were the instructions I got from Nubin Sonsera. I wanted to consult with Ronan, but they told me he was busy.

"I know I'm the newest council member," I told Predax as he helped me into my black coat. "What I didn't know was that every dirty job no one else wants to do is suddenly mine."

"A little like when you first become an apprentice." Predax gently moved my hands away and unraveled the mess I had made of my cravat. "You think that now you're not a student anymore things will be different, but you find out that from being on the top tier of students, you're now on the bottom tier of apprentices."

"I'd forgotten that." For some reason that made me feel better. When we were both satisfied that I was properly dressed to receive outside visitors, Predax followed me out of my rooms and down to the audience chamber always used for meetings with mundanes. We'd always been told that no *forrans* could work in this room. I wondered if anyone had ever tested that.

"They're waiting for us," Predax reminded me. "We don't want to look as though we've been waiting for them."

"I know," I said. "I've read those strategy books too."

I was surprised to see that the delegation from the Red Court consisted of only two people, a very well-dressed older woman in a lovely dark blue suit with gold trim, and an even better dressed younger man in a riot of color. Even his fingernails matched his cravat. I'd never seen such a thing. I immediately felt dowdy, but I told myself practitioner's colors trumped style every time.

"I am Riva Anden Deneyra," the older woman said after she'd got over the fact that it was just me here to meet with her. "Courtier of the Chamber of the Red Court."

I almost smiled; the even softness of her voice didn't hide the steel of command under it. She was used to getting her way. The sunlight coming in from the window highlighted the strip of white hair that rose through the dark red from above her left eye. She'd done it on purpose, of course, and it looked stylish, but what it said was "Yes, I *am* older, and don't you forget it."

"This is my associate Wittenslade Camdin Volden, a new member of the chamber." I caught him looking at me, and as our eyes met, I saw past all the silk and lace and color and ruffles and, yes, the slightly blue wig. There was someone much more intelligent, sensible, and shrewd under all that stuff. *Why the costume?* I wondered.

"I am the Practitioner Tamari Otwyn." How I wished for a third name. It sounded so imposing. "Member of the Council of the White Court. And this is my senior apprentice, Predax Ap Gervin. He will take notes of our meeting." The woman's lips tightened. Evidently no one had told her she could bring a secretary.

"Oh." The young man turned to Predax. "I think I know your family. I was at school with Jeller Ap Gervin."

"A distant cousin," Predax said. "I haven't seen him in years."

"Of course, forgive me for mentioning it," Dom Volden added. "It's so easy to forget how out of the world you really are."

I examined his tone for sarcasm and didn't find any. "Now that the formalities are over, shall we begin?"

"Just a moment," Dom Volden said. "If you could provide me with a pen, and some paper, I'd be happy to take notes for the Red Court." His grin changed his whole face. He clearly didn't think it beneath him to act as a clerk. "You can have a look at them afterward, if you'd like."

Dom Deneyra raised her eyebrows, but in amusement, not disapproval. Dom Volden was pretending this was all a game, an amusement of some kind. I think he knew that the only person he was fooling was his companion. *Why does he do this?* I wondered.

Predax passed paper, ink, and pen across the table and we waited until Dom Volden was ready to begin.

"Put simply," Dom Deneyra said in her smooth voice, "the Red Court would like to explore the possibility of opening trade negotiations between the two Courts."

"I'm not sure you can put any of that 'simply.'" I didn't bother hiding my surprise—after all, I *was* surprised. "You must know that the . . . coolness between the two Courts has existed for some time."

Dom Deneyra nodded. "To the point where it was difficult to arrange this meeting, yes." She leaned forward over her folded hands, brows drawn down. "Which is exactly the issue, I think. The present conditions are detrimental to both parties. Commoners who can't afford ever-increasing tariffs and fees are dying needlessly; artisans are not benefiting from new techniques; buildings, roads, and bridges are falling into disrepair, and the knowledge to fix them is not available."

"I understand that at one time, this was arranged a little better?" Dom Volden said looking up from his notes.

I took a deep breath. Wasn't this part of what Fenra had talked about? But I could see that this petition had to go to the whole council. "You're quite right. Our records show that there have been periods of time when relations between the two Courts were more open and friendly. You will understand, however, that this overture has to be taken to the full council?"

"That is why I am surprised to meet only with you." She leaned forward again. "We should be helping each other, not hindering. After the extraordinary aid given by a practitioner after the earth seizure three days ago, we were hoping the atmosphere had changed, that we could work toward easing hostilities. I've only talked about what you can do for us, but there are things we can do for you. Increased contact means better food, more variety, a bigger labor market, access to artisans. You wouldn't have to use up your science and theories in performing things ordinary people can do."

I leaned back in my chair. Of course, Fenra's fixing the rift and helping the injured gave the Red Court grounds to think we were well-disposed toward them—which was true, at least as far as Fenra went. According to what I'd read, the Dadian philosophy *did* call for better relations between the two Courts. When the philosophy was followed in the past, the City had flourished, and the two Courts helped and supported each other.

I decided to tell this woman the truth. "I'm sorry," I said. "All I can do is take your suggestions to the council."

Riva Deneyra stood. "I understand. Can you make sure that any reply comes to me?" She pulled a visiting card out of her vest pocket with thumb and forefinger. "There are some in the chamber who aren't as supportive of my proposal as I might like."

It seemed she also told the truth.

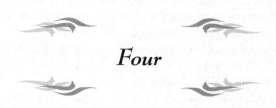

Four

FENRA

WHEN MY LAST patient left, I sat outside in the sun, my back against the warm stone wall of my cottage, breathing deeply and wondering what food I had in the house to stop the trembling in my hands. I did not open the eyes I had closed against the light until I heard Ione Miller's footsteps stop in front of me. The look on her face—lips pressed into a tight line, eyebrows drawn down—made me push myself to my feet and draw my stola closer around me.

"Come in, I'll get some wine." I stood at the table, pitcher in my hand, when I realized she had not followed me in.

She stood in the doorway, arms folded across her chest. "I've got three people down by the mill asking for you, Fenra Lowens. From their clothing, two apprentices and one practitioner. So you've already started inviting people here? Without checking with me?"

"I have not invited anyone." I hesitated, wondering if Predax or even Tamari had sent them. Well, so much for keeping out of sight until the council forgot about me. I knew I would draw the attention of the Court sooner or later, I was just hoping for later.

"Right now they're at the hostel. They've got a few coins between them, so we'll feed them today, but tomorrow they'll be your problem." Ione came in as far as the table, but did not take the cup of wine I poured for her. "Fenra, I thought we hadn't finished talking about this."

"We had not." I set cup and pitcher down on the table, next to an old leather pouch about the size of my hand. Elva had kept extra bullets in it. I sat down and pulled it toward me. "I wonder if this might get us started in the right direction." I loosened the cord and upended the pouch. Three irregular chunks of metal ore about the size of my thumbnail fell out onto the tabletop.

Ione dropped her arms and sank into the seat across from me. "Is that what I think it is?"

"If you think it's gold, then yes."

"Where did you—No! Don't tell me. I don't want to know." Ione took her lower lip between thumb and forefinger, studying the three little lumps on the table before lifting her eyes to mine. "Could others find it? We won't get a bunch of people digging us up, will we? My dad told me once about a gold find in the next county. People went crazy, he said."

"No one can find it but me," I told her. I dropped the chunks back into the pouch. "Not even another practitioner, not even if I explained how to do it." I was not entirely certain about this last, but as far as I knew, no one had the same connection with the World that I had. That was why it had needed me in the first place.

Ione swallowed, and nodded. She pulled her focus from the pouch and looked me in the eye. "Does the gold mean we don't get the other things we talked about? Better harvest, making the mill more efficient?" Ione was not turning down the gold, she just wondered what the village had to give up for it.

"Gold—money—in itself isn't worth anything." I pushed the cup of wine into her hand and poured another for myself. "It's only valuable in terms of what you can buy with it. I will be buying labor to build my school, lodging for students and teachers, including food. In order for there to be food to buy, there needs to be a good harvest, animals need to be healthy and numerous, grain needs to be milled for porridges and breads." I shrugged. "Bread needs to be baked. And the villagers need to be able to go to other towns to buy the things that are not made here."

"Or to attract the artisans to set up their shops here. If there are more sheep, or better wool, maybe we can persuade Jonsel Weaver to move her shop here, or send one of her daughters to start a secondary shop. Maybe even a goldsmith." Ione leaned back and smiled. "Yes, this will work." She took a sip of her wine.

TAMARI

"If we could return to the actual purpose of this meeting?" Ronan Sedges' voice was deep and resonant. Everyone stopped talking. *Wish I could do that*, I thought. "Practitioner Otwyn has met, on my instructions, with members of the Red Court chamber. Apparently, they want to have more cordial relations with us."

"Perhaps they got the idea from Practitioner Lowens' well-meant but not very well-thought-out actions with regard to repairing the rift." Omasi Dekadent was the chief examiner, a short, thin woman with long delicate hands. Her tight curly hair reminded me of Fenra, but Omasi's skin was much paler. The rest of the council were so much older than me they likely didn't remember their exams, but I was still a little afraid of her.

"Perhaps they were thinking along those lines already, and just took courage from a set of circumstances." I'd learned already that Nubin Sonsera had a sour view of the world. He looked like everyone's favorite uncle, a little round, a little jolly, with a cheerful smile. Like my mother used to say, looks can deceive.

"In any case, I suggest we ask Practitioner Otwyn, acting as Senior Lorist, to research past agreements and treaties between the two Courts to help us come to a decision."

Acting as Senior Lorist? That was news to me. Why this sudden sign of approval?

"If I may, before we begin." The speaker this time was Zavala Rankin. Until I came along, she had been the newest councilor, though that was long enough ago that no one remembered when she was voted in. "I think Tamari needs to focus her research. It's clear what the mundanes want from us, but how would *we* benefit from a more amiable association with the Red Court? What can *we* get from *them*? Would it be an equal exchange? Or, if unequal, how could we ensure it would be in our favor?"

"That is precisely why negotiations need to take place." I hung on to my patience with both hands. Had the council always been this slow and this frustrating? "We won't know what the mundanes have to offer unless we give them a chance to tell us."

"I can tell you right now, nothing." Nubin leaned back in his seat, tucking his thumbs into his belt. I don't know, maybe he thought it looked impressive.

"We overlook something." The quiet voice from the far end of the oval table brought everyone to attention—some of us literally. I don't think I'd ever heard Az Pilcuerta speak—or seen her move, for that matter. As far as I knew, she didn't have any official assignment on the council. Easily the oldest practitioner at the table, older even than my late mentor Medlyn Tierell, I'd begun to think she was a mummy.

"We would love to hear your thoughts, Az." Ronan clasped his hands on the table in front of him, leaning forward on his elbows. There was nothing but polite respect on his face, though some of the others shifted in their chairs and looked uncomfortable.

"This world does not exist for the use of practitioners only," the quiet rough voice went on. Obviously she couldn't speak any louder. "If it did," she continued, "there would be no mundanes. I know it's unpopular now to think this way, but as people with a better understanding of the world as it is, it's part of our duty to look after mundanes, to protect them from the worst the world can bring them, and prevent them from harming themselves through ignorance or want."

That sounded a little like the Dadian philosophy to me. If I'd known she saw things this way, I could have sent Fenra to her.

More shifting of chairs as several council members sat back, pretending they weren't interested. The old lady smiled and suddenly you could see the skull under her skin. *Just how old* is *she?* I thought. She waited until the sounds died away before speaking again.

"I told you it was unpopular, but that doesn't make it less true. We have a responsibility to the mundanes as fellow creatures of the world. We have been slowly distancing ourselves from them, and that has gone on long enough. The world is unbalanced, and this is a good time to bring that to an end."

"Are you serious? No offense, Az," Nubin hesitated a little at using her first name, "but things are different now from your day. It isn't our job to look after people who can't look after themselves." Nubin did everything but throw his hands in the air.

"To say 'no offense' does not make your words less offensive, young man." I stifled a grin. Az Pilcuerta's eyes had narrowed, and with her beaky nose she looked like a bird of prey. A dangerous bird of prey. But

I felt she was more amused than anything else. "I strongly advise you to consider what I have said."

"With respect, Az, and I sincerely mean *those* words, there are more than enough pragmatic reasons to open negotiations with the Red Court. If there are those of us," here Zavala Rankin looked around the table, "who feel uncomfortable with a more humanitarian position, they can ignore it. *They've* approached us," she added. "That gives us the advantage in any discussions."

When I returned to my office, a student I didn't know was waiting for me just outside my door. Like my mentor before me, I kept the office door open at all times, but no one could go in unless I was there.

"Practitioner Otwyn? You don't know me, I'm Hogar Prinde? I attend your lectures? On research methodology? I'm hoping to be a lorist one day?"

Hogar was obviously one of those people whose shyness is shown by making every phrase a question. I think I managed not to sigh out loud. The boy was taller than me and looked as if he was still growing. I could remember being this young, but I hoped I'd never been this annoying.

"What can I do for you, Hogar Prinde?"

"Well, I was talking to Predax, you know?"

"Try to say something without making it sound like a question," I said as kindly as I could, tapping out a *forran* on his shoulder. He blushed, and I felt petty, but someone needed to tell him.

"What Predax was telling me, that old philosophy—I mean, it means we could do more outside the White Court, doesn't it?" He winced.

"That's all right." I went around my worktable and motioned him to a seat. "That actually was a question. Go on."

"Well, those old records, the ones that show we used to be more out in the world, traveling around—I mean, I'm enjoying my studies, but where does it lead but more studying, and more research? What happens to practitioners who aren't good at research? If we traveled more, well, there'd be more for us to do, wouldn't—I mean, I think. So we'd need more practitioners—and maybe more of us could graduate. And from what Predax told me, we'd be doing more good." He lowered his voice as he said those words.

I sat forward, drumming the fingers of my right hand on my desktop. I'd learned the hard way not to do that with my practitioner's hand. "Have you gone out as a courier yet?"

"No, Practitioner, I was supposed to go last month. It's just that my warding and healing tests keep being postponed." It wasn't unusual for students who hadn't been marked down as someone's future apprentice to face this type of delay, but from what this boy said, there might be other reasons.

"I can look into that for you." I thought quickly through all the things I'd have to do to accomplish that. At least Hogar was far enough along . . . if I gave him his tests myself . . . if I could find the right courier to send with him . . . "How badly do you want to be a traveler?"

Hogar chewed on his lower lip. "Pretty badly," he said, his voice lower and firmer than it had been. "When I think about staying here and living here and doing the same thing all the time?" He shook his head. "I don't see myself as an inventor of *forrans*. When I think about it I get a sick stomach and," he shrugged, "I tell myself to stop worrying? But I don't really, at least not for long."

The odd thing was, I could remember feeling a little that way when I was an apprentice. I'd felt more comfortable on the Road than I had in the City. But then I began studying lore, and that feeling went away. A couple of others had felt the same way, but we weren't encouraged to talk about it. Did those feelings point to Fenra being right? Was the World trying to get us all back in motion?

"If you're sure, there's a place I can send you where you can get a different kind of training, training that will teach you better how to live on and off the Road, and what to do when traveling. But you might not be able to change your mind and come back. You might have to stay there, at least until you finish an apprenticeship." If he passed the third-class exams, he'd be a practitioner, and no one could say any different. And if he wasn't allowed to take the exam? Well, I'd cross that bridge when I came to it. We both would.

More lip chewing. "I'd like to go," he said finally. "I can't be unhappier than I am here."

Let's hope so. "Come with me." I got to my feet. "You have some tests to pass."

ELVANYN

Betrex Smith looked up from Elva's drawing. Ione Miller stayed bent over the table outside the mill, tracing lines with her index finger, her eyes squinted against the sun.

"So, what you're saying is this contraption can be driven by the mill wheel, and then I can hammer with it?" Betrex said.

"I've seen it work, and I studied the design. It could increase your production," Elva pointed out. "You can see how the face of the hammer falls in evenly spaced intervals, just like a person hammering."

"It will take your work away from you." Ione looked up, still frowning.

"People said that it freed them to do other, more interesting things with their forge." Elva looked from Betrex to Ione and back again.

"It's just a hammer," Betrex Smith said after thinking a while. "It can't design nor invent. But I'll tell you something it *can* do," he added, speaking directly to Ione. "It can make it easier for women to be smiths—or anyone who has the talent but not the strength."

Elva thought Betrex would have been rubbing his hands together if it hadn't been for the obvious skepticism of the miller. She had straightened up, but she crossed her arms.

"The village needs income it's not getting from Fenra," Elva told her. They'd all agreed that the fewer times the word "gold" was said aloud, the better. "An increase in production, both for the mill and the forge, means more trade, and that's something you'll always have, whether Fenra is here or not."

Ione dropped her hands to her hips. Her slow nod told Elva that she was coming around.

"It would mean moving the forge—" Betrex began.

"Not inside the mill," Ione protested at once.

"No, of course not," Elva said. "But here—" He laid out another drawing, showing the mill's relationship to its surroundings. "If the shaft came out of the wheel here, you'd have to trade off between milling and hammering. Whereas, if you have the shaft come out of the opposite side, across the mill race, then the forge can be set up here, on the other bank, and no danger to anyone." He paused, frowning. "We'd have to persuade these two households to move."

"Will Fenra help?"

"Moving people? If you think it's a good idea." Elva didn't, but then it wasn't his village. "She helped me with the design," Elva said. "I can describe, but I can't draw. I don't recommend that she help with the building, except maybe in finding the metals we need. Better that the device doesn't depend on the practice to work." The looks on their faces told him they understood. Using the practice to build something meant a constant drain on the energy of the practitioner. They knew from watching Fenra healing what *that* could do. "Even the buildings in the White Court weren't built by practice," he said.

WITTENSLADE

"If you're finishing admiring the drape of your coat, the carriage is ready."

Witt could hear the smile in Arriz's voice, so he didn't turn around. It wasn't a new coat, but it was one he particularly liked, a deep green, with black reverses, and gold trim on the sleeve cuffs, lapels, and pockets.

"Do you think practitioners are going to be impressed with your fashion sense?"

Witt laughed. "I don't dress for other people," he said for what might have been the thousandth time. "I dress for myself. And besides, she has very nice eyes." A little disturbing, maybe, but Witt told himself that only made Tamari Otwyn more of a challenge. Teach *her* to think she knew everything about him. *Hah.*

Arriz whistled as he began gathering up discarded and rejected clothing. "I don't think practitioners are allowed to, ah, fraternize. Come to think of it, I'm not sure we're allowed to either."

"There's no actual law against it." Witt straightened his cuffs again and turned around. "It's more a tradition."

"You haven't looked it up? You *have*!" Arriz's tone was half laughing, half shocked. "You're seriously thinking about seducing a practitioner?"

Witt didn't answer aloud, but he knew he didn't need to. Arriz was the only person who understood—Tamari Otwyn only *thought* she understood. He was looking forward to seeing her alone.

This would be his third meeting with the practitioner, but the first time alone, without Riva Deneyra. When Practitioner Otwyn turned out to be the council member designated to meet with them, Riva had suggested he could manage better without her. Witt expected Tamari to relax quite a bit once Riva wasn't there. Not that she'd been all that tense to start with, but she'd definitely warmed up since they first met. Always a good sign.

The apprentice who met him at the East Gate this time was new, a short, slim young man with very dark hair and eyes and very white skin.

"I'm here to meet Practitioner Otwyn," he said, an unexpected chill passing over him. "Predax—ah, Apprentice Ap Gervin usually escorts me."

"Yes, Dom, Apprentice Ap Gervin has other duties this morning?" The boy blushed for some reason and coughed. "I'm the practitioner's new apprentice, Hogar Prinde. The practitioner asked me to bring you to the rose garden. This way, please."

Witt couldn't figure out how practitioners chose the names for their patios. The one the apprentice took him to had no evidence of roses at all, being filled with water features, each one different, and each contributing its own tinkle of noise and sparkle in the sunlight. The boy indicated a stone bench that curved around a particularly lively cascade of water.

"If you will wait here, Dom, Practitioner Otwyn will join you presently." He inclined his head politely, turned and walked away.

Witt spent the first few minutes strolling through the patio, looking at the fountains. He could now see that there were in fact flowers in the rock gardens surrounding some of them, and lilies in a small pool whose fountain barely disturbed the surface of its water. He nodded. Someone had chosen the color combinations with a great deal of care. Still no roses, though.

When he heard footsteps approaching, Witt sat back down where the apprentice had left him, making sure the sun hit him at the right angle and that the skirts of his coat were spread in the most attractive way. He'd stood up three careful seconds after Tamari entered the path leading to where he sat, giving her plenty of time to notice him. His heart rate increased, and this surprised him. *Maybe Arriz was right,* he thought. He'd always found strong and powerful women attractive—even Riva Deneyra—and who could be more powerful than a practitioner? Their eyes met and again he had the feeling that she saw right through him—that she knew what he planned and was . . . not amused exactly, but tolerant, patient. Seduction would probably never have been a very good idea. Somehow this realization didn't bother him as much as he would have expected. He could feel his annoyance fade away under the influence of Tamari's gray eyes. *It's just infatuation*, he told himself, *that's all.*

"Good morning, Dom Volden." Tamari's face seemed stiffer, her voice on edge.

"I've asked you to call me Witt." He gestured at the stone bench and took the chance as she turned her face away to look her up and down. Her hair was all spiky, as if she hadn't bothered to comb it. He couldn't understand it. Usually, he wasn't attracted to women who didn't at least *try* to dress elegantly. Tamari seemed always to wear the same outfit, practitioner's colors of course, black shoes, white hose, yellow breeches, crimson waistcoat, white shirt and cravat, a black jacket with crimson reverses. Her cravat was badly tied, with one end hanging longer than the other. He itched to retie it for her. Or to take it off completely.

"I'd better not," she said. For a moment Witt had forgotten what she was responding to. "I might forget and call you 'Witt' in front of other people." This time Tamari gestured at the stone bench and waited for Witt to seat himself before she sat down on the verge of the fountain where she could face him.

Tamari didn't speak right away, a little line formed between her brows. The silence didn't bother him; he could use it to look at her. Finally, she took a deep breath. "There's been some—I'm afraid I have to postpone our discussions for a period," she said.

"Postpone." Witt crossed his legs and set his folded hands down on his knee. "Can you give me any idea of how long a 'period' might be?" *How long can Riva Deneyra keep her majority?*

"Short, I hope. But the council has another issue they need to deal with before resuming talks."

"Another issue?" She'd said "they," and Witt wondered if that was significant, as though she wasn't part of "them," as if she disagreed with the council. He waited, making it clear with his manner that he would go on waiting as long as necessary to get a better answer. *No use pretending*, he reminded himself.

"A practitioner—someone who would be very much in favor of a better relationship between the two Courts, by the way—is rumored to be starting a new court, and the council isn't sure yet what their response should be. Most think that's the more pressing issue at the moment."

Witt felt his jaw hanging open and closed his mouth. "A new court? What, Blue? Green? Checks? Dots?"

"I don't think she would care about the color." He was sure Tamari almost smiled.

"Wait, where is she getting practitioners for her new court? All the practitioners are here, aren't they?" At least, Witt thought, that was what the Red Court had always believed.

"That's just it," Tamari said. "There are practitioners leaving the White Court—most of them students and apprentices, sure, but a few third- and second-class practitioners as well. Which, well, it's making people nervous." She looked down at the edge of the water. "It makes some people angry." She looked up again. The movement of the water reflected in her eyes. "So right now, that strikes the council as more important than anything *we're* doing. But I want you to know that I'll stay on top of things."

"Maybe we need to meet this other practitioner, if, as you say, she's supportive of an alliance," Witt said, not at all sure he was joking. From the look on her face, Tamari didn't find it funny.

"I don't think I need to tell anyone what this means."

Witt found Descar Parta's obvious satisfaction mystifying. He knew there were people who didn't want a closer relationship with the White Court, but really. A mean, rat-like little man with a mean rat-like little face. Witt remembered his father saying that Parta had always wanted to be First Courtier but had never managed to secure the votes.

Now, however, several of his fellow courtiers exchanged similarly satisfied looks. Witt thought he should stir things up a little. "Pardon me," he said in his most bored tone. "I'm new here, and I'm afraid I, for one, have no idea what 'this' means." He waved his closed fan in the air with a languid hand.

"Basic strategy," Parta said, hands spreading wide. "The time to strike at your enemies is when their attention is directed elsewhere. If the White Court is distracted by this schism in their ranks, now is the time for us to make our move."

"And what move will that be?" Riva's sarcasm was barely in check.

"Muster a sufficient force of guards, with soldiers from the other counties, and take control of the White Court by force."

"But why bother? We've already started negotiations. I can't imagine it will take them long to sort out this internal problem." Witt yawned and did a poor job of hiding it behind his open fan. He found it hard to imagine that anything the Red Court could do would have any kind of impact on the White Court, but he found he felt an uncomfortable level of concern. *I'm not worried about Tamari*, he thought. *I'm not.*

"Which is precisely why we need to strike now!" Parta banged the table with his fist. Witt had thought that only happened on the stage.

"That doesn't answer Courtier Volden's question." First Courtier Valter Denson turned slightly away from Witt. He hadn't yet forgiven Witt for voting against his father's wishes. So he didn't call Witt by his first name, and Witt no longer called him "uncle." He turned back, but still didn't look at Witt directly. "I believe Parta is thinking that if we succeed in taking over the White Court, we wouldn't need to exchange service for service, we would have the upper hand. In effect, they would become our servants rather than our partners."

"We wouldn't have to trade anything of ours to get something of theirs, it would all be ours," Parta said, as if Witt didn't understand.

"We'd be trading the lives of every citizen who falls in the conflict," Riva said.

"A sorry price, but we would only pay it once. And don't forget, their guard is made up of citizens like ourselves. We might even persuade them to switch sides."

"I would vote against any such suicidal scheme." Riva laid both her hands palms down on the table in front of her. "You seem to forget that these are *practitioners*."

"If they really are as powerful and dangerous as you suggest, why haven't they already moved against us? Why aren't we already ruled by them?"

"Perhaps because they're so little afraid of us that they can't be bothered," Witt said. He meant to speak in jest, but as the words left his mouth, he had the uncomfortable certainty that they were true. "I would also vote against attacking them."

"We haven't arrived at voting yet," Denson said. "Will someone make a motion?"

"I move that we attack the White Court now while their attention is divided and take control of it." Descar Parta looked around nodding, as if he had already won.

"Second the motion." Of course, this quick support came from Erden Quant, always ready to agree with anything that seemed popular. Quant looked like he should have a squeaky voice, and Witt always found his booming baritone a surprise.

Witt didn't listen to the rest of the discussion. He knew how he intended to vote, and no one and nothing would change his mind. He told himself he was motivated by the loss of life—on both sides—the destruction of all the beauty he had seen within the Court, along with who knew what valuable artifacts. It wasn't that Tamari Otwyn might be in danger. He *wasn't* more concerned about her than he should be. Witt began paying attention again when his ears registered Riva Deneyra's voice.

"I urge you to remain with the peaceful option," she was saying. "We already have a majority supporting the diplomatic approach."

"I'm not so sure about that," Erden Quant said. "I supported your motion because I could see economic benefits in having a more sensible agreement with the White Court, but as Descar Parta suggests, if we can obtain those benefits at a relatively low cost to ourselves, I for one would support that action."

"People's lives are not a 'relatively low' cost," Riva reiterated.

Witt could have told her to save her breath. There might be one or two others who would feel the same way she did—those who might have children or even grandchildren who could be involved in the fighting—but it was clear to him that she had lost her majority.

"If no one else has anything to add, I call for a vote on the motion that we attack the White Court."

⟐

We turn our hands over and look at the palms. There is something missing. They are too smooth, too plain. We run the tip of one finger over the surface of the other palm. Something else is missing. We look more closely at our fingers. Ah. Our cheeks spread. A smile. We have no fingernails. We concentrate. There, we admire our work.

We don't have to look this way. In fact, we don't look this way. However, for some reason it seems we can think more clearly when in this shape. We didn't have to think before, or talk. Not until we had to speak with Fenra Lowens.

Now we have other work. Work that will push Fenra Lowens to greater efforts. We look out over the ocean, and it gives us an idea. Water. Water is always useful.

⟐

FENRA

Elva was out at the construction site with Tux Gradon, marking out new foundations with colored strings. Tux had come with the first group of students. I remembered him as a second-class practitioner who worked with animals. Using the practice to check, Tux found the old foundation of the existing building to be sound. Plenty of room to expand if we needed to. I had left it to Ione to sort out workers from among the villagers. There were always some who had experience, but if necessary, we would send away for more.

I found it difficult to carve out the time to create a curriculum for the new court, in between visiting the sick and injured of the area. Now that Tux Gradon had arrived, I at least had some help with the building aspect of things.

A light tapping on my door frame. "Practitioner Lowens?"

A young woman dressed in apprentice gray stood at the door biting her lip. Her short dark hair looked as if she had been running her hands through it, and her pale gray eyes were almost round. I tilted my head to one side and raised my eyebrows.

"I'm Teke Urgal, I'm the courier?" She chewed at the inner part of her lower lip. "I don't want to go back to the City and the White Court, Practitioner. I'd like to stay here."

Could I keep a courier? That would ruffle some feathers. "Where are you in your studies?"

"I've been studying agriculture." She took a short step inside. "I'd really like to work in the gardens, but, you know, all those posts are taken."

I had the feeling this was a longstanding complaint from students, and maybe even some apprentices. Even in my day advancement had been difficult, but now it appeared that a practitioner or council member had to die for anyone to advance. And since practitioners rarely died . . . Tamari was the last person to take first-class exams, taking Medlyn Tierell's place. She became a member of the council only after Santaron Metenari died. I could not help wondering if this state of affairs wasn't part of the World's problem: there were too many students and not enough practitioners.

With the gardens, it might be even more complicated. There were always practitioners who really hated leaving the White Court enclave. Elva once told me that this condition was known in the New Zone as agoraphobia. Those who suffered from it had difficulties being outside, or in any wide-open spaces. Some got to the point where they could not leave their homes. I had no way of knowing if the gardeners in the White Court suffered from this condition, but I knew they never left the Court. And since they also did not age, anyone waiting for a chance at a position could wait a very long time.

Teke took another step in. "Predax told us you want us all to travel, and that way the whole world could be my garden, couldn't it? I mean, the parts that didn't belong to anyone."

"Even those parts," I said. "Farmers and other landowners occasionally need help with their lands." I got to my feet. "When are you expected back?"

"I'm not, not really—at least, no one will be looking for me. When I said I was the courier, well, this isn't my route. I traded with someone else."

"But whose apprentice are you?"

"Oh, didn't I say? Practitioner Otwyn's. I passed all my exams ages ago, but I was still waiting to be apprenticed to someone. We're a bit—"

"Short of first-class practitioners, I know."

"Not just that. The thing is, lots of the older practitioners aren't taking new apprentices. There haven't been any new students in ages, and those of us who were ready to become apprentices have been waiting without much hope since Practitioner Metenari went missing. Practitioner Otwyn's the first new first-class practitioner in no one knows how long, and she's taken on five apprentices in the last week. I was lucky to be one of them. At least it means more of us can be promoted." She blushed.

I nodded my understanding. "I think you are being more pragmatic than selfish, so relax. Unfortunately, Tamari is only one practitioner; she will not be able to take on new apprentices indefinitely." Unless, of course, she sent all the willing ones to me. *And how long can she do that before someone notices and takes offense? Or worse?*

"Come with me." I led the courier around the west side of my house to Terith's stable. "You can leave Carith here for the night. In the morning I will teach you the *forran* that will help him return safely to the City."

"Then I can stay?"

"Of course."

"Can Carith stay as well?"

I smiled, shaking my head. "I am afraid not. It's one thing for me to take in students. It's entirely another to steal horses."

The letter came the next day. I turned the folded and sealed parchment over in my hands, remembering the letter that had come for Arlyn, almost a year ago now. That one had summoned him to the City, and brought us face to face with the Godstone. I fetched a thin silver knife to lift off the seal.

"Well, well." My eyebrows rose higher. It seemed that life *was* repeating itself, after all.

"Of *course* you're not going." Elva was cleaning his already perfectly clean revolvers, the parts spread all over the table. The letter now had oily fingerprints on it. Reading wasn't something he'd had to do when he was part of the White Court guard, but he had learned how in the New Zone.

"I do not see how not," I said, taking the letter from him. "If they are finally ready to listen to me, I need to give them that chance."

"What if they're just getting you to come so they can accuse you of creating the earth seizure?" Elva began reassembling one of the revolvers, his fingers selecting the right part without his looking.

"There's no mention of the seizure in this letter." I tapped the written surface.

He rolled his eyes upward. "An *academic* conference?" he said finally.

"Apparently they would like to discuss the founding of another court," I said. "I think they are trying to make a virtue of necessity. If I am successful, they will pretend it was their idea. And if I fail . . ." I shrugged.

"I don't believe it." Elva pressed his lips together and shook his head. "Make them come here! If they want to know something about the new court, here's where they're going to learn it."

"You could be right." I had to admit it. "But what if this is my chance to reach the whole Court? A little humility applied in the right place could go a long way." Elva still looked skeptical. "I know how hard everyone is working, but if representatives of the council come here, they will find half-built classrooms and lectures given by two practitioners in pastures where sheep are listening in. If I can make my case there, in the White Court, I can reach every member of the Court, on and off the council, and that will do more good than rumors. Tamari and Predax can only do so much alone."

He got to his feet and began pacing in the narrow space available in the center of the room, between the cooking fire, the tables, and my shelves of potions and scrolls.

"You know I am right," I said. "Nothing we have here will convince them to take us seriously. This may be our chance."

At first his face hardened, and his lips compressed, but finally he relaxed. "When do we leave?"

"I am the only one summoned."

"Oh no, not likely. You aren't going alone."

I knew that look. I had seen it on his face the first time we met, when he insisted on returning with Arlyn and me from the New Zone. I had not been able to convince him then, and now would be no different.

He could read my response on my face, and he relaxed, smart enough not to smile. He knew when he had won, he saw no reason to underscore it.

"We can use the locket," I said. "Quick there, quick back . . ." I let my voice die away as Elva shook his head.

"They know how long it takes to travel from here to the City," he pointed out. "And they will know if you don't pass through the City Gate. We don't want them to know you have another way to travel." He spun the chamber of the assembled revolver and clicked it shut. "We have no reason to trust any of these people. Remember Metenari? *He* was *so* smart he thought he knew what the Godstone was, and he thought he could control it. Now you're suggesting that we let people just like him—stupid, arrogant assholes—know there's a way to move from one place to another without passing through the space between? What do you think they'd use it for?"

"What do *I* use it for? Besides, they do not know how it works, any more than I do!" My voice was rising. Only Elva could bring out this side of me.

"Could you figure it out, knowing what you know?"

I opened my mouth and shut it without speaking. "Yes," I said finally. "It might take me a long time, but—"

"But you have a long time. You and every other practitioner." He took my right hand in his and pressed his lips against the back of my fingers. "You think of the White Court as a bunch of scholars, maybe misguided, maybe stuffy and out of date, stubborn. Even after all we've been through, you still think that way. I'm asking you to think again."

"But Metenari—"

"I grant you that he was more misguided than evil, but he couldn't have made more trouble if he'd been the evilest guy around. Besides, I'm a soldier," he said. "And I tell you that you don't give up a strategic advantage until you absolutely have to."

I thought. Medlyn Tierell had created the locket, and who knew how many more *forrans* that influenced time and space, and he had never told his colleagues about them, even though he had plenty of opportunity to do so. He had even withdrawn from the council, due to ill health he had said at the time, but there might have been more to it.

Still, there was someone else Medlyn Tierell had not told.

"There may be a small problem," I said. "I have already told Tamari Otwyn about the locket."

"But she doesn't know how it works?"

"*I* do not know how it works," I repeated.

"We'll just have to hope she won't tell anyone else."

She would keep it to herself if she thought of it as Medlyn's secret, I thought. But if she thought of it as mine?

Five

FENRA WENT FROM Ione Miller to Betrex Smith, to the practitioner Tux Gradon, giving last-minute instructions and accepting last-minute advice. Getting out of town always took longer than it should. Elva had been ready since dawn, and so, to give her credit, had Fenra, but everyone else seemed to realize only now, in the last minute, that their pet practitioner was going, and leaving them in the hands of people they hardly knew.

When Fenra finished with him, Elva caught Betrex's eye and jerked his head back, waiting until the man circled the still-talking practitioners and joined Elva where he stood next to his horse.

"Is everything ready?"

"I've checked the signal traps we set up yesterday, and they're all still in good shape. Tux has lent me a couple of the brighter students to keep watch in other ways. Are you sure this is necessary?"

Elva bit back a sharp response. If Fenra could underestimate the dangerous potential of the council after her experiences, he could hardly blame ordinary people for doing the same.

"An old teacher of mine used to say that if you take care of the possibilities, the probabilities look after themselves."

"So, this is because it *could* happen, even if there is only a small chance of it?" The older man looked unexpectedly younger when he grinned. "My old dad used to say we should never underestimate the depth of human stupidity."

"Sure. And practitioners are human, no matter what some of them would like us to think. If this invitation *is* some kind of trap, which *is* a possibility, they are easily stupid enough to come after us here, when they think Fenra is out of the way."

They reviewed the final details, what to hide or disguise if the wrong people showed up, who should stay out of their way entirely. Betrex was no fool, but when push came to shove, he was a smith, not a sheriff. Too bad Elva didn't have a couple of his deputies here, people who had been in enough scrapes to understand how bad things could get, and how quick it could happen.

Come to think of it, most of his deputies had some degree of practice—not exactly the same kind as here, but close enough. One or two of them at least would be thrilled to come here and learn more. If Fenra ever figured out how to open the gate again.

He'd mention it to her. Later. She had enough on her mind for now.

<hr>

FENRA

We rode as quickly as we could, but horses—and people for that matter—can only travel so far without rest. We stopped twice on the Road at Wayfarers' Rests, but I set up wards all the same, and not just to follow Elva's principle that you cannot be too careful. The people who had joined us from the City had confirmed rumors that the Road was becoming a dangerous place.

The first night as I was selecting rocks to anchor my wards, I felt the World shift around me. It spoke, but I could not make out any words. I could feel the plants and trees growing, feel their roots pushing into the soil, soaking up moisture and nutrients. The animals were giving us a wide berth, but I could still feel them, some under cover and dozing, some on the prowl, some on the wing. Underlying all of this I could sense a pattern, a pattern of which I was a part. The World's pattern, the one I was supposed to be strengthening.

Instead, I felt, or saw, rising waters. The Third Mode. Water surging over the banks of a river, far from the Road, flooding fields, pushing houses off foundations. Animals fleeing, drowning. People too. I disconnected, and I was just myself again. I did not doubt that what I had seen was real. Somewhere in the Third Mode a river had escaped its banks. There was nothing I could do, even if I had a quick way to get there. I wondered if this was how all practitioners were supposed to feel, if they were out of the City, traveling around as we were meant to do.

The City was a part of the World, though. Changes in the Modes started from the City and moved outward—though *outward* wasn't the exact word. Practitioners brought changes too, coming up with new ideas, so some of us did have to stay in the City, researching and experimenting. When did we begin to think that was all we should do?

"Fenra? You finished?"

"What? Oh, yes, that's it." I set the *forran* and joined Elva at the fire.

This was the same journey I had made with Arlyn. It was from watching him as he reacted to the changes in the Modes that I understood the truth about him. Every time we crossed into another Mode, Elva asked whether his revolvers had changed. Every time I reassured him that though his tunic, leggings, and sandals had become shirt, breeches, and clogs, and finally breeches, hose, shoes, shirt, jacket, and wig, his guns remained exactly as they were in the New Zone. He knew as well as I did that artifacts from the New Zone did not change here in the world, but he could not stop himself from asking, and I was happy to tell him. Like all mundanes he noticed no changes at all, so everything always appeared "normal" to him.

Rumors of the flood caught up with us as we passed through the Third Mode. Couriers were carrying the news of the flood to the City. I hoped the help being sent wasn't already too late.

When we got up in the morning after a comfortable night in the last inn, our two horses had turned into a one-horse barouche, and a riding horse. We left the riding horse to be returned to the village with the next courier and climbed into the barouche. Elva handed me the reins and took the seat on the right.

"Most people are right-handed," he explained when I asked him, "so an attack is most likely to come on our right, not our left." I had already noticed that when he was not thinking about it, he called the practitioner's hand "left."

We passed through the City's main gate and took the first right into the wide avenue that would eventually lead us to the White Court. With the reins in my practitioner's hand, I touched the emerald stud in my right ear. "If they have anyone looking, they will know I have entered the City."

"They're expecting you, aren't they? Maybe you should have left your earrings in the New Zone."

All practitioners wore earrings, from the time we became students. Our first pairs were usually plain metal knots, or spheres, and our final pairs, given to us when we passed from apprentice to practitioner, a precious gem of some kind. These were the ones we could not remove, though I had managed to when Arlyn and I were in the New Zone. There was debate as to the actual purpose of this jewelry. Most agreed that they were used to track practitioners, and when I was a student, our instructors certainly seemed to know where we were all the time. But that could have been their own use of the practice, and nothing to do with our earrings.

On the other hand, in the attic of a dilapidated old tower in the White Court—called, for some reason no one remembered, the New Tower—students being disciplined for some infraction sat, tracking the movements of the jewels in enormous, faceted crystals. My friend Hal and I had spent three days there once. No one had ever asked to see the reports we meticulously kept on the movements of those beads of light. With luck, nothing about that had changed.

"What about Terith?" Elva asked as we drew nearer to the White Court.

I sat up straighter, looking in the direction of Ginglen's Inn, as if I could see over the buildings. "He is well," I said. "He knows we are here." I turned to Elva and smiled. "Do not worry, he will not tell anyone."

I was surprised to be stopped by the guard at the West Bridge. It appeared we were expected, and the head of the watch insisted on sending for an escort. The second-class practitioner who arrived shortly after did not recognize me, though I knew him. We used to call him What Ah Fusspot behind his back. I could not remember his real name. He did not quite manage to meet my eyes when he spoke to me, though he did not seem to have the same trouble with Elva. He first took us to the stabling area, as if neither of us had ever been in the White Court before.

"Your rooms are in the Primrose Tower, Practitioner Lowens. Does your guard know the way to the barracks?"

"He will stay with me, thank you."

That raised his eyebrows. "Very well." Our guide led us right to the door of our rooms, but didn't open it, just to remind me he was not a servant. "The council wasn't sure exactly when you would arrive, so they've set your first meeting for tomorrow morning." He smiled at Elva. "You can rest today and prepare."

"Prepare?"

This time he almost looked at me. "You're going to give a presentation in the council chamber, aren't you? And then afterward we'll break up into groups—a councilor, a practitioner, an apprentice, and a student—to discuss the various aspects of the problem."

"Problem?" I was not happy with his choice of words.

He pressed his lips together, impatient with me. "This won't be easy, you know. You may not see it as a problem, but there will be issues to resolve. Can we support a second court? Can it be made self-sustaining? How would we apportion funding and the recruiting of new student practitioners? Will they all come to the City first and then be assigned? It's very complicated." He gave me a curt nod, turned on his heel, and walked away without saying anything more.

"'Complicated.' So glad he told me, I would not have known otherwise." Strangely, I felt reassured by this exchange. No one would spend this amount of time and effort on something they were not taking seriously.

"Well." Elva dropped the satchel containing his New Zone clothing and his spare cartridge belts on the oval table centered under the tall window. His left his guns where they were, holstered one under each arm.

"What shall we do with the rest of the afternoon?" I said. "Go into the City? Visit Terith?"

"I have a better idea."

Several hours later, Elva dressed in his New Zone clothes while I sat at the table in my dressing gown making notes. Should I focus on the logistics of the new court, or should I try to convince the council that I had spoken with the World?

"I think I'll go find out whether any of the guard are still speaking to me," Elva said. "They usually know all the gossip."

Elva had told me that it was different once, but since my time, the White Court guard has been largely ceremonial—checking mundanes in and out of the Court, escorting practitioners when they had to go into the City, that sort of thing. There were always a few who studied the martial arts more thoroughly, but for the most part, skill levels were average. Even though the guard was made up completely of mundanes, many apprentices, some not long from their own homes, often shared gossip and rumor with them. In fact, they tended to treat the guard better than did practitioners of long standing. Arlyn was the only first-class practitioner I knew who had had a close friend in the guard—perhaps his only friend. These were hard friendships to maintain, however, as the mundanes in the guard aged, and the practitioners did not.

I do not know how much time had passed when someone knocked on the door. I looked up from the outline I had almost finished. "Yes?"

"Fenra, did you ward the room?" I could barely hear Elva's voice.

I ran to the door and slid my fingers quickly over the jamb. "I did not." I turned the handle with my practitioner's hand, but the latch did not disengage. I took a step back and placed my palms together, relaxing myself and concentrating. I pulled my hands apart, watching lines of pale-yellow light connecting fingertip to fingertip, concentrating on the most powerful unlocking *forran* I knew. Slowly the lines took on a familiar pattern. I gathered it up in both hands and flung it at the lock. In the instant before it struck the door, I saw another pattern, different colors. A *forran* I did not know. Elva rattled the latch, but the door didn't open.

"I did not ward it, but someone else has."

"The locket will only take me to Tamari's office, or Medlyn's old rooms. I know of no other destinations." Elva had allowed me three more tries to open the door before he insisted on a change of strategy.

"The office," he decided. "If nothing else, we may get a clue as to whose side Tamari's on." I opened my mouth and closed it again without speaking. "Don't worry, we'll find a way out of this mess. We have before."

My shoulders relaxed. "We defeated the Godstone, and if we can do that, we can manage the council." I could feel him thinking on the other side of the door. "What?"

"Bring my cartridge belts, and any other weapons you've got."

Which would be exactly none. I no longer even carried a cane. "I will get there before you," I said. "Hurry, but be careful."

"That may not be possible." I could hear the smile in his voice. "But you do the same."

And he was gone.

I found the door of Tamari's office closed and the room dark. Both were unusual. My fingers were on the latch of the window shutters when I heard soft footfalls in the corridor. I stood against the wall where the door would hide me when it opened—unless, of course, it opened completely into me, but I did not think of that until later. The door swung open halfway. I had time to wish the invisibility *forran* would work when I stood on stone.

"Fenra?" A whisper, but I could tell it wasn't the voice I was hoping for. Tamari took a careful step into the room. "I know you're here," she said. "I can sense you."

I had forgotten she could do that. I wondered exactly what she was sensing from me. I stepped out from behind the door and pushed it shut with the tips of my fingers.

"I knew you'd be here." Tamari had my forearm tight in both her hands. I could feel her trembling. "They've taken Elvanyn. You've got to get away before they find out you're here."

I carefully lifted her hands from my arm and took several deep breaths, until my heart finally stopped pounding in my ears. "How—never mind, where have they taken him?"

"I don't know, I only saw him being led away. Hurry."

I made my hands and my jaw unclench, stroking the cartridge belts hanging over my shoulders. Made myself focus on the problem. They would have taken his revolvers, and his sword. Elva was without weapons. I would go nowhere without him. Finally, my breathing slowed down, and my brain sped up. They knew I would come for him, so they would keep him safe and well, thinking that it would bring me.

I would come, all right, but not when and how they expected. I would need help to free him, that was clear. I heard the soft hiss of gas as Tamari lit the wall lamps. *Why do all of this?* I thought. *Why did the council not simply tell me to stop?*

"I need help," I said aloud.

"Maybe I can find out where they're keeping him." Tamari did not sound very sure. "Once we know that, we can work out how to free him. But you should go. They know we've spoken before and they'll come here."

I ignored her and sat down on the edge of her desk, one hand wrapped around my locket, the other around one of the cartridge belts. "I will be fine." I looked her over carefully, taking in her eyes, and her trembling lips. Her hands were still. One of the first things they teach us when we become apprentices. Could I trust her? Only one way to find out.

"Go, find him," I said.

I waited until I was sure she was gone before I cracked open the door and examined what I could see of the hallway outside. Empty. Electric lamps gave off yellow light every twenty feet or so, giving the hallway an oddly striped look. I wondered why Tamari did not use them in her office. I slipped out, shut the door behind me, and set off in the direction of the outside stairwell. When I had been an apprentice here, most practitioners used the inner ones, even though the weather in the White Court is always fine during the day. I knew where I was going and how to get there, but I would be passing through only one courtyard where I could stand on earth, one place where my direct connection with the World could help me remain unseen, so I had to resort to the more mundane ways of avoiding notice, dodging into alcoves, stepping into shadowed spots, and looking unobtrusive. With luck I would not have to use it, but I prepared a sleeping *forran* just in case, and kept my practitioner's hand ready.

I made it to the old south tower with only one near miss. I crossed paths with a student in the vestibule of the tower itself, but he only bowed to me quickly as he ran out into the courtyard. *Probably late for a lesson.* I ducked around the main staircase and made for the stairs that curved upward around the inside of the outer wall of the tower. I stopped at the door halfway between the second and third floors, and opened it without difficulty. According to Arlyn, the door of his workroom had never needed a lock, since it could only be seen by people who knew it was there.

I hesitated on the threshold. The last time I had seen this room, its floor was red with Arlyn's blood, running along the grout lines of the floor tiles, spattering the glass-fronted cabinets. Today the room was immaculate. I could tell that no one had been here. The room had cleaned itself.

"Arlyn, I wish we had had more time." I missed him. "You could have shown me so much." My friend had designed some of the White Court's greatest *forrans*. Who knew what others existed, that we might never recover, now that he was gone?

The workroom door closed behind me as soon as I cleared the threshold. When I saw that I was unconsciously walking around to avoid blood that was no longer there, I stopped, took a deep breath, and set off straight across the room to the point on the far wall where I had once found the entry to Arlyn's vault.

The door to Arlyn's vault, like the one to his workroom, wasn't visible. In this case, however, even if you knew where the door had been the last time you saw it, you could not be sure of finding it there again. And if by some twisty chance you could find and unlock it, the door had a gateway just inside—part of the lock mechanism itself—that would send the unwelcome intruder to another dimension. Arlyn had called this place the New Zone, and it was where he had accidently exiled his best friend, Elvanyn Karamisk.

Even if the gateway no longer functioned as a trap, I was sure I would find it in place. Then all I had to do was power it. If, that is, I could find and open the vault in the first place. I closed my eyes and sorted through my memories for the pattern Arlyn had drawn for me. His pattern, unique to him, part of which formed the lock of his vault.

Once I was sure, I raised my practitioner's hand and began tracing the pattern in the air. The outer lines tried to shift, distorting the center, but I concentrated harder and managed to shove them back into place. I lowered my hand. Yes. That was it. It only took another few minutes to add colors to the lines, sage and a muted gold. I stepped back, my hand still lifted. Exactly right. I made sure it wouldn't shift again, and moved it slowly over the portion of the wall where I thought the door to the vault was hidden.

Nothing. I tried again. Still nothing. All right. I shook out both my hands, rotated my shoulders. Fine, the door wasn't where it had been the last time. I left that spot and scanned the rest of the walls with the pattern. Still nothing.

I sat down on the round padded stool that anchored the center of the room and pushed my hands through my hair, causing the cartridge belts to click against each other as my shoulders moved. If I could not find the door to the vault, I could not find the gateway to Elva's world, and I could not bring the help I hoped would be there.

TAMARI

I was so angry I could spit. I had taken everything the council said to me at face value, and look what had happened. While I was off flirting with Witt Volden—and my meetings with him had been the council's idea too—they'd been plotting this trap. Well, whether I liked Fenra Lowens or not, I couldn't let them get away with using me like this.

Problem. I had no idea at all where to start looking for Elvanyn Karamisk. Out in the City—or so I'd been told—you could find jails, cells, even dungeons, but so far as I knew, none of these things existed in the White Court outside of old stories. Who would we lock up? Some misbehaving apprentice? Using a locking *forran* too advanced for them on doors and windows would be enough to keep them in whatever room we chose to use. No need for special accommodations.

So, obviously, whatever would work for any apprentice would certainly work on any mundane. Which meant my search could be narrowed down by exactly no factors at all. Another, more helpful thought occurred that made me slow down even more. Wherever they were keeping Elva, wouldn't they be planning to keep Fenra there as well? So, either not an ordinary room or not an ordinary *forran*. Or both.

Why isn't logic ever my friend?

I reached the Patio of Horses and started across diagonally. The Filigree Palace had unused student rooms, two whole floors of them if I remembered correctly. Not perfect, but at least a place to start.

Just as I cleared the patio, I heard my name called. I hesitated before I turned around, but of course hesitating was enough to show I'd heard him. I turned around, holding my breath, but relaxed when I saw Predax chasing me across the patio.

"I thought it was you," he said as he caught his breath. "You're wanted at the East Bridge."

"It'll have to wait," I started to say, but Predax didn't let me finish.

"It's Courtier Volden," he said. "He insists on speaking to you, and only you, and he won't go away until he has. So . . ."

"All right, all right. Fine." What on earth brought him here? I didn't have time for this. "I need you to do something for me, without letting anyone else know."

I walked as quickly as I could to the East Bridge. The sooner I saw Witt Volden and sent him on his way, the sooner I could get back to finding Elva—unless, of course, Predax found him first. As I cleared the inner wall and reached the open area around the bridge, I saw the sun was setting. I couldn't remember whether it was supposed to rain this evening, but the clouds didn't look promising.

They had brought Witt into the guards' room, something they'd never done before. Of course, he'd never come without an appointment, and it was clear from their relief when I reached the doorway that they didn't know what to do with him. He turned around, his face lit up when he saw me, and I felt an odd sensation in my stomach, as if someone had lightly punched me. Witt looked exactly as usual, too well dressed, linen crisp, wig powdered, accessories matching down to his nail polish. But he didn't *feel* like his usual self, though the only outward sign was his index finger tapping rapidly at the top of his walking stick.

"Thank you for coming." He took a step toward me, hands outstretched, his voice as tight as his smile. "Could I have the favor of a private interview? As charming as these fellows are . . ."

"Thank you, Emmett," I said to the guard who had the evening duty. "I'll look after Dom Volden from here."

"Sure, Practitioner. We, uh, we haven't made a note of his visit." Emmett waggled his eyebrows at me. His eyes were smiling. He'd been a particular friend of mine when I was an apprentice, letting me and a couple of others sneak out unescorted, and it looked as if he was still my friend.

I motioned Witt forward. "This way."

I tried to avoid other people as we went. Witt was memorable enough in himself without drawing more attention to him. I could trust Emmett to keep Witt's arrival to himself. There wouldn't be any record, nothing official anyway. Romantic liaisons between mundanes and practitioners weren't forbidden, but they were rare. I thought about Fenra and Elva. Was their relationship what I thought it was? Or was there something more to it? Where *had* he gotten those strange weapons?

I slowed down almost to a stop, enough so that Witt looked at me with concern. I realized that I'd instinctively been heading for my office, a private space where I felt safe and in control. But Fenra was there. Would Witt speak in front of her, even if I told him exactly who she was? Did she need to hear what Witt had to say? Would her presence mean we weren't in private? Why *was* he here, anyway?

So, not my office, and therefore not my workroom, since the one opened into the other. There was only one private space left. With luck, what with the rain starting, we wouldn't meet anyone who would be more curious than Emmett.

"I haven't been this way before." Witt slowed down to examine an intricate mosaic of tiles on the wall of one entry, realized what he was doing, and caught up with me again.

"I have to say, I approve of the decoration in this wing," he said. "There's more here than I've seen anywhere else, anyway. So I suppose that means I approve of its presence, if not its execution." He turned his head to stay focused on a particularly irritating mural. At least, I'd always found it irritating.

"This building is all private rooms," I told him. "Traditionally, we don't change the painting or the tile work in the hallways and corridors. Some of this stuff is older than any of us." I turned into a wide alcove with three doors leading out of it.

"Now this I approve of." Witt stopped and examined the tile work more closely. "Simple geometric shapes, but whoever chose the colors knew what they were doing." He straightened and smiled at me. "These are your rooms?"

I almost smiled back at him. "You said you wanted privacy. We can't go to our regular meeting room and there's someone using my office."

"So this is where you live? I'd like to see that."

I felt heat crawl up my neck, but luckily he wasn't looking at me right at that moment, so he didn't catch me blushing. It had been quite a while since I'd had anyone into my rooms. In fact, when I had private meetings with people—with all the meaning that word might imply—I preferred to go to the other person's rooms. I liked to sleep alone, and I'd always found it easier to leave myself than to get someone else to.

My door was raised two steps from the hall floor, two steps made of stone with thick oak planks on the risers. I touched my practitioner's hand to where a door latch would normally be, and the door opened inward.

"Nice," Witt said, following me in. "Better than a lock."

I stood to one side, holding the door. Suddenly it was very important to me that Witt like my rooms. Would my choice of decor strike him favorably, like the tile work? Or would he wrinkle his nose, too polite to tell me straight out that he didn't like it?

I heard whistling coming toward us from the hall and shut the door.

I turned back to find Witt looking at the woodstove that occupied the space of what used to be a regular wood fireplace. It wasn't new here in the White Court, but from his interest I gathered they weren't common in the City. The door of the stove had been decorated with blue and green tiles in the same tones, if not in the same designs, as the fireplace mantle. I hadn't changed the hearth; it was still the same gray stone, wide enough to sit on. The darkened oak floors were covered over with Lestusan carpets in deep reds, golds, and greens. Witt set his hat, gloves, and fan down on the shelf to the right of the door, and leaned his walking stick against the wall.

He looked from the walls, painted in solid colors, to the high ceilings, to the windows with their small panes of glass. He scrutinized the gaslights long enough that I expected him to ask about them, but he surprised me.

"No table?"

I shook my head. "I work only in my office—or my workroom, of course."

"Where do you eat?"

I gestured at the single upholstered chair close to the woodstove.

"Off your lap?"

"Something wrong with that?" And irritation blows away nervousness.

"No, no. None of my business anyway."

Well, he wasn't wrong. "Will you sit? I can offer you an infusion, or hot chocolate. I'm afraid I don't have any wine."

He made a noncommittal gesture with his hand and refocused his attention on the woodstove.

Finally my patience ran out. "Dom Volden, you have something to tell me?"

"Call me Witt, please." He always said this, but this time his heart wasn't in it. He shot a quick glance at my face, looked away again, and cleared his throat.

"The Red Court is planning to invade."

"Invade what?" Practitioners rarely got involved with political disputes between Modes.

"You. The White Court."

I'm afraid my laughter offended him.

Fenra

I paced up and down in front of the shelves that held Medlyn Tierell's collection of models. Each one would transport you to a particular place, once you knew the right *forrans* and how to use them. But there wasn't a model here that would take me to the New Zone. My hand clenched into a fist, but I stopped myself from pounding the shelves. The New Zone was the only place I could think of to find the kind of help I needed—that Elva needed. The dimension where he had lived since Arlyn had accidentally exiled him there longer ago than anyone now living could remember.

I felt an ache in my practitioner's hand and found that I was gripping Elva's cartridge belt so tightly the edges of the bullets were bruising my palms.

The cartridge belts.

They weren't models of places in the New Zone, but they *were* artifacts from that place. And artifacts from that place acted in a particular manner when they were in this place. Could I use it? Would it work? I ran over to the bookshelf, pulled out the book with my name on the spine, and found the *forran* designed to trigger the models. There had to be some way for me to modify it enough to let the cartridge belts function as the models did.

I forced myself to stop once to eat, and twice to rest. I was itching with the need to hurry. Every minute I spent was a minute Elva might not have. But if I pushed myself to exhaustion, used too much of my own power, I could not succeed, no matter how perfect my *forran* might be. I could feel time slipping away from me, but time is what it took.

Once I was ready, I found a pack in the first closet I looked, filled it with rolls, dried sausages, fruit, and a flask of water from the food cupboard before standing in a clear spot in the middle of the floor large enough for me to practice without much danger of banging into anything if it didn't work.

I expected to find myself in the same hot, dry world where Arlyn and I had found Elva. I was completely unprepared for pouring rain.

Six

DRIER LAST TIME we met."

The voice seemed to come out of the rain itself. I backed away two steps, raising my practitioner's hand, prepared to defend myself. The chuckling didn't help.

"Is that you, John?" I lowered my hand while my heartbeat returned to normal.

"Expecting someone else?" John Bearclaw moved the reins into his right hand and offered me his practitioner's hand. It was just as callused and bony as I remembered.

"The rain worried me. I thought I had come to the wrong place." I put my practitioner's hand into his and he hauled me up onto the seat beside him. It was dry, he was dry, and the rain wasn't falling on me anymore. As far as I could tell in the dim light, John wore the same faded shirt and embroidered vest he had worn the first time I saw him. I had never seen him standing, so I could not be sure of his height. His skin color, though as dark as mine, was a result of the sun. The same white braids hung down out of the same black hat. His very startling green eyes twinkled at me.

"Nice trick, with the rain," I said, patting the dry seat.

"One you know," he said, flashing me a smile as he chucked to the horses. "Nice hat."

I could not help it, I laughed. That had been one of the first things he had said to me when we met. Though I could not feel the World here, laughing helped me.

"How did you know where to find me?"

"Rain told me where. Horses told me who." Obviously John's connection with his world had to be as strong as mine with my World. That made me feel better. The two places weren't so very different after all.

"The rain and the horses speak to you?"

"Not just me."

I smiled at the sound of laughter in his voice, partly because of John himself, partly out of relief. This proved what both Arlyn and Elva had told me, that the practice existed here, and therefore I was right to come here for help. "They do not speak to me," I said.

"Not yet," he said. "Your friend?"

I knew a change of subject when I heard one. "Arlyn Albainil is dead," I said.

"And the sheriff?"

"In trouble." His manner of speech was catching. "I am looking for help."

"In town. His office. His deputies."

"What about you, John? Would you come with me?" I did not know anyone here at all well, but at least John was not a complete stranger. And he liked me, though I had a feeling it might be because the horses did.

"Not my time," he said finally. I had no idea what he meant, but it was clearly the only answer he would give me.

Finally, the rain stopped, and the sky cleared, revealing a three-quarters moon. Allowing for the moonlight and the smell of wet earth, the landscape looked much the same as it had the first time I had seen it. The shadows of rocks, and of plants, mostly cactus, showed clear and sharp in the moonlight. I could smell the faint odor of blossoms brought to life by the rains.

When we reached the outskirts of town, the scent of flowers increased, and I could even smell grass. When we first met, John told me about the underground springs that were the secret of the town's existence, and of its gardens, trees, and fountains. At this time of night the streets were quiet, doors and shutters closed, blinds down. We saw the first window showing light as we turned into the main street.

"Doctor," John said as we passed the place, though I did not ask.

"I can help there if I'm needed." I had to offer, even though I could feel time passing like ants running across my skin.

"Obliged, but should be fine."

The second light was brighter, shining through the open door of the High Sheriff's office, Elva's office, where we had met. As John pulled up in front, the sharply outlined silhouette of a tall, thin man blocked the light in the doorway.

"Make a nice target standing there," John said without moving from his seat.

"You're the only one awake, my friend, and you wouldn't shoot me without warning." A light voice, but with a distinct rasp.

"Could be." John laughed. "Lady to see you."

The tall man stepped out from the doorway and came to my side of the wagon. As he stepped into the moonlight, I could see he wore a sword hanging from his right hip, and a single gun in a simple holster on his left. Confusing. Which was his dominant hand? The practitioner's or the right?

"Ma'am, I'm Donn Keeshode," he said, taking off his wide-brimmed, feathered hat and sweeping me an elaborate bow before replacing the hat and lifting both hands to help me down. "First deputy to Elvanyn Karamisk, High Sheriff of the Dundalk Territory, and for tonight, your host."

"Fenra Lowens," I said. Reaching down, I put my hands on his shoulders. He took hold of my waist, his long, thin hands stronger than I expected. He lifted me down as if I weighed nothing. I turned back to John, straightening my hat.

"Thank you, John. Will I see you again?"

"Depends." He nodded to me, lifted a finger to the deputy, and chucked the horses into motion.

"Where is he going?" I asked.

"He's got kin in town," Donn Keeshode said. "Louisa Blackthorn, who runs the dry goods store, is his niece." He offered me his arm. "This way, Practitioner Lowens. Let's get out of the rain."

I had not been paying attention and had not noticed that a fine rain had started again. "You know who I am." I took the offered arm.

"I didn't expect you, though I dare say John Carter did. No knowing what he knows until he tells you. But I've seen you before, and the High Sheriff told us about you before he left. Needs help, does he?"

"You are sure you were not expecting me?" I followed him into the square front room that made up the outer office. The wall across from the entry had two doors in it. One I knew led to Elva's office, but the other?

"Jail cells," Donn Keeshode said as he held a chair for me.

I remained standing and took a deep breath. "You know what I am thinking."

"Sometimes," he agreed. "Not everyone, and not all the time. I admit I cheated a bit just now. You looked at the door," he added when I lifted an eyebrow. "Though I might have been guessing."

I sat down on the edge of the seat he had placed for me. "But you were not." Wonderful. Tamari could tell how I felt and now this man could read my mind.

He smiled, taking the chair on the other side of the desk, and his eyes sparkled. He waggled his eyebrows at me. "No, I wasn't." He was enjoying himself, and for a moment I saw what he had looked like as a schoolboy. The same narrow face with the bladelike nose, the same mischievous twinkle in his eye, though the eyebrows might have been less bushy then. He would be about fifty, I thought, as mundanes judged age, the foxiness of his face exaggerated by the white tuft of beard on his chin and the pointed mustaches. He dressed completely in black, though his clothes were faded and dusty with use.

"Did the High Sheriff send you?"

I took a deep breath. "Not exactly. We were separated and I am afraid that he is being held—I believe as a hostage—to make me give myself up."

"Rude," he said, shaking his head. "Gentlemen don't draw ladies into traps. Someone needs to be taught a lesson." His mouth twisted in amusement, and he looked over his shoulder as the door behind him opened, barely, and an older man sidled in out of the rain, light glinting off the drops of water on his shaved head.

"Back then, are you, sweetheart? Managed to lose his nibs, I see." The old man winked at me.

"Lugg! Manners! Practitioner Lowens isn't *your* sweetheart."

"Ah, her and me is old acquaintance, aren't we, lovey?"

I had to admit that was so.

"Any little thing I can do for you then, *madame*?" Lugg said the last word looking at the deputy, opening his eyes wide in feigned innocence.

"Not at the moment, Lugg, thank you."

He turned to the deputy. "See? Manners. I'll go see if the abode is ready for her ladyship," he said with the same tone of false subservience.

"Does he read minds too?" I waited until Lugg was out the door before asking.

"No, but he has been with the sheriff a long time." Deputy Keeshode looked at the door Lugg had used with a fond expression. "Well, now, let's get back to business. Someone's gotta stay to protect the territory, but I think I can round up a few of the people you want."

"The people I want?"

"The people like you." He smiled again. "Like us."

I was happy to take his advice to eat something while he sent for the others. Not everyone he sent for was an official deputy, he explained, but all were people whom Elva had trained, people who could be trusted. After eating an enormous slice of ham spread with mustard between two thick slices of grainy bread, I dozed off, my head cradled in my arms, though sleep was the last thing I expected. I must have been even more tired than I thought.

I blinked. I was lying on cool pebbles. I heard waves and smelled the fishy saltiness of the sea. I pushed myself up to a sitting position.

The World sat cross-legged a few feet away from me, head tilted to one side, eyes narrowed. It still looked like Arlyn. It drew down its brows, pressed its lips closed. When its mouth opened, I saw the World had forgotten to carry the illusion of Arlyn inside.

"What's taking so long? This isn't good, Fenra, not good at all."

I swallowed. The world sounded so much more articulate than it had when I had first met it. Of course, it now had much more experience in speaking with me. It even managed to mimic frustration.

It stood, dusted off its hands. "Pay more attention. Work faster. Don't make us angry."

Voices woke me. Someone called my name. Donn Keeshode was down on one knee beside me, holding my hand. For a moment I thought he was going to kiss it. I used his hand to pull myself to my feet, my back stiff from the chair. *Don't make us angry?* What exactly did that mean? I shook off my worry and focused on what was happening in the sheriff's office. I would have to think about the World later.

The door to the street stood open while two men and three women exited. They weren't in uniform, exactly, but they dressed alike, wide trousers stuffed into tall boots, embroidered shirts with full sleeves, some in leather vests, some in jackets with fringed sleeves. All had wide-brimmed hats trimmed with feathers, or the fluffy tails of foxes and coyotes. They all wore swords and pistols, and some carried long guns as well. The last woman looked back over her shoulder and gave me what I thought was a look of apology. Donn saw where I was looking and his face hardened.

"Don't blame them, Donn." The man who spoke stood off to my left. "Too many have families to tend to. And the rest are afraid of going to another world." His eyes swung from Donn to me. "Ma'am," he said, touching his fingers to his brow in a salute.

"This is Randd," Donn said. The young man saluted again. He wore the same combination of chin beard and pointed mustaches as Donn, though he was far more striking, with white-blond hair, sun-darkened skin, deep blue eyes. It seemed likely he would be the hand-somest man of any group he found himself in. And from the way he kept catching his reflection in the window glass, he was aware of it.

"Lizz." A younger woman standing closer to the door carried sword, revolver, and long gun. Shorter than the men, she looked wiry and strong. A wing of dark blond hair fell over the tattoo of crossed keys on the left side of her face.

"Randd and Lizz will be coming along." Donn had two satchels open on top of the desk, into which he carefully packed boxes of am-munition, and two more guns. "We're lucky. These are the best magi-cians we've got. Besides me," he added with a grin.

"Maybe there's only two of us," Randd said as he handed Donn even more boxes of bullets. "But we won't disappoint." I did my best to show I believed him.

"Better bring guns for Elva," I said. Donn tapped the two revolvers already in the satchel and his grin became a smile.

He led us out into the street and around the corner, then down one of the narrower cross streets. There were already a few people up and about. A boy was sweeping off the boardwalk in front of the general store, and a light was shining through the open door of the stables. Donn turned in at the gate of the third house on the left. A small, single-story wooden building, with two gables in the roof. The central door opened directly into a sitting room, the width of the house. I knew at once the house belonged to Elva. And that Lugg had been there—not a speck of dust anywhere and fresh flowers in a crystal vase on the table.

All three deputies were obviously comfortable with each other, and with being in Elva's house. I had not seen that type of relaxed familiarity in a random group of people since my apprenticeship—it's absent even in some families. Though differing in age, size, and coloring, they all had the same look: fit, clear-eyed, relaxed in stillness, but ready to move, like cats. Maybe this was the look soldiers had, at least the ones who had been trained together.

Donn waved me into a chair. "So, what kind of fix is the sheriff in?"

"Is it his fix, or yours?" Randd asked me.

TAMARI

"I don't know what you find so funny."

I really *had* offended Witt, so I tried my best to stop laughing. At least out loud. Single practitioners out on the street *could* be at risk— we might live a long time, but that doesn't mean we can't be killed. That's why we usually took a guard along when we went out into the City. Just the same, the idea that the Red Court could invade the White was, well, laughable.

"I'm sorry," I said as soon as I could speak without grinning. "But I don't see any cause for alarm. Even counting both the Red Court guards and the City watch, there aren't enough people to, what? Storm the castle? And what would we be doing while all this storming goes on? Playing cards?"

"They're calling in troops from the other counties, and anyone who has ties of family or fealty with people in the City."

I frowned. The other Modes—or counties, as mundanes called them—did use soldiers, that was true. Sure, those Modes were farther and farther behind the further you traveled from the City, but anyone who could use a longbow, or a catapult, or a siege tower, would find they could use muskets and cannon once they got here. And yes, catapults and siege engines. They just wouldn't notice that the specifics of their weapons had changed.

"You have to admit, trained troops backing the City guards might turn the tide in our favor." Witt crossed his arms. "And there are plenty of young men both in and out of the council families who would think of this as a great adventure."

"People like you?"

"Yes, people *like* me, but not *me*. So stop looking at me like that. I've come here to warn you, if you haven't realized it." There was color in his face and all the banter in his tone was gone.

"Why *are* you here warning us?"

"I'm not." He paced around the room. "I'm here warning *you*." He stood at the window looking out. "I like you."

I sat down on the arm of my upholstered chair. He liked me. I could tell now that I looked for it. Even if his tone *was* a bit grudging. And what exactly did that mean? And why, exactly, did I feel so pleased? I hoped I wasn't blushing, and I was glad he was still looking away.

"Well," I said when I was sure I could control my voice. "Thank you. It was very thoughtful of you. Though I still don't see why you think we're—that I'm in any danger. The White Court is like a fortress. All we have to do is close the bridges—"

"*Like* a fortress isn't a fortress." Witt spoke quietly, but firmly. He turned away from the window and came closer to where I stood. "The Red Court has been making a study of your 'fortress' for generations. You think there aren't vulnerable points? And what if we defend the bridges? Where are your food supplies coming from? And as for why *now*, it's because they think this is a good time to strike, while your attention is distracted with your internal politics. And besides that, most of the council is greedy enough to try attacking you anyway, if it means gaining the upper hand."

"You mean, why should they share and treat with us if they can own us?" That sounded bad, but I told myself I wasn't worried.

"Something like that, yes."

"How can they be so stupid?" I said before I could stop myself.

"Look, we're not the ordinary people on the streets. We're all educated. We know how things work. We know you have artifacts and technology and machines that you don't share with us yet—for whatever reasons—but you're still just scientists and engineers when you come right down to it. Not some kind of spooky, deathless mages." Witt's face changed as if he'd just remembered something he'd just as soon not think about. I turned my hands palm up and looked at him, ready to wait.

"How old are you?" he said finally.

"What an odd thing to ask." I had no idea where he was going with this, nor why this question should have made him uneasy.

"Can you tell me?"

"Well, of course I can . . ." I crossed my arms and hugged myself, suddenly cold. I'd been, what? Seventeen when I first came to the White Court. I'd been apprenticed for years before passing my third-class exams, and then for more years still before the ones for second class. An opening finally occurred among the first-class practitioners, and I could become one myself. So now I was . . . what?

"To be honest with you, I *don't* know, at least not exactly." And since I was being honest, "Older than you, I'd say, maybe a lot older."

Witt swallowed. "Riva Deneyra says you practitioners have some kind of anti-aging tonics or something, that help you live longer. She never said, but I always thought that's why she was so anxious to come to some kind of accord with you."

"There's no such tonic, I'm afraid. No artifact." I could assure him of that. "We live a long time, but it's because we're practitioners, nothing more."

"Just that simple?"

"Just that simple."

"Is it breeding? You only have children with other practitioners and eventually longevity becomes part of your heritage." He nodded, satisfied with this explanation.

"That's not it at all. You must have noticed that new practitioners come to us out of the general population. In fact, most of us don't have children, and the ones who do—well, a very few of them are practitioners and most of them aren't. Just like everyone else." I couldn't let it sit there. The sooner they understood the truth, the sooner we could put a stop to all this invasion nonsense.

"But you're wrong about something else as well. It's not superstition, what the people think of us," I said finally. "We're not deathless, but we are mages."

"Whatever you say." Witt plucked his gloves from out of his hat and pulled them on, deliberately fitting each finger. "I'd better be getting back before they miss me." He straightened his cuffs as if he had nothing else to do this evening. "I'll let you know what I can," he said without looking up.

"Thank you." I stood holding the door open. "I'll walk you to the bridge."

It wasn't until later I noticed he'd left his fan behind.

We met even fewer people on the way back to the East Bridge. Witt walked just as slowly as he had when he'd come in, but he didn't seem to be admiring or examining the gardens and buildings we passed. I didn't hurry him.

The sky had clouded over and I wished I'd thought to bring my coat. I started to ask Witt why we were strolling along so slowly, but I shut my mouth without speaking. I enjoyed this, his company, even though we weren't speaking. In a few minutes it began to rain. I had already flicked the standard rain-shade *forran* before it occurred to me that there were plenty of arcades and sheltered spots where we could have sat together out of the rain.

"What did you just do?"

I didn't know a whisper could be so sharp. "I used a rain-shade *forran*," I said, and waited for him to ask.

"That wasn't science, then? You just . . . did it yourself?"

"We call it the practice. Hence we're called practitioners—"

"*Hence?*" It looked like I hadn't awed him for long. "That's why you're not worried about us," he said. "If you can control the weather . . ." He stopped talking and we reached the gate in silence.

Emmett sat at the square table in the guard tower where those on duty usually took their meals. When we came in, he left the card game he was laying out. "Just in time," he said, "the shift's about to change. I'll take him to the bridge." He made a beckoning motion toward Witt. "Here's an umbrella for you, sir."

Witt looked at it with his head tilted to one side. "Thank you, but I'm afraid it clashes." He indicated his clothing with a sweep of his hand before turning and offering it to me. I knew this custom had been growing popular in the City, but this would be the first time I'd ever shaken hands with a mundane. I put out my right hand to meet his and thought how lucky it was that the ritual didn't involve the practitioner's hand.

Witt squeezed my hand gently and gave me a short bow that somehow reminded me of Elva Karamisk.

"Stay safe," I said. "Good luck."

"I might say the same to you." He smiled like his old carefree self, and I felt better. He saluted Emmett with a finger to his hat. "Ready when you are, good sir."

Emmett picked up the lantern hanging ready and already lit to one side of the doorway and led Witt outside. The raindrops sparkled as they fell through the lantern's light. Emmett went as far as the near end of the bridge, and stood watching as Witt crossed. The East Bridge is a long one, and with the night, and the rain, I lost sight of him before he reached the other side.

Suddenly there was a flash of light, a deafening noise, a rumble that shook the ground and knocked me off my feet. Emmett stumbled, and the lantern disappeared. I staggered upright and ran for the bridge. Emmett got to his feet fast enough to bar my way. Without the lantern I couldn't see his face, but I could feel his shock and terror.

"No, Tamari, don't look," he said, his voice surprisingly even. He'd never called me by my name before, without any title at all, not even when I had been a student. "The bridge is gone. It's fallen into the ravine."

"Dom Volden—did he make it across?"

ELVANYN

For the fourth time, Elva examined the window, the door, and even the bricks of the fireplace. For the fourth time, he didn't find a way out. The door had no knob or latch—or at least none that he could see, he amended, thinking of the door to Arlyn's workshop. With practitioners you never knew. The window shutters had latches, but he couldn't move them. No tapestries for secret doors to hide behind, no part of any wall sounding hollow.

The room itself was comfortable enough, though it lacked a bed. They'd have to move him if they expected him to sleep. Two wooden armchairs with cushioned seats, carved backs, and curled legs sat by the fireplace. A pedestal table with a round stone top polished smooth. Probably marble, from the graining. A cupboard, but nothing inside it, not even a tablecloth, or an old clay cup. Nothing he could use as a weapon. He sat sprawling on one of the chairs, right leg hooked over the arm, and frowned at the clean fireplace.

"Not even a loose brick to crunch someone with." He rotated his shoulders. He felt naked without his guns. He wondered where Fenra was, and when she would come for him.

A noise outside the door warned him in time to stand up. He put his back to the fireplace and got as ready as he could, shaking out hands and feet. They never came one at a time, so there was no point in pulling any tricks like hiding behind the door holding one of the chairs over his head. Just as he suspected, when the door opened, a guard with a crossbow came in pointing it at him. *More accurate than pistols?* he thought. When the guard stepped aside, Troy Rennard, the captain of the guard, came in. Elva leaned one elbow on the mantle.

"Well, what do you know," he said, "I expected someone else."

"Which you might have gotten, except for me." Rennard pulled one of the chairs to the table and motioned to Elva to take the other. "You disappeared a little abruptly the last time."

"I didn't exactly have a chance to proffer my resignation."

"Which means you're technically still a guard here. Still under my command, and that makes it my business—and no one else's—to find out why you're here now."

Actually true, as Elva knew. It was part of the bargain made with the practitioners when a guard was first formed, a kind of protection, security against being abused. Just like the *forran* that prevented the apprentices from practicing on mundanes within the Court.

Of course, that meant only his status as a guard kept him safe from practitioners. As soon as Rennard discharged him, this protection disappeared. Elva pulled out the other chair and sat, crossing his legs. "As for why I'm here in this room, I was dragged here, of course. Otherwise, I'm 'here' for Fenra Lowens, just as I always have been. She was invited to attend a meeting of the council. She decided to accept, and I came with her. It seems that the invitation was false, and the council has something else in mind for her."

Rennard nodded, silent, his head tilted to one side. "They mishandled that badly, didn't they? Luckily for you, since making that error helped convince them to leave you to me. I told them it would be a waste of time to interrogate you," he said. "You always have the same answers. You wouldn't tell me where Practitioner Lowens is even if you knew. And you don't know, do you?"

Elva smiled.

"I suppose if someone asked you where you think she might be, they'd get a different answer."

Elva smiled again and shrugged.

"You don't happen to know how she got out of the room she was in?"

Elva scratched at an itch behind his left shoulder. "I don't even know *that* she got out. Can I trust what any of you tell me?"

"What were *you* doing wandering around? Where were *you* going?"

"Looking for you, of course." Elva enjoyed Rennard's look of wary confusion. Funny how the truth had a way of throwing people off guard.

"If we let you go, would you persuade her to go home and be a nice little class three? Go back to healing villagers and let go of this idea of a new court?"

Elva shook his head slowly from side to side. "I wouldn't even if I could. Not after what I've seen."

"Meaning what?"

"Meaning she's right, and the council is wrong." Elva hesitated, his mouth dry. He remembered the beach, and the being that was the manifestation of the World. A being made up of sand and stones and sticks and grasses. And wind, and water. "The World is real, alive," he said. "I've seen it, her, whatever, with my own eyes, waiting for us all, practitioners in particular, to do our jobs and keep it and ourselves healthy."

"You sure this isn't one of Fenra Lowens' *forrans* talking?"

Elva grasped the edge of the table and leaned forward. "If she's the class three you say she is, then she couldn't do that level of *forran*. And if she could, why would she? My word, my testimony, isn't going to change anyone's position."

"You're telling me—"

The floor trembled under their feet and the table danced a few inches to the left. The two men looked at each other.

"Maybe that's the World telling you."

WITTENSLADE

Blinked. Dust in his mouth. And his eyes. Heavy weight on his legs. And sharp. He could move his fingers. And his toes. He coughed. Pain in his side. Gasping, taking shallow breaths. He closed his eyes.

Voices. His legs free. Hands on his arms, his legs. Lifting. Sharp pain in his side.

When Witt woke again, it took him several minutes to understand where he was. Certainly not in his own canopied bed, the sheets smelling of sandalwood and the air of beeswax candles. His throat was dry and scratchy. He coughed, gasping when the pain in his side knifed through him.

"Easy, Dom. Not so fast. You've got a couple of cracked ribs, I think." Witt couldn't focus on the speaker's face, but she had a kind voice, and helped Witt ease himself—with short, sharp breaths—to a sitting position. "I can strap you up, but it'll hurt quite a bit getting your coat off."

In the uneven light of the moon and the flickering lanterns, Witt could see the woman was dressed in the uniform of a Red Court guard. "If I lean forward and put my arms behind me," he said, "you should be able to pull off the coat by peeling the shoulders down and yanking on the sleeves. If that doesn't work, you can cut it off." *Goodbye, favorite coat.*

There must have been too much pain after all. When Witt woke up again the moon had moved, and he was sitting up, still in his shirt, his chest tightly wrapped. He took an experimental breath, and while it was shallow, it didn't hurt as much. His coat, still in one piece, had been hung over his shoulders, a blanket covered his legs. He didn't know how long he had been unconscious this time. Around him voices murmured, feet pounded, and hooves clattered. The moving lanterns made him dizzy, and he had to shut his eyes again. Finally, things seemed to quiet down, and when he opened his eyes, a man sat on a stool just to his left.

"Can you tell me your name?"

Witt cleared his throat, stifling a cough. The voice wasn't familiar, but the tone of command was. The man made a gesture and someone else held a water container to Witt's lips. The edge of the metal cup was cold. He nodded his thanks. "Wittenslade Camdin Volden."

"What were you doing on the bridge, Dom Volden?"

"I don't know." Something urged caution. He hadn't told anyone except Arriz where he was going, and he thought it best to go with his instincts. "What bridge is it?"

The voice of authority didn't answer the question directly. "From your position when we found you, you were coming from the bridge. If anyone on this side had seen you approaching it, you would have been stopped from crossing. So, again, what were you doing on the bridge? Where were you coming from?"

"I don't remember. I don't even know what bridge you're talking about. But I'm a courtier, surely I can be wherever I like."

"War has been declared against the White Court, Courtier Volden, and you seem to have crossed the East Bridge just before we destroyed it with explosives. I'm afraid you'll be wherever *I* like until I get some answers."

Witt stifled the urge to cough again. He must have breathed in some dust. "And you are?"

"Field Commander Fendall Dorst Vanaldren, of the County Forces."

Well, that explained some things, anyway. People from the outer counties sometimes forgot just how important the Red Court was—or at least they pretended to forget.

"You say the East Bridge? The bridge to the White Court?"

"That's right." The commander nodded.

"You may not know—I don't know who was told—that we, that is the Red Court, were trying to negotiate a trade agreement with the White. In case there was a chance, you know, to avoid outright war. I guess that must seem naïve to you. Well," Witt continued when he got no response. "Probably made a good distraction for you people, anyway." With luck the man wouldn't be able to tell that Witt was making it up as he went along. Though now that he thought about it, negotiations did make a good distraction, for anyone who was planning something else. "Courtier Riva Anden Deneyra—"

The left side of the man's mouth twitched. Apparently, the widow's reputation traveled even into other counties.

"She's in charge of the negotiation," Witt continued, as if he hadn't seen anything, "and I'm thinking she must have sent me with a message or something. Maybe even some fake information that would lead them to a false sense of security so that you would be able to act." *There, that pile of confused nonsense should help convince the man that I'm an idiot.* "I'm a terrible actor, so she might not even have told me what was going on, in case I gave it away. I can't think of any other reason for my being here." Witt blinked. Was he talking too much? Must have been the knock on the head. He blew a breath out carefully and then pressed his lips closed.

"We can check with Courtier Deneyra?"

"Of course. Would you like a personal introduction?" The look that flashed across the man's face was gone too quickly for Witt to know what it meant.

"Perhaps another time, Courtier Volden. Just now I'll have one of my junior officers escort you to your home. I ask you not to leave the City without clearance. I may have more questions for you," the man added as if the thought had just occurred to him.

"Certainly, Commander, whenever you please. I wouldn't miss this excitement for the world."

Following the commander's order, a young officer appeared in a small two-seater carriage. Witt had to be helped first to his feet and then into the seat. He hissed with pain but clenched his teeth against any other noise. It might be helpful in some future situation if he made a good impression now, and he guessed that whining wouldn't help. He thought the young officer detailed to go with him would resent being taken away from the action, but on the contrary the boy was happy to be given an excuse to explore the City, bombarding Witt with questions once he realized he wouldn't be snubbed. Witt did his best to find answers about the buildings they passed, and what the Red Court was like inside, and the White Court for that matter, and what it was like to be a courtier and if there was a theater season and were there dances, and hunting, and horseracing and was it true that it was always summer in the City?

Once they reached his house, Witt sent the now-reluctant young officer back to his commander. He could tell there was nothing the boy would like better than to come in and continue talking, but both of them knew it wasn't possible.

Arriz met him at the door, the housekeeper and butler hovering behind him, their faces white. All the lights in the house were out, only the front hall showing dim candle lanterns. All three servants were still fully dressed, despite the lateness of the hour. Suddenly Witt noticed just how dusty and disheveled his clothes were, to say nothing of the state of his lace cuffs.

"Dom Witt! We heard there was fighting, are you all right?" Arriz reached out with his hands, as if fully intending to check for himself, but the presence of the other servants prevented him. Arriz was nothing if not an expert in decorum.

"Some cracked ribs." Witt held up his hand as all three of them stepped forward. "Just from something falling on me, nothing serious."

"I'll send for a healer." The butler turned away, heading for the servants' wing.

"We'll have to handle it ourselves, my friends. We've declared war and the White Court is under siege. We won't be getting any practitioners until all of this is over. Not healers nor anything else."

The looks of shock on their faces echoed what he'd been thinking himself. Complain about them, sure, find ways to fine or tax them, of course. But no one could remember the last time—if it had ever occurred—that the City hadn't been able to call on the White Court. Witt thought about Riva Deneyra and her assisted childbirths. What would pregnant ladies near their terms do for help now?

"Right now, I'd like nothing more than a bath if there's still hot water. Arriz, you'll have to be careful helping me off with my clothes."

Seven

MY KNEES SUDDENLY felt rubbery, and I sank down in the chair Donn pulled out for me.

"Okay, what's the plan?" he asked. "Storm the White Court, rescue the sheriff, and disappear into the night?" Donn rubbed his hands together, his mustaches quivering above his smile.

"*Victorious*, Donn, don't forget. 'Disappear into the night' *victorious*." Randd perched on the edge of the table and grinned at the older man. These two had a special bond, I thought.

"*My* immediate plan is food, and sleep," I said. I thought I detected a tremor beginning in the fingers of my practitioner's hand. "Right now I doubt I can move all of us at once, and I am sure moving one or two at a time is bad strategy."

Donn rubbed at his forehead. "Sure, I wasn't thinking. There's more ham in the icebox, and biscuits and apples. If there are eggs, I could make you an omelet, or—"

"Ham and biscuits, Donn, thank you." I think if I had not stopped him, he would have gone on offering me choices until I dropped from exhaustion. I made a quick meal and Donn showed me to a bedroom opening off the sitting room. I was almost asleep when I noticed that the bed smelled of Elva, clean sweat, gun oil, and cedar wood. That helped me drop off.

Someone was tapping my leg. Gentle but firm. I did not want to wake up. I dreamed Elva and I were walking through a dark forest. I could feel the rich hum of the World under my bare feet. I kept looking over my shoulder, but I saw nothing that looked like Arlyn. I rolled over. Lizz immediately stepped back away from the bed, open hands raised to shoulder height.

"Just me," she said, as if I had woken up threatening her. "You rested?"

Was I rested? My mouth was dry, my eyes gritty, and my shirt sweaty. I had removed jacket, waistcoat, cravat, and boots, but had slept in the rest of my clothes. I thought back to my little house in the village. My plants, my books and scrolls. The sound of rain tapping on the rocks outside my door. This bed made that one look like a pile of grass, but I had slept better there.

I swung my feet down, sat up, and reached for my boots.

"There's clean linen," Lizz said from the doorway. She indicated the clothes press against the wall under the window.

I thought about wearing what would obviously be Elva's clothing. "That's all right," I said. "There will be clean clothes of my own where we are going."

She raised her eyebrows, but did not ask. Eventually, I supposed, I would get used to her reluctance to speak.

Randd waited for us in the sitting room. The table held four packs.

"We must bring ammunition," I said. "Bullets. Not just for you, but for Elva as well."

"Taken care of, ma'am." Randd tapped the pack nearest him with a forefinger. "Some in each pack. Lucky we all carry the same caliber."

I had no idea what he meant by that, but he seemed pleased, and he seemed to know what he was talking about.

"Where is Donn?"

"He's gone to see about the horses."

"We are taking horses?" I had a momentary image of the four of us, along with three horses, all crowded into the vault. Would we fit? Would I be able to move us all in the first place?

Lizz grinned, as if she thought I meant to be funny, but Randd did not. "Donn told us you didn't take any last time, so he's stabling ours while we're gone."

"You would prefer they went with us?"

"Of course. A Free Scout without a horse is like a fish without fins. But I understand it ain't possible." Whatever he understood, he still looked at me with hope in his eyes.

"I am sorry, Donn is right. We cannot take horses with us, but we can certainly acquire some where we are going." My own horse, Terith, was enjoying a holiday in the stables of the Ginglen Inn, and I was sure the proprietors, Ginglen and Itzen, would be happy to find us more— if I ever had the opportunity to ask them.

At that moment Donn returned, carrying a scuffed and dusty old saddle, at the sight of which Randd rolled his eyes upward, shaking his head. "Aren't you ever going to clean that thing?"

"What do you mean? It *is* clean."

I gathered this was an ongoing joke between the two men. "If you are ready." I picked up one of the packs on the table, turning it to put my arms through the straps.

"Here," Randd said. "Let me take that. You have enough to do."

I shook my head, ignoring his outstretched hand. "It makes no difference," I said. "Whoever is carrying it, I still have to move it." They exchanged glances, then all looked back at me.

I put out my practitioner's hand, palm up. "Put your hands on top of mine, and hold on, do not just place them there."

"Hey," Randd said. "We're all left-handed."

"It's your practitioner's hand," I said. "It's one of the very few things that mark us off visually from the mundanes."

"'Mundanes?' I don't like the sound of that." Randd curled his lip.

"You should hear what they call us when they think we're not listening." I smiled and shrugged my right shoulder. "Everyone has a word to describe others unlike themselves. It doesn't have to be negative. Though in fairness," I added, "it often is."

Once we were all holding hands, I noticed a faint glow surrounding them. *Their practice*, I thought. Would it help, or hinder? I pulled the locket from under my shirt and opened it with the thumbnail of my right hand.

Fog spilled out. Lizz grunted, Randd sucked in his breath, but Donn only chuckled. A wave of relief washed over me. They were practitioners enough to see it.

"Can you see patterns?" I asked.

Donn and Lizz nodded; Randd wrinkled up his face, eyes squinting.

"Colors?" I asked. The same nods, the same squinting.

"Each of us—and hopefully of you—has our own pattern. When

you learn how to use it, your practice improves and becomes stronger and more complex."

"Wait," Randd said. "I can see something moving." He turned his head, looking up, as if he could see the pattern as it expanded and settled around us. He squinted again and shook his head. When the fog disappeared, we were standing in Medlyn Tierell's vault. I lowered my practitioner's hand and released the others from the locket's *forran*.

"Holy mother of god," Donn said.

"What do you see?" Arlyn had seen nothing but empty shelves and cabinets when I had brought him here. Without power, or the *forran* I had created and used on Elva, there was nothing else to see.

"Books," Lizz said, her grin wide as she spun slowly around.

"What beautiful wood," Donn said, drawing his fingers along the edge of the nearest shelf. "I've never seen anything like it."

"This is your world?" Randd wrinkled his nose, clearly not impressed

"No," I said. "This is M—my vault." This wasn't Medlyn's vault anymore, it was mine. Time to start thinking of it that way. Every time I entered the vault I felt more at home, all the familiar things helping me relax. "It can be any size, created with the practice to house things of value." I thought of an experiment. "Donn, would you go to that chest and tell me what you see inside it?"

"Sure." He smoothed his mustaches with the back of his hand and strode across to the chest on the far wall as if he was an actor coming out for his bow. He flung the chest open and drew his sword at the same time, then peered in, his mustaches twitching and his brows drawn down in a frown. "Nothing," he said without turning his head to look at me. "What should be here?"

"Thank you, Donn. Would you close it, please? Lizz, would you try the same thing?"

Shrugging, Lizz crossed the room to the chest and lifted the lid, setting it carefully back against the paneled wall. She took a quick step back. "Clothes," she said, her astonishment clear even in the single word.

Donn hurried over. "Clothes." He turned to face me. "I swear the chest was empty when I looked. Is this your magic?"

"Not mine," I said. "The practitioner who trained me." I reminded myself that one day, when all of this was over, I would study Medlyn's *forrans* and learn how he did all this. I joined Donn and Lizz at the chest and took out underclothes, trousers, jacket, waistcoat, shirt, cravat, and gloves. I suppose my boots and hat were considered clean enough. I smiled at Lizz. "I told you there would be clean clothes waiting for me." I unbuttoned my soiled jacket. "While I change, would the three of you please go around the room and, one at a time, open each cupboard and chest?"

By the time they had finished, we learned that Lizz could see everything in the room, including all the books, scrolls, and models on the shelves. All the receptacles worked for her, every time she used them. Both Donn and Randd could see the books and scrolls, but Randd saw only some of the models. Both could find food and drink in the cupboards, but not items in the chests.

"What do you suppose it means?" Donn said.

I finished buttoning my trousers and picked up my waistcoat. "I cannot be sure, but I believe it might tell us what class you would be, if you were practitioners in my world. Lizz might be able to pass the first-class exams, for example, whereas you two might be second class only. Or," I added as Lizz grinned at the two men and snapped her fingers at Randd, "it might simply mean that the two of you would need more training. But when it comes to power, Lizz scores higher, and therefore has more options open to her."

I tied my cravat and pulled on my jacket, tugging on the cuffs to straighten the sleeves. "If you are ready, we should go now. We will be arriving in the office of Tamari Otwyn, who is an ally." Or at least I hoped she was. "But I ask you to be prepared to defend yourselves, as I have no way of knowing what's happened in my absence." I paused with my practitioner's hand stretched half toward them. "Can any of you fight right-handed?"

"Of course," Randd said. "All of us." He pulled his revolver out of its holster with his right hand, spun it around on his index finger, and caught it, ready to shoot. "We train for both."

Donn took his position on my right, with sword drawn, Lizz on my left, revolver in her hand, and Randd facing me, pointing his revolver at the ceiling.

I opened the locket.

Tamari

I thought about Witt for what felt like hours, my mind spinning and spinning—what had happened to him? Where was he? Was he all right? How could I find out? I must have fallen asleep finally, my head on my folded arms. I didn't hear anything so much as I felt a movement in the air. I lifted my head and looked into the barrels of two pistols aimed right at me. A quick glance to the right showed me the point of a sword. I just had time to take in the shapes of the figures, wide-brimmed hats, long hair, when I saw Fenra's face behind them.

"Are you trying to scare me to death?" I lowered my practitioner's hand. I have no idea what *forran* I meant to use. I sat back in my chair and looked at Fenra. "I didn't know whether to wait here or in Medlyn's old rooms." I rubbed at my temples and massaged the sore spots under my eyebrows. "Glad I guessed right."

"Do you know where Elva is?"

I nodded and pushed myself to my feet. "Predax's got some friends in the kitchens, and they were able to tell him that food is being sent into the old Griffin Palace. The upper floors aren't in use anymore, and they've put him into one of the suites. But Fenra—" I felt strangely as though I was about to betray something—"are you sure we should rescue Elva first? Aren't there larger issues just now?"

She gave me a most peculiar grin. "There are no larger issues," she said. Somehow, this made me feel better. I thought that if our roles were reversed, she would help me rescue Witt.

"Are there others shut up with him?" The thin man with the impressive mustaches sheathed his sword.

I blinked at him. "We don't have holding cells like the Red Court. If there's a problem, we just confine the person to their rooms with a *forran* they can't break."

Fenra's eyes unfocused and narrowed. I assumed she was picturing the building and sorting out her own memories of it. "We can get there through the gardens, if the door hasn't been blocked."

"There are guards in the gardens," I said. "And some of the third-class practitioners are helping them."

"That would be why we're here," the thin man said. "They're not likely to give us trouble."

I had no idea why he would think so. I looked from him to the other two. I'd never seen this kind of clothing before. It looked like pale leather, or maybe suede, and the younger man's jacket had fringes. All three were armed to the teeth with pistols and swords, and the two younger ones had long guns. "Who are you people?"

"Friends of Elva's," Fenra said. "Donn Keeshode, his first deputy, Lizz Weston, and Randd Greggson."

That explained their odd clothing and weapons. I *had* seen something like them before. Elva Karamisk had some similar stuff. "And how, exactly, are they going to help?"

"They're practitioners."

"Practitioners? What class? Who trained . . ." My mouth dried. Had Fenra been training people already?

"We're not from around here," Randd Greggson said. "We're soldiers. You'd be surprised what kind of training that gives you, and how fast it encourages you to learn. Most people won't even see us or hear us—though I'm not so sure about smelling us." He shot a glance sideways at the older man, who just grinned back.

Fenra started for the window, but Randd held her back.

"Let me," he said, signaling to Lizz. He flattened his back against the wall to the left of the window and rolled his head until only one eye peered over the frame. The young woman did the same from the other side.

"Four people leaving, running," she said. "That same uniform." She nodded in my direction.

That was when I noticed that Fenra wasn't wearing practitioner's colors, and shut my eyes, clutching at the edge of my worktable, part of me shocked, and another part wondering how she did it.

"How are we going to get to Elva without being seen?" I asked, after taking a few deep breaths and opening my eyes. "I can lend Fenra practitioner's colors, but the three of you are pretty noticeable."

"We'll start by going out the window." From his tone, it seemed Donn Keeshode was having a marvelous time. I half expected him to rub his hands together in glee. "We can be next to invisible when we want to be."

"We've done this before," Randd added.

"You've climbed out of a window into a courtyard full of practitioners?"

"It's not full of practitioners now." Donn swept his arm out to show me how empty it was.

"Fine," I said. "We're on the third floor. Are we going to jump?"

"I can," Lizz said. "Likely the only one, though."

"Do not look at me," Fenra said. "I can climb, but not float. That level of control is beyond most practitioners." She looked around the office, frowning. "Is there anything we can use to make a rope?"

"Wait." Lizz shrugged out of her pack and unbuckled the straps. She searched through it for a moment, pushing things one way and another, until she pulled out a compact package. She passed it up to Randd and re-closed her pack. "Told you we'd need it."

"*That's* a rope?" I think my voice squeaked. What Randd unraveled looked more like packing cord to me.

"Sure," Randd said. "It's silk, just about the strongest material there is. A hemp rope this thin wouldn't hold us up, but this will easily." He glanced around the room before knotting one end of the silk cord to a leg on the massive desk. "That should anchor it." He looked at me a wicked grin. "In case of accidents."

"Let me go first," Fenra said. "I can help if something goes wrong on the ground."

They all acted as if none of this was unusual. I crossed my arms.

Fenra sat down on the windowsill before passing the cord around her body and taking a turn of it around one hand. She nodded at Donn and swung her legs out over the sill, first checking to make sure the courtyard was still empty. As Donn belayed the rope, she swung herself out and began half walking, half hopping down the wall, just as easy as you please, like she'd been doing it all her life. As soon as she reached the bottom, Randd pulled up the cord. He and Lizz weren't quite as graceful as Fenra, but they reached the ground without trouble.

"From the look on your face, this is all new to you." Donn smiled at me. "Here, let me tie you on, and I'll lower you."

I couldn't believe it, but I actually nodded. *I'll be fine*, I thought. After all, I'd just seen three people go down before me, so I knew it could be done. But what if the strain of three people was all the rope could bear? What if it chose this moment to give out? What if he dropped me?

Donn patted me on the shoulder and gave me the kind of smile your father might give you when he didn't want you to be scared. "I won't drop you," he said.

I believed him, but I didn't relax. How had he known what I was thinking?

"I could see it right on your face," he said, his eyes shining.

"I feel *so* much better now." Oddly, I actually did feel better. Donn had managed to take my mind off the drop outside the window for several seconds at least. He finished knotting the cord under my arms, and all my fear came back.

"Here." Donn made sure the knot of the rope was in front, just above my breasts. "Hang on tight."

"I don't think—"

"Don't think. Look at me. Just keep looking at me." He took several turns of the rope around his arm and picked me up. Before I had time to react, he had lowered me out of the window, leaning back as the rope took my weight. I kept my jaw clenched, and my eyes on Donn's. After the first few feet, I tried to use my feet against the wall like the others had, but without much success. I was lucky I didn't break an ankle. I hadn't begun to finish worrying when someone's hands were on my ankles, guiding my feet to the ground. As soon as I let go of it, Donn followed me, lowering himself hand-over-hand before landing lightly on his toes, absorbing the impact with bent knees. He gave the rope a sharp tug, and it collapsed on the pathway in front of me. Before I could catch my breath, they all disappeared. One moment Lizz was coiling up the rope to replace it in her pack, the next, I was completely alone. I thought I saw a faint glow over by the pomegranates, but when I focused on it, there was nothing there.

I hadn't believed Fenra when she'd said these people had practice. I don't know what irritated me more, that I knew they were there and couldn't see them, or that I couldn't disappear myself. Well, maybe I couldn't, but at least I knew where we were going.

I'd meant to stroll innocently across to the arched opening in the wall that would take me out of the far end of the garden, but as I went, I found myself walking faster and faster, until I was almost running. The idea that around me, in the shadows made by trees and hedges, there were people silently slipping along, unheard and unseen, scratched at my nerves. By the time I was halfway through the garden, about where the fig trees were planted, I was running full out. Just as I passed the roses, stepping out onto the graveled section of the path, two guards in full uniform stepped in front of me.

"Practitioner Otwyn. Is there something we can do for you? You were running."

I had to catch my breath, no way to disguise it, but it gave me a chance to think. "No, I was just trying to get inside before the rain starts."

"There's no rain scheduled for this evening."

"What? Of course there is, it rains every Third Day night."

"It's Fourth Day, Practitioner." I heard exactly the tone of amused tolerance I hoped for. Many of the guard treated practitioners as if they might need help putting on their boots. Better they should think I was a bit absent-minded than that I was running for a reason. And what about my companions? Could I distract the guards enough that they could use their "invisibility" to get past them and out of the garden?

"Fourth Day? Here I've thought it was Third Day since I got up. No wonder none of my apprentices came to their lessons." I took a final deep breath and lowered my hand from my side. "Well, thank you, guardsmen. Good night."

"Just a moment, Practitioner Otwyn. This end of the garden is off limits at the moment."

My heart pounded, and my smile felt stiff. The guard spoke politely, but firmly, and I wanted so badly to just nod and walk away. However, I didn't think it would have been in character for me, as a practitioner and councilor, to give in meekly and not ask questions, since the guards were, in point of fact, employees.

"I'm a member of the council," I said, "and I've heard nothing about this."

～

WITTENSLADE

Witt rolled over and caught his breath as a muscle in his back spasmed and his left leg cramped. Breathing careful and shallow, he managed to roll over to the side of his bed and struggle upright. The pain in his ribs was only excruciating this morning.

"How are you feeling?" Arriz opened the curtains, but the light he let in seemed pale and washed out. Exactly the way Witt felt.

Witt wriggled his toes in the sheepskin rug beside his bed. Even that little movement reminded him of every stone, beam, and chunk of rock that had made his acquaintance the night before. Arriz had set up his favorite breakfast on the table nearest the window: flaky rolls, fresh butter, marmalade, and, of course, crispy bacon. Witt's stomach rumbled. He grabbed his robe from where it lay across the foot of the bed—or rather he tried to. He stopped, hissing, with his arm half extended.

"Let me." Arriz swept up the garment before Witt could try again and held it open for him. Witt winced as he fit his arms into the sleeves, but it was certainly easier than trying to pull it on himself.

Regardless of the sounds his stomach made, Witt hadn't expected to have an appetite, but after tasting the first careful mouthful, he didn't stop until the plate was clean. He set down his coffee cup on its saucer. "Have Fordon bring the gig around," he said. "I have to go out."

"I'll have him bring the curricle. You're not driving yourself."

Witt started to protest, but a twinge in his neck made him think again.

With Arriz driving, it didn't take them long to reach the Anden Deneyra House. It was close enough that Witt would have walked on a day his muscles were following his orders. His tutor had once told him all the courtiers' houses originally stood alone, each with its own drives, gardens, and walls. Slowly, the Red Court had grown out to surround and swallow them up, enclosing them within the great curtain wall, built in response to and in imitation of the walls surrounding the White Court. Witt often thought that from above the whole place must look like a child's toy box, dozens of architectural styles all brightly colored, and all jumbled together, sometimes with the most jarring effect imaginable. Though Witt had to agree that after a while a person could get used to just about anything, no matter how ugly or in what bad taste.

Like last season's lapels.

The widow's house still retained a small garden at the front, with a large enough circular drive for a carriage to be driven in and then out again. Arriz drove directly to the widow's front door, hopped out, and came around to help Witt descend.

"I don't need help," he growled, all the more annoyed when his legs almost gave out under him. With a hand under his elbow, Arriz supported Witt to the door, where a foot . . . servant, Witt remembered, smiling, answered his knock, and took the visiting card Arriz handed her. Witt braced his legs until he could stand by himself, and patted Arriz on the shoulder before he followed the servant into the west sitting room, where he was asked to wait while the woman checked whether her mistress was "at home" that morning. After a while Witt stood up and walked around the room, more to keep his muscles from stiffening again than from any special curiosity regarding Riva's furniture and ornaments. He smiled at a particularly sentimental shepherdess, not at all Riva's style, he decided. In fact, nothing in the room looked as if she had chosen it.

It could have been a pretty room too, well-proportioned with unadorned columns, if it weren't for all the family portraits covering the papered walls. *From the look of that nose*, Witt thought, *these must be Riva's late husband's family.*

A few minutes later he heard the servant returning and turned to look out the window. It was silly to feel guilty at being caught looking around, but he felt what he felt.

"Courtier Camdin Volden, my mistress will be with you shortly, if you don't mind waiting. May I serve you with anything?" She indicated the six matching decanters that sat on a silver tray between the portraits of two old granddads with particularly ugly whiskers.

"Thank you, not just now."

Witt heard the snick of the latch as the servant closed the door of the sitting room behind her and gave the woman time to return to her work before he opened the door, holding the handle to prevent any telltale sound. He held his breath, moved his head from side to side, slowly. At first he heard nothing, and then, faintly, the murmur of voices as a door on an upper floor opened.

One of the voices he recognized immediately as Riva's. The other, a man's voice, sounded familiar, but he couldn't place it immediately. The voices grew louder, and Witt pulled the door almost shut, placing his eye to the crack and watching the man descend the staircase. Witt made a silent whistle. When he had spoken to the field commander the night before, he'd had the definite impression that the man didn't know Riva Deneyra, and yet here he was walking down the widow's staircase while she personally escorted him to the door. What was going on? Witt tapped his leg with his fan. While the commander had questioned him, it had occurred to him that someone might be using the negotiations to distract attention from an alternative plan. Now, seeing the officer in the widow's house, he had an idea who that someone was. He felt so stupid.

Witt was standing at the window with his hands clasped behind his back when the servant returned.

"The mistress is ready for you now, Courtier Volden. Please follow me."

Witt followed the woman up the curving staircase that gave the entrance hall its feeling of grandeur, glad for the cold marble banister. They stopped on the second landing, and she led him down a long hallway with pale pink walls, carpeted in green and gold. Witt wasn't being taken to the room the Field Commander had been in, he realized, which had been on the first floor. Finally, the servant stopped, opened the door, announced Witt, and stood back out of the way.

Riva sat behind a desk made from pale wood with an inlaid leather surface. She should have been dwarfed by the size of the thing, but she had such presence that she managed to dominate it. Witt could tell right away she had furnished this room herself. Along with only a few portraits, the paintings were mostly landscapes in the new sublime manner, showing craggy rocks and stormy seas.

"Bring coffee and tarts, Jellen," Riva instructed the servant. She smiled at Witt and with her quill pen indicated a guest's chair facing her across the desk. She rested the pen on its stand before moving several sheets of paper into a folder.

"My dear, you look dreadful. Sorry to be so blunt, but should you be out of bed? Whatever happened?"

"A bridge fell on me."

A look of genuine concern drew down her eyebrows. "You were *there*? Why?"

Remembering the still-unexplained presence of the field commander, Witt decided to stick to the story he'd given the man. "I have no idea. I don't remember going that way at all. I thought perhaps you might have sent me."

"I certainly didn't." She frowned, lips pursed. Jellen returned with the coffee service, poured out two cups, put cream in Riva's before handing it to her, and then made sure both cream and sugar were close to Witt's hand before leaving the room.

Witt put down his cup and added cream to it before lifting it again. The way his forearms trembled, he thought he couldn't risk using both hands at once. "Then what was I doing there? Watching the action? But I didn't have a carriage, or friends with me . . ."

"Are you sure? I can think of several of your 'friends' that might have run away in panic when the bridge blew, leaving you to the soldiers."

Witt lifted his brows as if in appreciation of her observation. She was right, some of his friends would have done exactly that. He'd better agree with her. "I suppose so. I hate to think it of them, but it is possible."

"Sorry not to be of more help." Riva took a delicate sip of her coffee, set it down on her side of the desk, and put a tart on the edge of the saucer. She wouldn't eat it, Witt knew, but her gesture freed him to help himself. He did so, stopping himself by force of will not to stuff the whole thing into his mouth at once. He took a single bite and set his tart on the edge of his own saucer. "How did the assault happen so quickly? I thought the Court had only agreed on the idea in principle."

"Last night Valter called for an emergency session of the court. We couldn't find you—now I understand why—but we had enough for a quorum. I don't know who brought him in, but Field Commander Fendall Dorst Vanaldren was waiting in the wings, ready to come on stage. He gave such a rousing description of what he had in mind that the next thing I knew an immediate attack had been motioned, seconded, and passed."

"You voted against it?" Her smile didn't change, and after a long pause, Witt's suspicions solidified and he added, "You didn't vote against it, did you?"

She moved her head to the left and back again.

Suddenly everything fell into place. Living with his father—and card play—had given him plenty of practice in keeping what he thought off his face. He was especially glad of it now. He saw everything that had happened since he first took his seat in the Red Court with new eyes.

"This was your plan all along." Witt put his coffee down. Suddenly he didn't want it. "All that stuff about diplomatic negotiations—that was just to keep everyone's attention away from what you were really doing." He sat up straighter, pain making him wince. *She used me.* "And I suppose we were spying out the lay of the land when we were in the White Court."

Riva sat silent for a moment, sipping her coffee, looking directly at him as if deciding something. Finally, she spoke. "If you're waiting for an apology, I'm sorry. I'm sorry," she added when Witt started to speak, "that you were inexperienced enough to be manipulated. It's a lesson that hasn't cost you so very much, after all. We will get what we wanted, though not in the way that you expected it." Her smile became a little bigger.

Witt managed to chuckle—he hoped convincingly—and waggled his finger at her as though she were a naughty child. It might not fool her, but it would let him save face. It would also give him time to plan his revenge. He had stopped his father from using him, and now he would stop her.

FENRA

As soon as I stepped onto the stone pathway I lost my invisibility, but I could not reach the other end of the patio if I walked only in the flower beds—and there were thorns. However, I still knew how to move quietly, and take full advantage of the shadows cast by the gas lamps and the moonlight. I froze, holding my breath, as two guards walked past me into the garden. As long as I could remember, this part of the Griffin Palace had been used more as a thoroughfare than an entrance hall. The building hadn't been in regular use since before my time. The back corridors and stairs showed signs of being recently swept clean by someone who did not know how, leaving the corners still thick with dust and, from the smell, mice droppings. The lower, tiled portions of the walls were still intact, but the painted walls were scabby with damp. It surprised me that the council would allow this kind of neglect.

I crossed the open space quickly and slid myself into the shadow created by the stairwell.

It felt like hours until the others joined me in the shadows. I counted them, twice.

"Where is Tamari?" I wished I could stop doubting her, that my stomach didn't clench when she was not where I expected her to be.

"Two men in uniform stopped her and escorted her away."

I flexed my hands. It must have been the two I had avoided. "Arrested?"

"Not that I could see," Donn said. "She chatted with them, waving her hands as if she was telling them a story."

"It can't be helped." I thought that if she were not, in fact, arrested, Tamari at least knew where to be if she wanted us to find her. We waited where we were, in the safety of the shadows, but no one came after us. It seemed she had not betrayed us.

"This way," I murmured. I focused on Elva. I could have found him anyway, I think, but being so close it was like seeing a flare of light in the distance, like a lighthouse. Except that instead of warning me away, it called me in. When we reached the top floor, we crept down the corridor to the left, and stopped at the first turn when we heard voices. I shut my eyes and breathed more easily than I had in hours. One of those voices was Elva's.

Donn tapped me on the shoulder, smiling as he lifted his eyebrows. I nodded, and when he held up first three fingers, then four, and lifted his shoulders, I held up two fingers on my right hand, and one on my practitioner's hand. Two guards I meant, and Elva. He nodded and passed the information in the same silent way to the others. I made sure I had their attention and patted the air in front of me, waiting until they nodded before I turned back to face the corner. I rubbed the palms of my hands together and concentrated on the *forran* I used to put patients to sleep. I had used it against a guard once before, but I could not be sure it would work the same way against two of them. When I was ready, I took the pattern of light and tossed it around the corner, hoping we were close enough for the *forran* to reach the guards.

Randd motioned me back. He squatted down, and then used the same technique of peering around the corner at knee height that I had once seen Elva use. He straightened to his feet.

"Sound asleep," he said, grinning. "That's a good trick; can you teach it to me?"

"A question for another time, I think," Donn said. "But it would save a lot of bullets."

A throat cleared as we rounded the corner. "What took you so long?" Elva said.

Tamari

I accompanied the guards until we were well out of the patio before I stopped.

"Well, thank you very much, but I think I can find my rooms from here." I smiled, nodded, and turned away. Not that I was planning to go there. Either my office or Medlyn's old rooms, that's where Fenra would come looking for me.

"I'm sorry, Practitioner Otwyn, but you'll have to come with us. Captain Rennard will want to see you."

"What *now*? What's this about?"

"New rules, Practitioner, since the bridges went."

"Security's tightened," the second one said. "The same for everyone."

"Oh, very well." I tried hard to sound exasperated and not nervous. What new rules, and when had they been made? I walked out in front of them, so it looked and felt more like I was leading them than like they were escorting me. They let me stay in front, which made me feel a little better. Whatever this turned out to be, I wanted it over as quickly as possible.

The Blue Tower had been built right up against the wall at the west end of the White Court overlooking the river Garro. It housed the guards' barracks and their kitchens, and had its own interior patio for leisure purposes, though I understood many of the married guards lived with their families in the quarters just within the walls.

When we walked into his ground-floor office, Captain Troy Rennard glanced up, marked his place with a thin strip of parchment, and set his book aside.

"Good evening, Practitioner Otwyn."

"Good evening, Captain. These gentlemen wanted me to report to you."

He looked surprised, glancing from me to the guard standing behind me on my right.

"Sabord?"

"Yessir. We were relieved at the end of our watch, and as we were returning to quarters we found Practitioner Otwyn in the North Gardens, heading for the Griffin Palace. We explained that anyone out at night needs to account for themselves."

"I apologize, Practitioner, but those new measures were introduced this morning by Chief Practitioner Sedges."

Chief Practitioner? Where did that title come from? "I missed the meeting," I said. "I was just telling your men that I've thought it was Third Day ever since I got up. I'm afraid this whole thing—the bridges and everything—has shaken me up a little."

"Understandable. And what brought you to the North Garden?"

"As I just said," I allowed my tone to get a bit crisper, "I thought it was Third Day, so I was trying to get inside before the rain started. I didn't know the garden was off limits . . . ?" I let my voice die away, inviting him to fill in the blanks.

"Not as such, Practitioner Otwyn, we're just checking. Keeping you all safe. That's our job." His tone was facetious, but his smile didn't reach his eyes.

"Well, if that's everything." I glanced at his book.

"Of course, thank you for your understanding. You men are not dismissed."

But obviously I was. I nodded at each of them in turn and strolled out. I didn't go far, however. There was more going on than Troy Rennard was admitting to—such as a meeting no one had bothered to tell me about—and whatever it was, it troubled him. I went down on one knee as if to tie up my shoes and listened.

"You men, come with me."

"But sir, you don't think that Practitioner Otwyn—"

"No, of course not. Just making doubly sure everything is as it should be. Practitioner Otwyn is under no suspicion."

Well, I knew a lie when I heard one. *Thanks, Fenra, thanks very much.*

Eight

ELVANYN

ELVA CHECKED THE room over again for possible hiding spots, weapons, and escape routes and found nothing. Again. No hollow-sounding areas in any of the walls, no loose bricks, no cupboards large enough for a person, no furniture heavier than a bamboo table—with the glass top missing. There wasn't even an opening in the door he could see through or use to distract or bribe the guard—not that the White Court guards were very bribable, at least not for something this serious. Sneaking a bed mate into your quarters without permission or changing your watch with someone else's—that would be easy.

He knew he didn't have to do anything more than sit tight and wait for Fenra to come—and she would come, he was certain of that, though if coming for him put her in any kind of danger, part of him preferred waiting in this room forever. She was important, and more than just to him. The World was counting on her.

He heard noises in the corridor and reached automatically for a weapon, but the captain had taken his revolvers and his sword. He stood against the wall, as close to the opening edge of the door as he could. He shook out his hands, flexed his knees, and took a couple of deep, steadying breaths. He'd learned a move or two in the New Zone that might come in handy now. Then he heard voices, one voice in particular that made his breath come easier, and his heartbeat faster. Only a moment before, he'd tried to convince himself that he didn't really need her to come for him.

"What took you so long?" he said through the door. He rubbed his hands together and waited for the door to open.

FENRA

When I heard Elva's voice, my muscles relaxed and I breathed easier. I turned my face away from the others and blinked away sudden tears. "Did you get bored waiting?" I said, trying to keep my voice steady. I put my palm flat against the door. I knew that Elva was doing the same on the other side.

"I'll say. And I'm getting hungry."

"Time to get you out of there." I knelt to examine the lock more closely. An ordinary, keyed lock, I thought. But then my sight blurred. I blinked, and shook my head, but the lock stayed blurry. I sat back on my heels and blew out my breath.

"What is it?"

"This is warded." I explained what happened when I focused on the lock. "I cannot use a *forran* on something I cannot properly see."

Elva struck the door with his fist. At least, I hoped it was his fist.

"What about picking the lock?" Donn asked.

I straightened to my feet and dusted off my trousers, to give me time to harness my temper. "If a lock has been warded against practitioners—"

"Sure, but what if it's been warded *only* against practitioners?" Randd spoke, but it was Lizz who shrugged her shoulders at me.

"Can any of you pick a lock?" Obviously, my training hadn't been as thorough as I had thought.

They all ducked their heads and looked at each other sideways.

"Well," Donn said finally, his mustaches quivering as he tried not to smile. "It's a skill you don't brag about. People are apt to get nervous. Tend not to invite you in for a drink."

"But?"

"Yes, of course they can all pick the lock!" Elva called from the other side of the door. "This is no time to be coy. Get me out!"

Lizz and Randd stood to one side and bowed to Donn with mock solemnity. The old man grinned, cracked his knuckles, and pulled a flat leather case, like a note case, out of an inner pocket of his jacket. He went down on one knee and squinted through the lock with one eye.

"Can you see it?" They were practitioners also, in their own way, and in that moment, I thought the ward might also work on him.

"Not to worry, ma'am," he said. He picked two thin metal rods from an assortment in the leather case before putting it down to one side. Still on one knee, he inserted the lock picks into the mechanism of the lock and began to manipulate them. I realized I was holding my breath, and released it, only to find myself holding it again a moment later.

After what seemed an eternity, Donn sat back and opened his case again, returned one of the picks he'd been using and took out another.

"Want me to do it?"

"Mind your manners."

A much shorter time passed, and I heard a sharp click, as the lock released.

Elva yanked the door open from the inside and had me in his arms before anyone could take another breath.

"We are not alone," I reminded him, though I clung to him just as tightly.

"Hello, fellas," Elva said over my shoulder, without letting me go.

"Sheriff." The three of them spoke in unison.

Elva's arms loosened and I stepped back, but not far. "Who else did you bring?"

Both Randd and Lizz looked at Donn and the older man's smile dimmed a little. "They all wanted to come," he said. "But you know most of them have families, people who depend on them."

"Who did you leave in charge?"

"Susann."

"Good choice." Without saying anything else, Elva shook hands with Lizz. "Randd," he said, putting out his hand. "Good to see you."

Randd smiled as he shook Elva's hand. "I'm here for Donn, see if I can persuade him to be a Free Scout again, so don't get above yourself." Elva punched him lightly on the shoulder with the side of his fist. I was not sure what this meant, but there seemed to be nothing but good blood between them.

"Where to from here?"

Before any of us could answer, all four of them looked down the corridor in the direction we had come. Donn glanced at the walls.

"This place is too wide," he said. "Everyone into the room." I started to protest as he shoved us in, but he ignored me and shut the door.

"We can easily defend the doorway," he told me. "Only two can come at us at a time, and there are four of us to take turns keeping them off. Do they have guns?"

"Flintlocks," I said.

"These are only guardsmen, doing their jobs." Elva set his hand down on the older man's shoulder. "I know them. Let's not kill them if we can avoid it."

The old man nodded. "Hmmm. If they don't shoot, we won't, but if they do, we kill them."

Both men were serious.

Donn went down on one knee again, lock picks in hand, and this time locked the door from the inside. I motioned him away as soon as he had finished. By this time even I could hear quiet footfalls approaching us. I could not tell if a practitioner was with them, but warding the door from this side felt like a good idea. I rubbed my palms together, pulled them apart, and blew the red pattern that appeared into the lock.

"This can only buy us some time," I said to Elva. "We need to get out of here."

"Which we can do whenever we like." He tapped himself on the chest, just where a locket would rest if he were wearing one. "I say we negotiate first."

"Who can we trust?" I said.

"We have the boss," Lizz cut in. "I vote we go home."

Not my home, I thought, and I could not help the World from there. "I cannot—"

"What about Tamari? And Predax, for that matter?" Elva interrupted. "Where are they?" It was as if he knew I wanted to avoid the subject of a return to the New Zone.

"She left the garden with two guards," I said, "though it isn't clear whether she was under arrest. She *did* help us." They were all watching me. "We must make sure she is safe." All three deputies nodded their agreement, though Randd looked less convinced than the others.

"Karamisk." I thought I recognized the voice that called from the other side of the locked door, but Elva held up his hand, shaking his head, before I could answer.

"Captain Rennard, it's good to hear your voice," he said. "If you've come for me, it's only fair to warn you I'm not alone."

"How did they—never mind. Karamisk, you and your friends should give yourselves up. I guarantee you won't be hurt."

"Do you? That's interesting. What about being tricked and imprisoned? Where's your guarantee on that?"

A pause. "I had nothing to do with the trick that brought you here."

"I know you didn't, Rennard," Elva said in a much softer voice. "But you aren't the one who calls the shots, are you?"

Silence.

"Exactly. I know I can trust *you*, and your people. But we can't trust that idiot Sedges and the rest of his bloody council." *Don't mention Tamari*, he mouthed at us. I understood; if she was not yet suspected, perhaps we could keep it that way.

"You can't get out of that room. If I don't come back with you, they'll just leave you there until you starve."

More silence. We all looked at each other in the flicker of the gas lamps. I shrugged and pulled out the locket.

TAMARI

At least if they had arrested me, I might have had some glimmer as to what was going on. I guessed that Fenra, Elva, and their friends managed to get away, since Captain Rennard and four of the guard had turned up empty-handed and annoyed. Sadly, there was no way I could ask without raising suspicions. I wasn't even supposed to know Elva was being held. Of course I was happy that Fenra and her friends got away, but I found myself more than a little annoyed that they'd just gone off without me. Not that I would have gone with them, necessarily, but it would have been nice to have the option.

I fell asleep holding Witt's fan, and spent all night jolting awake, thinking that I'd heard him calling me. I got up exhausted and depressed. I had some fruit and day-old bran muffins in my sitting room, but no coffee, so I went down to the central dining hall. The courtyards and patios I crossed through seemed full of people. Students hurried from one area to another, gathering in groups to whisper to each other, and then moving quickly along when any senior practitioner approached them. After all that bustle, I found the dining hall unusually quiet, and almost empty, the high ceilings with their intricate carvings deadening any sounds.

Three practitioners sat at a table for four under the arched windows directly across from the door. The lattices on the lower halves of the windows were closed, but I could see the distant mountains through the top halves. Tellen Fitzen waved me over when she saw me in the entrance. I usually sat alone, or with Predax, but today I didn't want to make a point of refusing the invitation, so I made my way through the tables to take the empty chair.

"Tam," Tellen said as soon as I'd given my order. "Guess what? Wuten's just passed his first-class exams."

"That's wonderful, congratulations." I remembered him as an apprentice, but as he wasn't an apprentice of mine, I hadn't been involved in his examinations. It seemed the council had finally gotten around to promoting someone to replace Metenari as a first-class practitioner, just as I'd been promoted to take his vacant council seat. "Welcome to first class."

"Thank you. I was not expecting it so soon."

"So." Tellen leaned forward. "What's this special council meeting this afternoon?"

"First I've heard of it." I poured myself some coffee from the pot on the table and tried to ignore the uneasy twist of my stomach. "I've been busy the last few days, so I'm not up to date."

"Or you do not want to tell us what's going on," Wuten Aligari said. I hadn't noticed it before, but he had the same accent as Fenra.

I started to give him a sharp reply, but then I let it go. As a recent first class, Wuten probably thought he had to assert himself.

"So, will you tell us, then?" Tellen asked again; she was like a cat after a rat. "Once you know what the special meeting's about?"

"Oh, come on." I didn't know the name of the third practitioner at the table. "It's about the attacks, what else could it be? Everyone says the guards aren't doing well at all."

"Speaking of which, Tam, there's a couple of them heading this way. They seem to be looking for you."

"Excuse me, Practitioner Otwyn?"

"Yes." I didn't recognize the guard that stood at careful attention an arm's length from my side of the table.

"Your presence is required at an emergency sitting of the council."

I swallowed the last mouthful of coffee out of my cup and pushed myself to my feet.

"You can't be serious." Az Pilcuerta's voice shook, but I thought it was more from anger than from age. Her practitioner's hand formed a bony fist on the tabletop. "You are proposing that we merely ignore the Red Court's aggression?"

"What aggression?" Nubin Sonsera said, chewing on the edge of a thumbnail. "They've probably just messed up some repairs or maintenance or something. And even if they blew up the bridges on purpose, this isn't the first time we've been isolated from the City, and it probably won't be the last. We don't need the City, or the Red Court, for that matter."

"I'll remind you that this time the 'isolation' isn't our idea." Az's voice sharpened with distaste, but maybe she just didn't like people who bit their nails. "*And* I believe I'm correct in saying that in the past the bridges were cut off only after great preparation in terms of laying in food stocks, animals, seeds, et cetera." She looked at me with eyebrows raised, waited for my nod before continuing. "There's been no such preparation this time."

I thought about the chests and cupboards in Medlyn Tierell's vault. Had he started experimenting with ever-filling vessels for just this type of emergency? Would Fenra agree to use them if we should start running out of food? Clothing? Should I say anything? It would certainly give Fenra some badly needed bargaining power, if nothing else. The others were still talking, so I decided to let it rest for the moment. I couldn't reveal her secrets without first discussing it with her—even if a part of me still thought they should have been my secrets.

"What do *you* suggest we do?" Ronan spoke with a mild tone, but I could tell his decision had already been made.

"Negotiate." Az hit the tabletop with the palm of her right hand in emphasis. "At least find out what precipitated these attacks. Why have they broken the truce?" She fixed her pale eyes on me. "Tamari, you have been talking with representatives of the Red Court. Can *you* tell us anything?"

"I didn't see this coming at all," I told them. "The people I met with were sincerely looking to improve relations between the two Courts.

They were disappointed when I told them we would have to postpone our talks." At least, I thought, Witt had been disappointed. Riva hadn't been with him at the last meeting—something I hadn't thought significant until now.

"Do you think that in itself might be the cause of the attack? When their envoys told them about the delay, could that have motivated them?" Ronan was doing his best imitation of an elder statesman.

Before I could answer—in the negative, as I knew from Witt that wasn't the case—Descar Parta spoke up again.

"Are any of us seriously suggesting that we have anything to worry about? Even if this is an attack—something I'm not at all sure of—the Red Court is just trying to frighten us. Now that they've shown us, as they think, who's boss, we'll be hearing from them, they'll tell us what they want this time, and we'll decide whether to give it to them."

And how are they going to manage to speak to us? I kept my thoughts to myself.

Just as I expected, though the discussion went on for much longer, the council didn't come to any final decision. When we were adjourned, I left before anyone could recruit me for their side of the argument and headed straight for my office. If I was right about being followed, that wouldn't raise any eyebrows. I had to decide what to do. I didn't know whether Fenra and Elva would come back for me—or what plans they had for me if they did. They had obviously managed to free Elva—the feelings of the captain and the guards with him were clear. I let myself into my office and this time made sure to shut the door behind me.

For a moment I stayed leaning against the door, eyes shut, breath ragged. When I opened my eyes, I saw something that had my hand reaching for the door handle. I took a deep breath to steady myself before stepping forward. I'd left a short stack of parchments on the right-hand side of my desk, a new *forran* I was trying to work out. Now a perfect miniature model of a windmill, carved with fine detail from a single piece of holly wood, sat on top of my parchments, like a paperweight.

I hadn't needed Fenra to tell me about Medlyn Tierell's modeling hobby. He'd been my mentor too. When he faded, I took over his office, so I knew he hadn't left any models behind. Also, I knew where most, if not all, of his models had gone. Only Fenra could have put this windmill on my desk. I rested the fingers of my practitioner's hand lightly on the surface of the wood. It felt cool, smooth, and somehow made the skin on my hand tingle.

Setting my teeth, I slid my fingers down until I could take a firm grip and picked it up. On the top of my pile of notes sat a single quarter-page sheet, folded in half. The tingling increased as I picked it up and opened it.

I read over the note and folded it again, tapping my lips with the edge.

FENRA

The vault felt like home. The others fetched out provisions, happy that the jug was pouring wine when I held it, and beer when Randd did. I could spend the rest of my life just learning Medlyn Tierell's *forrans*. Not the first time I had had that thought. Wouldn't be the last.

"You'll forgive my mentioning it, ma'am." Donn accepted a cup of wine from me. "But you look like death came for a visit and left you behind by accident."

I braced myself with one hand on the table and set the jug down. Elva took my elbow and lowered me into my chair. The headache I had tried to ignore surged up and washed away everything else. Leaving without Tamari felt horribly wrong. Not that we could have done anything for her from that room. But if I went back, and if I could avoid the guard . . .

Did she need to be rescued? Was she under any kind of suspicion?

Someone put a biscuit in my hand. It smelled of chocolate. Two more biscuits and another glass of wine later I took a deep breath and found them all watching me. Elva smiled.

"Feeling better?"

I nodded. "I will once we decide what to do about Tamari." Maybe she would be able to talk some sense into someone like Captain Rennard.

"I think the room has an idea for us."

"What do you mean?"

"While you were resting, Lizz decided to check the other cupboards and chests." Donn nodded toward her. She shrugged without speaking.

"That's where she found the biscuits," Randd put in. "But then she checked those cabinets over there, and look what she found."

A pen with a malachite shaft, and a gold nib. A corked and wax-sealed bottle of ink. Five quarter-page sheets of good-quality paper made from linen and hemp. A blotter.

"Apparently I am to write her a letter."

TAMARI

I'm embarrassed to say how long it took me to decipher the note. The Watchmaker's Garden? Not the place I would have chosen for a secret meeting; orange trees don't give a lot of cover. I was still wondering how to answer Fenra when someone knocked at the door. I folded the note and put it back under the windmill. "Come in."

Predax stuck his head around the door and lifted his eyebrows when he saw I was alone. "Bad time?" he said. "You never close your door."

I pushed away from my desk and ran my hands through my hair. I needed a cut. Everything was so entwined with everything else, there wasn't any way to tell only part of the story. Finally I took the note out from under the windmill and handed it to him. He puzzled over it until I almost took it back. I felt better about how long I'd taken to work it out.

"I'm to meet her in the Watchmaker's Gardens."

"How sure are you that this comes from Fenra?"

Of course, he didn't know the significance of the model. "Completely sure. What are you getting at?"

"Maybe she doesn't know she can trust you. You disappeared when they were rescuing Elva and you never came back—and you didn't get into any kind of trouble afterward. That could look suspect."

I never thought of that. "But she knows—"

"Nothing she can be sure of. I'd better go with you. She knows me, she trusts me. I'm your proof."

"What if we're seen?"

"What could be easier to explain? I'm your apprentice," he added when I tried to protest. "You're showing me something special about the light, or you could be training me in a particular *forran*."

"Fine." I nodded. Good thing one of us had a flare for intrigue. "But what brought you here in the first place?"

He put the note back under the windmill before answering. "Some of us apprentices have been offered a chance to sit for our third-class practitioner's exam."

No one had ever been able to tell me where that expression came from—not even Medlyn Tierell, and he was Senior Lorist before me. The exams weren't taken sitting down. "You make that sound like a bad thing."

"You tell me." He looked around the top of my desk as if searching for something specific before raising his eyes to mine. "If I were ready for the exam—which I'm not—wouldn't they come to you? Why come to me first?"

I pursed my lips in a silent whistle. "In fact, I should be the one asking for you to be examined. Who, exactly, has approached you? Members of the council?"

"No, just two of the senior practitioners. That's why I thought I'd better let you know. If practitioners are acting without the consent of the council . . ."

Like Fenra, I thought. "You sure they're not recruiting for Fenra?"

"*We're* the ones recruiting for Fenra. Anyone who's heard about her plan comes to us first."

"Of course." My head was spinning.

Predax tapped the model windmill with the index finger of his right hand. "Are you going to answer this?"

Luckily my brain had come up with a response while we talked. "No," I said. "She left a note for a reason, and she won't be coming back to check for a response."

"We'll have to go anyway," Predax said, nodding.

WITTENSLADE

"I don't like this," Arriz said. "Since when does the court meet in the Horse Grounds?"

"For the last time, Arriz, I don't know." Witt shook his head at the offered cravat. "The darker one matches my nails better." He could still feel some stiffness in his shoulders, and his bruises had turned a truly disgusting shade of yellow green.

The Horse Grounds, the largest open space in the City, had been used for mallet ball as far back as anyone could remember. He wondered if Tamari could tell him when horses were first used in the game. He wondered if she was safe and happy.

He wondered if he would see her again.

"You're not doing yourself any good worrying about things you can't do anything about."

Witt grimaced. "Lucky for me, you're the only person who reads me that easily." *The only person I can relax around.* "I'll walk, so a light coat, please."

Of all the courtiers, he lived the closest, so he waited until the last possible moment to arrive fashionably late. Riva Anden Deneyra nodded to him from under her parasol, and he stayed beside her once he'd made his bow. *Let her think I haven't seen through her.*

"Dare I ask what this is all about?"

"I'm sure you *would* dare, but I'm not the person who can give you an answer." Riva tilted her head to where the chief courtier stood conferring with Field Commander Vanaldren. *Still pretending she doesn't know the man.* "I've already asked him," she added. "All he says is we'll know in a moment."

Beyond the commander Witt could see men and women in uniform following the directions of a small, plump man with a shaved head. They seemed to be assembling something out of the type of materials used to build houses and carriages, he thought. Plenty of strange, cogged wheels, thick belts made from layers of felt, and large flat panels of laminated wood. A little bit like the inside of a huge wooden clock. A broken clock.

Someone had given this gathering some thought. Servants began to circulate with cups of coffee and small pastries, tarts stuffed with cream and strawberries. Finally, they were called to order, and asked to approach the contraption. Witt helped the widow with her chair. The chief courtier and the field commander gestured to the plump man to speak.

"Courtiers, thank you for your attention. I am Jondrel Hansu, head of the engineering college. What we're about to show you is based on a smaller version, found in the Second County. There, it is used for the transportation of produce over—"

"If you would, spare us the history lesson and get on with the demonstration." That sounded like the chief courtier.

"Of course, Dom, of course." Hansu turned away and signaled to two men standing one on each side of the device, in front of large wheels. The men began turning the wheels, aided by shafts sticking out from the . . . well, from the rims. Witt didn't know what else you could call them. At first the men really leaned into it, the wheels turning slowly as if stiff, but soon other parts of the device began to move, more smoothly and more quickly as the men continued to turn the now freely turning wheels. A platform inched its way out of the front of the device, extending itself just above the men's heads. As a second piece began moving out, following and at the same time overlapping with the first, the men at the wheels were relieved by two others.

"What in the name of the Maker . . ." From the murmurs and gasps around him, everyone else was just as surprised as he was.

The platforms continued to extend until they reached the second tier of permanent seats on the far side of the stadium. The engineer made another signal and two people in military uniforms hopped up onto the platform and ran across to the seats, turned about smartly, and ran back again.

Witt found himself on his feet, clapping his hands and yelling. The engineer, clearly pleased with the response, grinned from ear to ear. "Doms, I give you the cloud bridge."

"I don't understand," one of the others said when they had gathered around closer to the device. "We destroyed their bridges and now we're going to build them new ones?"

"Not at all, Dom, no, not at all." Before Hansu could continue, Commander Vanaldren stepped forward.

"Doms, you are looking at the basis of our strategy." He gestured at the expandable bridge with his sword hand. "We've destroyed the bridges, so the practitioners can't attack us. But they think they're safe, that they can just hide in their court and ignore us, make us wait for them. But with this cloud bridge, we can take them by surprise. By the time they realize they're in danger, it will be too late. We will have them all under our hands."

A surprise attack, Witt thought, his mouth drying. Practitioners can be killed if you take them by surprise.

Witt took his chin in his hand and tapped his lips with his index finger. He hoped he looked intrigued, and not horrified, by what he saw. Apparently he was right to worry about Tamari's safety.

FENRA

"I'm going with you," Elva said finally, in his sheriff's voice. "I know how the guard behave, and what their schedules are like."

"Fine." I stood up and dusted off my clothes, though they were perfectly clean. I had found a guard uniform to fit me in the same chest the others had been in.

"Who's with me?" Elva asked.

"All of us," Donn said. "Not likely we'd stay behind."

I started to protest, but stopped, remembering what Elva had said the time I planned to leave him in the vault alone. What if something happened to me, and I was unable to come back for them? The food baskets would give them food, and the pitcher drink. But they gave the items they thought were needed, not what you asked them for. How long, Elva had asked me then, would it take for the pitcher to give him poisoned wine? I looked around at the others. The chest had given us uniforms enough for all of us. Not even inanimate objects thought they should stay.

I rubbed my face with my hands. "Fine. Elva, we are under your orders." The truth was, any of them had far more experience with this type of undertaking than I had.

"Here's where we'll come out," Elva said, pointing at the map he'd made for the others. "We'll go to Medlyn's old rooms in case Tamari is being watched. And here," he tapped the plan, "is the Watchmakers Garden. We'll get there two hours early. If she's reported us to the captain, he'll want to set up a team to take us by surprise. It's a common strategy, one we'll get around by setting up even earlier. I'm betting we'll see them long before they see us."

We knew that as of a few days ago Medlyn's rooms hadn't been reassigned to anyone. Apparently, the tower had become unfashionable since his time. Inside the building, we counted on the guard uniforms to help if we met anyone. Once outside, the others had their practice to keep themselves unobserved. I found it disconcerting that I could now see them clearly, or at least the soft human-shaped glow that was the evidence of their practice. I had to keep reminding myself that no one else could see them. Elva had no practice to help him, only generations of experience. My "you do not see me" *forran* worked best when I stood directly on the ground, but I discovered once we were in the open that the rain worked just as well.

I liked rain. Even before I had met the World, I had spent so much of my life living in the Outer Modes that I had a farmer's feeling for how important rain could be to forests, crops, and animals. The others felt much the same way, which surprised me until I remembered the scrub desert of the Dundalk Territories. I had been told the town existed only because of springs deep under the ground. They brought their water up using windmills, I thought, my eyes going to where Elva shifted through the shadows under the rows of orange and medlar trees. Had that been Elva's idea? He knew so much about waterwheels, maybe he understood windmills as well.

Once we reached the garden—with only one close call when a student had almost tripped over Lizz, she was so well hidden—we first determined that no one was hidden there already, waiting for us, and then spread out into the spots Elva had chosen for us. We were placed in such a way that we had eyes on all entrances to the garden, but we could still come together in defense—or in offense, I imagined—quickly.

Then came the waiting. After a while I began to shiver and had to say a quick *forran* to keep myself warm. With the clouds overhead hiding the stars, I could not judge the passing of time. I wished I had a pocket watch like the others, though there may not have been enough light to see it. Surely the two hours had passed? No one else moved, however, so I tried to be patient.

Finally, after I had begun to think she was not coming, Tamari entered the garden from the far corner, with Predax just behind her. She put out a hand to stop him advancing, hesitating for only a moment, her eyes flicking to each one of us before settling on me. I had forgotten that sensing people was part of her power. She crossed the path toward me, almost running. I stretched out my hands to her, but she waved me away.

"Keep your hands free," she said. "You may need them. The White Court is under siege. The troops in the City have destroyed the bridges. If you have somewhere to go, go!"

I was still deciding how to react when I heard Elva yell. "Fenra, here, now!"

I grabbed Tamari's right arm with my own right hand and dragged her with me toward Elva's voice. She resisted at first, surprised, but Predax helped me by taking her other arm, and we ran to the porticos we had come in by. They looked delicate, but carved as the stone was, they were still wide enough, and sturdy enough, to give us protection.

Before we got there, guards came pouring into the gardens. Elva and his deputies had guns out and were firing before I could even react.

"Try not to kill them," Elva called out.

"Sure, why make things easy?" I heard Randd mutter.

The moment came when the firing stopped. We took advantage of the rest to reload the revolvers. Of course, the guards were likely doing the same with their pistols. Lizz took her long gun out of its harness and checked its action.

"I think *she* set us up," Randd said as he pushed the last bullet into his revolver.

"Really? Then how do you explain this?" I saw that Predax was holding Tamari up, his arm around her waist. She had her practitioner's hand to the side of her neck, and blood was seeping through her fingers.

"Lay her down, now! Keep your hand over hers, do not let go." I knelt beside her, rubbing the palms of my hands together.

As I pulled them apart, Predax sobbed once, and relaxed his grip.

"Don't move!" I pulled my hands apart. Pink glowing lines extended between my fingertips. I threw the *forran* over her, watching it as it spread. Nothing. This time, rubbing my hands together, I realized I was kneeling on garden soil. We were under a tree, behind a statue of a bull. This time I reached downward as well and drew strength from the World itself. It had helped me with healing once before, and perhaps it would again. "This is one who will help us," I said, hoping the World could hear me. "Please."

Now I saw a pattern form around Tamari that wasn't mine. Quickly, I joined mine to it, watched as it sank into her. She took a deep gasping breath that sounded as though it hurt.

I looked up. Elva stood above me, watching us. The others stood in a circle around us, facing outward. All three had their revolvers in hand.

"I didn't bring them." Tamari's voice sounded raw. "I swear." I saw from the change in their postures that Donn, Lizz, and Randd were all listening to us.

"You could not tell you were being followed?" Donn said.

She started to shake her head and grimaced. Predax helped her sit up. "For days now, since the bridges went down, I've been sensing unease, unhappiness, worry, and fear. How could I distinguish these people from everyone else?"

"And why would they have shot her?" Predax sounded indignant.

Tamari waved his words away before I could answer. "That proves nothing," she said, her voice stronger. "I can think of at least three explanations."

"Well, don't list them now." Donn spoke over his shoulder, his eyes still focused outward. "A single person coming toward us, Sheriff. Hands in the air."

"Keep them covered."

"Teach your grandmother."

"Stop right there," Elva called out to Captain Rennard. "I'd rather not kill anyone. We've been shooting over your heads, but we don't have to. We'll go, and you can say you never found us."

"If it was only you, Elva, maybe, but *she's* supposed to be in league with the Red Court. I can't just look the other way while she escapes."

"If she were in league with the Red Court, she'd be over there right now, not boxed into the corner of the garden. Use your head, man."

Before the captain could argue further, he was interrupted by three rapid explosions, followed by a deafening clamor of gunshots, screamed orders, clash of steel, and finally, the deep tolling of a bell. All the guards I could see, including the captain, froze, their heads lifting and turning slightly toward the sound.

"I hope this whole thing hasn't been a distraction, Elva Karamisk. I hope you're all as innocent as you say."

With that, he made a signal with his pistol, gathering all his guards together, and disappeared into the shadows.

"Whatever this is," Donn said, "it's more important than we are."

"Maybe we should go and find out?"

Sand is fun. It looks solid, but isn't. It feels different under our feet, depending on whether it's wet or dry. It even moves differently, depending on whether it's wet or dry. We pick up a dry fistful of it and let it pour slowly out of our hand. *Like sand through an hourglass.* We don't know where that thought comes from. For a moment we can't tell where the sand stops and the hand starts.

We turn back to our sandcastle and are using our fingertips to shape slate tiles on the roof of the great hall when we feel Fenra, reaching out to us for help. We don't have time for her in this moment, so we just send some reinforcement and continue with the slate tiles. We dust off our hands and stand up. There is a spot on our back we cannot reach, and it itches. We would roll in the sand, but we think the sand caused the itching.

We walk around our creation to see it from every side. Perfect. Brave turrets, thick walls, busy courtyards. We lift our hand, and the sea enters and destroys it all.

Nine

ELVANYN

W
HAT DO YOU see?" Elva called up to where Randd perched on a third-story window ledge.

"I don't believe it," Randd called down to them. "It's some kind of a platform, layers of wood, then there's this sort of contraption on the other side, lots of pulleys and weights—kind of like a giant clockwork." He looked out again. "The platform reaches all the way across. This end's resting on the rock just outside the gate." He lowered himself until he was hanging from the ledge, let go, and landed neatly beside Lizz.

"A ghost bridge." Elva sounded almost approving. "I've never seen one before, but I've heard about it." He pointed down. "So that's why they attacked the practitioner's gate and not the other. On this side the wall is set back at least fifteen feet from where the bridge started; that gives them enough support for this end of the ghost bridge." He shook his head, lips pressed tight. "Let's go."

"Just how good is that gate?" Donn asked as they ran toward the noise of fighting.

"Oak planks," Fenra said. "Steel reinforcement. Nice thick beams."

Elva shook his head. "Maybe, but so far as I know, it's never been closed. There's no telling what shape it's in."

"Who let that happen?" Donn said, his hand under Tamari's elbow.

"Defense was never a priority." Tamari had a hand to her side. Predax supported her other side, but both were panting. "No one ever thought they'd . . ." She waved her hand toward the gate.

"We thought we were safe," Predax added when Tamari ran out of breath. "What could mundanes do to the White Court?"

By the time they reached the gate, City soldiers had already crossed the river, and were inside the gate—which didn't, as Elva had foreseen, close easily—and were engaging a squad of guards much smaller than it should have been. Captain Rennard and the few guards with him had charged into the fight, the captain yelling orders over his shoulder. This gave the others heart, but as Elva had once learned the hard way, guards were guards, and soldiers, soldiers.

"Randd, Lizz, up top." He pointed to the unfortunately only ornamental battlements on the buildings nearest the gate. The deputies didn't bother going in to look for stairs, they climbed up the side of the building, their New Zone practice finding finger and toe holds other people couldn't see. Elva didn't blame anyone for the flimsy defenses—when he had been a guard here, he'd thought they were fine himself. Only his long experience in the other world had taught him differently. "Donn, you're with me. Fenra, Tamari, light this place up. They'll need to see who they're shooting. Then take cover."

Luckily Fenra knew what he needed, and it took only moments to explain to Tamari. Both practitioners created balls of illumination—not fire, exactly—and threw them into the air to hover over the fighting. It took only a little longer for Randd and Lizz to reach their positions and for the first rifle shots to crack through the air.

There wasn't a great deal of cover between them and the gate, but Elva didn't consider that a problem. He tucked himself in behind a pillar and motioned Donn over to another.

"The enemy have flintlocks." Elva raised his voice over the noise. "Shorter range than our guns, and much less accurate. Still, take care," he added when Donn brushed his mustaches with a satisfied smile. "A stray shot to the head will kill you just as completely as one deliberately aimed."

"No one lives forever," was the reply Elva had expected. Reckless and foolhardy were both words that people used to describe his senior deputy. On the other hand, he was also known as Donn the Lucky. Donn shot deliberately, picking his targets carefully and hitting each one. With no time to reload, after six shots he holstered his gun and drew his sword. Elva took just as much care, shooting first with his right hand, and then with his practitioner's hand. When both guns were empty, he holstered them, and drew his own sword.

As opponents began to drop around them, the White Court guards rallied and fought more fiercely. Donn shouted out encouragement and warnings as he ducked, parried, slashed, and stabbed. Elva saw a woman he recognized but whose name he couldn't remember go down in front of a soldier and leaped into the space she left. She still had her sword and slashed the man behind the knee just as Elva ran him through.

Slowly the City soldiers were pushed back, until finally, with creaks and squeals that made Elva grit his teeth, the gate could be shut on them. Under Fenra's direction three apprentices helped practice into place the bars and locking mechanisms that hadn't been used in centuries. Elva took a deep breath and leaned against a nearby wall. Some of the guards around him were patting each other on the back, grinning, as they wiped sweat from their faces. Others looked dazed and had trouble meeting anyone's eyes.

Elva recognized that look, equal parts exhaustion and an unwillingness to examine too closely what they'd done. He remembered feeling the same way, once upon a time. *They've never shot at living targets*, he thought. *At least, nothing that shot back.* They'd have trouble sleeping for a while. Of course—he looked around at the bodies—there were those who would never have that trouble again.

Elva tore a sleeve off one of the City corpses and wiped the blood off his sword. Nothing worse than sheathing a bloody sword. He would clean it properly later, along with his guns. Sword sheathed, he signaled to Randd and Lizz that they could come down from the rooftops.

"Karamisk!"

Elva looked around at the familiar voice. Captain Rennard made his way toward him, stopping once or twice to exchange words with one of his guards. From the way Rennard's arm hung down, it was clear he had been shot in the shoulder. He put out his uninjured hand and Elva shook it.

"That was impressive shooting," Rennard said. All things considered, Elva had been thanked in worse ways.

"We've had a lot of practice." He knew the captain would understand that he used the word in the non-magical sense.

"Then we were lucky you came in on our side."

They both looked around at the creaking of metal and wood from the far side of the wall.

"They're pulling back the ghost bridge." Elva searched for the familiar silhouette of tightly curled hair and his heart skipped a beat until he saw her. Fenra was circulating among the wounded. She had taken off her shoes, walking barefoot despite the dirt and blood. She and Tamari were together, examining a young woman's arm. Fenra spoke, Tamari nodded, and Fenra moved on to the next injury.

"Fenra." She finished tracing a *forran* on a man's forehead and headed toward him. "Can you set fire to that bridge?"

"I can try." Breathless, she didn't say any more, but headed up the stone stairs that led up to the top of the gates. Her bare feet made no sound.

Elva waited, expecting at any moment to hear yells, commotion, even pistol shots from the other side of the wall, as the soldiers realized what Fenra was doing, but they never came. Instead, Fenra came back down the stairs, gray-faced, trembling, and leaning on a guard. When she caught his eye, she shook her head. Elva ran toward them, mentally cursing himself. Of course she'd run out of energy. After moving them all here from the vault, creating the lights, and healing people, it was a miracle Fenra was still on her feet. As it was, only direct barefoot contact with the World kept her up and moving. As she passed them, many of the guards thumped her on her shoulder, or patted her back in sympathy. Elva couldn't remember ever seeing a guard touch a practitioner so casually. He took her from the guard helping her and slipped his arm around her waist.

The guards' obvious approval made what came next completely unexpected.

Ronan Sedges pushed his way through the groups of guards, students, and apprentices, still trying to pull themselves together.

"Fenra Lowens, you are under arrest," he said when he reached her. He looked around. "Captain! Escort Practitioner Lowens to the Lion's Tower."

Silence fell among the guards standing closest, then murmuring as the news was passed back to those further away.

"On what charge?" Rennard's tone was respectful and calm.

From the look of surprise on his face, Sedges hadn't expected any opposition. "Sedition," he said. "Attempting to undermine and overthrow the authority of the White Court."

The captain looked around him, mouth twisted to one side. "I don't think that's what happened here. I think if it weren't for Practitioner Lowens and the reinforcements she brought with her, you and I would be having a different discussion, most likely with the commander of the attacking soldiers."

"Are you defying the direct order of the Chief Practitioner?" Everyone could hear the capital letters in the man's voice. Elva held his breath and saw Fenra touch the locket. Donn and the others all moved quietly toward them.

"Yes, I am. My orders come from the full council, not from any one member, regardless of what he calls himself. The full council put me in charge of the defense, and I am conscripting Practitioner Lowens and her escort."

Sedges looked at the still faces around him.

"With due respect, sir," Rennard added, "you won't find any guard who wants to arrest these people."

"The council will meet at once."

"Yes, Practitioner."

TAMARI

Not everyone on the council would meet my eye. I'd wanted Fenra to come into the council room with me, but as she wasn't a member, it wasn't allowed. She wasn't far, just in the anteroom; she was safe enough out there, with her escort around her. I wondered where they came from. Their guns were a design I'd never seen before, and there was no denying they were effective in the right hands.

I missed the first comment, but I heard Nubin Sonsera's question.

"I'm surprised you are so willing to let these people join forces with you," he said to Captain Rennard. "Were they not the very ones you went to arrest in the gardens?"

Rennard, his arm in a sling, was having trouble holding on to his patience. "I'll point out that none of my guard were killed during that fight. Their injuries were little more than scrapes and bruises. Given their performance at the gate, if Practitioner Lowens' people had wanted to kill us, we'd be dead. I take that as a clear sign of good faith."

I wanted to put in my opinion, but decided it was smarter to keep a low profile. They'd get to me soon enough.

"Where did they get those weapons, and who are they, anyway?"

Now everyone looked at me.

"Fenra Lowens was Medlyn Tierell's favorite apprentice," I told them. It hurt to admit that, but it was true. "He taught her things—*forrans* included—that he taught no one else, not even me." I wasn't going to say anything about Xandra Albainil, or Arlyn, as Fenra called him. "Medlyn was more than usually skilled. I'm not surprised that Lowens can do things we've never heard of." *The World helped her, too,* I thought, though I wasn't sure how.

"Is this why you've been supporting her? In the hope that she might share some of this knowledge with you?"

If I agreed, it could restore me to the favor of at least some of the council. But this "what's in it for me" attitude is probably what started the World's problems in the first place. Fenra was right, the World needed and deserved better than this. That was enough reason to tell them the truth. *We're all in the same hole now.*

"No," I said. "I supported Practitioner Lowens' original petition because any of us should be given an opportunity to address the council, and even the White Court as a whole. Whether we agree with her or not, we should have given her the chance."

"So, you approve of her setting up her own court? Luring students and apprentices away in defiance of established practice?"

Here Ronan Sedges gave me a hard look. This was getting us off topic, and quickly. I raised my left eyebrow and stared right back. I almost shrugged. If they couldn't see for themselves that this whole discussion was at best a waste of our time, and at worst suicidal, there was no point in my trying to tell them.

The captain cleared his throat. "I understand your disagreement with Practitioner Lowens' approach to the practice. I'm no judge of that. But I also know that whatever her position might be, she isn't trying to take over the White Court and take us all prisoners. Those people out there, they *are*." The captain pointed with his thumb in the direction of the West Gate. "So, I suggest that you set aside your philosophical differences until the more immediate problem of the Red Court is solved."

"The enemy of my enemy is my friend, is that what you're saying, Captain?"

"That's what I'm saying."

Ronan sat back in his chair, chin in his practitioner's hand, tapping his cheek with his index finger. My mentor used to stop us from doing that. Never use your practitioner's hand for casual movements, he used to say. Finally, Ronan let his hand drop to the arm of his chair.

"A good suggestion, for now," he said, thinking we couldn't hear the emphasis he put on "for now." *Fenra can't trust him*, I thought. Not that there was much chance she would after he'd tried to arrest her. "Very well, Captain, what do you suggest should be our next move?"

Rennard turned his right hand palm up. "It's been a long time since I studied strategy. The White Court guard has always been trained for defense, and defense is clearly not going to be enough. We need people who think offensively as well. We need Elvanyn Karamisk."

FENRA

"Can't say I think much of your council, not if they made that yammering gasbag their chief. Give him a fat cigar and he could be any politician I've ever met." Randd stopped pacing back and forth and stood looking out into the courtyard below us. We were waiting in the bamboo chairs on the third-floor gallery, just outside the anteroom to the council chamber, where we had been asked to wait. Elva hadn't wanted us to be shut up into a room.

"Unfortunately," I said, "the type of people who want to be in charge of things like the council are very often yammering gasbags." I decided I liked that expression. I also wondered what a cigar was. I closed my eyes and leaned back against the stone wall. If I didn't get some rest and something to eat, I would not be able to walk out of here, let alone use the locket.

"The balls of light—" This was Lizz. "Can you teach us?"

I answered without opening my eyes. "I believe so. I can see your practice when you use it, and that may be the first step. We should try."

"As useful as that might be, right now we need information," Elva said.

"We need a spy." From the way Donn smoothed his mustaches, I could tell he saw himself in the role. "We need to know more about the enemy, so we won't be taken by surprise again."

I shifted in my seat.

"You've thought of something." Elva crouched down in front of me and took my hand.

"I might know a way to get a message out if we can . . ." I let my voice fade away as the captain exited the council chamber. I tightened my grip and Elva pulled me to my feet.

"I suggest you all come with me," the captain said, making gathering motions with his uninjured hand. "They've decided to leave you free and accept your help—"

"Mighty good of them." "Then what's the problem?" Lizz and Randd both spoke at once.

The captain confirmed my good opinion of him by ignoring them both. "It's not often someone makes them compromise, and they'll be sweeter to handle if they don't find you smack in front of them just now."

"What about Tamari? Is she in trouble?"

"She's in more danger of discipline than you are, if that's what you're asking. They can't do anything to you, at the moment, but she's still part of the council. They could call her to account, even expel her." All this time he ushered us down the gallery, further from the council chamber.

"She would be safer with us," I said, slowing down. Only Elva's hand under my elbow kept me on my feet. "I do not trust those people to deal fairly with her—or with us, for that matter."

"Especially once we've pulled their nuts out of the fire and they don't need us no more. These ain't people who do gratitude real well." Randd shot a look at Donn, who shrugged and smoothed his mustaches.

"Good thing we are not in this for their gratitude," I said.

"Remind me again why we *are* doing this?" Elva lifted both eyebrows.

I grinned back at him. "Because we can."

TAMARI

I braced myself when the guard waiting outside the council chamber approached me. No one had said anything about discipline, but most of my fellow councilors still weren't meeting my eyes. I told myself that I knew what I was getting into when I decided to help Fenra, but my heart sped up anyway.

"Practitioner Lowens' compliments." The uniformed woman spoke so quietly, none of the other practitioners heard what she said. "She would like you to join her."

"Lead the way." The sooner I got away, the better. Out of sight, out of mind, my mother used to say. As the guard fell into step beside me, I noticed a few satisfied looks. Some of the council evidently thought I was being detained. While the others didn't look happy about it, they didn't stop it either. *Good to know who your friends are*, I thought.

I expected the guard to take me to my office, or maybe one of the smaller study halls. Instead, Fenra had chosen to go back to the orange garden. She sat on one of the stone benches eating what appeared to be a meat pie. I could smell the onions, and my stomach rumbled. Elva had been speaking, but fell silent as we joined them. I saw Predax hovering in the background, the ankle he'd injured last night apparently healed.

"Thank you, Sabord," Elva said. My escort gave him a sharp salute and turned back the way we had come.

"It's good you're here for this, Tamari," he said as I took a seat. "You know we can leave the White Court whenever we want to," he began.

"Just a second, boss." The older man, Donn, held up a finger. "I think I see where this is going, and I know I speak for Lizz and Randd when I say that we're not going anywhere if it means leaving you behind."

Elva nodded, his lips pursed, but his eyes smiling. "I was going to say I don't think we should tell anyone, not even Captain Rennard, that we have this ace up our sleeve." He nodded at Fenra and waited until he collected nods from everyone before continuing. "All right, then." He crossed his arms. "What none of you know is that we also have a way to get into the Red Court—that is, the Court itself, not the City."

I lifted my right eyebrow. Fenra only nodded.

"And that's something else we tell no one," she said. "We will use it if we must, but our goal right now is to restore a balance between the two Courts, not win a war."

"Still don't like this council of yours," Randd said.

"None of us do," Elva said. "But at the moment, we both want the same things, so . . ."

"The enemy of my enemy is my friend?" I asked. *And doesn't* that *sound familiar.*

"Something like that," Fenra said.

"To give Rennard the kind of help he needs, *we* need information. Fenra may have a way to contact someone on the outside, so the question is, who?"

"What do we ask?" Randd said.

"Until we know *who*, *what* doesn't matter," Elva pointed out. "Whoever it is has to be both trustworthy and willing to take on what may be a considerable risk."

"Witt," I said before I even knew I was going to. They all looked at me, waiting for me to explain. "Wittenslade Camdin Volden," I added. *Let him still be alive,* I thought. It seemed I needed to know he was safe more than I needed to know anything else. Until that moment, I hadn't really known how I felt about him. "He's the courtier I was talking to when negotiations were still possible."

"A *courtier*? An actual member of the Red Court? Someone we can trust?" Donn got to his feet and shook his head.

"He warned me," I pointed out. "He came specifically to warn me that the Red Court was planning to attack us."

"Was he warning the White Court, or was he warning *you*?" Fenra said.

"I don't know," I admitted. "Both, I hope." There, now it was out in the open.

"I am not sure I can send the messenger to someone I do not know myself. On the other hand, I have never tried." A line appeared between Fenra's brows.

"Send the messenger to Oleander," Elva said. "He's a lampee we know, a runner," he added before any of the rest of us could ask. "He shouldn't have any trouble finding this courtier, and there isn't anywhere he can't go."

Fenra nodded, her face clearing.

"What if somebody stops him? And reads the message?" I asked. "Won't we be putting both him and Witt in danger?"

"I have a way around that," Fenra said.

Elva clapped his hands. "All right. Now we need to know what to ask."

"You work on the message, while I fetch the messenger."

FENRA

I have always known Terith was not a horse—or at least, not only a horse. Horses are lovely creatures, but they do not know what you are thinking, and they cannot communicate their thoughts to you—two things that Terith could do quite easily. I knew he would come if I called to him. We had done it before, but never from such a distance. I told myself that with the practice, distance didn't matter, the *forran* did. I had found Arlyn in places that didn't even exist. I should be able to reach Terith when I knew exactly where he was.

We were already in the garden, so once I had dusted pastry crumbs from my hands, I took off my shoes and stockings and stood directly on the soil of the nearest flower bed. I still did not know how much this direct connection with the World helped me, but even if it only boosted my confidence, that would be something. I flexed my toes in the soft earth, feeling the warmth in the loam, the organic matter, even the worms a layer or so under my feet. When I was ready, I pictured Terith in his stall at Ginglen's. His head poking out as if to look at me. I reached out with my practitioner's hand and began the summoning *forran*.

I could not be sure where I went, not at first, though both Elva and Tamari said afterward that I had not gone anywhere at all. I caught a glimpse of the beach, but I concentrated harder, and it faded. It seemed to me as though I floated away, like a leaf in a soft breeze, and then I was a bird, flying high over a beach. I flew as fast as my wings would move, with the wind behind me pushing me even faster, and then I floated far above the earth. And finally, I stooped, and landed on the forearm of a dark-skinned woman who waited for me in a garden.

I blinked my eyes open. The largest raven I had ever seen perched on my forearm, shifting his feet, fluttering his wings for balance, and looking at me with a very familiar eye.

"Where did he come from?" "How did you do that?" Everyone spoke at once.

I felt a big smile on my face. Then I was nothing, and nobody.

We wish she would stop calling on us for petty minor unimportant things. She should be saving her attention and her strength to suit our purpose, not that of these unimportant beings. This is not the best way to use her time. It would be better if we could stop this draining of our energy, however small it is, but we have chosen her as our agent. It is too late to train another. Still, she should obey us more strictly. We must think of some way to ensure this.

ELVANYN

When Fenra collapsed, the raven did not let go of her arm, just rocked a bit to steady itself. Tamari ran to Fenra's side, while Lizz tried to convince the bird to stand on her arm instead. Elva motioned them both away, taking Lizz by the upper arm when she didn't move.

"The bird should let go."

"No hurry." Elva kept his grip. The bird looked at him, his eyes dark and familiar. He knew where he had seen those eyes before. Elva swallowed and nodded to him. He cawed, hopped off Fenra's arm, and began tugging at her sleeve with his beak, as if to drag her over to the center of the flower bed. Elva stooped and picked up Fenra's shoulders, swinging her around until her whole body lay on the carefully raked dirt between the flowering bushes.

Once she was positioned, the bird shook out his wings and paced up and down the length of her body.

"Terith?" He should have felt stupid even thinking such a thing, and yet . . . the bird stopped pacing, fixed his left eye on him, and bobbed his head like a parrot. He let out another call, and Elva lifted his hand, patting the air. "Keep it down," he said. "We don't want anyone coming to investigate the noise."

The bird flapped his wings and settled down by Fenra's head.

"Is it safe?" Tamari approached the bird but stopped when he turned to look at her.

"He is," Elva told her. The raven rubbed his beak on Fenra's cheek. "There, you see?"

"What is it, boss?" Randd took a step closer, his hand outstretched.

"*He,*" Elva said again. "He's . . . her horse." Elva always understood that Terith wasn't a horse, but understanding something was not the same as seeing it. He turned to Tamari. "Can *you* explain it?"

"I've read about it, of course," she said. "We've all been shown the *forran* to create a familiar, theoretically, at least first-class practitioners have. But there's not much call for them nowadays, and I don't—didn't—know that anyone outside of the old records had ever done it."

At that moment Fenra took a deep breath and struggled to prop herself up on her elbows. She looked fine, but Elva thought her lower lip trembled. Terith jumped onto her shoulder and rubbed his head against her cheek. Fenra sat up, smoothed his feathers, and looked around. "It worked."

"Why didn't you tell us it would knock you out?"

"Because I did not know." Fenra took Elva's hand and hopped to her feet as if she'd just had a long, restful nap and was ready to go dancing. She glanced down. "How did I end up here?"

"Terith made it clear all of you needed to be touching ground."

"Thank you," she said crouching down and patting the dimple in the soil where her head had been. She dusted off her hands and turned to them. "Now, is the letter ready to go?"

She took it from Tamari and read over the lines the other practitioner had written. "You used squid ink? And this parchment has never been used before?" Tamari nodded. "Good, that should help."

"She brings a bird that's really a horse here by thinking of him, but she's not sure she can manage with fresh parchment and squid ink?" Donn said, but he smiled.

Fenra sat down on a marble bench and smoothed the letter flat on the stone. She closed her eyes, took two deep, steady breaths, and placed the index finger of her practitioner's hand on the last word in the letter. "I will leave your name," she told the other practitioner, "to test whether the *forran* is working, then I will remove it as well." She traced the letter backward with her fingertip, word by word, and as she passed them, one by one, the words disappeared, until the paper was blank again except for the younger practitioner's name. "Here, Tamari, can you read it now?"

Tamari, a wrinkle between her brows, took the page gingerly between thumb and forefinger. Once she had it in her hands, her frown changed into a laugh. "Yes! Yes, I can. Oh, you have to teach me this."

"Be sure I will." The others crowded around.

"I can't see anything." Donn reached out to touch the parchment and Fenra stopped him with a gesture.

"That's because your name isn't on the page." Tamari had stopped laughing, but still had a smile on her face. "This is a very old way of sending special documents by mundane couriers. The records say it fell out of use when the White Court had enough students and apprentices that they could be sent instead."

Fenra took the paper back, erased Tamari's name, restored two others, and rolled it up tightly. She patted her pockets until she found a small stick of wax. With her practitioner's hand she melted wax onto the scroll and sealed it with her thumbprint. She handed the scroll to Terith, who took it delicately in his left claw.

"Be careful."

⌐⌐⌐

OLEANDER

Fenra Lowens said once that she didn't think his parents had named him Oleander. Maybe they had, maybe they hadn't. All he knew for certain was that his mother—before she'd taken his little brother to get his cough looked at and never came back—had called him Ollie, which he figured had to be short for *something*. One time he'd delivered a red-flowered shrub in a clay pot, and when he'd asked, they'd told him it was oleander, and that he should watch out, it was poisonous. That had been good enough for him. It had taken quite a bit of threatening and pummeling to get the other street kids to call him that, but he finally managed.

He'd spent the whole morning running messages back and forth from the Red Court to the army posts set up where the West Bridge used to be. Something big going on, that was clear. He'd have unsealed the messages, and read them, if he'd been able to. Unseal? Easy as a biscuit, and no one would ever know, but the reading part, *that* he couldn't do. Now that things had slowed down, he could take a break, and maybe eat something. He followed his feet to Bridge Square and the Ginglen Inn. Ginglen Locast and his partner, Itzen

Morlant, didn't run a public house, their kitchen served their paying guests only, but Oleander thought he could scrounge a meal in exchange for news. Maybe he couldn't read, but he could use his ears and eyes.

Oleander walked right around into the mews that ran behind all the buildings on this side of the square. He figured he'd get a warmer reception if he didn't show up at the front door like he was a guest. A long face looked out of a stall, but it wasn't the horse he expected to see. "Hey, boy." Oleander stroked down the horse's muzzle. "Where's Elva then? Huh? Know where he is?"

"You there—oh, it's you, Oleander." Itzen, tall, thin, pale, followed his voice out of the kitchen door and strolled down to join Oleander in front of Terith's empty stall. "Where in the Maker's name is Terith?"

"How should I know? I just got here."

Itzen stopped short of the stall's door, brow wrinkled, and lips twisted to one side. "You just got here?" He peered closely at Oleander without moving his head. "Terith was already gone?"

"'Course he was." Oleander wouldn't have thought that Itzen could get any paler. The man looked like he would faint, and Oleander, using both hands, took him firmly by the forearm. "Come on, you need to sit down." Now he was being helpful, a meal was practically guaranteed.

Itzen allowed Oleander to lead him into the inn's kitchen, where he kicked over a stool to sit the man down near the door. He nipped back into the hallway and stuck his head into the dining room across the hall. Ginglen stood near the cold fireplace, talking to a well-dressed middle-aged man. *Trader*, Oleander thought. He caught Ginglen's eye and beckoned to him with a jerk of the head. For a moment Ginglen looked annoyed, but then he must have figured Oleander wouldn't be calling him for nothing.

"What is it?" Ginglen managed not to growl as he came out into the hall.

"Itzen—he's all right, just came over faint. I've got him sitting down here in the kitchen and—" Oleander was talking to an empty hallway. Before he could follow the innkeeper, Ginglen came out of the kitchen with his arm around Itzen's waist.

"I'm fine, I said."

"You don't look fine. Go on ahead, boy, open the doors for me. We'll take him into our sitting room."

Oleander had never been in their private sitting room, but he knew the way. He crossed through the entrance hall, passed the reception desk with its ledger and little brass bell, opened the door on the far end, and stood to one side, waiting to be invited in. Ginglen lowered a still protesting Itzen into an oversized upholstered chair and spoke over his shoulder to Oleander.

"Go tell Rasah that Itzen's ill and she's to watch the dining room. Come back with a glass of water."

"I'm not ill, I'm just surprised, that's all."

"When did you last eat?"

Oleander left them bickering—seemed that's what married people did best—and ran to the kitchen, gave the cook the message, and ran back again as fast as he could while carrying a glass of water. Whatever was going on, he didn't want to miss any of it.

"I tell you, the boy says he didn't take him," Itzen was saying as Oleander handed Ginglen the glass and then closed the door to the hall. Ginglen paused with his hand on a cupboard door, and gave Oleander a hard eye.

"Don't look at *me* like that. You couldn't pay me enough to touch *her* horse."

The two men exchanged a glance and Ginglen shrugged. "It's not like anyone can steal him, I suppose." Ginglen took a small glass jar of green powder out of the cupboard, tipped some into the glass where it fizzed, and handed it to his partner. "Drink this."

"I told you, I was startled, that's all." But he finished the drink just the same, making a face as he swallowed.

Oleander eyed another chair, but the likes of him didn't sit down in company. That's just the way it was.

"Oh, for the Maker's sake, boy, sit down." Itzen's color was coming back. Oleander wondered just what exactly the green powder was.

He looked at the upholstered seat and hesitated. He took off his jacket, laid it down outside up, and sat. "What's the worry? Fenra's the only one can take Terith."

Ginglen took the glass from his husband but left his other hand on Itzen's shoulder. "Of course, she might have needed her horse, nothing more likely. She would have taken pains not to involve us unnecessarily. But . . ."

"You still want to know for sure." Oleander finished Ginglen's sentence for him. "It's always better to know," he added when both men looked at him with eyebrows raised. "Then you can get ready for what might come." He got to his feet. "I'm just here to tell you the military is getting very busy for some reason, and to ask for news about Fenra and Elva. Looks like you don't know more than me, so I'll be on my way." He pushed his arms through the sleeves of his jacket, careful not to strain the seams in the shoulders. He couldn't afford a new jacket just now. "Unless you've got work for me?"

Ginglen shook his head, first at Oleander, then at Itzen when he tried to stand up. "Not just at the moment, I'm afraid. Ask me again tomorrow—oh, and stop in the kitchen, get yourself something to eat."

"Yes, Dom." Oleander felt his grin spread wide enough to crack his lower lip. "Thank you, Dom. Very good of you, Dom." He bowed three times, each time tugging on his cap.

Ginglen flapped his hands in the air. "Just get out of here, you brat."

Oleander touched the brim of his cap, seriously this time, and ran off, whistling. He'd been right about the meal. Ginglen and Itzen were good people.

The lady in the kitchen was happy to fix him up a plate. Stewed onions and turnips, some chopped chicken, a little overcooked by this time in the afternoon, a wrinkled apple almost past its prime that she must have just taken from storage. Oleander had eaten much worse, that he'd actually had to pay for. The big chunk of bread she balanced on the edge of the plate more than made up for the meat—nice and light, the cook must have made it herself that morning.

"Mind, I'll need the plate back," she said, handing it over.

"Yes, Dom Rasah, I'll eat right outside." He indicated the mews door with a tilt of his head. He knew just the spot, the stone corner of the raised herb bed. At this time in the afternoon, the stone would be warm from the sun. He set the plate down carefully, balancing it between the dirt and the stone edging, picked up the apple, and took it down to Elva's horse, holding it out on the palm of his hand.

"Here you go, boy. You need this more than me." The horse carefully lipped the apple into its mouth and tossed its head at Oleander.

It was warm out in the sun, and the boy took his time with his meal. He was just wiping up the last of the gravy with the last of the bread when he heard a bird's cry far above him and he looked up, hand shielding his eyes against the sun. A bird, probably a hawk, a tiny silhouette against the light. The silhouette got bigger and bigger, until finally, too fast for him to even put down the plate he still held, a huge raven—the biggest he'd ever seen—landed on the wall beside him. He had never been so close to a bird this big ever in his life. He figured he should stay still. Very still.

"Nice bird," he croaked. Clearing his throat might give the wrong impression. "Good boy."

The bird tilted its head, first one way, then the other. Thrust out its wings and refolded them so suddenly that Oleander didn't jump until after the bird was quiet again. It looked at him some more. There was something familiar about that look. Oleander swallowed, his mouth dry. It couldn't be—the idea was crazy.

At that moment, he saw a small roll of parchment in the raven's left claw. He'd been carrying it in his talons and now stood on it. When he saw that Oleander had noticed the paper, the bird hopped a step back from it, leaving it to roll free just within Oleander's reach. For a minute Oleander stayed frozen in place, and then, slowly so as not to spook the bird, he reached out and picked up the scroll. Most writing was just marks on a page to him, but he recognized the letters on the sealed edge of the scroll as his own name. He could read that, street signs, and the names of most shops. He unrolled the page, held it up to the light, and squinted, but as usual, that did no good. In fact, he wasn't sure there was anything on the paper at all. He shot a glance over at the door to the inn. For sure someone in there could read.

The bird shook out his wings again and gave a harsh cry, just as if he was saying, "What are you waiting for?"

Oleander kept his eyes on the raven as he slowly rose to his feet and backed away toward the door. Too late he realized he'd left the plate behind. On the one hand, maybe the bird would have attacked him if he'd picked it up. He took his lower lip in his teeth. Maybe the bird would be gone when he came back out.

He found Itzen first, sharpening knives in the kitchen.

"Itzen," he said. "Can you read?"

"Of course. Whyever would you—" The man's half-insulted look changed when he realized what Oleander's question meant. He didn't mind; he was used to people's reactions when they found out he couldn't read. "Here, what have you got?"

Oleander handed over the paper and hovered at the man's elbow as Itzen's eyes flicked back and forth over the page.

"Where did you get this?"

"From this really huge raven. He landed on the wall outside and he had this in his claws."

Oleander followed Itzen out the back door. He should have known the man would want to check for himself. Naturally, the bird was gone. "I swear, there was a bird here."

"I believe you." Itzen spoke like a man not paying attention to what he was saying.

They found Ginglen making entries in an accounting ledger when they entered the private sitting room. Itzen handed Ginglen the paper. Oleander fidgeted while the other man looked at it, turned it over and back again. Wasn't anyone going to tell him what it said? Wasn't it *his* letter? They wouldn't even have it if it weren't for him.

Finally, Ginglen looked up. "Well, what do you think?"

"The boy hasn't read it," Itzen put in before Oleander could say so himself. Not that he was embarrassed or anything.

Ginglen just nodded, without that special oh-no-poor-thing look Oleander usually got. "On the outside there's your name, and on the inside, it says 'Ginglen or Itzen, give this to Wittenslade Camdin Volden if he is alive. If not, send it back.'" He rolled up the parchment again. "Lucky for us the man's alive, since we don't know how to send it back."

WITTENSLADE

"There's a street runner with a message he says he'll only give directly to you."

Witt sighed and pushed his hands through his unbraided hair before he remembered that Arriz hadn't brushed the powder out yet. Who would send him a runner? The Court had its own messengers, a friend would have sent a servant. Even the military would send some low-ranked soldier.

Which left who, exactly? For some reason he thought of the widow, but she fell into the category of the Court—or, if you used the term loosely, of a friend. When she'd sent him messages in the past, it had always been one of her pages. That's what you kept pages for. Witt had a couple himself.

"Witt?"

Only Arriz would call him that, and only when they were alone. "Send him away, if he can't state his business, or even who sent him. I'm not seeing him. Not now."

Later that afternoon, Witt attended an informal tea at the home of his cousin Tillenslade Volden, who had just become engaged. No one there seemed to care or even notice that there was a war going on. As he strolled home by way of Randoff, Witt noticed a boy walking parallel to him on the other side of the street. He didn't look away when he saw Witt look at him. The boy looked a little older than the usual street kid, taller, and with an intelligent face. The boy saw he was being examined and grinned, not at all embarrassed or abashed. He was well enough dressed, though with clogs rather than shoes, and bare legs. But his hair was neatly pulled back and braided, and his clothes, though plain, were clean. Someone looked after this boy. Though from the look of confidence on his face, Witt thought he looked well able to take care of himself.

Witt stopped walking and so did the boy. As far as Witt could see, he wasn't armed. He beckoned him across the street.

"Are you the boy who has something you'll only give to me personally?"

"I am if you're Dom Camdin Volden."

From the look on his face, this runner knew exactly who he was.

"What is it?" In answer the boy handed him a loosely rolled scroll of thick, heavy paper. Whoever sent this message could afford good quality.

Witt frowned. "The seal is broken."

"Yes, Dom, but if you look closely, you'll see it's addressed to me. I had to open it to find out I was to bring it to you."

Witt turned the paper over and checked the other side. "Your name is Oleander?"

"Yes, Dom."

"You know it's a poisonous plant?"

It seemed impossible, but the boy's grin grew larger. "Only sometimes, Dom."

Witt grinned back, then returned his attention to the scroll. He hoped he kept his face from showing any shock when he read the first line.

"To Wittenslade Camdin Volden, from Practitioner First Class Tamari Otwyn, greeting."

He let the scroll roll shut again. "Do you know what this says?"

"No, Dom, I can't read." The boy must have read skepticism on Witt's face. "I can't even see it, anyway. No one can but you."

Which meant the boy knew *something* about the sender.

His mind made up, Witt tucked the letter into his sleeve. "Come with me."

The boy Oleander knew his job, keeping a carefully regulated three paces behind Witt all the way back home. The look on the footman's face when he saw the boy was coming in—he clearly recognized him—was priceless. Witt waved the boy to follow as he ran up the curving staircase to his personal suite. He hesitated and then went back to look over the railing to the entrance hall below. "Oh, and Kendril, send up some chocolate, and an assortment of rolls."

"Very good, Dom."

Arriz greeted him with an impassive face when he saw Witt was not alone. "The messenger I turned away before. Have a look, see what you think."

Kendril came in with the chocolate. "Over by the fireplace, Kendril, thank you, and thank Cook." He waited until the servant had closed the door behind him. "Help yourself," he said to the boy. "I've already eaten."

Oleander's eyes grew rounder, and he nodded, once, before going over to the table. Witt noticed that he picked up the cup and saucer in one hand and the pot in the other before pouring the chocolate. *Someone's trained him*, he thought before returning his attention to Arriz.

"I don't see anything," Arriz said, handing the scroll back to Witt.

The boy cleared his throat for attention and swallowed the piece of cinnamon roll he had in his mouth before speaking. Witt hoped he wouldn't choke. "No, sir," he said. "That's because your name's not on it."

Witt looked from the boy back to the paper and took it from Arriz. He read aloud to save having to repeat himself.

"The first line says it's from Tamari Otwyn," he said.

"The practitioner? And we know that how?" Arriz said.

"I should think by the fact that no one can read it but Dom Volden." The boy was concentrating on his ham bun, but Witt could hear the eyeroll in his voice.

"Play nice, gentlemen. She goes on to say, 'If this reaches you, and you answer, I will know you are alive.'" Witt's hand trembled. Why would she—of course, she wouldn't know whether he had made it across the bridge. Sometimes, in his dreams, he wasn't sure himself. Tamari had been worried about him. A part of him felt lighter at that thought. Arriz cleared his throat and Witt went on reading.

"'You have shown yourself to be my friend in the past.'" Witt felt his cheeks grow hot. "'We have turned back the assault made using the ghost bridge—' Hah! I like that better than cloud bridge. 'Any information you could give us would be welcome, though I understand if you would rather not. If you are willing to help us, answer this letter by writing directly onto the parchment under our names. Your writing will replace mine. Whatever you can tell us with regard to plans or further attacks would enable us to avoid more bloodshed.'"

"Nothing less than treason." Arriz's voice was flat, neutral.

Witt looked up at his man. "I think I'll need something stronger than chocolate."

Ten

T HE COUNCIL WANTED to separate us, give us rooms in different parts of the Court.

"You'll each be able to protect a different area, spreading
out the good you can do." Deka Omara looked around at us and smiled.
She met everyone's eyes but mine. She was not in the council herself,
but as the newest second-class graduate, she had been given the often-
unpleasant task of assigning rooms and workspaces.

"Thank you," Elva said, smiling, "but we'll stay together."

"It's not even good strategy," Donn pointed out kindly, as Deka
opened her mouth to argue. "Separating us lessens our effect and it's
rotten for communication."

Deka had no choice but to agree. She finally led us through two
patios and an arched tunnel of roses to the north wing of the Granite
Palace, which, like so many of the older buildings in the White Court,
hadn't housed practitioners in years. I am not sure how Deka managed
it, but when we reached the hallway that led to our rooms, there were
already two students cleaning them, with an apprentice to supervise.
Each small suite consisted of a bedroom with a bathing room attached,
and a good-sized sitting room. The furniture—couches, chairs, small
tables, hassocks, and armchairs—was in an older style, heavy and dark,
probably why it hadn't been removed for use elsewhere. Plenty of
down-filled cushions made the rooms comfortable, once the apprentice had shown the students how to refresh them. A simple *forran* they
would probably use in their own rooms once they got back to them.
They had cleaned two suites and were moving into the third when we
reached them.

The apprentice straightened almost to attention when he saw us coming. "Practitioner Lowens. If you wouldn't mind using these rooms until we clean the other three—"

"We'll only need four rooms altogether," Elva said.

"Three," Lizz corrected.

"Donn and Lizz and I will take turns keeping watch," Randd said. He and Lizz smiled identical smiles. Clearly there was no point in arguing with them. The students brightened up and hustled into the third suite, moving far more briskly than they had been. We gathered in the room Elva chose for the two of us, talking of random things until students and apprentice had gone.

"Wait." Donn held up his palm toward me as I was about to speak. I blinked when Lizz started singing in a clear alto voice, a rhythmic tune I had never heard before. Donn gestured us all closer to him. "The singing will cover our talk and help Randd while he checks the rooms," he whispered.

"For what?" Small *forrans* and cats kept even these disused rooms clear of mice and other vermin. Most of the time. Since housekeeping *forrans* were regarded as training for students, they had been known to fail.

"Listening devices. Randd can sense them." Donn smiled. "Don't know how he does it, myself, but he's very good."

I shook my head, lips parted, a little embarrassed. I had not thought of the council spying on us.

Elva patted my arm. "You don't have our experience," he said as if he knew what I was thinking. "But then again, we don't have yours. Most New Zone mages are Free Scouts or gunslingers—"

"Or law bringers," Donn added.

"Or law bringers," Elva agreed with a smile. "They're especially skilled in anything that might help them survive—"

"We hear better," Donn interrupted again. "See further, move faster. Look." He waved a hand at Randd.

The gunslinger stood in front of the portrait of a practitioner I did not know, a sour-faced woman with her blond hair in a tight bun. How was it that pleasant, happy people never had their portraits painted? I drew my attention back to Randd as he passed his practitioner's hand over the painting without touching the actual paint, stopping with his fingers hovering over the painted ear. My skin prickled, and when I concentrated, I could see a faint glow of light outlining his hand between his palm and the surface of the paint. He looked back at Donn, nodded, and tilted his head toward his hand.

"Seems we were right not to trust these people," Donn murmured. He brushed back his mustache and smiled. "Guess they don't trust us." Lizz shrugged and continued to sing.

"I've never seen one like this," Elva said. "In fact, I wouldn't believe it was a listener if it wasn't Randd saying so. Fenra, is there anything . . . ?"

I appreciated Elva's faith in my talents, I really did, but just then I wished his faith wasn't quite so strong. "Go on singing, Lizz, until I tell you to stop."

Randd stood to one side of the painting, his finger pointing at the spot where he had detected the listening *forran*. I nodded my thanks and placed the palm of my practitioner's hand as lightly as I could on the surface of the painting, taking care not to touch the ear itself. I felt a small residue of Randd's energy, and I thought for a moment that I could see the shape of a strange pattern.

Now that I knew what to look for, I could feel the pattern made by the listening *forran*. I wished I had the time to figure out who designed it. It hadn't been left in operation in these long disused rooms; that would have drained the energy of the practitioner who installed it. It could only have been recently activated. Such a thing could be done easily by any apprentice, or student for that matter, who had been given the *forran*'s key.

The elements of the painting warmed under my hands. I could trace the oil all the way back to the flax seeds it was made from, and the warm dry soil they'd grown in. The pigments in the paint spoke to me; the hemp of the canvas I traced all the way back to the plant, and I could smell the pungent odor of the field it grew in. There was even a hint of the pine trees that provided the turpentine that thinned the oil. I ran my hand over the maple frame as well, though it had nothing to do with the listener.

I felt how the *forran*'s pattern was a thing apart from the elements of the painting, something foreign that tampered with and misaligned them, pulling their natural forms askew. Breathing softly, I reached into the patterns of the oil, pigment, hemp, and turpentine and tweaked them back into their original forms, restoring them to themselves. No longer anchored, the listening *forran* disappeared, floating away like smoke from a fire. I looked at the others and nodded.

Lizz let her voice die quietly away. Randd slipped in through the door, and I realized he had gone to check the other rooms.

"The one next along, but not the last one," he said. He frowned at the painting.

"Did anyone see the apprentice go into the third room they cleaned?" Everyone shook their heads. "Then the students didn't activate the *forran*, the apprentice must have done." I rubbed my face and rolled my shoulders, trying to get the tension out of my muscles. "Might as well take care of it now."

The room next door was mirror image of ours, allowing the plumbing to use the common wall between the bathing rooms. The walls, however, displayed no artwork of any kind. When I looked at Randd, raising my eyebrows, he pointed out a small but perfect conch shell decorating the mantelpiece.

"How beautiful," I said for the benefit of anyone who might be listening. "Look at the iridescence." After the complexity of the oil painting, the conch shell felt simple. It was all of a piece, completely itself, except for the same *forran* I had felt on the painting. For the elements of the portrait, they'd been together so long that the portrait itself had become their natural state, the state to which they wished to return. The conch shell, perhaps even more than the painting, wanted to return to its natural, unsullied condition.

I did what anyone would do when confronted with a beautiful seashell. I picked it up and held it to my ear. Silence. I was so startled I almost said something. Instead, I breathed into the shell, soothing it with my breath, blowing the listening *forran* away. When I finished, I held the shell to my ear again, and heard what I should have heard, the sea. For a moment I saw the waves, heard them rushing up the beach, smelled salt air.

Randd completed another sweep of our rooms before he let us sit down. Exhaustion made my knees weak and my hands tremble. I took the glass of wine Donn gave me in both hands.

"Won't they notice they can't hear us?" Randd said, frowning again at the portrait.

"They will most likely blame the apprentice for not practicing the *forran* correctly," I said. "How long should we wait for an answer from Tamari's friend?"

"If it was up to Tamari, I think we'd be waiting as long as it took."

I glanced up at Elva and our eyes met. He raised his left eyebrow in the way that meant, "Are you thinking what I'm thinking?" Tamari had a certain unmistakable look on her face when she said Witt's name. I set my glass down on the small table to my right and pushed back my hair with both hands, trying to tidy away the loose strands.

All three deputies suddenly looked at the door, so the knock didn't surprise me. *Improved hearing*, I thought. Randd took two steps back, pulled out his gun, and aimed it at the center of the door. Lizz took the spot to the left of the opening, and Donn put his hand on the latch. He tilted his head at an angle, as if he was listening.

"It's a servant," he said.

"Anyone can be armed, Donn," I said. Donn smiled at me without moving his head. He lifted his eyebrows, looked for and received nods from the others, and cracked the door open just enough to see into the corridor. He looked through the crack, tapped Lizz on the shoulder, and both of them stepped back from the door. A young woman in a kitchen smock pushed an elegant high-wheeled cart made of wrought iron and glass into the room. She managed to bring it all the way into the room without looking up once. Her clothing proved she was neither student nor apprentice, and with a little shock, I realized I had forgotten how many mundanes lived and worked in the White Court.

"Supper," the girl said. "With Practitioner Otwyn's compliments." Wherever she was right now, Tamari had thought about us, and sent us food.

"Thank you," Elva said. The girl swiveled her eyes sideways at him, saw that he was looking at her, paled, and scurried back out into the hall. Donn stuck his head out and watched her until she reached the first turning.

"Why would she be afraid of us?" Donn shut the door and looked around at us.

"Maybe the food is poisoned, and she knows it." Randd ran his fingers quickly over all the plates, cutlery, napkins, and finally the cart itself.

"Nothing," he said.

"Why would Tamari send us poisoned food?" Donn picked up an empty plate and handed it to me.

"We don't know that this actually came from Tamari," Elva pointed out.

"Ah." The old man nodded. "Not that it matters. I'm sure that one of us—"

"It won't be poisoned," I said.

"Did you use a *forran* to check?"

"I will if you like, but no one is going to kill us while they still need our help. So long as we stay useful, we stay safe."

When nothing was left of the food but crumbs and streaks of sauce on the plates, Elva stood up and stretched. "We need sleep," he said. "I'll take the first watch."

"No, that you won't do, Sheriff." Donn crossed his arms and leaned back until his chair balanced on its back legs. "Senior officers don't take part in the watch if there are at least three subordinates." With his thumb he indicated Randd, Lizz, and himself.

"We're not at war, Donn."

"Wrong again, Sheriff," Donn said, smoothing back his mustaches. "War is exactly where we are."

Splitting up, even if just to the room next door, made me a little nervous, but all five of us would not be able to rest comfortably in any one of the suites we had been given, and rest was paramount. Elva and I stayed in our sitting room when the others left, Donn to take the first watch in the corridor, Randd and Lizz to sleep until it was their turn. In spite of the third suite, they all chose to sleep in the one next to ours.

"I know I should sleep." I rested my head against the back of the couch. The students had done such a good job cleaning that the upholstery, which had to be decades old at the very least, smelled fresh and new. "I'm exhausted, but I cannot shut off my brain."

"You didn't kill anyone." As usual, Elva knew exactly what kept me awake.

"Not this time, no. I did, however, make it easier for others to kill." My stomach had soured, and I wished I had not eaten after all.

Elva sat down next to me, turning and adjusting me until I lay half in his lap, my head on his shoulder. He smelled of the sea. He had smelled that way since he had almost died on the World's beach. "You're definitely an accomplice to killing, I won't argue that. I don't know if it helps, but what you did isn't murder. You were protecting us, and besides, those people knew who they were attacking, and had to expect that we would fight back."

"Mundanes on one side, practitioners on the other? I think I know on which side the bets would be placed."

"Really? Where *were* all these practitioners? I only saw you and Tamari—no one else came to help but a few students and apprentices like Predax. No one else sees the danger. The important thing is, you didn't practice anyone to death, and don't try to tell me you don't know how."

"Oh, I know how." I shifted until I could look Elva in the face. "I have even done it, once or twice, when someone has been dying in great pain, of something I could not heal." I watched his face, but nothing in it changed. "I know what you are trying to do, and I appreciate it. But I still feel terrible—" I blinked back tears and waited until I could be sure my voice would stay level. "And it will take time for that to pass."

"I've known people who didn't have any trouble killing, who even seemed to enjoy it. I won't have one as a deputy. They're unreliable, even in the short run."

"Between the troubled and the untroubled, where do you stand?"

He took a long time to answer. "About halfway between those stone killers and you, I think. I can kill when it's necessary, to defend myself or someone else. I also don't mind making the decision myself. But I don't go looking for the opportunity."

"And the others? I have heard them talk a great deal about their honor."

"They wouldn't kill someone just for insulting them, but they'd be happy to break a few bones, should the need arise."

"I will remember that." I must have fallen asleep. I do not remember talking of anything else.

Breakfast arrived on the same beautiful wrought-iron cart, but this time a young man brought it. Randd checked it over just as carefully as he had the night before. As we ate, we considered what we knew about the assault, and what we would need to deal with another.

"Map would help." Lizz had just refilled her cup with the last of the coffee when we were interrupted by a knock on the door. Donn signaled to the others and once again they took their positions.

"A guard," Donn whispered, throwing the door open and leaping to one side in the same motion. The young woman wearing a guard uniform at least a size too big took one look at the barrel of Randd's gun and stepped back, her hands up.

"The compliments of the chief practitioner and would Captain Karamisk and his deputies meet with him." Her voice was so thin and high pitched we could barely understand her.

Elva put himself between Randd and the door, pushing the barrel of Randd's revolver to one side. "It's Sheriff, not Captain. Is it just Ronan Sedges? Not the full council?" he asked, while Randd holstered the gun.

"I don't know, Dom. Sheriff, I mean. I'm just meant to bring you." Her tone lowered and she sounded more like a human being and less like a mouse.

I got to my feet and picked up my jacket from the back of my chair.

"Oh, not you, Practitioner Lowens." Her voice got higher again. "Just the sheriff and . . ." She gestured at the others.

"You're new," Elva said. "I haven't seen you before. We'll be with you in a moment, if you don't mind waiting." He closed the door softly in the young guard's face and motioned us all away from it.

"Unacceptable." Donn's mustaches quivered. "It's an insult to Fenra to exclude her."

I stifled a smile. Apparently, Donn also felt himself responsible for my honor. "Ronan Sedges still thinks of me as a third-class practitioner who causes trouble. There's no reason as far as he can see to include me in any strategy sessions."

Donn shook his head. "Back home he'd be asking for a pounding."

"Don't be too hard on the council of practitioners," I said. "They are all out of their depth. As for Ronan Sedges—" I shrugged. "At least he is not one of those who like to be on the top of the heap but run as soon as things get difficult."

"We're not going without you, no matter how commendable he is." Elva pulled his coat on over his holstered guns. "We wouldn't leave you alone here anyway." He shrugged to settle his jacket and opened the door. The guard had been standing with her back against the opposite wall, and she straightened and saluted before she realized what she had done.

"Guard, my compliments to the chief practitioner, but tell him it's all of us, or none." Elva tilted his head to one side, taking in the young woman's appalled expression. "Never mind, we'll tell him ourselves."

When Elva realized we were being taken to the council room, he stopped and waited for the guard to notice we were not still behind her. "We would prefer to meet in an open space," Elva said. "The third alcove off the Patio of Horses will do. All of you go ahead," he added, turning to me. "I'll go with the guard." I heard him asking for her name and saying something about a map as they walked away.

The alcoves Elva referred to were open on the patio side, allowing for air circulation and a view of the fountains. Enough light came through the narrow, stone-latticed windows at this time of day for even the finest detail work. The stone floors, patterned with inlaid tiles and marble, were cool under our feet. I had never sat in one of these alcoves before. When I had been a student, and later an apprentice, these spots were reserved for senior practitioners, whether council members, mentors, or both.

We were not there long before servants brought low cross-framed chairs, cushions, and side tables. These were set up in two rows facing each other. Donn and I took two of the chairs on one side with Lizz and Randd leaning against the wall behind us, arms crossed.

Elva joined us, carrying a long wooden tube, bringing Sedges and Nubin Sonsera with him. Behind them came Tamari and Captain Rennard. A little knot of tension in the back of my neck released. Tamari did not appear to be in the captain's custody; we would have at least one person on our side. Tamari, Sedges, and the other councilor sat down across from us, while Captain Rennard took up a position against the wall behind the others. More servants carrying trays of cool drinks, grapes, apricots, nectarines, and cherries followed them in and set up on the small tables beside each seat. I heard murmuring behind me and reminded myself to explain the mixture of fruit later.

"I'm sorry to see you still mistrust me." Sedges gestured to where Randd and Lizz leaned against the wall. He did not look sorry to me, unless a curled lip and narrowed eyes were signs of sorrow. "Will your bodyguards not take seats?"

"They're colleagues, not bodyguards," Elva said. "And they prefer to stand."

Sedges leaned forward, his hands braced on his knees, trying to demonstrate openness. "First, I want to apologize." He looked us both in the eye before continuing. "I lost focus on what is most important to the White Court. I completely underestimated the abilities of the mundanes, and I'm grateful for your intervention and your help. It's obvious that you understand a great deal more about this type of confrontation than we do, and we hope you will join with Captain Rennard to take charge of our defense, and, when the time comes, our offense."

"There's no doubt they'll try the ghost bridge again." Elva poured himself a glass of iced orange juice. "But next time they'll be more careful. For one, they'll make sure they have more people on this side of the river before they begin another assault."

"Can the guard be prepared to repel this assault? With the help of your people of course, Captain—I mean, Sheriff." Nubin Sonsera did his best not to sound frightened.

"There are only thirty guards," Rennard said. "And our main job has been policing visitors to the White Court and escorting anyone who has to go into the City. We drill carefully and often, but last night's engagement was the first real fight most of us have ever had."

"They did well, for unseasoned troops," Donn said.

Elva lifted his hand. "I didn't get a chance to mention siege engines, such as catapults or towers. Would they have this technology?" he said, turning to me.

"It's possible. Most of these weapons existed long before gaslight and might be found in other Modes." I saw Sedges take note that I spoke about the Modes in front of people he thought of as mundanes. "They've just never been used in the City before."

Sedges leaned back, gripping the arms of his chair. "It seems that we are very lucky to have you on this side of the valley."

"So, we have to destroy the bridge, right? Once they see they can't reach us, they'll give up." Nubin Sonsera's hands fluttered in the air. This careless moving of his practitioner's hand made me uneasy. When had this started? Tamari cleared her throat and shifted backward in her chair.

"To destroy the bridge," I said, "we would have to wait until it had extended, which would mean the deaths of everyone on or near it."

"But they are our enemies, aren't they? We can't let the deaths of mundanes stop us from defending the White Court."

I knew the World would disagree. "I would suggest a different plan."

ELVANYN

Elva signaled and Randd came forward, sliding a map out of the narrow tube and unrolling it in the open space between the chairs. He placed dishes and pitchers where they would hold down the edges of the paper scroll, which tried to roll up again.

"Where did you get that?" Sedges was clearly not happy they had a map of the White Court.

"I gave it to them." Everyone turned to look at Tamari.

"I'm not sure that I approve—"

"I could have drawn a map," Elva cut in, "and I'm sure Practitioner Lowens could as well. This saved time."

"It's just buildings and elevations," Donn pointed out. "Stuff we need to know to mount a good defense." The older man held on to his temper remarkably well, all things considered. Elva smiled. These people didn't know how lucky they were.

"If there isn't anywhere for the ghost bridge to rest on our side, they cannot use it." Fenra tapped the map in three places. "We propose removing these sections of earth, leaving only the underlying bedrock."

"That's not possible," Sedges said.

"I believe it is." Elva kept the amusement out of his voice. "I've seen Practitioner Lowens do far more difficult things than that." Like ask vegetation to move itself for her. Like turn a horse into a raven— though that might have been Terith's doing.

Sedges wiped the frown off his face as soon as he realized it was there. "Wouldn't that be dangerous?"

"Not if it's done right," Fenra said. "As Lorist Otwyn can confirm," she nodded at Tamari, "the White Court stands on what was a granite promontory, later practiced into an island for greater security. What I propose removing is really just centuries of accumulated silt." She tapped the map again. "Removal won't affect the underlying granite."

"That all makes perfect sense." This unexpected agreement came from Sonsera. "Once they see what we're capable of, they'll surrender."

"How soon do you think you can be ready?" Sedges looked up from the map, skepticism on his face, if not in his voice.

"Give me a day to prepare."

Elva knew there was no point in telling Fenra that one day's rest wouldn't be enough to restore her. Anyone could see the dark marks under her eyes. She would kill herself at this rate, and then where would the World be? He needed to talk to her, but she listened best when they were alone.

Tamari stayed behind when Sedges and Sonsera finally left to prepare for a meeting to inform the rest of the council. Judging from the stiffness in Sedges' back, he wasn't happy.

"Don't you have to go, too?" Donn asked Tamari.

"I've already heard everything he's going to tell them," she said. "I'd rather stay here and help."

"Besides," Captain Rennard pushed himself off the wall and took hold of one of the vacated chairs, "there's still food and drink on the tables. First rule of soldiering, eat when you can." He moved his chair and Tamari's to form a circle with the others. Randd and Lizz pulled up chairs for themselves.

"That actually went a great deal better than I expected," Tamari said after helping herself to a slice of melon.

"Sedges is too ready to let us do what we want." Fenra's voice sounded full of doubt.

"Of course. We're his scapegoats if something goes wrong." The captain looked around at their faces. "But I'm sure you thought of that."

"*I* didn't think of it, thank you, and now I'm depressed." Tamari bit into her second piece of melon.

"What if our plan works?" Elva was glad to see the smile on Fenra's face.

The captain shrugged. "He'll find a way to take the credit and then get rid of us."

"I had better stick with Tamari," Donn offered. "She's just not suspicious enough."

Wittenslade

He told himself it was just curiosity that brought him down to the ruins of the bridge that almost killed him. It was even partly true. He wanted to get a closer look at the mechanism of the ghost bridge—he really did like that name better than cloud bridge. The place looked entirely different in the daylight, thank the Maker, not so much like the spot where he almost died. He craned his neck upward, squinting against the sunlight, trying to make sense of the monstrous mass of wood, iron, and gears. This whole business was nothing but a waste, no matter what Riva Deneyra said. His lips pressed together, he drew in a deep breath through his nose. The widow had lied to him, had tried to use him. He couldn't let her get away with that.

He carried the still unanswered letter in his breast pocket. He wanted to help Tamari, and helping her would settle with the widow too. No reason he couldn't do both. *Besides, it's only courtesy to let her know I'm still alive.* The boy Oleander was ready to act as go-between for as long as Fenra Lowens wanted him to.

"Witt, you old dog! Why the long face? Not here to join up, are you?"

He'd been expecting someone in authority to question his snooping, but this voice belonged to an old friend, Colyardin Antorn Benfett.

Witt flicked his fan open and closed. "I'm afraid I'm occupied elsewhere," he said, in the pompous tone they'd made so much fun of when they'd been at school together. Col's father had gambled away most of their property, leaving just enough when he'd killed himself to feed and house his wife and Col's younger siblings. Witt's friend had struck out on his own and joined the army as a lieutenant. He wore colonel's eagles now, along with a scar under his left ear.

"That's right, I heard you took over your father's seat in the Red Court. I would have sent condolences when I heard the man died, but that would have been hypocritical, wouldn't it?" The two old friends laughed. Col's father had been a kind, charming man with an unfortunate weakness. Witt would have traded fathers without hesitation. At least, he straightened his lace cuff, he liked to think he would.

"What does bring you here, then, if you're not joining up?"

Witt gestured upward to the machinery. "Curiosity, pure and simple. I saw the demonstration in the Horse Grounds, and I wanted a closer look. How goes the invasion? You can imagine the type of reports we get at the Court."

"Prettified for consumption by noncombatants?"

"Exactly."

"I was just about to go off duty. Let's go somewhere and catch up."

"They let you take coffee breaks?"

"Now, now. This is serious. We don't call them that."

After speaking with one or two subordinates in less clean uniforms, Col led Witt not out of the area entirely, as he had expected, but into a nearby house, and up to the third floor.

"Merchant's place," Col said over his shoulder as they mounted the curved staircase. "Commandeered for the duration."

"I hope he was well compensated." Witt looked around with interest. The furnishings were not so very different in style and quality from his own.

"*She*, as it happens. We think so, but I doubt she does. I don't even want to think about what army cooks are doing to her kitchen."

"I suppose she'll appeal to the Court, and one day I'll get to decide if you have to give her more money."

The servant Col had shouted at on their way in—clearly a low-ranking member of the armed forces rather than an actual servant—came in at this point with a tray containing cups, the coffee pot, a cream jug, sugar bowl, and plate of apple tarts. All the delicate porcelain matched beautifully, and Witt wondered if they would still be intact when all of this was over.

"Come here to the window," Col said once they had poured their coffees. "This is the reason I wanted this house."

Witt gave a silent whistle. The view from the window astonished him. The White Court, perfectly framed in the opening, sprawled across its rock foundations, an imposing jumble of red stone towers and white walls, with turrets and fanciful roofs and greenery peeping out everywhere.

"Incredible," he said in his natural, unaffected voice. "You miss out on this view when you live in the Red Court."

"All the houses on this hillside have more or less this vista," Col said. "We'll see how long they can go on keeping it to themselves now that more of you rich types know about it. Although I suppose you could get so used to it that after a while you wouldn't notice it anymore."

"I suppose," Witt said. "Then again, not everyone would want to look at the White Court every day, no matter how beautiful it is."

Col slapped him on the shoulder. "Sit down, relax, let's have something to eat." Witt followed his friend to where high-backed upholstered chairs sat to either side of the refreshment table. Col poured him another cup of coffee and offered him a tart. "Take one, they won't stay fresh forever."

Witt laughed, spraying powdered sugar over himself. "Remember that? Denton caught with his hands in the bun bin at midnight?"

"'But Professor Etnown.'" Col imitated the higher-pitched voice of a child. "'They won't stay fresh forever.'"

They exchanged a few more anecdotes of their school years, trading information on what their companions were up to now. Finally, Witt thought he could turn the subject back to something more serious.

"What's your take on how the first use of the ghost bridge went?" Witt asked. "'Moderate success' is what the report said."

"Yes, well, since we didn't get a glorious victory, we're now calling it a trial run. I'm not revealing any secrets when I tell you it didn't go as well as we'd hoped. In many ways, I don't think our hearts were in it. Since that woman fixed the great fault, and saved all those lives, it's almost impossible to convince people—even some soldiers—that practitioners are the enemy."

"That surprises me." Witt dusted sugar off his fingers with his napkin and picked up his coffee. "People are usually afraid of them."

"Not so many now, and even those who still are, are afraid for the wrong reasons. Stories their parents told them as children to make them behave."

"'Go to sleep or the practitioners will come for you.'"

"Exactly. Grownups are more likely to be angry, or feel deprived, as if they're entitled to the results of someone else's work. They've forgotten that these people have talents—"

"Wait a minute." Col's use of the word "talents" in the plural surprised him. "How long have you been living in the outer counties? When I knew you, you weren't so superstitious. You laughed at the kids who believed in magical powers. Practitioners are just scientists, working out theories they won't share on how the world around us works." Tamari had told him differently, but he wasn't sure he believed her. It was hard to think of her as dangerous, still less as some kind of witch.

Col shrugged, keeping his eyes fixed on his coffee cup as he turned it in circles. "It's as good an explanation as any other," he said. "I don't want to sound like some old granddad, but I've seen some things that can't be explained. Science, magic, who really knows? I can tell you for certain I've never seen the kind of lighting they used the other night, and that somehow my men were being killed by guns even though we were well out of range of any pistols or rifles that we know of."

Witt nodded, remembering the widow's take on it. Did it really matter how practitioners could do what they did? "So, what's next? The bridge is awfully expensive if we're only going to use it once."

"Not at all. We were too arrogant. Our mistake was to assume that White Court guards were like Red Court guards—that is, not soldiers. We needed more people than we sent over, many more. We won't make that mistake again. And we won't attack at sundown either, we'll wait until the slow part of the night. Their lights can work for us as well as against us. And we'll take precautions, now that we know the range of their guns."

Witt started to ask another question when a sound from outside drew them both to the window. At first, they saw nothing that could account for the rumbling they could feel in their bones. The sky was clear. Then Col grabbed Witt's forearm and pulled him closer to the window.

"Look."

Witt looked in the direction his friend pointed, squinting against the glare of sunlight on stone. At first, he didn't see anything. And then he saw a strange shimmer—like a heat shimmer—passing over the White Court. The trees he'd noticed earlier, the ones that bordered the edge of the promontory, and the bushes growing at different heights in the rock and earth that led down toward the water, looked like they were moving, even though there wasn't any wind to speak of. Witt straightened. More than just moving. For a moment the trees and bushes seemed to be walking down the face of the cliff— then, with a horrible tearing noise, they took a part of the cliff face with them down to the water below, crashing into the river, sending up sheets of water. The shoreline of the island was nothing now but rocky cliffs, sheer all the way from the White Court's curtain wall to the river.

Witt followed closely as Col ran of the room, their feet slapping down the marble staircase almost in unison. Out in the square in front of the house they found soldiers running to their posts, pulling on uniform jackets and hats as they ran. Some called to others, asking what had happened, but none of them seemed to know.

Witt stayed with Col all the way to the field commander's quarters, drawing as little attention to himself as possible. For the first time in his life, he wished he dressed more drably. As long as no one noticed him, they wouldn't send him away. The command post itself was set up in the open, complete with a stool, a strategy table, and maps. Behind it stood the commander himself, the only one of his officers perfectly calm; even his color hadn't changed. Either this was nothing new to him, or it was the best act Witt had ever seen. The older man looked up from a map on his desk. "Colonel, you have a report?"

"Yes, sir. The entire outer edge of the White Court has fallen off into the river—at least, I'm assuming it isn't just happening on this side. The view from my rooms shows nothing left but sheer cliff."

"Meaning there's nowhere for troops to gather." The commander tapped the map in front of him with a stylus.

"Worse than that, sir." Witt hadn't noticed the engineer, Jondrel Hansu, now that he wore a uniform. "Even if they left the gates open for us, the bridge won't reach. It's too short now."

The commander glanced up without lifting his head. "How much time to make it longer?"

"Making the bridge longer isn't just a matter of adding material to the moving end, sir. We'll have to take the whole thing apart and re-configure for new stresses . . ." The man stopped talking, his eyes taking on a faraway look. "It could be weeks."

"Respectfully, Commander," Col said, "what would we do if we got across? Crawl up the walls like spiders while they shoot at us from above?"

"If we have to, Colonel Benfett, if we have to." The commander nodded slowly, looking at but not seeing the map in front of him. "I was hoping it wouldn't come to this, but they've left us no choice." He lifted his head. "Colonel, have the cannon brought up." He looked back at the map. "They're not the only ones who can make the earth move."

Col grabbed Witt by the arm, taking him along as he left to follow his orders. "Go home," he told his old friend. "Sorry, but here you'll only be in the way." True, but that didn't make it any easier to hear. Witt returned to his carriage, whistled to his horse, and began driving home. *Cannon will destroy the walls*, he thought. *Maybe more than the walls*. Did the council really care how many practitioners lived, so long as some did?

FENRA

When I woke up, I stayed quiet for a few minutes, watching Elva reloading his pistols, spinning the cylinders the way he always did after cleaning or reloading.

"Where are the others?" I asked.

"I've got Lizz and Randd training the guard." He flipped the cylinder closed and picked up his other gun. "Their rifles are breach-loaders—single shots," he added when I raised my eyebrows. "Not repeaters like ours, so the first thing they need to do is learn to shoot in pairs, one shooting, one reloading."

"Lizz and Randd have experience in that?" Elva had been living in the New Zone an unknowable length of time—ever since his friend Xandra Albainil had tucked him away for safety and then created the Godstone. Xandra had not been able to return for Elva until only a few months ago.

"Just because we use the Westminster repeating rifle doesn't mean we don't know how the others work," he pointed out. "There are lots of the older long guns still around." He holstered one revolver under his right arm. "If you look after your guns properly, they should outlive you."

"What about Donn?"

"He's with Tamari. He doesn't think she's safe, and he's figuring to pick up some practice from her."

I nodded. "She has the aura of a teacher, I think."

We both spun around at the sound from the window, Elva raising the still unholstered revolver to cover the intruder, lowering it again when we saw it was Terith. He passed through the narrow stone lattice that covered the window without difficulty. Now I saw why he had chosen a raven shape, rather than something larger.

The paper Terith carried had been resealed, and the wax showed the impression of an animal that must be the emblem of Tamari's friend Witt. I broke the seal and unrolled the scroll.

"Whose name is on it?" Elva tried to read over my shoulder.

"Tamari's."

"Then how can you read it?"

"It's my *forran*." I skipped through the personal part of the letter, and read the final paragraph more carefully. When I looked up, Elva was watching me with a frown on his face. "Cannons," I said. "They're bringing cannons."

Over the next few days, Elva and his deputies trained everyone they could get their hands on—a cook could reload a weapon for a shooter—and I tried to teach the other practitioners to locate and fend off incoming artillery. Many of the older, first-class practitioners had trouble taking instructions from me, and since most had not been out of the White Court in decades, their practice now involved more theory than application. There were even some who had developed new *forrans*, but never tested them. The idea of feeling in the air for the cannonballs was almost more than they could manage.

Ronan Sedges surprised me by ordering everyone, even council members, to at least try. The oldest of them, Az Pilcuerta, caught on very quickly, and helped persuade some of the others to apply themselves more, if only to stop the old lady laughing at them.

Everyone knew at least one *forran* to make objects move—usually for calling objects like your hat or your cup of coffee to your hand, things that didn't use too much power, and saved time. Stopping objects from moving was something most had never tried.

"I don't think we want to make these projectiles approach us faster," Tamari pointed out to those inclined to argue. With one eye on Tamari, Donn worked closely with Az Pilcuerta. Apparently, he had picked up the *forran* for calling things to you rather quickly, and he was trying to teach her how to feel for objects in the air.

I showed Tamari the sketch I had been working on. "With this *forran*—" I had scribbled some instructions as well, "—we should be able to push the cannonballs. They'll still move forward, but at a different angle."

"We'd do better to stop them entirely," Tamari said, looking over my shoulder. "Or send them back where they came from."

"If someone would like to work out that *forran*, they are welcome to. Remember also that it might not be cannonballs. It can be other, more dangerous things, like exploding shot, or fireballs." I shivered, thinking about the things Elva had told me about.

We soon learned that pushing down the objects we were using as practice models as they approached us was the easiest strategy—after all, down was a natural direction for them. Unfortunately, the practitioner doing that could not do anything else. It took all their concentration and power to make objects change trajectory—to make the missile drop, in the case of cannonballs, into the river. Stopping it entirely was much harder to master, and took even more energy, though it might be more useful in the long run. One of the younger first-class practitioners actually managed to throw the missile back, but none of the others, including me, could do it.

Continued training, however, uncovered a serious problem with this line of defense: practitioners very quickly became too tired to achieve any consistent results. These weren't specialized *forrans*, carefully designed for anyone to use with top efficiency, just sketchy ones pared down roughly into essential parts. Each practitioner had to come up with a variation of their own, which they might or might not be able to explain to the others. It didn't help that the more we trained, the longer it took to recover from the effort.

"We will have to work in shifts," I said to Tamari after one particularly tiring session. "And concentrate our efforts. Elva and the captain are spending the morning picking out the areas most likely to be targeted by cannon fire." I had no idea how they made their decisions; I was only happy I did not have to do it.

Tamari patted me on the arm as we parted. If she felt as tired as I did, she would have to stop and rest somewhere on the way back to her rooms. I saw Donn appear from behind a hedgerow and join her. Good, he would look after her. I sat down myself at the first stone bench I passed. Could I call upon the World for help? Was there something it could do?

The mountainside startled me. Before this, I had always met the

World on a beach. At first, I thought I had made a mistake, but the wind blew my hair back off my face, and I saw the rocks just up the hillside from where I stood move and shift in a familiar way. Perhaps it had given up appearing as Arlyn. I no sooner had that thought when suddenly the movement resolved into his familiar shape. It had not improved its version of Arlyn since we last met, and to be truthful, I preferred it that way. It would be worse dealing with a perfect replica. This way I always knew exactly who I was talking to.

"Thank you for meeting with me." It did not acknowledge me directly, but the Arlyn-face seemed to smile, and I could feel it listening to me. I had helped it, saved its life, in a way, but I still did not know whether I was in any understandable sense important to it.

"You have not progressed as instructed." The mouth moved properly, but the inside still wasn't real, and the voice rattled and scratched, almost indistinguishable from the sound of moving pebbles and rocks. Or Arlyn with a very sore throat.

"I am afraid not," I said, sitting down on a handy rock. I leaned forward, my hands clasped between my knees. "The Red Court has attacked the White, and this conflict is distracting everyone who might help us." I cleared my throat. This would be the first time I had ever asked it for more than just strength. "Is there anything you can do to help us put an end to it?"

"That work is too small for me," it said. "Conflict is your work, practitioner's work. Clear away those who aren't helping us."

"Practitioners are being killed," I said, not sure what the World meant. "Which means they cannot be helping you."

"Killed." It stayed silent for a long time, beginning to thin and drift away around the edges, before solidifying again. "Move some to the outer Modes. Enough for our purposes. I'd help you do that."

Enough to do the necessary traveling and maintaining that the World required of us. Not much doubt now what it meant. I felt suddenly cold. I thought I had sensed a change in the World before, but now I was sure. It had stopped worrying about what were in fact parts of itself no matter how small. When, and why, had this happened?

"We can do our work more quickly and more efficiently the more of us there are." I waited but got no response. "You will return to the way you should be much more quickly."

Another long pause. How much time was passing in my part of the World?

"And how long must we wait for things to happen 'much more quickly'?" It shook its head. "Who knows, perhaps we should do more harm. Perhaps that would encourage people to listen to you. That's what we will do if you delay much longer. Keep yourself safe."

Of course it wanted me to be safe. It had waited who knew how long a time until someone it could communicate with directly appeared. Perhaps it did not have enough time to wait for another one.

Who was "we"?

Eleven

TAMARI

I HAVE NEVER TRAINED so hard in my life as we did for the next few days, not even before taking my first-class exams. Elva thought it would take some time for cannon to be brought from other Modes, especially since they were used more at sea than on land. If they waited to adapt naval weapons, we'd have even more time. We found out quite quickly, however, that the more we trained, the more energy we used, to the point where if we carried on for too long, we became useless. Everywhere you went you'd be likely to find a practitioner napping in the sunshine, or asleep head down on a dining table.

"Will the cannon change when the army moves them into the City?" Donn had assigned himself as my bodyguard, and nothing I said or did changed his mind.

"I don't think so," I said. "Or very little. There are things that evolve so slowly that they don't change much over only two or three Modes."

"So, no clockwork rifles, then." Donn brushed back his mustaches, looking relieved. So was I once he explained. The idea of a machine that would crank out several hundred bullets at a time made me feel sick.

"If the City guard doesn't have a weapon of that kind, then no one does. It's the City that sets the standard for the other Modes, and there are only flintlocks here, you said so yourself."

Suddenly I heard a dreadful whistling sound and Donn rolled me over the wall we had been sitting on, pushing me to the ground and lying on top of me. The whistling was quickly followed by a loud crash and a thud that made the ground and the walls around us tremble. I heard people yelling, screaming, and I tried to get up, but Donn shoved me down again.

"They may have more than one." His lips were so close his mustache tickled my ear.

"More than one *what*?" I said, still struggling to throw him off.

"Cannon."

"I'm supposed to be stopping them," I yelled. When Donn didn't move, I said it again and shoved against him. This time he released me and helped me to my feet. I took a look around and wished I'd stayed down. Another wall just like the one we'd hidden behind had been shattered into pieces. Everywhere people were bleeding or holding what were obviously broken limbs. A leg in a guard's uniform stuck out from a pile of red stone and chips of glass. I started toward it, but Donn pulled me back.

"Your job is stopping the cannon," he reminded me. I wanted to argue, but I followed him to my assigned spot on the curtain wall.

I saw many others running for their positions as I ran to mine. By the time we were organized, and we were able to slow down the attack, a lot of damage had already been done. We managed to get at least a dozen cannonballs to fall into the river, but there were at least as many that we missed. Elva and his deputies—this time I managed to convince Donn to go as well—were everywhere, figuring trajectories and using their enhanced eyesight to point out incoming missiles to the practitioners at the walls. I couldn't take my attention from what I was doing, but I thought there were fewer of us than I remembered from training.

Finally the rate of incoming cannonballs slowed enough for us to take turns and help each other. We were feeling pretty proud of ourselves, though drained and tired, until Elva pointed out something none of us would have noticed.

"We're lucky the Red Court have only enough cannon to attack from this side." He swept off his hat and dusted it against his sleeve. "If more cannon arrive, we'll have real trouble."

More cannon? My hands shook and I was glad to be sitting down. Had Witt lied to me? Had he known that there were already cannon in the City? But in that case, why say anything at all? Without his warning we would have been in far more serious trouble. I was still picking fruitlessly at this thought when I saw Predax weaving his way toward me. He looked just as dirty as I was, and he seemed to be favoring his left leg again. He stepped close and whispered into my ear.

"What? Now?" He nodded, lips pressed together. Just what we needed, an emergency council meeting.

From the look of the other council members, everyone else felt the same. Az Pilcuerta showed signs of hasty washing, but many of the others were like me, covered in dust and streaked with sweat and dirt. I took in the number of clean faces around the table, Ronan Sedges among them. He cleared his throat.

"I don't need to tell any of you the extent of the damage to the southern wall and the danger that damage represents." Ronan looked around, making eye contact with each of us. Was it my imagination, or did he linger longer on me? "I'm calling for volunteers to lead rebuilding teams."

We looked at each other. We were all strong on theory, but usually City engineers were called in when there was actual building to be done.

"Now, I know what you're thinking, we can hardly call in City engineers. So, I'm asking for volunteers to practice the walls back to full strength."

"That's ridiculous." I may have been the only one who spoke up, but everyone had to be thinking the same. "It's all we can do to fend off the attacks. We certainly couldn't maintain building *forrans* at the same time." If we used *forrans* to build walls, or anything else for that matter, we had to leave them running, in a manner of speaking, otherwise the walls would collapse as soon as the practice keeping them up stopped. It didn't work exactly that way with living things, otherwise we wouldn't be able to heal people, but keeping walls up meant a steady drain on the practitioner's energy.

"Even rebuilding wouldn't be enough." Az Pilcuerta's voice trembled with exhaustion. The old woman was near the end of her strength. "It's clear the mundanes won't be satisfied with just cutting us off, as they have been in the past. They'll keep up their attacks until we surrender or they destroy us. You'll see, the damage they've done to the south wall is only the beginning. We have to stop them now, while we still can."

Several of the others spoke up, pointing out that sturdy walls would keep the Red Court at bay while we were working on a more permanent solution. None of this argument felt real. I began to get the creepy feeling that I was watching a play, and from the look on Ronan's face I could guess who had written the lines. Could I be the only one who felt this way?

"I wonder," Nubin Sonsera said, with exaggerated innocence, "if we couldn't use some of the new second- and third-class practitioners to build the walls. Maybe even a few of the more promising apprentices. Many of them can't do the *forrans* for turning away the missiles, and this would be a way for them to help."

"No." Az Pilcuerta cleared her throat and her voice grew stronger as she continued. "Apprentices and students are our future. We can't afford to let them fade by draining them. Without them, there would soon be no White Court."

"We were all apprentices and students once," I said. "And third- and second-class, for that matter. We're not worth more than they are. If it's wrong for us, it's wrong for them."

"With respect, Az, Tamari," Ronan said. "There's no future if we don't survive the present. As it is, I don't see that we have any choice but to use what resources we have. The White Court is more than any one of us."

"Would it be such a tragedy if a few of the lower classes faded? They aren't likely to get much in the way of advancement. We don't need to replace any first-class practitioners, or any council members."

Once again, I had the feeling that someone had written his lines, but I shut my mouth on my automatic protest. I myself had become a council member because Medlyn Tierell had faded.

"I object to the proposal that lesser classes and apprentices be used to build and maintain walls." Az's voice starting to fade. I hoped that wasn't a bad sign.

"I also object," I said. There were one or two others who agreed with us, but of course, we were voted down.

"Then we are in agreement that lesser classes and apprentices be used as discussed," Ronan said once the full vote was taken. "I nominate Practitioner Otwyn to lead the team."

I was almost too shocked to speak. "But I voted against it."

"Exactly what makes you the perfect supervisor. You would be far more careful of them than someone else."

I couldn't argue with that. In fact, I might be so careful that no one would be in danger at all. I was thinking about ways and means of doing this when my attention was drawn back to the meeting by a comment that slid into the discussion so smoothly I knew it was planned.

"If we had the practitioners and apprentices that were lured away by Fenra Lowens, we wouldn't be in this predicament now. We would have more than enough practitioners to spread out the work without fading anyone."

Again, I felt I watched something rehearsed, but they were all such bad actors. What could be the point of blaming Fenra? She didn't arrange the invasion of the Red Court. It was on the tip of my tongue to tell them that there was a way to both contact the others and bring them here quickly, but luckily Ronan spoke before I could make that mistake.

"I think we have to consider what Practitioner Lowens' part has been in all of this." He did his best to sound as though he deeply regretted having to say that. He was a better actor than most of the others.

"You're not suggesting that she arranged for the Red Court to invade us?" I couldn't stay quiet.

"I know that you consider her a friend, Tamari, but there's more to her than being Medlyn Tierell's apprentice. What else do we really know about her?"

"She's involved somehow in Santaron Metenari's disappearance, isn't she? Her and that strange guard who's always with her. Where did *he* come from, by the way, and how does he know so much about the White Court?"

"And who are these new friends of his? Where did they get their weapons?"

"I can't believe this!" Donn was right, I was too innocent to be allowed out on my own. "These people have just finished saving your lives."

"I hope she's satisfied with what she's done," someone said, just as if I hadn't spoken. "The people she's taken away could make a difference between victory and defeat."

What victory? I wondered, rubbing at the pain in my temples. If this conflict didn't stop, there wouldn't be any winners, only losers. "Again, I'd like to point out that without her helping us we'd be much worse off than we are."

"I'm not so sure of that, but let's say that it's true. We can let her solve the problem of the Red Court, and then . . . review her actions."

I didn't bother to ask what that meant.

"She's certainly a bargaining chip, no matter how you look at her."

I stopped paying attention when they dropped the subject of Fenra and began debating whether we should be launching our own projectiles. How had the White Court lasted so long, with people like this in charge? Then I remembered Medlyn Tierell—and surely there had once been more councilors like Az Pilcuerta, sitting back now with her eyes closed. The Court had been run by different people once.

⟜

WITTENSLADE

Witt pulled a nail file out of his sleeve pocket and started smoothing the already perfectly manicured nails of his left hand. He ignored the disgusted mutter from a courtier to his left, the studied silence from everyone else, and finally the affronted tapping of a fingernail on the surface of the table. He didn't look up, or show in any way that he was aware of the other courtiers. Yes, he was being deliberately rude, but there was nothing anyone could do about it except challenge him to a duel, and none of these old farts would dare. He started filing his right hand.

He was fed up with the lot of them—Riva Deneyra especially. He knew his animosity stemmed from her having tricked him, from her thinking he was too stupid to figure her out—and, if he had to be honest, from the knowledge that she wasn't *entirely* wrong. He'd been overconfident, and that was stupid.

"In any case," Descar Parta said, as if someone had just been speaking, "the guard at the City gates report the arrest of two White Court couriers this morning. They're being taken into custody as we speak." *And don't you just love that*, Witt thought.

"Whose custody?" From her tone, Witt would almost think that Riva didn't already know the answer.

"Why, the military, I believe."

"They should be brought here, to us, to answer for their crimes," Valter Denson said.

"Let me remind you that these are prisoners of war, not criminals."

Riva spoke with authority, but she couldn't quite keep a note of laughter from her voice. *She wants to be First Courtier.* She was making Valter out to be an unrealistic fool, and positioning herself as the savior of the day. Witt almost choked on the thought. It would explain everything, from her tricking him onto her side, to her introduction of her pet field commander. Witt slipped his nail file back into his sleeve pocket before anyone could see his hands shaking.

With rage, he told himself. *I'm not frightened, I'm angry.*

"Nevertheless." Riva kept her tone oh so reasonable, this time with no hint of laughter. "We should interrogate them ourselves, not merely rely on what the military decides to tell us." This would be the first open acknowledgment of what Witt had told his friend Col, that the courtiers weren't as well informed as they thought they should be.

"That's precisely why I've instructed the field marshal to have the prisoners brought directly to us." Valter Denson smiled a tight-lipped smile. Maybe Riva wasn't as subtle as she'd thought.

"While we're waiting for them to arrive, we have time to address the resistance we've been getting from the people. Ever since that practitioner woman fixed that rift, support for the White Court is on the rise."

"Oh, come now, Erden." It appeared a crack existed in Riva's cool reasonableness. "You've brought this up before. Exactly why should we care about this so-called support?"

"You wouldn't be so cavalier about it if you'd seen what I've seen." Erden Quant was one of only three courtiers who didn't live in the Red Court proper. "People are starting to say that the White Court would have been helping them more all along if we hadn't been putting obstacles in their way. There are people standing on boxes on street corners, haranguing the passersby, and a great many are stopping to listen."

"The wine traders have handed in a petition. And we've received several requests for aid from the Second and Third Counties—forest fires, flooding, that kind of thing." Nothing pleased Descar Parta more than to see Valter criticized.

"And another one just arrived from the Merchants Guild, exhorting us to do our utmost to force the White Court into submission," Erden hurried to point out.

"So as usual the 'people' are divided in what they want, and we have to decide for them," Valter said. "Nothing new in that."

Witt didn't like the way Valter said "people" as if, somehow, they weren't. He thought he knew exactly what would qualify someone to be "people" in the way Valter meant.

A discreet tap turned everyone's attention to the door. A servant Witt didn't recognize came in without waiting for an invitation.

"Your pardon, First Courtier, an officer insists you are expecting him."

Not just one officer entered after Valter Denson had given his nod, but three. The first one in was Witt's friend Colyardin Antorn Benfett. Col's uniform looked dusty, and Witt now saw that one of the others had a tear in his sleeve. Col's two juniors looked nervous, even as they stood to attention, but Col was as relaxed as if they were all at a garden party.

"First Courtier." Col inclined his head to a precise angle, but didn't acknowledge the rest of the court in any way. Witt remembered that his friend was actually related to two of the other courtiers, and had, in fact, been engaged to the niece of a third before the family lost their money.

"You've brought the prisoners?"

"I regret to say we have not, First Courtier." Col didn't sound at all regretful—courteous, but not regretful. "We were set upon in the streets by an armed mob and were relieved of our prisoners."

"How armed?" Valter's cold tone echoed his disbelief.

"Some with cobblestones, others with swords, and three with pistols." Col's tone was still cool and relaxed. Witt realized that his old friend had his hand thrust into the opening of his jacket, using it as a sling. It wasn't mud on his sleeve, but blood.

"This is outrageous! Explain how it is possible that trained soldiers could be overcome by a mob of shopkeepers and servants."

Now Col turned to face Descar, tilting his head as though he examined a strange specimen. Though the angle was wrong for him to see it, Witt knew that Col had raised his right eyebrow.

"I don't answer to you, Courtier Parta. I answer to Field Commander Vanaldren, and I will explain to him," Col said. "The field commander will tell you what he wishes you to know. And now, if you don't mind . . ." As Col turned to leave, he caught Witt's eye. Witt could have sworn his old friend was laughing.

OLEANDER

At this time of day, even the streets of the Red Court were full of people, mostly workers. The crowd sure hadn't been happy when they caught on to it that the soldiers were escorting two White Court couriers. Maybe the Red Court and the army thought it was a good idea to arrest practitioners—even though these guys were only apprentices—but the people whose lives and homes had been saved when Fenra fixed that crack in the earth felt a little differently. Between the pushing and shoving, the shouts and yelling, thrown cobblestones, and even a couple of pistol shots, it hadn't taken much for Oleander and a couple of his pals to winkle those two couriers right out from under the noses of the soldiers escorting them.

Though he suspected the colonel had been smiling at least a little, even though he had his hand clapped over his upper arm.

The crowd was also real helpful when it came to sneaking the couriers away. The horses went one way, with someone else entirely on their backs; meanwhile, Oleander smuggled the two couriers into another alley, through a tenement where he knew the family (they were having what smelled like braised pork cutlets for dinner and Oleander's stomach rumbled), and across two roofs, along the top of a stone wall where one of the couriers almost slipped off and had to be steadied, and finally down into Witt Volden's garden.

Never mind the guards; security in the Red Court was a joke, Oleander thought, and not for the first time.

"Stay here," he told his charges, pulling them into a rose-lined path. "No one comes this way, not even the gardener." He pointed out how the bushes were full of drying rosehips. "When the hubbub dies down, we'll see about moving you out of the Court."

Luckily the regular staff were well used to seeing him around the place by now, though he got the occasional curled lip from Kendril the footman. Ignoring both Kendril and the cook's assistant (she smiled at him), Oleander ran upstairs, knocked on the door to Witt's rooms, and went in without waiting. He found Arriz in Witt's dressing room, carefully dabbing at a stain on a crimson coat.

"Vinegar," Oleander said when Arriz looked up. "That's what me mum always used."

"You can't fool me, your 'mum' never had any vinegar." Arriz turned his attention back to the sleeve. Holding the material up to the daylight coming in through the window, Arriz tilted his head to one side, raising his eyebrows. "That's got it."

In the meantime, Oleander threw himself into the chair Witt used to put his shoes on. "A chair just to put your shoes on," he'd told his disbelieving friends on the streets, many of whom didn't own any shoes, let alone a chair for putting them on.

Arriz stood, returned the coat to its padded hanger, and opened the closet's right-hand door. "What brings you here just now? Witt's at a council meeting."

"Yeah, well, I think I can guess at least one of the things the council thought they'd be doing but won't be after all. Though his courtiership can have a go on the subject, thanks to me."

"I shudder to think what you might mean by all of that."

"I've brought him someone to talk to. Two someones, in fact."

Arriz froze in the act of shutting the door. Finally he closed it, careful to make no noise, and turned to face Oleander, folding his arms and leaning back against the closet doors. "Someone others also want to interview?"

"Sure, call it an interview if you like. But when it's soldiers taking care of the questioning, I'd call it something else."

"Quit making a mystery, Oleander. Tell me who you've brought here."

"Two White Court couriers arrested when they tried to come in the gate, liberated on their way to the chamber."

"And now?"

"Now in the rose walk that's never used by anyone." Oleander grinned at the look on the valet's face. "They'll be safe there, don't you think?"

"Maybe. But I don't think we will."

FENRA

"We need a different strategy." Elva made sure he had our attention. Randd and I sat with him at the table in our rooms; Lizz stood leaning her shoulders against the door. "Pretty soon now, we'll be running out of everything, including energy enough to defend ourselves."

"There are other missiles they could be using," Randd pointed out. He turned to me. "Would it be harder or easier to ward off fire or gas bombs?"

I had to shrug. "I have no idea. I am not sure the *forrans* we are using can be modified any further, or whether that would make them harder to use."

"How long would it take to make new *forrans*?"

"Anywhere from five minutes to forever," I said.

"We need to do more than defend ourselves, we need to go on the offensive," Randd said. "Carry the battle to them. We've bought ourselves time, now let's use it."

"This sounds like Tamari's description of the last council meeting," I said. "Remember that we do not wish to crush them, just restore a balance of power."

"Tell *them*," Lizz said.

"Up until now we haven't attacked them, and they probably don't think we can. They've had it all their own way." Elva looked at me from under his brows and smiled. "If only we had a way to get to them," he said innocently. "We could destroy the cannons directly."

Stifling a smile, I looked them over. "Who goes with me?"

"You don't need to go," Elva said. "All right, yes, you need to do the moving, but you should stay here. I'll go, I know how to sabotage cannon."

"Should be one of us," Lizz said.

"We have a better chance of not being seen," Randd added. He held up a finger and we all fell silent. I could hear two sets of faint footfalls, growing closer, and someone trying very hard to control her breathing. Elva put his hand on his revolver, as did Lizz. Randd put his on the hilt of his sword, and joined Lizz, each standing to one side of the door.

A single knock, a whisper. "Fenra?"

"Tamari," I said, though all of us recognized her voice. Randd released his sword and opened the door. Donn gave a smiling nod to the others as he came in, but Tamari came straight to me.

"The council is planning treachery," she said. "You've got to get out of here."

"What about needing us to stay alive?" No one but me heard the edge in Elva's voice.

"They're just waiting for the right moment, and then they'll come for you. They don't mind using you—apparently they don't mind using anyone." A look half desperate and half angry flitted over her face. "They talked about your being some kind of bargaining piece with the Red Court."

"And they'll convey this idea how?" Elva asked before I had a chance to.

Tamari frowned and sat down. "They didn't say, but they didn't seem worried about it."

"I was wrong, you do have to go," Elva said, turning to me and putting his hand on my forearm.

"Tamari as well," Donn said. "If Fenra disappears, they'll know who told us, and she won't be safe here." I could see from her face that Tamari had not thought of this. Too innocent to be safe, just as Donn had said.

I nodded. "Someone who knows about cannon must come with us."

"Donn." Elva neither looked nor sounded happy. Nor was I, but I understood. Someone Captain Rennard trusted had to stay behind, and that meant Elva. "I'll have Lizz, Randd, and Predax with me." He looked at me then, his eyes smiling. "We'll try to keep everyone here alive while you carry the war to the enemy."

"Except this isn't a war, and they aren't the enemy."

"The council thinks it is, and they are," Tamari said. "As the meeting ended, we were discussing how to make direct attacks on the Red Court forces. After all, if we can move cannonballs one way, we can move them the other." For the first time, Tamari did not look as though she disagreed with the council. She looked from one face to another, as if to gauge our responses. Finally, she looked at me. She and I were the only two practitioners in the room—for this I could not count Donn and the others. They were soldiers and had a different perspective. Right now the three of them watched us, faces impassive.

"We cannot just kill people." Even setting aside what would best help the World, I had spent the better part of my long life healing people, not killing them. I was not sure I could explain why mundanes were important, but I had to try.

"Would you cut off your right hand?" I asked Tamari.

"Of course not."

"Why not?" I shrugged. "It's not your practitioner's hand."

For a moment her mouth hung open, as she searched for an answer. "It's still a part of me," she said finally.

"Mundanes are the World's right hands." I watched Tamari's face as the idea took hold of her. Her lips pressed together, but she nodded. She did not like it, but she understood.

The others very kindly gave Elva and me a moment to ourselves, or at least as much privacy as they could by turning their backs and pretending they were not in the room. I had cut Elva's hair just a few weeks ago, but it was already long enough to start curling.

"Make sure you come back," Elva whispered into my hair.

"Make sure you stay alive," I whispered back.

"It feels like Medlyn." Tamari ran her hand over the dust-free surface of the round table in the vault, though I knew she did not refer to it. "His office and his workroom don't, not anymore, but this place feels like he could walk in any minute."

"I wish he could." From her pale smile, I could see Tamari felt the same way. "I always feel calm and safe here." My knees suddenly buckled and both Donn and Tamari rushed to take hold of my elbows and lower me into one of the armchairs. Donn went straight to the cupboard and brought out the pitcher, and a basket full of rolls my nose told me were stuffed with thinly sliced cured ham and smoked cheese. And tomato, I noticed as soon as I bit into one.

Donn took one of the rolls for himself and, munching, went to check the rest of the cupboards, closets, and chests for anything else useful.

"This is interesting." He held up the lid of a chest with the hand that didn't hold the roll. His tone drew Tamari across the room. I swallowed the bite I had in my mouth and braced myself to stand up.

"It *is* interesting." Tamari lifted out a complete set of clothing. Linen underclothes, shirt, and cravat, woolen breeches, stockings, shoes . . . a short jacket with a dark blue body and pale blue sleeves. "A servant's livery. An upper-class servant, from the quality of the materials." Tamari looked back into the chest. "There are two more suits of clothing, and I'll bet each of them fits one of us." Tamari handed me the jacket she held.

"The vault has given us a way to stay unnoticed when we enter the City." I turned the jacket over and inspected the bone buttons.

Tamari made a small sound in her throat. "What is it, my dear?" Donn turned with the last bundle of clothes in his hands.

"I've seen these outfits before." Tamari ran her hand along one sleeve. "This is Witt's livery." She turned a white face to me. "I mean, we already knew Medlyn had *forrans* that manipulate space and time, but how can the chest hold Wittenslade Volden's livery?"

I kicked off my shoes and pulled off my stockings. I sighed. "I wish I knew," I said, and not for the first time. Once we were dressed, we checked our packs. Donn carried his extra ammunition and his own clothes. Tamari and I had to be satisfied with food and drink. I also found two blank letters of credit in the bottom of the basket the ham and cheese rolls had been in.

"Too bad we don't have any more guns," Tamari said, watching Donn draw and re-holster his revolver until he was satisfied with its place on his hip. To anyone else it would look like a flintlock pistol.

"I was not sure we could use them," I said. "It seemed safer not to try."

"But what about our practitioner's colors?" Tamari stuck out a leg and frowned.

"Clothing from the vault doesn't change," I reminded her. "Just like things from the New Zone."

When we were ready, I moved a tall, square side table, inlaid with green leather, to a clear spot on the floor and asked the others to join me around it. I selected one of the many models on the shelves, a replica of a fountain in the Red Court, and placed it in the center of the table with the open book of *forrans*. For this I would not be needing the locket.

"I have reached this fountain once before," I told them. "According to Elva, it's within the Red Court precinct itself. Are we ready?" When they both nodded, Donn with a bright smile, Tamari took my practitioner's hand in her right, Donn took hers in his right, and I took his with my right. As soon as the circle closed, I began the *forran*.

I do not usually feel the transition, but this time a sudden wash of icy cold, then burning hot, swept through me, and I had the sensation of tiny insects crawling over my skin. All this took only fragments of seconds to happen, but it seemed much longer when finally my heels and feet struck heavily on a familiar surface. I could smell the sea. I saw nothing, heard nothing. But I smelled the sea. Slow as a sunrise, the darkness around me grew lighter, and I was standing on the beach once more. It was then I realized neither Tamari nor Donn was with me. This time I did not panic, I did not try the locket. I knew why I was here.

Elva

"You'd think these people didn't want to be saved." Randd examined an imaginary spot of rust on his revolver with great attention. Elva knew just how the man felt. Without Fenra here to goad them, the practitioners had stopped training regularly, and fewer and fewer of them came out to stop the cannonballs—which, as Elva and the captain had pointed out more than once, only put a greater strain on the ones who did. A couple of council members agreed with them, Az Pilcuerta among them, but not even the old woman's seniority could stop Ronan Sedges from concentrating his attention on rebuilding and fortifying. True, most of his rebuilt walls resisted the missiles better than the original ones, but Elva could already see they would run out of practitioners before the City's army ran out of ammunition.

"Forget the practitioners." Randd polished the imaginary spot with a cloth. Lizz sat on the window ledge, looking out into the courtyard where the guards, at least, were still training. Elva had moved Lizz, Randd, and himself into the guard barracks after Fenra and the others left. They were probably safe in their assigned rooms, given that he and his deputies were still the White Court's best defense, but Elva knew better than to put his complete trust in the council.

"We're not here for the practitioners," Randd continued. "Well, for Fenra and Tamari, sure. But we're really here for *them*, aren't we?" He pointed into the courtyard with his chin. "The practitioners can look after themselves. It's our job to look after everyone else. As usual." He smiled. Lizz laughed and threw a heel of bread at him, which he caught with his practitioner's hand. He stopped smiling when a noise from the courtyard drew his attention, and he straightened to his feet.

"Boss, come see this." Elva and Randd joined Lizz at the window.

Where there had been the controlled chaos of training, with rows of guards fencing in one corner and others reloading rifles in another, there was now a chaos of people running, calling out, resuming jackets they'd taken off for training, and picking up weapons.

"Let's see what—"

Before Elva could finish, they heard running up the stairs and along the corridor outside their room, and a young guard, honey-blond hair escaping from her braid, appeared panting in the open doorway.

"Sir, if you could come, they're throwing something else now, some kind of smoke—"

Elva cursed and checked the set of his guns as he ran toward the door. "Tell everyone to stay away from the smoke, keep the others back from it. Don't breathe it in, whatever you do. Go!" The girl was halfway down the stairs as Elva shouted the last order after her.

"Smoke bombs, you figure, boss?" Randd pulled a bandanna out of a pocket and tied it around his nose and mouth. It wasn't much, but anything might help.

"We'll be lucky if that's all it is," Elva said as they ran downstairs. "It could be sulfur, it could be—hell, it could be anything." Where were Fenra and the others? How close were they to stopping the cannons?

The courtyards and patios were in uproar, glass from broken windows, clouds of evil-smelling gas, people calling for healers. Some of the few practitioners on the walls left their posts to help, letting in even more of the new missiles that broke open on impact.

Elva heard Captain Rennard calling for those on defense to leave their patients and get back to the walls, but only a few heard him and obeyed. Whether it was the shape of the new missiles—more cylinders than spheres—or the distraction of the screaming, the practitioners were clumsier, letting more and more of the shots through. A practitioner he thought he knew stood up as Elva came near, looking from the wall to the student at her feet, indecision clear on her face. Elva grabbed her by the arm.

"Can you call a wind?" Fenra could, but how general a skill was it?

"Well, yes, but—"

"No buts, do it."

"I can do it, Sheriff." Someone else in apprentice gray. "This way!" he called to someone Elva couldn't see.

Elva turned to Randd and Lizz. "Split up," he said. "There's no one for us to fight. Get everyone indoors and tell them to close their windows."

The three of them separated, picking up guards as they went who helped them move everyone indoors. By this time, even the guards who wouldn't sit with them in the dining halls were happy to follow their orders, particularly when it became obvious that the clouds of gas avoided them. It seemed their ability to go unnoticed worked almost as well on the gas from the bombs as it did on people. For the first time, Elva wished he shared at least one of the particular talents of his deputies.

"Get inside." Randd pulled a coughing guard to his feet. "Don't follow me, get away from the gas."

Everywhere people were taking off cravats and scarves, tying them around their lower faces, others shutting doors and windows, caulking narrow cracks along edges with bits of cloth and crumpled paper. Unfortunately, the White Court never had cold weather, and the buildings were designed to allow for a free passage of air.

As the bombardment slowed, the practiced wind could finally make headway against the smoke. Guards began going hall to hall, tower to tower, checking that windows were closed, that no one was lingering in patios or courtyards. Coughing, Elva pushed yet another window closed as Randd and Lizz joined him.

"What's Fenra doing? Why are those cannons still firing?"

Elva had no answer.

"Boss, we can't hold out much longer." The longest statement he'd ever heard Lizz make.

"Sheriff?" The young woman speaking was a practitioner Elva didn't know. She must have been a recent second- or third-class, since she wasn't helping to defend the walls. "The council's having an emergency session. They'd like you to attend."

"Of course."

The young woman led them away, down a courtyard away from the council chamber.

"We're going the wrong way." If he hadn't needed to watch where he put his feet, Elva would have shut his eyes and shaken his head. He should care about this, should even protest, but he couldn't seem to keep his thoughts straight. He cleared his throat, checked to make sure his guns and sword were handy.

Without turning around, the young practitioner said, "We can't close the windows in the council room. We're using the south lecture hall twelve." When he had first lived here, there had only been three south lecture halls. With so few practitioners, why would they now need twelve?

As they passed into a small square, guards appeared out of nowhere and surrounded them. Randd and Lizz pulled both guns and swords, but Elva held up his hand, not really surprised. What else could they expect from the council?

"No point in killing these people just because some practitioners are scared," he said, smiling at the young woman who had led them into this trap. "Besides, there's nowhere for us to go." As two of the guards stepped forward, hands out to take their weapons, Elva drew his own guns. "On the other hand, maybe we should shoot everyone here and then barricade ourselves in somewhere while we're still armed. What do you think?"

The guards—none of whom Elva knew well—looked at one another. Clearly, they weren't ready to die because of an order from the practitioners' council. The young practitioner, paler than she had been, said, "This way please," in a voice they could barely hear. They followed her to a doorway. Elva let Randd and Lizz enter ahead of him.

"Let me remind you of something." Elva spoke directly to the young practitioner who held the door. She wouldn't meet his eyes, but he didn't need that to know she wasn't very happy about her assignment. "We could prevent you from doing this to us, but not without hurting people." He looked around at the guards. "Maybe even killing them. Please, remember that."

She pressed her lips together, saying nothing, though Elva heard some whispers from the guards behind her. She closed the door and Elva turned to Randd and Lizz.

"Sorry to get you into this."

"Hey, you gotta die sometime."

"You'd think the practitioners would still want our help." Randd holstered his gun and re-sheathed his sword. Lizz snorted. "The gas can affect them just as much as the mundanes."

"Don't count on it," Elva said. "I think it's far more likely that they'll surrender, figuring that they can still get good terms, before too much more damage is done."

"So where does that leave us?"

"Just as you said, we all have to die sometime." Elva put a fist up to his mouth as he started to cough again.

TAMARI

"Where's Fenra?"

Under other circumstances, Donn's shocked face and the way he spun around looking for someone who wasn't there would have been funny. But I didn't feel like laughing, not one little bit.

I checked my clothes, relieved when I saw that Fenra had been right, they hadn't changed to practitioner's colors. Looking around, how-ever, it was clear we weren't anywhere near a fountain, or a courtyard, or any place in the Red Court, or the City for that matter. It had been a while since I traveled on it, but I knew the Road when I saw it. Though I'd never seen it like this, pavement cracked, with the mortar between the stones almost worn away; weeds, and in some spots baby trees growing up in the drainage ditches, which weren't properly lined with rock and gravel. "I have no idea what Mode this is," I said. I looked around again, but the sight of more trees and more underbrush didn't tell me anything. Since when had the Road been in this kind of shape?

"I take it we're not where we expected to be." Donn now had his revolver in his practitioner's hand and his sword in his right. Some-how, he managed to keep an eye on the Road in both directions, and the forest around us, all at the same time.

"Not even close."

Donn nodded. "Elva's gonna be very annoyed with me," he said. "I am supposed to be keeping the two of you safe, and I've already lost one of you." He looked up and down the Road again. At the moment there was no traffic, but how long would that last? "What now?"

I looked up and down the Road myself. "Maybe we should look for help."

Donn sheathed his sword, but kept his revolver in his hand. "Which way?"

I shrugged, wracking my brain for more details—any details—that might give me an answer. "It's been so long since I've been out on the

Road, I can't be sure what's ahead, and what's behind." Was Fenra's village around here someplace? If we were anywhere near, we'd get more than just help from the villagers. There were practitioners there. I shrugged, and heard the crackle of paper coming from an inner pocket. At least the letters of credit had come along with us. "Let's start walking," I said, picking out one direction. "Wherever we end up, we'll be able to buy or hire some transportation."

Donn helped me crawl out of the drainage ditch on the side of the Road. We had only been walking an hour or so—the sun hadn't even moved in the sky—when suddenly the earth started moving under our feet, and a great crack, maybe three feet wide, opened in the Road. If it weren't for Donn, I would have fallen into the crack myself, instead of just rolling into the ditch.

"What was that?"

"An earthquake," Donn said. "Don't you have them here?" When he was satisfied that I could stand by myself, he let me go. "No matter, even back home they don't happen everywhere. Lots of people have never experienced one."

"That's not it," I said, looking around at the fields beside the Road. Was something dangerous going to come out of nowhere and kill us? "Nothing like this happens to the Road. If there's anything wrong, the couriers fix it, or report back to the Court. There isn't any place practitioners haven't been—or there didn't used to be, anyway." I thought about what Fenra had told me. How long had it been since practitioners stopped traveling regularly? If things were this bad here, who knew what was happening in the Modes once you got away from the Road?

We continued walking, hopefully toward the village, but I found myself putting my feet down gently, softly, as if I might set off another of these earthquakes if I wasn't careful.

✦

FENRA

At first, I thought it was the same beach as usual, but after I turned my back on the wind that blew off the water, I saw subtle differences. More sand among the pebbles, for one thing, and fewer shells along the highwater mark. The wind brought the smell of salt, vegetation, and something burning. I spun around when I heard the sound behind me, took two steps before I knew it, and sat down without really meaning to.

"Where are the others?"

"You'll see them again." The stiff shrug was not completely unexpected, and did nothing to reassure me.

I shivered, my skin suddenly like ice. My hands and feet seemed to belong to someone else, and my head was full of buzzing. Even the sounds of the sea were somehow faint and far away. *Good thing I am already sitting down*, I thought. Under similar circumstances I had once asked the World where Elva was, and it had told me he was safe. Why had it not given me the same answer now? The World had not been so indifferent when I first knew it. Nor had there been earth seizures, nor storms, nor floods. Why were things getting so much worse?

Finally, I felt I had control enough to speak. "Why am I here now?" *And how did I get here?* This made the second time that the World had stopped me when I was moving from the vault using the models. I had always thought the vaults were spaces apart from anything else, but if the World could interfere with mine . . . or was it just me? I was definitely a part of the World, and if the vault was part of me . . . My head started to ache.

"Why isn't this working? We've given you time, what are you doing?"

Impatience? "It's been hardly any time at all," I said, starting to lose my own patience. "The earth seizures, the floods, they're interfering, distracting people who should be helping us. Is there any way you could help with them? Control some of it? Meditation?" I added, hoping it would understand me.

It made a slashing motion with its hand. "That was to remind you all what's at stake, and who is in charge."

It did it on purpose. Everything around me suddenly felt far away, as if I were surrounded by nothing but space. The seizures weren't part of its illness, I thought as soon as my brain started working again. Of *course* this being did not feel like the World as I first knew it. This was *not* the World as I first knew it. And suddenly, I knew what had changed. I knew where I had encountered these attitudes before. The Godstone. This was the World with the Godstone restored. With the

Godstone's knowledge, its experiences, its self-absorption and arrogance. The Godstone had brought with it impatience and indifference, making the World less warm, more pragmatic, more cruel, more ruthless. No one—including the World itself, had expected any change like this.

I could not think of anything to say, now that I knew what I was talking to. It began to pace with its hands behind its back. More confirmation—the World had never done anything so human looking.

"First the White Court wouldn't help you, and now the Red Court is distracting it from listening to you." It stopped pacing and faced me.

"We are working toward a solution," I said. "I am certain that—"

"No." More head shaking. "We see the answer. Let them destroy each other. You'll be able to do more once these stupid ones have cleared themselves out of the way."

"You are wrong." I clasped my hands to stop their shaking. This sounded like political strategy to me. All that time it was separated from the World, all that time it thought itself to be Xandra Albainil, the Godstone had been learning things, human things. The cold practical perspective that was Xandra's, the arrogant confidence in its own judgment.

"Every person who dies or is injured is part of you." Perhaps I could appeal to its sense of self-preservation.

Nodding. "Perhaps so. But cutting away the detritus will restore me much faster. A new start, a new Court, with you in charge. You will return, help them destroy each other." Had this been where it wanted to go all along? Was it—had it created the conflict in the first place? Just then I could not know what to think.

"The Courts aren't a bad tooth you need to pull," I said. How was I going to persuade it to listen to me? Individuals weren't important to the World, any more than individual skin cells were important to me, but these were people to me, not skin cells. Somehow, I had to save them.

"Really? Pruning to allow for new growth certainly feels like the right thing to do."

"It isn't always," I pointed out. "Some plants shouldn't be pruned at all, and others can be killed by pruning in the wrong way. Or at the wrong time."

It stood perfectly still. "That's true," it said finally. "You're the healer, that's why we chose you. But this is still taking so long." Its movements told me nothing about how it felt. The Godstone hadn't brought the concept of body language with it.

"Wait." I had an idea. "I could not get practitioners to move before, when they were too comfortable in the White Court, but they are not so comfortable now."

The World looked at me the way a teacher, still waiting for the correct answer, looks at a pupil.

"Some practitioners and apprentices have already moved, those who were willing to listen to me. I will be able to persuade the others to relocate now that the White Court is no longer an impenetrable refuge." I had no idea if that was true, but neither did the World. "Once I move them away, they will have to travel, just as you want them to do. Give me more time, and I can do this with no more loss of life."

"Hmm. It shouldn't be too difficult to move even the unwilling ones." It thought more. "Very well. You've helped me before, so I will give you some time, but don't take too long."

And then the beach was empty, and I stood alone, shivering from more than the breeze.

Did I really think I would find anyone who would now be willing to move? Perhaps, but not enough, and not fast enough. All I had done was buy time to end the conflict, before the World ended the Courts.

Twelve

FENRA

E LVA AND I had once used the model of a bridge to move to another Mode, but the World had wanted to speak to me, so it
had split us up, sending Elva to the bridge, and bringing me to
this beach. That time, when the World was finished with me, it sent
me to join Elva. But this time when it disappeared, I still stood alone
on the multi-colored pebbles, with the water still almost as pewter as
the sky. Until that moment I had not worried about Tamari and Donn,
thinking the World had sent them to the fountain in the Red Court,
but if it did not send me after them, how could I be sure?

I wasted no more time, but used the locket to return to the vault,
and the model fountain to enter the Red Court. Luck was not with me.
It was full daylight, perhaps midday, not late evening as I expected. The
sides of the shallow bowl forming the base of the fountain were slick
with mold and algae, so I lost my footing immediately and landed hard
on my backside in warm, slimy water. Worst, the splash brought guards
running toward me as I slipped and staggered my way to the edge.

Misdirection, I thought.

"Did you see them?" I scanned the square around us, not looking
directly at the guards at all. "They pushed me in. Little practiced brats,
they ran away laughing, but they won't be when I catch up with them."
I stood on my toes to peer around the taller of the two guards. I almost
slipped again.

The shorter guard took my arm as I sat on the rim of the bowl and
swung my legs over. She helped me to my feet, made a motion as if she
was going to brush me off, hesitated when she saw just how slimy I
was, and stepped back.

"Did you get a good look at them?" the taller guard asked.

Hah. If I am a victim, I cannot be a criminal. "I was in before I noticed them, and then they ran off that way." I pointed toward the gate. "Boys, I would say, but I cannot tell you much more." I paused, but neither of them mentioned any others who had also fallen in the fountain today, so where *had* Tamari and Donn gone? I took off my cravat and tried to wring water out of it. I looked down at myself with perfectly genuine disgust. If the Red Court wasn't going to use the fountain, they should have the good sense to empty it.

"I've been telling them for months they should drain this stupid thing," the shorter guard said to the taller, who nodded with a look that said he had, in fact, heard her say that before. More important, they were no longer concerned about who I was, and how I had arrived there.

"That's Courtier Camdin Volden's livery, isn't it?" the female guard said. How she could tell what the colors were under the wet and the slime was more than I could guess.

"It's only my second day." I put a little trembling into my voice. "I got turned around and was coming across to ask you for directions when those—" Shaking my head, I took off my shoes one at a time and shook water out of them.

"No harm done," the man said. "Unless the courtier's going to dock you for ruining a set of clothing. Take that street there." He turned away, pointing, and proceeded to give me detailed directions on how to reach Witt Volden's house.

I thanked them for their help and set off in the direction I'd been given as briskly as I could considering the state of my shoes and stockings. I waited until I was out of sight to rub my palms together and murmur the simple drying *forran* we were all taught as students. The last time I had used it had been to dry off one of Ione Miller's helpers who had fallen into the mill pond. My clothes were still wrinkled and dirty, and brought me more than a few sidelong looks, but at least I no longer squished.

WITTENSLADE

"Let me guess, you've some kind of wager going, don't you?" Colyardin Antorn Benfett asked when he found Witt beside the looming mechanism of the ghost bridge, looking across the ravine. Witt couldn't be sure without a spyglass, but both the wall and the towers of the White Court looked rougher around the edges, as if they'd taken some damage from the cannons. Col would surely have asked anyone else to explain his continuing interest, but luckily, Witt already had a reputation for being frivolous and easily bored.

He flicked open his fan. "Now you're going to tell me how inappropriate it is to wager on people's lives."

"Why? Clearly you already know, and it hasn't stopped you. Now tell me, what's the wager, and how can I get in on it?" Col leaned against the base of the ghost bridge, ankles and arms crossed.

Witt's laughter was genuine. "First tell me what's on for this morning. It might have some bearing on the bet," he added when Col hesitated.

"Ah! Well, you might find this interesting in any case. Until now we've been firing regular cannonballs—five-, ten-, and fifteen-pound shot." Col's hands moved around each other, miming spheres of different sizes. "They cause damage on impact—when they can get through, that is. The practitioners are using some kind of destabilizers—maybe projectiles too small to see—to push most of our cannonballs aside, or into the river." He waved his hand at the Garro below them. "These new ones we're trying now are an entirely different shape, so, first, it could take them a while to recalibrate, and second, these will explode on impact, releasing sulfur gas." Col spread his hands and wiggled his fingers, showing how the gas would disperse.

"Sulfur gas? But surely that's—"

"Poisonous? Don't look at me like that, Witt. The field commander's willing to use anything we can to end this as quickly as possible." Col shrugged. "At least if this convinces them to surrender, we won't have to starve them out. That would kill a lot more. We've got a batch ready to go, and we're preparing another now."

Witt took his eyeglass out of his waistcoat pocket, unfolded it, and peered through it to examine the cannon nearest them, trying to give himself time to control his face, and his feelings. He knew Col well enough to know he wasn't happy about what he was saying. Witt needed to go home right now, send for Oleander, and get this new information to Tamari as soon as he could. If they were warned and ready, they might be able to defend themselves.

But he couldn't just rush off and leave Col standing here. He had to keep his cover as a bored, curious courtier or he would never learn anything else. Col wanted in on the imaginary bet. Witt had to pretend there really was a wager, and he could think of exactly the right person to help him do that. It would help his cover, give him a reason to leave right now, and the perfect—and credible—excuse for returning and exercising his curiosity.

"I'll have to clear it with the others." Witt tapped his chin with his eyeglass. "I'm sure there won't be a problem, but we agreed not to include anyone else in the wager without checking."

Col cocked his thumb and "shot" Witt with his index finger. "See that you do and get back to me soon."

Witt left Col to resume his own duties and swung himself into his curricle. Though every fiber urged him to get home as soon as possible, he told Arriz, "We'll have to stop by Nevin Hamm's." He explained to Arriz as they navigated the narrow streets around the bridgehead and headed uphill toward the more moneyed part of the City and the Red Court. By the time they got to Nevin's house, Arriz had helped him refine his story.

"Let me out here," his valet said as they reached the right corner. "I can get home faster on foot, and I'll send for Oleander right away." Witt slowed down and Arriz hopped out, running down the main street while Witt turned the corner. He would have preferred that Oleander stay with him, but the boy had refused, claiming he had to be free to move around.

When he reached his friend's house, he secured the reins, jumped out of the curricle, and used the brass knocker vigorously. When the doors opened, he entered without waiting to be invited, patting the servant on the shoulder as he passed. He'd been in and out of this house for years, and the servants knew him.

"I know he's still asleep," he told the man. "I'll run up and wake him myself." Once upstairs he flung open the double doors to Nevin's suite, did the same to the bedroom doors, crossed the carpeted room, and yanked aside the heavy velvet curtains.

A groan came from the bed.

"By the Maker's balls, Edsen, I swear I'm going to fire you for this." The voice was little more than a croak.

"Isn't Edsen," Witt said, throwing himself into the chair that stood by the bedside and propping his feet on the edge of the mattress. His friend murmured something into his pillow that long acquaintance allowed Witt to understand.

"It's *not* that early in the morning, and besides that, it's *never* too early to collect on a bet." Another murmur. "That's right, you *don't* owe me money, but I *do* owe you."

That brought his friend's head up off the pillow. "You do?"

"'Course I do, from last night. Don't you remember?" Witt counted on Nevin remembering nothing whatsoever about most of the night before. Lately that was more likely than not.

"It's starting to come back to me." Nevin propped himself up on his elbows and squinted at Witt through sleep-fogged eyes. "Remind me of the details."

"We were betting on how observant people were. You remember, Guidon bet you that you couldn't remember how many horses there are in Chief Courtier Fennella's statue, and you said—"

"Trick question." Edsen sat up and rubbed at his eyes. "Lions, not horses."

"Exactly, so we made him pay up. And then I bet you there are seven cannons along the edge of the Garro River, and you said there were only six."

Nevin lowered his hands. "And how many are there?"

"Six."

"Huh." Nevin twisted his face and looked uncertain.

"Of course, if you don't think I owe you any money . . ."

"Now, now, not so hasty." Nevin threw off his covers, revealing a silk nightshirt whose strong yellow color did nothing for his complexion. Witt tossed him the dressing gown draped across the back of the chair. "Sure, I remember. It was five hundred, wasn't it?"

"Well, I was going to say three, but since you remember so exactly . . ." Witt shrugged. "I should have known better," he added. "You've been winning bets on the setup of the encampment all week."

Nevin managed to look smug. "And don't you forget it."

Witt paid his friend, refused the offer of breakfast on the grounds that he had an assignation, and left as quickly as he could.

"There's a servant none of us know waiting for you, Dom, another of these ones who says she needs to speak to you in person. I put her in the kitchen."

"She'll have to wait—hold it, who is she from?"

"Uh, she's wearing our livery, Dom, that's why I thought we should keep her until you got back."

Witt paused, his foot already on the staircase. "Our livery? It's not Oleander?"

"No, Dom, this is an older woman—well, younger than me, but older than the boy."

"Oleander's not here yet? Fine, fine, tell the woman to come up. What is it?" he added when the footman didn't go.

"She looks like she's been sleeping in her clothes, Dom. Or as though she put them on wet and wore them until they dried."

"Give her fresh clothing, then, if you think I'll be offended by her appearance, but be quick." Honestly, sometimes Witt wondered what some of his servants would do without him. Most, he knew, were superbly competent and capable people, but in every household, there were always a few . . .

The woman who was shown into his sitting room five minutes later was fully as tall as he was, slim, with fine bones, dark skin, and tightly curled black hair. He had never seen her before in his life, but there was no doubt about the livery. The question was, who was she, and how did she get a set? There were enormous fines for any tailors or cloth merchants who copied either the colors or fabrics of any courtier's house.

"Good afternoon, Courtier Camdin Volden." Her voice was well modulated, her accent faintly Ibanian, but overlaid with a great deal of education. That didn't mean she wasn't a servant, but still didn't explain what she was doing in his livery.

"My name is Fenra Lowens," she said after sitting down in the chair he offered her—definitely no one's servant, since a real one wouldn't have sat down. "You have been using my stationery."

Witt stood momentarily speechless. "*Practitioner* Lowens?"

"Have Tamari Otwyn and Donn Keeshode reached you?"

❦

Fenra

It was too early to be worried, but I caught myself rubbing my palms together more than once. I wished I could think of a *forran* that would tell me where they were. Once more I promised myself that I would take the time to read through Medlyn's book. If we lived long enough.

Time worked differently on the beach, and even if Tamari and Donn had arrived before me, it might have taken them longer to find Volden's house. Tamari likely had not been in the Red Court for years—if ever—and Donn had never been here at all. *I will not worry yet*, I thought. I clasped my hands together on the table in front of me and tried not to think of them.

Which meant I had leisure to worry about the poison gas. Tamari and Donn were most likely safe, but what about the others? What about Elva?

We could do nothing until Oleander came with the scroll.

"Are you sure you won't accept a change of clothing?" Witt asked me for the second time after we had been waiting in silence no more than a few minutes. "Even a clean livery, if you won't take something of mine?"

"Thank you, but I am sure. It wouldn't be a good idea for everyone to know you are hiding a practitioner in your house."

"But how is anyone to know you're not a servant, or a friend of mine?"

His lips twisted to one side, he seemed really concerned, as if the state of my clothes genuinely distressed him. "Trust me, they will know."

He turned away and pulled at a bell cord next to the door. Another young man, dressed in the same colors but in much better fabrics than mine, appeared immediately at the door.

"Arriz Abalaga, my valet," Witt said as soon as the man shut the door behind him. "Arriz, this is Practitioner Lowens—yes, Oleander's Practitioner Lowens. While we're waiting, can you help her look less as though she's been dragged through a hedge backward? And before you ask, no, she can't change her clothes."

It startled me, but I smiled when, other than raised eyebrows, the valet did not react to my introduction. Apparently, he was not concerned that Witt was now harboring practitioners in the house. Later I might learn the two men could not be trusted, but at that moment I had very little choice but to accept their help.

"My dear, you look just as though you'd fallen into a stagnant pond and dried off all anyhow." Arriz leaned closer and took a sniff. "Smells like that too."

Witt took a step toward us, face concerned, but relaxed when I held up one hand. My smile felt stiff. "I know the *forran* for drying things out," I said to Arriz. "The theory, I think you call it. But the wrinkles and the smell I cannot do much about."

Arriz pulled a brush out of nowhere and frowned as he applied it to my right shoulder. "What do you generally do with soiled clothing, then?"

It was my turn to lift my eyebrows. "Wash them if I am at home, give them to the laundry if I am not."

"So why do you know the, uh, the *forran* for drying clothes?" Arriz took my right wrist in cool fingers and brushed vigorously at my sleeve. I coughed.

"A person who has been rescued from a river needs to be dry and warm as soon as possible, and someone with a bad fever but only one set of clothing or bed linens needs them to be dried." Arriz signaled me to turn and lift my practitioner's arm.

"You're a healer, then? Have you worked here in the City?"

I could tell Witt had a particular reason for asking, but though I waited, he said nothing more. "I have been working in the outer counties ever since leaving the White Court." I remembered just in time to use the mundanes' word for Modes.

"Lift both arms and shut your eyes." Arriz put down his brush and picked up an atomizer from a sideboard. Once I had my eyes shut, I felt a soft mist on my exposed skin, and smelled carnations.

"Open your eyes. Now, sit down here and let me do something with your hair."

I appreciated being clean, but I was still anxious about Tamari and Donn. "What if they have been arrested?" I said aloud without thinking.

"We'd know, wouldn't we, Arriz?"

"Definitely. Servants always know everything. You should remember that, Practitioner Lowens."

"Call me Fenra," I said. "How long do we wait for them to arrive before we get to work?"

"Excuse me?"

"We have to stop the cannons. People are dying."

Just at that moment, another servant opened the door. "Oleander, as you requested, Dom."

"Excellent, send him up." Witt turned to Arriz. "Do you think he's hungry?"

"The odds are good." Arriz began to braid my hair, starting at my forehead. It felt strange, but very secure.

"Sandwiches, tea, and cream biscuits, please."

Witt waited until the footman left before turning back to me. "Oleander divides his time between this house and another, and I think we're both feeding him three meals a day. And tea."

"He can certainly eat," I said. I had once seen four meat pies disappear so quickly the boy might have used a *forran* on them.

Moments later we heard running feet coming up the stairs and along the corridor toward us. Oleander appeared, panting, his smile fading when he saw me. He liked me, but it was Elva he loved. He managed to put a grin back on his face as he bowed and pulled the letter out of the front of his tunic.

"Good to see you, Fenra," he said, as he handed it to me.

"And you. The sheriff was well the last time I saw him." Oleander would not ask, but of course he wanted to know. I scanned over the lines on the paper.

Witt had been surprised when Oleander gave me the scroll. "How is it you can read that?" he said. "Your name isn't on it."

"It's my *forran*," I said without looking up. I sat down in the nearest chair.

"There's already been a gas attack?" I asked Witt.

"What? Col didn't tell me anything like that—" He pressed his lips together. Whoever this Col was, Witt was not happy with him.

"I must go," I said, standing up. "It's Elva," I told Oleander. He grabbed the wrist of my practitioner's hand.

"Take me with you," he said.

"You can't go," Witt said at the same time.

"My . . . friend is dying," I told them.

"What about the gas bombs?" Witt said. "How many more will die because you don't stay to stop them?"

"There is no larger thing," I said.

"Which means what, exactly?"

I pulled the locket free of my shirt without answering. I had chosen Elva once before, and it had been the right thing to do. I had to hope it still was.

TAMARI

We hadn't gone far before I started to worry. Should we have gone the other way? Were we wasting valuable time? We needed horses. Walking could take us weeks to get back to the City . . . unless, of course, we commandeered the horse I could hear heading our way. Where there was one horse, there might be two.

Donn and I stepped off to one side of the Road, signaling the rider as soon as he got close enough to see us clearly. For a second, I thought he wasn't going to stop, and I couldn't believe it until I remembered that for the first time in years I wasn't wearing practitioner's colors.

"I can't stop," he said, even though he just had. "I'm on White Court business." He wasn't even looking directly at me, but over our heads toward, maybe, Fenra's village. It felt so strange not to be acknowledged. Did all practitioners treat mundanes this way? Did I? Clothes or no clothes, he should have recognized me.

"Hadler Pensalyn. Look at me more carefully." I saw his eyes widen and his brows rise.

"Practitioner Otwyn? How . . . ?"

"No time for that now. Where are you going?" And what, now that I thought about it, were the other students and apprentices who were caught outside the White Court doing right now?

"To Fenra Lowens' village." The boy dismounted, holding the reins in both hands. "The White Court is under siege, and they need to know."

"When did you leave the City?" Donn put in.

A momentary crimping of the lips. "I never reached it; I turned back when I saw the troops. There wasn't anything I could do," the boy added, his eyes shiny. "I carry messages and fix bad spots on the road—that's all. I've only been a full apprentice a couple of weeks . . ."

Donn put his practitioner's hand on the boy's shoulder and gave him a little shake. "You did the right thing. Look at me." Donn waited until Hadler looked up before continuing. "What would getting caught have done for anyone?" I could tell that some practice was happening between Donn and Hadler. I could feel it, almost see it, a glow linking them. Not a *forran* exactly, but when it finished Hadler stood a little straighter, with half a smile on his face. I'd have to get Donn to teach me how to do that.

"Are we far from the village?" I asked.

"No, maybe half an hour's walk. Did you want to take Baanith?"

Donn shook his head before I could answer. "She's already tired," he said. "And even if we switch off, she'll still be carrying both of us."

I hesitated for a second, but Donn was right, we couldn't both ride. "You go on," I told Hadler. "Tell them we're right behind you."

Hadler looked from Donn to me and back again, his pinched look coming back. "Should I tell them? About the Court, I mean?"

Now it was my turn to look at Donn.

"If you can, sure," he said to Hadler. "If not, don't worry, we'll tell them."

It really was only a half hour or so until we reached the village, but I felt so hot and so tired, it seemed to take all morning. I don't know what Hadler told them, but quite a large group of people were waiting for us when we finally reached the center of the village, and they didn't look happy to see us. Almost everyone there looked like they hadn't slept in days. Their clothes were dirty and torn, and there was a smell of dank, stagnant water everywhere. The open area couldn't be called a square, exactly; it wasn't paved except in a couple of spots where stones had been let into the ground, probably where soft spots recurred when it rained. What was most impressive, however, was the enormous mill—river-stone foundation, half-sawn logs above. A stocky woman with graying hair, muscular arms crossed, waited for us a pace or two in front of the rest. Just at her shoulder was a much larger man, even more muscular if it was possible.

The person who really caught my eye, however, was the middle-sized man with the sharp nose and the wispy brown hair, dressed in black sandals, yellow leggings, and a crimson tunic over a white undertunic. Practitioner's colors. He saw me studying him and came forward, his right hand out for shaking.

"Practitioner Otwyn, you probably won't remember me." His grip was firm and dry. "Tux Gradon, second class. We have met, but . . ."

"Of course." I wasn't lying, I really did remember him. He smiled.

The woman came forward then, her hand outstretched. "Ione Miller," she said. "I'm the headman here. This is Betrex Smith. Your boy didn't want to tell us anything, but he seems pretty spooked. What in the name of the Maker's mother is going on?"

It took the rest of the afternoon and into the evening to explain and describe everything that had happened since Fenra had left them. Fortunately, we were able to do it sitting down, and we could eat while we talked.

For a few minutes after we finished, the only sound was Donn and me chewing and swallowing. Tux had gone all pale, and somehow looked more serious than he had before. Ione Miller and Betrex Smith sat watching each other, as if they were communicating between themselves silently. Finally, she spoke.

"I want to help you," she said. "But I don't see how. No, Tux," she said when he began to speak. "We can't spare you, or any of the others, for that matter." She turned back to me and gestured around us with a trembling hand. "We've had a flood—for no reason we can make out—and we're still cleaning up—"

"There's people missing," one of the others put in. "And animals."

"An important part of the mill was broken, and it'll take Betrex here who knows how long to fix it. That's not even counting the animals acting strange—rabbits trying to bite people, chickens flying—"

"And there's things that come out of the forest," the smith put in. "People who've been dead for months, or years. We lost an adult and a child before Tux figured out what was going on and dealt with it. We need him here."

Fetches, I thought. I wanted to argue with them, but I couldn't. The village needed Tux more than I did. It was Fenra Lowens I needed. My stomach clenched and I put down the biscuit I had in my hand without biting into it. Where was she? My mind was blank, but fortunately, I wasn't in this alone.

"Can you give us horses?" Donn asked.

Hadler's horse had ridden most of the way to the City and back again, so the villagers gave us two others, very sturdy, a gray and a black, just a size up from ponies, really. The useful kind, good for practically anything from plowing to carrying practitioners. I wasn't worried—the horses would change as we crossed through the Modes. Donn, however, checked them over thoroughly, looking at their teeth, and examining hooves, and running his hands over their legs. I had no idea what he was looking for, but eventually he smiled and nodded to the miller.

"They're in fine shape," he said. "Thank you." I felt a little guilty that I hadn't thought to thank her myself.

"They're sturdy," she said, "but mind you don't ride them too hard. People tend to think they're stronger than they look—and they'd be right—but they've a breaking point like anyone else."

"Let me see what I can do about that." Donn stroked down the head of the gray pony, the one nearest him. Donn was a tall man, and he had to lower his head a little for their foreheads to rest against each other.

Again, I felt that some practice was happening, but beyond the same faint glow I'd already seen, I still couldn't see anything. I reached out and put the index finger of my practitioner's hand on the back of Donn's wrist. I could feel a flow of energy going back and forth between him and the horse. When he finished, he turned and did the same with the other horse.

"I've shared some of my own magic with each horse," he said when we asked him. "Making them—like me—a little stronger, a little faster. It just increases their natural stamina, strength, and speed."

"Can you do that with any horse?" The smith had a speculative look.

"It doesn't last." Donn's smile said he'd heard this question before. "If you do it too often, they'll forget that it fades away, and they'll hurt themselves trying to do something they can't do without the magic."

"He means the practice," I said, in answer to the miller's and the smith's puzzled looks.

What these beasts could do, I found out once we were back on the Road, was trot along, not very fast maybe, but for hours and hours. In the end I fell asleep in my saddle, only waking up when Donn nudged my knee with his.

"What?" The light told me we had ridden through the night, and my mouth was dry.

"The horses stopped by themselves." He hopped off his mount, and I lowered myself a bit more carefully, my muscles stiff and my thighs sore. When I joined Donn in front of the horses, I covered my mouth with my practitioner's hand, to stop all the air from leaving my body.

There was no Road.

FENRA

"Fenra!"

Even as I spun around, Predax pulled me into a hug. I could feel him trembling.

"Where is Elva?"

"I've never been so happy to see anyone in my life." He leaned his forehead into my shoulder.

"*Elva.*" He would tremble a good deal more if he did not take me to Elva *now*.

"In the guard barracks," he told me over his shoulder as he took my right hand and led me out of Tamari's office. A stab of guilt soured my stomach. That formless guilt you feel when your head knows you are not culpable of anything, but your guts aren't so sure.

"They tried to lock him up, Randd and Lizz too, but the guard wouldn't let them and they had to let them go."

Predax continued to toss words at me as we ran, telling me as much as he could of what had happened here in the White Court. I saw nothing as we went, just a blur of patios, and colored tiles, and greenery and splashing water. Finally, we ran through the gateway to the barracks.

From further down a short corridor, I could hear someone coughing. I followed Predax into the room and stopped in my tracks. Elva lay on his side, coughing into a basin held by Lizz. She looked up as I knelt beside her. I smoothed Elva's hair back off his forehead. His skin felt clammy, and his eyes took longer than I liked to focus and recognize me.

"Fenra." Voice weak, he reached for my arm. "Everything . . . falling apart . . . take deputies and go."

I held up a finger to stifle Lizz's protests. Of *course* none of them wanted to leave him. I did not want to leave him. Nor anyone else, for that matter. "Hold him up." I waited until Lizz had him braced against her shoulder before I took Elva's face between my hands.

"No time," he whispered.

"Nothing but time," I said. I concentrated. I could feel the damage the gas had done, his lungs filling with liquid, struggling to get oxygen out into his body, his pulse slowing, his heart laboring as fluids gathered around it. Each part trying its best to do its job, and in doing so, further damaging other parts. I leaned over his body and began to breathe into his mouth.

I heard Lizz say "Randd" in a tone that any other time would have me looking around for the danger, but at that moment, nothing distracted me from Elva. First, I tried the *forran* I always used to fix Arlyn's lowness—it pervaded the whole body, and I knew it so well I could modify it on the fly.

I suppose I should not have been surprised when I heard waves moving over the beach and smelled the sea. My heart rose into my throat and I almost lost my concentration. Just in time, I realized that this wasn't the beach where I met with the World, but the gentle sandy beach I associated with leveling Arlyn. I was not surprised to find that Lizz had come with us. She was still holding Elva up against her shoulder, which meant she touched me through Elva. What did surprise me was that Randd was also with us, his hand on Lizz's shoulder. I pushed these thoughts away. I had no time to consider how this had happened, nor what it could mean.

Randd knelt to help Lizz support Elva's other side. I did not notice until afterward that they were propping him against what I thought of as Arlyn's rock. Elva was breathing better now, despite the damp air moving slowly through his lungs. But he was not yet out of danger. I sat back on my heels and rubbed my face with trembling hands. I would have trouble standing up. I needed sleep, but Elva needed me.

"Here." Lizz held out her practitioner's hand.

"We can lend you our strength," Randd said, taking hold of my upper arm.

"I do not think I know—"

"Not our first rodeo. Relax, give it a try." Lizz took a grip on my right arm, and Randd on my left.

For a moment I felt a faint sizzle run up and down my body, but it disappeared so quickly I could not be sure it had been there in the first place. Lizz began to hum. I focused on my pattern, thinking that I could somehow enfold the others into it. Instead, two glowing auras appeared, so bright as to stun me. There might have been patterns within them, crystalline and chaotic, not precise and delicate like mine.

"Focus," Randd said in my ear.

It seemed our practices knew each other, their differences unimportant, dancing and weaving patterns and light through, and over. Lizz, and then Randd, copied bits of my pattern, making it larger, brighter, and multicolored. Lizz began to sing aloud, until all three of us glowed intensely, colors almost blinding. I saw tiny sections of my own pattern in their auras, repeating themselves in the glow that surrounded us all, resembling nothing more than a crazy quilt, put together out of scraps of cloth—some printed, some plain—and snips of threads, beads, and buttons.

One of us laughed, or perhaps we all did. We stretched out the moving, living pattern we had created and wrapped it around Elva.

The colors warmed, and brightened even more. Elva took a deeper breath and then another. He opened his eyes. Now they were clear. He smiled, reached up and brushed my cheek with the backs of his fingers.

"You look tired," he said.

"I love you too."

"You shouldn't have wasted your strength," he said in a voice much stronger than before.

"First, I do not consider it wasted; and second, we have had this argument before, and you did not win then either."

Lizz laughed. We were all sitting cross-legged on the sand watching Elva, ready to catch him if he slid off the rock. His eyes looked bruised, his hair ebony black against the pallor of his face. I took his hand, cool and callused, in mine.

"I feel so much better." He took a deep breath and smiled as he let it out slowly. "The cannons," he said, struggling to sit up. "We've got to get back." Lizz and Randd both held him down.

"We *are* back." Lizz did not sound surprised. Elva was on the floor, with his back against the bed, but otherwise nothing about the barracks room had changed.

"In a manner of speaking, we never left," I said. I helped Elva sit up. When it was clear he could manage on his own, Randd handed him his holsters and his revolvers. Once he had checked them and settled them as he liked, he touched each one in turn, frowning slightly when his fingers did not find his sword at his side.

"The World is playing its own game," I told them. "It will not help me stop the conflict—in fact, I begin to think it might be responsible for it. It wants to leave the Courts to destroy themselves and begin with a clean slate."

"Does that even make sense?" Randd looked from me to Elva.

I sat down at the small round table and rested my chin in my practitioner's hand. I was not as tired as I should have been, but my legs still felt rubbery. "The World has changed. It is more impatient, unwilling to wait to return to full health in a natural manner. And it is less compassionate. I think—" I stopped short of saying it. I had not told Elva about the World appearing as Arlyn.

"It doesn't mind if people get killed, so long as it gets what it wants?"

"Something like that, but yes." I rubbed at my forehead.

"Say it." Elva's hand rested on my shoulder.

"I hear the Godstone's voice when the World talks to me. What if it brought back all the things it learned and experienced while it was lost? What if that changed the World?"

"So. Let's give it what it wants." Elva pushed himself to his feet, pulled me over to him, and sat me on the edge of the bed. He looked around the room.

"Tell me what you mean," I said. "My brain is not working well."

"The White Court is suffering from these attacks more than it ever expected," Elva began.

"You got that right," Randd added. "The gas made it a whole new ballgame. Practitioners are in the same danger as the rest of us."

Funny that Randd saw himself as a mundane, given what we had just been able to accomplish together.

"Right." Elva fetched his sword from where it lay on the table. That's what his roaming fingers had missed. "They'll be wanting to evacuate, and that's a service we can provide."

I began to understand, and it made me smile. And here I had been worried about getting them to leave.

"What about the ones who won't go?" Randd asked the question before I could. "Some of these guys aren't very smart, but the idea of leaving them behind don't sit well."

"We can trick the really stupid ones," Elva pointed out. "Or at least some of them."

A noise at the window drew our attention. Terith the raven tapped on the shutter for our attention.

"Maybe someone else has a few ideas."

Thirteen

DEEP BREATH." DONN held me up by my elbows. "And again."
Finally, my vision cleared, my breathing slowed, and I realized the Road hadn't completely disappeared, that it continued on the far side of the break. The *very* far side. It looked as if someone had taken a huge prybar and wrenched the two sections apart, revealing layers of rock and earth underlying the surface. The sharp edge looked crumbly, and I backed further away. Fenra had fixed the fissure in the City, but I had no idea how.

Donn looked over the edge and grunted. "I don't see us climbing down and climbing back up again." He turned back to me. "And certainly not with the horses."

I shivered and looked away. "I'll take your word for it." I'd never been much of a climber.

Donn rested his practitioner's hand on his sword hilt, the other on his pistol, completely relaxed. He looked at the horses, at the cliff edge, at the horses again.

"In my world there's a thing called steeplechasing. I saw it once. It's a race; the horses have to jump fences and hedges and wide pools of water." He looked over at me without moving his head. "Some of those water jumps weren't much smaller than this." He tilted his head toward the rift. "And they gave the horses no trouble."

I blinked. "You're not suggesting . . ." My mouth had stopped working properly, and I cleared my throat. "These aren't jumping horses, they're—they're *ponies*."

Donn shrugged, lips pursed, mustache standing out. "Wouldn't they change with the Mode? Become their equivalent in that part of the World, right?" I had to nod. "So right now we need jumpers. Why can't we have them?"

"Because that's not how it works, and we haven't changed Modes." I threw my hands into the air. "There's no inn here, there's not even a Wayfarer's Rest." *Unless it was lying at the bottom of the new ravine.* I kept that thought to myself.

"I wonder." He beckoned me over to where he was standing. "Does the Road look different on the other side of the rift?"

I shuffled nearer to him and looked, squinting my eyes. I wanted to tell him no, but I had to be honest. "I'm not sure," I said finally. "Maybe." I shook myself. This was still nonsense. "You mean to tell me that you think the horses will change halfway over this abyss?" I waved at the empty space at our feet. "What if they don't change? Or they don't change into jumpers?"

"What if they do? What if we work on them a bit first?"

"Work?" I couldn't believe I was even considering this hare-brained idea. Why didn't I just turn around and . . . and what?

"Practice then, or whatever you call it. Look what Fenra can do with Terith."

"Fenra is older than I am, more experienced. Her connection to the natural world is closer than mine—and I'm pretty sure Terith isn't even a horse." I couldn't be actually considering this, could I? I rubbed my face, leaving my palms covering my eyes. "Any ideas about where to start?"

Donn patted me on the shoulder and led the horses over to the edge of the rift.

"We need you to jump that." Donn sounded exactly as though he thought the horses understood him. "Carrying us. We're going to help you, but you'll be doing most of the work."

I should have been expecting it, but it still made the hairs on my arms stand up when the horses looked at the gap, at each other, the gap again, and back to Donn. I couldn't tell whether they had agreed or not, but evidently Donn could.

What had Fenra said when we were training to deflect the cannon-balls? "Think of your Pattern. More often than you realize, it's a part of what you do when you perform a *forran*." Maybe there was something in my pattern that would help me now. "All right, what do we do? What makes a horse a good jumper?"

"I think it's mostly that they've been trained to jump."

"Not helpful."

Donn grinned. "They'll try, that's all we can ask. First we've got to lighten their loads, then we'll see about enhancing their strength and general balance."

We started by removing all our gear, our packs, saddlebags, sleeping rolls, extra blankets, everything the villagers had given us to make traveling more comfortable. When I finished, Donn stood frowning at the stirrup in his hand.

"I think we'll need those."

"They're heavy," he said without looking up. "Every piece of metal equipment is heavier than we actually need them to be."

I picked up one of my horse's stirrups. "For safety, you mean?"

"Exactly. Racing horses have everything lighter—saddles, stirrups, shoes, everything. Strong, but as light as possible."

I rubbed my thumb over the metal in my hand. Patterns. They helped, they enhanced, and you could use them to modify any *forran* that you already knew.

"That's an interesting look," Donn said. "Have you suddenly remembered a spell for flying?"

I held up my hand, palm toward him. Not flying, but maybe something else that could help.

"These stirrups and the other pieces are iron, right? Is gold lighter than iron?"

"On the contrary, it's heavier."

"Oh." Maybe not such a good idea after all. "So turning the iron into gold won't help."

Donn stroked his mustache. "You can do that?"

I nodded, smiling at his tone. "Gold works better in certain *forrans* and it's not always readily available, so . . ." I shrugged.

His brow furrowed, and he shook his head. "No, even if it isn't heavier, it's too soft."

"Is there a lighter metal that wouldn't be too soft?"

Donn stared into space while I chewed on my upper lip. "There's copper," he said finally.

"Copper." I knew what it was, of course, but it didn't have any practical use that I knew of, so I wasn't familiar with its essence. "I don't know copper, not the way I know gold," I said. "I don't think I can do it without a sample."

Donn went back to the pile of equipment and rooted around until he pulled up his belt pouch—not the one he kept bullets in, he still wore that. He emptied the contents of this one onto the palm of his hand. A small comb, and an even smaller pair of scissors. *For his mustache*, I thought. There were also three buttons, two silver pieces, and another reddish-brown coin.

"Here," he said. "It's a copper pence, I keep it for luck."

"We're taught there's no such thing." I took the coin with the thumb and index finger of my practitioner's hand.

"Nonsense," Donn said. "Everyone knows there is."

I put the coin in the palm of my right hand and placed my practitioner's hand over it until I felt the cool copper warming. I pulled my hands apart and held the coin in the net of light that formed between my fingertips. I rotated my hands until I was satisfied I had examined the coin from every possible angle. I saw exactly how it wasn't gold, everything about it that made it not gold. I called up the *forran* that would turn iron into gold. I took my pattern and laid it over the *forran*, using its lines to tweak it, until wherever the original *forran* meant "gold" it now meant "copper." But would it work?

"Only one way to find out." With the coin held tight in my right hand, I grasped the metal stirrup with my practitioner's hand. I saw exactly how the iron was iron, and everything about it that made it not copper. And I spoke the *forran*, the new copper-making *forran*.

When I opened my eyes, I was holding a perfectly formed copper stirrup. "It *is* lighter," I said. "I wasn't sure it would be."

"Never doubt me," Donn said. "Now the rest."

There's a surprising amount of metal involved in horse equipment, or "furniture," as Donn called it. Just the same, we were finished far too quickly for me. I wouldn't have minded more delay at all. My hands shook as I resaddled my horse. I could have said I was too tired to continue, but I would have been lying, and the gap would still be there waiting for us to jump over it. "What if it doesn't work?"

"We'll probably be dead, so we won't care." *Not comforting.*

Donn had practiced the horses while I was transmuting the metal, and they actually seemed pleased, prancing a little and shaking their heads. I don't know what it was Donn said to them, but they were treating this whole thing like an adventure. We'd decided that Donn should go first. He was the better rider, and he was confident that his plan would work. I'd be encouraged by his success. At least that's what I told myself.

"We need to get our weight over the horse's shoulders," Donn told me. "Imagine yourself as so light you're hardly weighing the horses down at all." He took my hand, bowed over it and kissed my knuckles. "See you on the other side."

He led his horse to the starting point he'd calculated was far enough from the edge to give him enough speed to carry him over and swung himself into the saddle. The distance looked too short to me. I had both hands over my mouth as they flashed past me, Donn standing up in the stirrups, leaning over his horse's shoulders, just as he'd told me. Suddenly they were in the air and I held my breath, breathing again only when they landed neatly on the far side of the crevasse. Donn took off his hat, threw it into the air, caught it, and bowed to me, at least as much as he could while still in the saddle.

"Your turn!"

I nodded, and smiled, and lifted my hand. Just as if I wasn't shaking inside. My horse and I took our places at the starting point. I could feel him crouching, his legs like springs, getting ready to fly forward.

"We can do it," I whispered to him. He flicked his ears at me, and somehow that made me feel better. I stood in the stirrups the way Donn had shown me. *I hope this doesn't take long*, I thought. The muscles in my thighs were already starting to complain. I kept my eyes front, looking out between my horse's ears. I didn't look down; I tried not to think about the rocky chasm in front of us. Closed my eyes as the horse launched himself from the edge. "I'm very light," I said over and over through clenched teeth.

I felt my horse's front hooves hit dirt, not air. Just as I was congratulating myself on getting to the other side safely, and beginning to breathe again, I felt my horse's left rear hoof slip off the edge. He scrabbled with his front hooves, trying to get his weight up onto the three legs that had made it. My thighs began to loosen, and I felt myself slipping backward.

Then Donn was beside me. His practitioner's hand grabbed the bridle, and his right hand grabbed the collar of my tunic even as his horse braced its feet and pulled backward. This time I saw the aura of light clearly. My horse straightened itself, all four feet once more on solid ground, and I slid off, my heart thumping and my arms and legs shaking. I think there were tears in my eyes. I still had the reins in my hands. The horse stood with his head hanging down, his sides heaving, his skin twitching and covered with sweat. I knew just how he felt. When I managed to look up, Donn stood next to my horse, running his hand over its shoulders and face, rubbing its nose. His own horse looked over his shoulder and seemed to speak to mine. I closed my eyes and tried to take deep breaths.

When I opened them again, Donn was squatting on his heels next to me. The horses were calmly investigating the grass verges, looking for something to eat. Suddenly, for them, what we had just done was all in a day's work.

"Can you stand?" Donn offered me a hand and I let him haul me to my feet. I straightened my tunic and slapped dust off my breeches. I thought I had lost one of my shoes, but Donn found it just a meter or so away from where I had rolled when he hauled me off the horse. I held it in my hand, puzzled, as though I'd never seen anything like it before. A shoe. Not a sandal, not a clog. Donn was right, the Mode *did* change. But how here, in the middle of nowhere? No inn or even Wayfarer's Rest to mark the border?

I looked up the Road in the direction of the City. What else waited for us?

We found out a few days later. As we got closer to the City, we met more and more people heading out of it, some walking, some riding, some in carriages or wagons. We stopped two young men carrying backpacks, obviously brothers, and asked what was going on.

"The City's collapsing," the taller one told us, a note of hysteria underlying the exhaustion in his voice. "Streets cracking open, buildings falling in." I looked at Donn and he was thinking the same thing I was. The fissure in the Road.

"Does the Red Court still stand?"

The man spit to one side. "Of course it does. I mean, there's rumors of trouble even up there, but I don't believe it. They know how to look after themselves."

"And they're not doing anything to protect us from those practitioners, neither." This came from the shorter brother. "This is all their doing. They've invented some kind of earth-shaking theory, how else could something like this happen? If you want my advice, you'll turn around."

The chaos on the Road was nothing compared to what we found in the City. We didn't see as much damage as we'd expected from what the brothers had told us, but the streets were full of people, some clearly evacuating, others still arguing about whether to stay or go. A fistfight broke out between what looked like two sisters, but we passed them without learning the cause. Some streets were eerily empty, others blocked by the people trying to get out of the City. We learned that a completely clear street usually meant a fissure somewhere along the way. Fortunately, none of these were as wide as the crack in the Road, and we were able to jump them without too much strain. In fact, the horses gave the distinct impression of having a wonderful time.

We expected to be stopped at the gate of the Red Court, and we were.

"Returning to Courtier Wittenslade Camdin Volden," I said to the guard barring our way.

"You've picked a fine time to come home." The man turned to someone we couldn't see in the guardhouse inside the gate. "Run and tell Courtier Volden we've got two of his people here and find out what he wants done with them."

While we were waiting, we'd had time to realize that we didn't know the way to Witt's house, and that since we were wearing his livery, it might be awkward to ask. Luckily for us, a boy came back with the messenger, though he wore street clothes, not livery. As soon as we were away from the guards, the boy introduced himself quietly as Oleander and shook hands. "This way." After too many turns to remember, he led us to a huge door painted a bright yellow. A footman answered his knock, looked us up and down, and rolled his eyes.

"At least you're cleaner than the last one."

As the door closed behind us, I heard a clattering on the stairs and suddenly my nose was buried in a mound of scented silk and linen with Witt inside it. He hugged me so fiercely I could hardly breathe. I think I hugged him back. Over his shoulder I saw Donn with a peculiar smile on his face, which relaxed when he saw I was watching him.

"Where's Fenra?" I finally managed to ask. "Why are the cannons still working?"

"A letter came and she left before I could stop her."

"Just like that?" I couldn't believe it. What could possibly be more important than destroying the cannons? I felt I was going to be sick. Until that moment I didn't realize how much I'd been counting on her to tell us what to do.

"Why didn't she wait for us?" I asked, hearing the hollow sound in my voice. "I don't know what to do about the cannons." I sounded hopeless, and that was exactly how I felt. Donn took his copper pence out of his pocket, flipped it into the air, and caught it.

"Oh now, let's not be hasty."

FENRA

I opened Tamari's letter with relief, not surprised at her ice-cold tone. Alive and angry with me was infinitely better than the alternative. Terith hopped up to read it over my shoulder. "They're safe," I said. "They're with Witt, and they plan to destroy the cannons this afternoon." I looked up at the others. We were in the guard barrack rooms Captain Rennard had given Elva.

"Does that mean we don't have to evacuate the White Court?" Elva sat on the bed next to me and I turned to look at him. His eyes still looked tired. We had saved him from dying, but only just.

"What if something should go wrong?" I asked. "I say we continue."

"Good. We'll use Predax's network to get the news out."

"My what?" Predax stood leaning against the outer wall, his arms wrapped around his chest.

Elva turned to him. "Your network, all the people you know. In no time at all you managed to let everyone know that Fenra was opening a new court. You can do the same now." He turned to me. "He'll let everyone know that Fenra Lowens is willing to help anyone who wants to leave the White Court."

I rubbed at my forehead with my practitioner's hand, careful not to disturb Terith. "Elva, I cannot move the whole court, and even if I could, it wouldn't be quickly enough."

"I doubt you'll have to." Randd picked up the coffee jug from the lone table in the center of the room and began topping up everyone's mugs. "Judging by the idiots we've seen on your council, there'll be a whole bunch who won't go."

"How many can you move before you're too tired to continue?" It was the longest sentence we had ever heard from Lizz.

"Unfortunately, there's only one way to find out," I said. "What happens when I have to stop and rest?"

"Too bad you can't borrow energy." Elva leaned back and closed his eyes. I took his mug of coffee away from him and handed it to Randd, who set it on the table.

"I would not know how to begin."

"We do it." Lizz gave me a tiny smile when I stared at her.

"You mean you give energy to each other?" Lizz nodded. "So you can give it to me?"

Lizz took a sip from her mug. "We've done it."

"You have done—" I knew Randd and Lizz could combine their practice with mine, we proved that healing Elva . . . "The singing," I said finally. "It didn't just cover the sound of our voices, it also helped Randd find the listeners, and then it helped us on the beach. But are you not worried—the Godstone could absorb someone else's power completely."

"We don't do that." From her tone it was obvious that Lizz thought me an idiot.

"Are you sure? It's one thing for you to give me energy, but I need to be able to consciously control it, draw it from you as I need it. Perhaps I could modify the *forran* I use in healing." I knew I could give strength to others; plenty of healing *forrans* involved something of that kind. "In theory, it should be possible." I looked from Lizz to Randd.

"Here." Lizz stood up and held out her hands, one to me and the other to Randd.

This time it was far easier for me to see the auras that surrounded Lizz and Randd when they practiced. I saw latent patterns in the light, and I worked to encourage them. Lizz said it gave her a headache, but she persisted until I could see the patterns clearly. As soon I could, I brushed away Lizz's headache.

"Thanks," she said.

"Do not thank me yet," I told her. "That establishes that I can intentionally take away pain, it doesn't prove I can do the same with energy. Let me try with you alone, Lizz. If it works, I will add you, Randd." When they both nodded I shut my eyes.

Remembering the time I tried to manipulate Arlyn's pattern, I reached carefully into Lizz's, and tweaked one of the lines I thought I saw. I needed to get it loose without pulling the entire pattern out of shape, to connect with her without overlapping.

"Itches." Lizz rolled her shoulders. "Magic didn't."

She meant that lending me practice didn't itch. "Does it hurt?"

"Just itches. There, it's gone."

Once I had one of Lizz's lines in my hand, I laid it alongside the one of mine. Slowly I coaxed a little brightness from her line, until finally the two blended, and I could feel Lizz's practice directly. I felt my lips broaden into a smile as Lizz began to sing, and I felt her strength surging through my body.

"Elva, watch her closely." He knew the first signs of fatigue well, having seen them often enough in me. He knew what to look for in Lizz.

Performing the same *forran* with Randd was much easier. I could feel power running through me and circling back through them. They were both smiling at me. I could feel the same smile on my face. We all relaxed back into ourselves.

I took my locket out. "For our plan to work, I will need to draw power from you while I am in the vault—moving you back and forth with me will defeat the purpose. Let us find out if this will work even if we are not physically close," I said. I opened the locket.

Standing in the vault, I could not see their patterns, but I could feel their energy. I felt my shoulders relax.

I opened the locket again, returning in time to hear Predax and Elva talking strategy.

"I'll start rounding up the council," Predax said.

"No," I said. "Get Captain Rennard." I turned to the others. "We will move the mundanes first. They are the most at risk, and they should have guards with them."

"They won't all agree to go," Elva reminded me once Predax was out the door.

"We will move the ones who do," I said. "And we will send some of the guard with each group." Terith called to me from the windowsill. "After I send a message to Tamari."

TAMARI

"Wow," Oleander said once Donn had explained the significance of the copper pence. "Can I see that?"

"Keep it," Donn said, handing him the coin. "It's lucky." Oleander took the coin in one hand and shook hands with the other.

"You're all right," he told Donn with a grin, pushing the coin into the pouch on his belt. "So, when do we get this play on the stage?"

Donn laughed and swatted the boy on the back.

"This isn't a game we're playing," Witt told them. I was glad someone said it.

"Don't be too sure," Donn said. "We all know a game means winners *and* losers."

Witt had ordered lunch to be brought up to us, and Terith arrived with a message from Fenra while we were eating.

"They're evacuating the White Court," I read.

"Then we can relax?" Donn looked over my shoulder, though he knew he wouldn't see anything on the page.

I shook my head as I read on. "They say not everyone will be willing to go. We're still on."

Witt rubbed his hands together. "What are we waiting for? Let's go."

As we went out the door, Oleander carried a meat pie in his hand, and I was sure he had rolls in his pockets.

The carriage ride gave me too much time to think. Donn's idea should work. What we could do with stirrups and bits, we should be able to do with cannon, if we could get close enough—which turned out to be no problem at all.

"This area of the City has been evacuated since the start, to create room for the military," Witt said when I asked him. Which explained why we weren't fighting our way through streams of people going in the opposite direction. Even when we reached the area overseen by the military, nobody stopped us from approaching closer.

"They're used to seeing me here," Witt said as he stopped the carriage and tied off the reins. "And they're all too focused on what they're doing to pay us any mind, unless we get in the way."

"Which is exactly what we need to do," Donn said, making a big show of helping Witt down from the carriage, like any good servant. In no time at all, we were at the line of cannons. Each of the five cannons had only three soldiers working them. One to push in the powder bags, one to load the cannonballs and use the ramrod to pack them well in, and one to place and light the fuse.

"Fine," I said. "One of us will distract the men—"

"Gunners," Witt said with the air of being helpful.

"Fine, gunners, and the others will break the gun."

"It might be more complicated." Donn took my elbow and drew me to the side, where I had a better view of the gunners at work. "You see those buckets?" He pointed at half a dozen leather buckets lined up a few paces back from the line. "Those are full of oil to cool the barrels when they get overheated," Donn added. "Which means the barrels may well be too hot to touch."

"But that should make it easier," Witt said over his shoulder. As his servants, we couldn't stand beside him. "You don't have to weaken the whole barrel, just one spot will do. What? I've read books."

I raised my eyebrows and waited for someone to explain.

"If the barrel heats unevenly," Donn said, "*and* we introduce a weak spot, it will explode without our having to do anything more."

I couldn't help looking at the gun holstered to Donn's hip. "You mean that could explode anytime you use it?"

"This?" Donn tapped his revolver and shook his head. "Not at all. A cheap gun, maybe, but this is a Swift and Lennon, one of the best guns made. No weak spots. The sheriff uses Popes, but I don't like the long barrel."

"Wait," Witt said. "If the metal of the barrel is so hot, how are you going to touch it to make it weaker? Can you do your science from a distance?"

Donn and I looked at each other. I hoped I looked as calm as he did, because inside I was screaming with frustration. Then I had an idea.

"I can remove heat from a distance," I told them. "We often have to do it when creating *forrans*—doing experiments," I added for Witt's benefit. "But that means that, Donn, you'll have to weaken the metal yourself. Are you sure you can?"

"Anything for a lady." He touched his finger to where his hat brim would normally be.

"And if you expect the cannon to explode, you'll have to get out of the way pretty quickly," Witt pointed out.

"Faster than a speeding bullet," Donn said with a grin.

"This one," I said, pointing to the middle cannon with a tilt of my head. "It's smaller than the others, but from where it is, we could set off the others near it. A chain reaction. Complete confusion. *And*, there's only two soldiers setting it up." Donn took up a position on one side of the cannon we'd chosen, holding Witt's hat and fan as if he'd been asked to wait there. It was strange how no one seemed to take notice of servants. Almost as good as being invisible.

I silently reviewed the *forran* for removing heat, making sure I hadn't forgotten it. The last time I'd used it was to prevent glass tubes from breaking. When I was sure I had it, I recited it under my breath, as quietly as I could. This type of *forran* always worked better for me if I spoke it aloud.

I didn't see any change, but Donn must have felt something. He nodded, and Oleander dashed in, grabbed the ramrod, and ran off with it. Both soldiers chased him—something I was sure they'd be disciplined for later—and as soon as they were well away, Donn placed the palm of his practitioner's hand on the middle of the barrel, the spot where it began to taper. The soldiers were on their way back with their ramrod—and without Oleander, I was happy to see—but they weren't worried about Donn at first. They called to him to back off, that the weapon was dangerous and that he was in the way. Again, no one takes a servant seriously. Donn smiled and nodded, and then suddenly leaped forward, carrying both men to the ground with him.

I have to say, the explosion was impressive. Unfortunately, we only managed to set the next cannon on fire. *No chain reaction.* I could hear Donn cursing from where I stood.

We had managed to injure one of the soldiers. I had just run over to where Donn was helping her with her broken arm, when a voice came from behind us.

"You three are under arrest. Come with me, nice and easy, and no one will get hurt."

WITTENSLADE

"I am a courtier of the Chamber of the Red Court," Witt said for the fifth time. "You have no jurisdiction over me." Witt didn't know why he kept repeating that. It accomplished nothing and didn't make him feel any better.

"You are under military jurisdiction," the officer holding them said. He hadn't bothered to introduce himself, which Witt took as a bad sign. "You are all three guilty of espionage and sabotage. It's the field commander will decide what will happen to you." He grimaced as though he smelled something bad. "Those fops up in the Court would probably just let you go."

They weren't being kept in a prison only because there weren't any prisons in what was, after all, a residential neighborhood. Instead, they were put in a small room at the top of a house, right under the roof, so the ceilings were slanted. There was a window, round, small, and high up on one wall, and no furniture except a single stool. The servants' rooms in his house were much nicer.

"Won't you sit down?" he said to Tamari, gesturing at the stool. For some reason she was leaning on the door, palms pressed to the wood, as if she were listening to it.

She shook her head. "It's not a lock," she said to Donn. "Just a bar and maybe a wedge. No mechanism I can practice on."

Donn shook out his hands. "Let me give it a try. Might need a trick from the old school."

"Like a crowbar?" Tamari shook her head, but Witt was glad to see she was smiling.

Donn stepped abruptly back from the door, knocking Tamari into Witt's arms. The door swung open, and Witt took a deep breath,

"Col," Witt said, reaching to take the man's hand. "You have to get us out of here."

"I don't know how you think I'm going to do that, or why you think I should."

The coolness in his friend's voice made Witt take a step back. "Look, I'm sorry—"

"Sorry that you took advantage of our friendship to spy on us for the White Court?"

"I wasn't spying!" Witt swallowed. "All right, maybe I was, but you yourself said you wanted the conflict over as quickly as possible. You didn't seem to care then who was on what side." Witt forced his tone into something less combative.

"Even if I wanted to help you—and that's definitely a big 'if'—I'm not precisely in good favor at the moment. Something else I can thank you for."

"Colonel—" Tamari began.

"Save it. I've spent the morning trying to convince the field commander that you're just hapless idiots, and I didn't have any more luck than when I wanted him to evacuate from this promontory. With all the earth seizures, we could fall into the river gorge any minute. But no, he wanted to do one final bombardment, see if we couldn't bring them to their knees."

"He thinks *practitioners* are responsible for this? The seizures, the storms?" Tamari obviously couldn't believe what she was hearing. "Doesn't anyone remember that it was a practitioner who closed the original fissure and saved all those people?"

"It seems a logical conclusion," Col said, turning to Witt. "Don't you remember? We saw them break off the edges of the Court ourselves."

"Which means we wouldn't have had any trouble breaking off this bit of land if we wanted to," Tamari pointed out. "And if we *had* wanted to, we would have done it as soon as the cannon bombardment started."

"*WE?*" Col took a step away from all of them, as far as he could get in the small room.

"Col," Witt said. "At least let Tamari go. It's not her fault." This was Col, his old school friend, and Witt knew that under this understandable anger Col wanted to let them go.

"No," Tamari said. "Let Witt go. Tell them I tricked him, that he's innocent."

Witt could see right away she'd made a mistake. Col couldn't overlook that she was a practitioner. He couldn't let them go now. Witt saw Col's face harden and his lips compress, and he left them without saying anything more.

In the end it wasn't the field commander who came, but Riva Anden Deneyra. She went straight to Witt when she came in, as if the other two weren't there. Perhaps she'd forgotten that she knew Tamari.

"Witt, you absolute fool, what did you think you were doing?"

Well, that made it clear they weren't likely to get any help from her. Was there any way to get through to her?

"Courtier Deneyra, listen." Tamari stepped forward as much as she could in the small room. "Reality is much bigger than you think. If we don't finish our mission, it's not going to matter which Court comes out on top. There won't be any Courts at all."

If anything, her face became stiffer, though Witt thought he saw a shadow of what looked like fear pass over her face. "It's you who don't know what's at stake," she said, addressing Witt as if Tamari hadn't spoken. "If you understood anything of what's been going on, you wouldn't have been such a fool."

Witt gritted his teeth, trying to think of something to defend himself, but he realized he was past the point of caring what Riva thought of him. "Riva, why are you here?"

She stared at him for a long moment, then blinked and turned to Tamari. "Practitioner Otwyn," she said. "There is a place for you in my household, if you wish to take it. You would be under my personal protection."

Witt opened his mouth, but found he had nothing to say.

"You mean that you'd protect me—" Tamari's sarcasm was sharp enough to cut. "—so long as I did what I was told and didn't make a fuss. Maybe you'd even let me out for a walk every now and then, with appropriate attendants, to make sure I was 'safe.'"

"I'm giving you a chance to choose where you'll live." The woman glanced at Witt and then back to Tamari. "Soon you won't have that option."

"I'll stay with my friends, if it's all the same to you."

Riva lifted her eyebrows and looked as if she had something more to say. Instead, she shrugged and turned back to Witt.

"I thought you were just being taken in," she said. "I found you easy to trick, and I assumed they did as well. But I see now that I misjudged you. You *are* a fool, but not the kind I thought you were." She gathered up her skirts as if she had been sitting down and was about to stand up. "Good luck to you, Witt Volden. I wish I could have helped you."

FENRA

First, I moved Predax into the vault. Randd thought Elva was a better choice, but we needed someone the mundanes and soldiers would trust, and that meant he had to stay in the Court.

"Start with these models," I said, once Predax had overcome his shock and surprise and was able to listen to me. "Place them on this square table, one at a time. As we use one to move people, remove it and replace it with the next in line." Predax drew down his brows and nodded. He drew a finger along a replica of a swinging bridge as if checking for dust.

"We'll be right back," I said, and opened the locket.

"I don't understand why you can't move at least some of the guard into the City." Captain Rennard looked from Elva to me and back again, as if he wasn't sure which of us he needed to persuade. Elva just smiled and began to inspect one of his revolvers.

"I only have one anchor point in the City. It's smack in the middle of the Red Court, and since I cannot move more than four or five people at a time, it doesn't strike me as good strategy."

Rennard did not like it, but he knew I was right. "Very well. How close to the City *can* you move us?"

I was not interested in helping him with his flanking maneuver. "Captain, even if you had enough soldiers to attack the Red Court— something I doubt—my intention is to take everyone here to safety. I am not offering you a military advantage, I am offering you an opportunity to continue the safekeeping of the White Court—which I understand is in fact your mandate."

"It's this way." Elva re-holstered his revolver and took out the other one. "We're not moving everyone to the same place. Every group we send is going somewhere unfamiliar to them, maybe even dangerous. We want some of the guard to go with each group, to keep them safe if necessary, or just to help them if that's all that's needed."

"What about the practitioners?" This question didn't mean that he had given in, just that he wanted more detail. We did not have time for this.

"We will send at least one practitioner with each group, if they are willing to go. But believe me, Captain, we will be doing this my way."

It took a little longer to convince him, but we were well started before the afternoon was over. Predax's network and the guards Rennard sent brought all the mundanes who were willing to escape—most if not all of them—and then we started on practitioners. The first two came in smiling a little, looking around them as if they had never seen a barracks room before, which, when I thought about it, was very likely true.

"I'm Tellen Fitzen, and this is Wuten Aligari. Is Tamari Otwyn here? She would vouch for us."

"You do not need vouching for," I told them. "We will take anyone who is willing to go." I was happy to see that they had brought packs and walking sticks with them.

"Can you move us both together?" Wuten asked. "It's been some time since either of us was out of the Court."

"Certainly," I said. "Stay alert when we leave you. Even the Road is not as safe as it should be. Have you brought what money you have?"

At that moment, Ronan Sedges came barreling through the door. "Practitioner Lowens, this time you've gone too far. I must insist that you immediately cease. These are not decisions for you to make."

"I'm not making decisions; I am moving only those people who wish to move."

"You are destroying the morale of the White Court at a time when we must all support each other to the utmost." He might have gone on, but a snort from Lizz brought him up straight, indignant and blustering.

"Donn's right, this guy *is* a yammering gasbag," Randd said. He and Lizz grinned at each other.

"You two." Ronan turned to Tamari's friends. "I forbid you to go anywhere. You haven't cleared it with the council—"

"Hang on," Elva cut in. "They can't go, or they can go but only if the council authorizes it?"

"Tell you what, gasbag," Randd added as Ronan continued sputtering. "How's about we move you right now? Do you need to ask for permission?"

OLEANDER

The fun had definitely gone out of the day. Only the fact that he hadn't been wearing livery saved Oleander from being caught up with the others. When he saw Witt's colonel friend, he waited, just in case the man was coming to free them, but no. Oleander had a couple of friends like that himself. Though to be honest, most of his knew when to look the other way—which, come to think of it, wasn't exactly honest, was it?

But he did know who *he* could trust, and as soon as he got away from the soldiers, he headed for Ginglen's Inn. Not that he went straight there. He wasn't an idiot. Making sure no one followed him only took a few minutes of backtracking, two walls climbed, and one trip through the tanner's yard. And he didn't go in the inn's front door either, but went round to the mews as usual, and through the kitchen door. Hearing voices, he turned into the kitchen, and found both Ginglen and Itzen with the cook, discussing the amount of sugar needed for a cake. All three stopped talking and looked round as he came in.

"From the look on your face, it's not good news."

"Nothing for you to worry about, Doms." Oleander knew immediately that both men thought he was here to tell them that the couriers they had hidden in their attics were about to be arrested—and Ginglen and Itzen along with them. Witt's house would have been roomier, but it was also full of servants, at least some of whom would gossip about their master's private business.

"Come through, you can tell us what's happened." The two men led Oleander through the inn, across the entrance hall, and into their private apartments. Oleander had been here so often recently he felt almost at home. He plopped himself down onto his usual chair, noticing for the first time that his legs were rubbery. *More tired than I thought.*

"They've been taken prisoner," he began.

"Wait, boy. Start again, *who* have been taken prisoner?"

Oleander took a deep breath, wondering how far back he needed to go. "Tamari Otwyn and Donn Keeshode came from the White Court to destroy the cannons."

"How—never mind, go on."

"They made one blow up." Oleander couldn't help grinning at the memory. "That set off a second one, and the next thing I knew, a bunch of soldiers came and 'escorted' them away." Oleander held up his hand to stop the next interruption. "I'm not dressed in Witt's livery, so no one knew I was with them. No one sees people like me," he added, knowing he'd be understood. "I got away, no problem."

Itzen stood up and began pacing up and down in front of the fireplace. "Will Dom Volden be able to pull strings? Who do *we* know in the guard?"

"That's just it," Oleander said. "It's not the Red Court as has 'em, it's the military. Know anybody there, do you?"

"Even so, the prisons are under the control of the guard—"

"You're not listening." Oleander got halfway to his feet. "The military aren't using any Red Court prison, nor any City prison neither. They've got them in one of the houses they took over at the riverside, right in the middle of things, with soldiers all around them."

Itzen stopped pacing and pushed his hands through his hair. He looked at Ginglen and raised his eyebrows. Ginglen shook his head.

"We'll have to think of *something*," he said.

"I already did." Oleander pulled the rolled-up parchment out from inside his tunic. "You guys are going to have to write the letter."

FENRA

I read the letter aloud to Elva and the others since they couldn't read it for themselves.

"Donn in jail." Randd shook his head. "Worst thing for a Free Scout—I don't care if he *has* settled down just lately."

"According to Oleander, they were able to put at least two of the cannons out of commission." Elva touched each of his guns and the hilt of his sword.

"Can't leave them there."

I could not tell whether Lizz asked a question or made a statement, and I did not think she knew either. She looked tired, the corners of her mouth drooping. Randd looked to be in better shape—his eyes had their usual sparkle—but it was clear they both needed rest. Feeding me energy wasn't as draining as using it themselves, but it still took its toll. I looked at the palms of my hands, turned them over. They looked unfamiliar. Thinner. My head felt heavy and I propped it in my hands.

"She can't show up in the fountain again." Elva's voice.

I must have dropped off. It sounded as if I had missed some of the discussion.

"Terith," I said. Lifting my head took unexpected effort. I pushed myself upright, hands against the edge of the table, and straightened my back. "Maybe I can use Terith as a focal point," I said. They all turned to look at the raven sitting calmly on the back of one of the chairs. It tilted its head to one side and shrugged its wings. "I can do it with Elva." I looked at him. Terith should be just as easy. If it worked. Terith bobbed his head, flapped his wings a few times, and flew out the window. "Looks like he agrees." I straightened. "He can go right where they are, and so can I."

"You need rest," Elva said. "Or at least eat something first."

"It's faster to get food in the vault." I stood up, grateful that my legs at least seemed to want to carry me.

"Don't waste any power taking me back to the White Court," Predax said, as I filled my mouth with lamb stew. "It's quiet here, and to tell you the truth, I could use some of that." He gestured at the models still left on the shelves. "I can use the time to organize the ones we haven't used yet." We had not been able to use all the models. Almost half of them didn't work—likely because the Modes they came from no longer existed. Fixing the World should change that. The disappearance of Modes had been one of the signs that the World was ill and needed the return of the piece of itself known as the Godstone. I almost wished we had not been successful.

"We may not need any more," I said. "I have the feeling time is running short."

Terith surprised me by being in Ginglen's Inn and not the room where the others were being kept.

"The room's too small," Oleander said as he helped brush my coat. "What if, you know, there isn't room for you to fit?"

What indeed. It had never happened before, but then, most of my experience had to do with beaches. I could not risk it, so I followed Oleander through the streets by what he assured me was the shortest route—barring taking to the rooftops, something I no longer had the skills to do. Likewise, we did not take the horses Ginglen offered us—that would have drawn the wrong kind of attention. Still, that we were at the army camp in under half an hour had more to do with the lack of people on the streets than the route we took.

"I have a parcel for Courtier Camdin Volden," I said in my best imitation of an upper-class servant's voice. I could feel Oleander in his hiding spot off to my left.

"No visitors," the sergeant said again. A little spark in his eye told me he was enjoying himself. Not a bad man, really, just monumentally bored.

"I am not a visitor," I protested. "I am a servant."

"What's all this, Sergeant?"

The man snapped to attention so fast it would have been funny any other time. I did not recognize the voice, though the accent was virtually identical to Witt's. Upper class, for all that his uniform looked well lived in.

"Servant to visit the prisoners, Colonel."

"What's the master being held for?" I asked. "The house is in an uproar, Colonel. None of us know anything. Please tell me."

"Espionage and sabotage," the man answered. "Using a practitioner's device to damage the cannon." I did my best to look shocked and appalled.

The cannons had been silent for several hours, but as if the man's words had been a signal, at that moment the bombardment began again. Surely at some point they would run out of ammunition?

"Search the parcel," the colonel said. "If there's no weapons, let her through."

"But Colonel—"

"Something on your mind, *Sergeant*?" The man raised his right eyebrow.

"No, Colonel, not at all."

"It's my responsibility. I won't forget."

The man looked relieved. "Yes, Colonel, thank you."

"Not at all. Carry on." The colonel nodded to me, the corner of his mouth lifting as if he saw something pleasing, then he strolled away with his hand resting on the hilt of his sword.

The sergeant took his time searching through my parcel—again, not out of pettiness, but out of boredom. It didn't matter; the parcel was for cover only, and all he found was clean body linen, a fresh shirt, a packet of coffee, and a bar of chocolate. He handled everything carefully, and let me refold the clothes, after he broke off a piece of chocolate for himself. Once I packed everything up again, he signaled to one of the lower ranks standing against the wall.

"Take this lady to the guardhouse."

I knew there wasn't a guardhouse, but I supposed that using military jargon made everyone feel better.

I chattered away to the private, even though she did not respond very enthusiastically. She also did not notice Oleander's progress through the short streets that brought us to the house being used for the prisoners. He had told me that no one in the military would know the streets as well as he did, regardless of how long they had been occupying the neighborhood. He was right. When we arrived at the front door of what by Red Court standards was a modest home, Oleander was only a rooftop away.

The bars and grates on the windows explained the choice of housing. At one time this must have been used as a warehouse, before being converted into a private home. There were two guards at the entrance, but once my escort explained who and what I was, and mentioned the colonel, they let me into the house with only the usual amount of grumbling. It's one of the privileges of junior ranks to grumble about the vagaries of senior ranks. That's true even of practitioners. Perhaps especially of them.

"Up the stairs all the way. You'll see the door on the left," they told me.

The door on the left opened into what had obviously been a servant's room, with nothing more than a bed, a stool, and a small chest. At first glance, the room appeared empty, but that didn't fool me.

"Am I interrupting something?"

Fourteen

WITT WATCHED TAMARI and Donn Keeshode out of the corner of his eye. What was their relationship? Father and daughter? The older man watched everything and everyone, but his eyes always returned to Tamari. Was he a bodyguard? Of course, he *was* much older—he had naturally white hair, for the Maker's sake—so that probably meant he at least saw her as a daughter. Donn caught Witt watching him and smiled a reassuring smile. Witt had no idea what the old man thought he needed reassuring about. Witt stopped leaning against the wall, stood straighter, tugged down on the points of his waistcoat, and straightened his cuffs.

Witt didn't know how Tamari and Donn knew someone was coming when he couldn't hear anyone on the stairs himself, but he didn't mind hiding at all. He also couldn't figure out exactly how or even where they were hiding, but he assumed it had something to do with one of their theories. All he knew for certain was that he couldn't see them, and he assumed they couldn't see him.

When the door swung open, he didn't need Tamari's "Fenra!" to recognize the dark woman dressed in his livery.

"And the others?" Donn's voice had a tension Witt hadn't heard from him before.

"With Elva." Fenra tossed the parcel she carried onto the floor. "Quick, join hands."

This would be a little tricky, since she stood in the doorway, unable to come all the way into the narrow room. Witt took Tamari's hand at once. It fit into his perfectly, warm and dry. Fenra held his other hand, and Donn stood between Fenra and Tamari. However, he just hooked his arm through Fenra's, leaving her hand free. With it Fenra pulled a gold locket with blue enameling from under her tunic and flicked it open with her fingernail.

Nothing happened. Witt could tell that the others expected something from the way Tamari's hand tightened on his. Fenra let go of his hand and rubbed her face, rubbing at the skin around her eyes.

"I am more tired than I thought," she said.

"Rest," Witt said. "Sit down." But the practitioner shook her head.

"We do not have time." She reached out with her practitioner's hand and took Tamari's right hand, pulling her gently onto the landing. She was then able, with her right hand, to take Donn's practitioner's hand, and at her sign Donn took Tamari's practitioner's hand in his right.

"We have found that I can draw on Randd's and Lizz's energies when my own are low—"

"Like a battery," Donn said.

Fenra smiled at him. "Exactly. It does not hurt them, and we can take it in turns to rest and eat. I would like to draw upon yours now." When both the others nodded, she added, "Tamari, focus on your pattern. Donn, concentrate."

Witt hadn't felt so out of things since his father shut him out of his study when Witt was a child. He saw absolutely nothing different in his companions. In fact, they stood so still, he couldn't be sure they were breathing. He touched Tamari's hand and breathed a little easier himself, reassured by the warmth of her skin. He could even feel a little sizzle, or so he convinced himself, something that made the hairs on his arms and the back of his neck stand up. Without intending it, his mind drifted. He got all the way to the seventeenth verse of "The Donkey and the Monkey" when all three sighed and let go of each other. He didn't know what they'd done, but he had to agree that Fenra looked better, her eyes brighter and her skin less gray. Even her curly hair seemed bouncier.

"Let us try again."

They took up the same positions as before, all connected and touching. Fenra opened her locket, and, again, nothing happened.

"If you don't mind my asking," he said. "Exactly what is *supposed* to happen?"

Fenra, eyes and lips squeezed shut, didn't answer.

"We should move from here to Fenra's vault," Tamari said. "A safe place only she can reach," she added when Witt lifted his eyebrows.

Donn put his hand on Fenra's shoulder. "You are strong enough," he said. "I can feel it." Tamari nodded when he looked at her. "There is something else wrong."

"Can you move just yourself?" Tamari asked. "I know that isn't what you came for," she said. "But if you can't rescue us, you're needed elsewhere." Witt wondered if he would be brave enough to say something like that.

Fenra opened the locket she still held in her hand.

"Nothing," she said—rather unnecessarily, Witt thought. "If it's not me, and it's not the locket, what is it?"

"It can't be the Red Court," Witt pointed out. "We're none of us practitioners. Could it be someone from the White Court?"

"No. In order to interfere with the keys to someone else's vault, you would have to know how the key was made—not easy to learn in the first place, and in the second, it hasn't left me since my mentor gave it to me."

"Has this ever happened before?"

Fenra didn't answer right away. She had exactly the look of a servant who had just found out who *really* broke the crystal vase. "Yes," she said finally.

"Who is it, then? Who's blocking you?" Witt said. The other three exchanged glances. "That's very annoying, you know, that 'Ooh, we know something you don't know.'" He sat down on the cot and crossed his arms. "Why don't you just tell me, and then we'll all know."

Tamari looked like she was trying not to cry. "It isn't some*one*, it's some*thing*."

Witt swallowed, untied his cravat, and retied it. Everyone knew the stories about things that preyed on travelers, how it was never safe to leave the Road, and lately the Road itself wasn't as safe as it used to be. "What kind of something?" he said. Something that could interfere with a practitioner's theories? He wasn't sure he wanted to know after all.

"It is the World," Fenra said in a tone that made Witt shiver.

"The what?" Maybe this was some weird kind of practitioner's metaphor.

Fenra waved her hand in a way that took in everything round them, not just the room they were in. "The World is a living entity. We are all part of it—all of us—and we have not been performing to its satisfaction in a very long time. It has decided to take matters into its own hands. So it's pruning us."

"Pruning us." Witt jerked off his wig and scratched at his scalp. As he tossed the wig aside, he saw his hands were covered with powder. What would Arriz think?

"Yes, in a way," Fenra said.

"But if it needs us, why would it *prune* us?"

"To clear the way for new growth."

"But that's . . ."

"Extreme? Excessive? Suicidal? Yes, that's what we all think," Fenra said. "It may not have started this war between the Courts, but it is taking advantage of it. All the earth seizures and storms—that's to speed things up."

"And to get us to kill each other," Tamari added.

"Yes. And that."

Donn put his arm around Fenra. Witt felt his eyebrows crawl upward. He didn't think he'd find a hug from either of those two reassuring. Fenra relaxed, however, and rested her head on the older man's shoulder.

"It's too bad the sheriff can't ride to our rescue."

Fenra looked up.

FENRA

Even with the extra strength Donn and Tamari had given me, my brain was clearly not working at top efficiency. Otherwise, I would have thought of Elva long before this. Thought of him as a solution, that is, not just as himself. For his sake I had been able to move to the New Zone, without either Arlyn's dimensional gate, or the locket—and I had moved myself, Donn, Lizz, and Randd back again. Was it the connection with the New Zone? Would working with an entirely different world allow me to do as I wanted?

I stood up and held out my hands. "Let us try this again."

OLEANDER

After he'd waited at least an hour, Oleander realized he had no way of knowing whether his friends were still up in that attic or not. The guards changed, but apparently no one thought to mention that a servant with a parcel had gone in, so no one expected her to come out again. True, none of them looked very bright.

Finally, that officer, the one who was supposed to be Witt's friend, turned up and went inside. Sure enough, he came barreling out again a few minutes later, calling for the guard and yelling like an angry rooster. He sent one of the idiots at the door up to the room, and the other to go for reinforcements while he waited at the door. What good he thought that would do, Oleander didn't know.

He checked for the hundredth time that the scroll was still tucked into the front of his tunic, and pulled his belt tighter, just in case. He let himself roll off the wall he was lying on and landed neatly on the other side. With all the soldiers running around, it took him almost twice as long to leave the military area as it had taken to get in. Once he was back on ordinary streets he lost no time, running most of the way back to Ginglen's Inn like a street boy with an important message.

Which, when you thought about it, was exactly what he was.

It started raining again when he was no more than halfway there, making the pavements and cobbles slick, and forcing him to slow down again. No matter; there was sure to be a fire in the kitchen.

ELVANYN

Lizz and Randd weren't watching him, but Elva stayed sitting down anyway, breathing deeply. Maybe his legs would hold him up— probably—but maybe they wouldn't. His lungs moved air in and out without difficulty, but only a few hours ago he'd had the feeling that his lungs were turning into liquid, and that it was only a matter of time until they drowned him. His hands weren't sweaty or trembling, but while he didn't think he'd have any problems shooting, he wouldn't last too long with a sword.

Checking that his revolvers were fully loaded always made him feel more relaxed. Almost as though they'd been waiting for him to holster the weapons again, four more people appeared in the room. Fenra smiled at him, and he reached out his hand to her. "Who's our new friend?" he asked, tilting his head toward the only one of her companions he didn't recognize. The last time he'd seen anyone dressed in this much silk, satin, and velvet had been in the New Zone, at the court of Louise the Fourteenth, when all the courtiers competed to impress the queen with the extravagance of their clothing. Except maybe this guy was more colorful.

"Wittenslade Camdin Volden," the fop said, coming forward with his hand held out. "Witt for short."

"Elvanyn Karamisk." Elva shook the man's hand. "Call me Elva. That's a real strong grip you've got for someone dressed like a peacock." The man laughed; Elva liked that.

"It's in the nature of a disguise."

"I would hope so."

Suddenly the whole room shifted violently to Elva's right, throwing him to the floor, his pistol digging into his ribs. He let Fenra's hand go in time not to drag her down with him, but she and Donn were the only ones still on their feet when the earth seizure stopped. Plates and mugs had bounced off the tables and smashed, and a whole jug of wine broke and spilled on the flagstone floor.

The shutters blew back from the windows with a snap, and the glass blew in. Randd, Lizz, and Donn threw their hands into the air and deflected most of it to either side before it had time to do any real damage. Witt had a small gash on his forehead, but that was the worst injury, more bloody than dangerous.

"Twister," Donn said. "Look." He pointed out the now bare window to a thread of darkness that connected the sky to the ground. "We've got to get undercover and fast, before it gets any closer."

TAMARI

I couldn't believe the noise, and the shaking. I'd seen with my own eyes the damage the World could create, but I hadn't yet seen it while it was actually happening.

The floor jumped again and Fenra grabbed my arm. Luckily Witt was holding me up by the other, or we both would have been on the floor.

"This has gone too far," she said, her voice loud in the sudden silence. "We must contain it, prevent it from going to such extremes. We must find a way."

"If it's lost control of itself," Elva said, "it will kill us all, and itself as well."

"Either it does not know, or it does not care."

"Can you reverse any of this?" Elva said. "Like you did the fissure in the City?"

Fenra shook her head, lower lip between her teeth. "Small pieces, here and there, perhaps, but even with everyone's help, we cannot reach all the damage fast enough. As we fix one spot, another will break out." She rubbed her forehead, focusing on a spot in the middle of the room. She looked around at us as if she were counting us. "We cannot reach every part of the World at once, but we can reach the World." She stood up and held out her hands. "Come, all of you."

"All of us?" Elva said.

"Who would you leave behind? Besides, I have a feeling."

She pulled out her locket.

WITTENSLADE

The silence was so sudden Witt's ears hummed. From somewhere behind him Predax the apprentice ran up, looking between Fenra and Tamari as though he wasn't sure who to help.

The Lizz woman hissed.

"I beg your pardon." Witt released the grip he had on her upper arm. She rubbed at the spot and gave him the tiniest of head shakes. From the way they relaxed, everyone except him had been in this room before. Looking around, Witt thought he'd never seen a room so empty and so interesting at the same time. Before he'd had a chance to examine the wooden paneling—how did you panel an oval room without leaving any seams in the wood?—Fenra called them all to attention.

"We are moving on from here," she told them. "I will need you to stand in a particular formation."

Eventually they were all standing where she moved them, forming a loose six-sided figure with Fenra in the center.

"Each practitioner place their right hand on me and give your practitioner's hand to the person next to you. Elva, you and Witt can use whichever hands you like, just as long as one is on me, and one on the person to your left."

They shuffled around until Fenra was satisfied. Witt was pleased to find Tamari on one side of him, and the other woman, Lizz, on the other.

"If this works, we should find ourselves on a beach," she told them. "The World should join us there, and we will contain it." Witt thought she was trying a little too hard to sound certain.

"If it will let us," Tamari said.

Fenra closed her eyes tight, puffed out a breath, and opened them again. "That *is* the question, isn't it? It should want to work with us, but it is not itself right now . . ." She shrugged, but in such a way Witt thought she had an idea.

Elva laughed. "We all have to die sometime."

Fenra didn't smile at him, but the others grinned. She shut her eyes and began to breathe deeply. Lizz began humming softly under her breath a tune that Witt thought he should recognize. Within minutes they were all humming, some the same tune, others in a kind of harmony with it. Elva looked at him and nodded before shutting his eyes. *He's the only other normal person here*, Witt thought. Probably best to follow his lead. He shut his eyes.

He wasn't sure when it started, but after a while he found himself humming along with the rest. He thought he should be able to hear singing—it felt like the words were only just out of his hearing. The air shifted around him, and he felt sand beneath his feet, a breeze smelling of the sea on his face. Witt opened his eyes on a fresh sandy beach and started to take his hand off of Fenra's shoulder.

"Do not let go!" she called out. Witt tightened his grip immediately, a cool sweat breaking out on his back. "No matter what, do not let go."

Small chance.

Fenra

When I opened my eyes, I was relieved to see the sandy beach where I used to level Arlyn Albainil. I had hoped that coming here was something the World would not stop, and it seemed I was right. I also hoped this meant that I would have more control over what happened. I should not have been surprised when I saw the World sitting on the rock where I had always found Arlyn, but I was shocked at how old and worn it looked—perhaps as Arlyn would have looked if he had ever grown older.

"What do you want?" it said. "We didn't call you."

"You are ill," I told it. "You must let us help you." I saw it hesitate, and for a moment I had hope. Then it rolled its eyes and crossed its arms.

"Because you've been doing such a good job up to now?"

"You're doing no better," Elva said.

"Great. Now we're hearing from mundanes."

"Well, I know what *we're* hearing from, and it isn't the World," Elva said. "Don't forget we've met before, and even I can tell you're not yourself."

"Really? What are we, then?" But it had hesitated again, as if it meant to say something different.

"You absorbed the Godstone," I told it. "And it has changed you."

"Impossible. It's us and we're it. All the same thing."

"You *were* all the same thing," I said. "But when the Godstone existed apart from you, it became something more, or something less. It learned to live as an individual—"

"A selfish, self-centered, arrogant, know-it-all individual," Elva cut in.

Not helping, I thought. "That personality came back with the Godstone," I said. "Your judgment could be impaired. You may have lost control."

"Nonsense!" And yet it wrapped its arms around itself, as if for comfort. Suddenly it dropped its arms and strode toward us. It limped, and I could see, the closer it got, that if nothing else it was losing control over its shape. Its image of Arlyn was less like my old friend than it had ever been—and obviously so. The chaos that had always shown in its eyes and mouth had spread, its skin and clothes now crackling and flaking. It continued toward us, but its feet and legs dissolved away. Suddenly the Arlyn avatar faded away completely, and the World became as I had first seen it, a monstrous human shape made up of swirling bits of sand, rock, and seaweed, shells, driftwood, and bits of polished glass.

"You cannot hold your shape."

Its human shape disappeared, and a wind began to whirl around us, picking up the bits of glass and pebble and sending them circling, closer and closer, faster and faster. Pieces struck us, stinging, until Tamari and I had to use a *forran* to keep ourselves from being injured. Finally, the full force of the World struck us, knocking all of us to our knees.

"Don't let go!" I screamed over the sudden tearing, grinding noises. "It wants to weaken us." As long as we stayed together, we would be safe. Or so I hoped.

But I knew that eventually we would tire.

And then, out of nowhere, Witt began to sing. I could not hear him with my ears, but I could somehow feel the notes and words through the physical bond that still connected us. He was no practitioner, but he was a part of the whole, as important a part as any. I did not know the song, but it spoke of the sea, and fishermen, and the day's catch and how the sea was both friend and foe, providing and taking away. How happy the fishermen were to set out each morning, and to return each night. A bouncing merry song that made you think of warm firesides and wine.

First Lizz, then Donn and Randd began to glow, their magic forming full strength. Brightness informed and surrounded them, exposing their patterns—or what I saw as patterns—swirling and moving within the almost blinding light. I threw out my own pattern, and then Tamari added hers, strong and complicated, though through our physical connection, I could feel her trembling.

The wind sweeping through our circle softened and slowed, as if it too watched the light and listened to the song.

"Hold it," I said. "Draw it in." Just like fishermen and their nets. This had been Witt's message.

We stopped resisting, drawing it closer to us, using its own strength to bring it into the net we created with our bodies and our patterns. I heard Predax scream, and his pattern flickered, steadying almost at once, but fainter.

Witt's voice began to falter, his throat not up to the task. Before his song could fade completely, Lizz began a new song, and we all felt a surge of strength. She sounded as though she were laughing. And then it struck me. *She is not part of the World, not she, not Donn, not Randd. It will not affect them the way it affects us.* We could use their magic; it would be the difference that would save us.

Elva's voice joined in, and then Donn's and finally Randd's. After a few moments I heard Witt singing a harmony, using only notes and not words. Each word, each note, drew in more of the flotsam that made up the World's avatar, holding it safely within the shimmering net we made with our bodies, and our patterns, and our practice. It strained to push its way out, surging and fading like the waves on the beach around us, but we braced ourselves and clung to each other. The brightness that was the New Zone's magic spread to cover all of us.

Suddenly we were surrounded by vacuum, no air, no sound. Tamari fell forward but before she could hit the ground Witt and Elva had her around the waist, supporting her. I felt a thrill of panic run through us, until I realized we could still "hear" singing, as if through our bones. Then I saw only the brightness, sweeping round us, holding us, filling us with strength. I could smell the desert.

For a moment I saw Arlyn's face, with the Godstone looking out from his eyes, but then the eyes changed, and Arlyn smiled, and faded away. We still held the World, and bit by bit we put the pieces back together, but in a different configuration. The more we managed to fit, the easier it became, as if the World no longer fought us. Some of it was in danger of blowing away, but we were patient, and watchful, until even the tiniest bit of the World was tucked into place.

We were sitting on the rocks that overlooked the mill pond. People had been using them to sit on forever, and they were worn smooth, if not exactly comfortable. Elva, his shirt sleeves rolled up, his revolvers resting on top of his jacket, was trying his luck with a fishing line, even though I assured him there were no fish in the water.

"It went too far," I told him. "The World I spoke to in the beginning—

the World you met—it understood that we are all equally important parts of a whole, understood without thinking about it, without knowing there was anything to understand. When the Godstone came back to it . . ." I waggled my hand in the air.

"Tainted," Elva suggested.

"Yes, tainted is a reasonable word. It brought with it the practitioner's habit of analysis, of assessment and judgment. Once it began questioning itself, it lost perspective. Lost control."

Elva rolled over onto his elbow to look at me. "Ione Miller said a letter came for you today. Anything I should know?"

I pulled the scroll from the front of my tunic. It snagged on the locket on the way out, and I was careful disentangling it from the chain.

"Donn says the earth seizures and extreme weather seem to have faded considerably, in some areas stopped entirely—at least, that's the news he gets from travelers on the Road."

"And the Road itself?"

"He has sent a troop of third-class practitioners to patrol it, and to check towns and villages. He also says that people are beginning to move back into the City, now that the more extreme damage has been fixed."

"Won't that drain a lot of practitioners?" Elva coiled up his line, stuck the hook into a bit of wood, and slipped it all into his pocket.

"They are not building anything, just restoring the . . . well, I suppose you could call it the landscape," I said. "Flattening upheavals and getting the rivers back into their own beds, things like that. As for the buildings—" I smiled, "—Witt says he can get the Red Court to pay for restoring the City."

"How is he planning to do that?" Elva stood up and gave me his hand, pulling me up after him.

"It appears the old field commander—the friend of Riva Deneyra?—was fatally injured in the chaos that followed our escape. Witt's friend Colyardin Antorn Benfett is now the commander of the military."

Elva tried to whistle and grin at the same time and wound up choking on spit. "When do you suppose all the practitioners you moved will find their way back to the White Court?" he asked once he stopped coughing.

"It should take a while. Predax and I chose the models we used very carefully."

"What will happen when they figure out that by 'saving' them you were actually getting them to do what you wanted them to do in the first place?"

"Honestly, I doubt it will occur to most of them. In the meantime, Tamari and Donn are setting up a new council."

"I had a feeling Donn would want to stay."

I nodded. Lizz and Randd were staying with their old friend, in case he needed their support, but we both thought they would one day be asking me to send them back.

Movement further down the path showed Tux Gradon walking up toward us.

"Looking for us?" Elva called out. He stood up and gave me his hand.

Tux waited for us to reach him, puffing slightly. Clearly the man was not getting enough exercise.

Elva tapped him on the belly. "If it's an emergency, you should have sent one of the boys."

"Not an emergency as such," Tux said with a grin. "It's just that there's a horse at your cottage, Fenra, and no one knows where it came from."